Sarah Adams was born and raised in Nashville, Tennessee. She loves her family, warm days, and making people smile. Sarah has dreamed of being a writer since she was a girl, but she finally wrote her first novel when her daughters were napping and she no longer had any excuses to put it off. Sarah is a coffee addict, a British history nerd, a mom of two daughters, married to her best friend, and an indecisive introvert. Her hope is to always write stories that make readers laugh, maybe even cry – but always leave them happier than when they started reading.

To learn more, visit: **www. authorsarahadams.com**
or follow Sarah on Facebook and Instagram: **@authorsarahadams.**

Raves for *The Cheat Sheet*!

'A laugh-out-loud romantic comedy' Sophie Sullivan

'As slapstick funny as it is both sizzling and sweet' Chloe Liese

'The perfect mix of laugh-out-loud entertaining and intensely tender'
Devon Daniels

By Sarah Adams

The Temporary Roomie
The Off Limits Rule
The Enemy
The Match
To Catch A Suitor
Seeing Mary
To Con a Gentlemen
The Cheat Sheet

The Cheat Sheet

SARAH ADAMS

Published by arrangement with Dell, an imprint of Random House, a division of Penguin Random House LLC, New York

Originally self-published in the United States by the author in 2021

First published in Great Britain in ebook in 2022
by HEADLINE ETERNAL
An imprint of HEADLINE PUBLISHING GROUP

First published in Great Britain in this paperback edition in 2022
by HEADLINE ETERNAL

10

Cataloguing in Publication Data is available from the British Library

ISBN 978 1 4722 9703 7

Offset in 10/15.51pt Minion Pro by Jouve (UK), Milton Keynes

Printed and bound in Great Britain by Clays Ltd, Elcograf S.p.A.

Headline's policy is to use papers that are natural, renewable and recyclable products and made from wood grown in well-managed forests and other controlled sources. The logging and manufacturing processes are expected to conform to the environmental regulations of the country of origin.

HEADLINE PUBLISHING GROUP
An Hachette UK Company
Carmelite House
50 Victoria Embankment
London EC4Y 0DZ

www.headlineeternal.com
www.headline.co.uk
www.hachette.co.uk

To my best friend, Chris. Thanks for always taking jokes way too far with me, and giving me so much material for my books.

Also, you're super hot. So that's awesome too.

AUTHOR'S NOTE

Readers, please be advised that on-page panic attacks are portrayed. As someone who experiences anxiety and panic attacks, I hope that I have given this subject matter the care and sensitivity it deserves.

CHEAT SHEET:

A piece of paper the quarterback has on his wristband to easily reference plays to be called.

The Cheat Sheet

1

BREE

Balancing two cups of burning hot coffee and a box of donuts while trying to unlock a front door is not easy. But because I'm the best friend a person could ever ask for—which I will remind Nathan of as soon as I make it inside his apartment—I manage it.

I hiss when I turn the lock and a splash of coffee darts out onto my wrist through the little hole in the lid. I have fair skin, so there's a one million percent chance it's going to leave an angry red mark.

The moment I step inside Nathan's apartment (which really should not be called an apartment because it's the size of five large apartments smooshed together), the familiar clean and crisp scent of him knocks into me like a bus. I know this smell so well I think I could follow it like a bloodhound if he ever goes missing.

Using the heel of my tennis shoe, I slam the front door shut with enough gusto to warn Nathan that I'm on the premises. *ATTENTION ALL SEXY QUARTERBACKS! COVER YOUR GOODS! A GREEDY-EYED WOMAN IS IN THE HOUSE!*

A high-pitched yelp sounds from the kitchen, and I immediately frown. Peeking around the corner, I find a woman wearing a light pink shorts-and-camisole sleep set pressed into the far corner of the wraparound white marble kitchen counter. She's clutching a butcher knife to her chest. We're separated by a massive island, but from the way her eyes are bugging out, you'd think I was holding matching cutlery against the jugular vein in her neck.

"DON'T COME ANY CLOSER!" she screeches, and I immediately roll my eyes, because *why* does she have to be so screechy? She sounds like a clothespin is pinching the bridge of her nose and she has recently inhaled a whole balloon full of helium.

I would raise my hands in the air so I don't get knifed to death, but I'm sort of loaded down with breakfast goods—goods for me and Nathan, *not* Miss Screechy. This isn't my first rodeo with one of Nathan's girlfriends, though, so I do what I always do and smile at Kelsey. And yeah, I know her name, because even though she pretends not to remember me every time we meet, she's been dating Nathan for a few months now and we have met several times. I have no idea how he spends time with this woman. She seems so opposite of the type of person I would pick for him—they all do.

"Kelsey! It's me, Bree. Remember?" *Nathan's best friend since high school. The woman who was here before you and will be here well after you. REMEMBER ME?!*

She releases a big puff of air and lets her shoulders sag in relief. "Oh my gosh, Bree! You scared me to death. I thought you were some stalker girl who broke in somehow." She sets the knife down, raises one of her perfectly manicured eyebrows, and mumbles not so quietly, "But then again . . . you sort of are."

I narrow my eyes at her with a tight smile. "Nathan up yet?"

It's 6:30 A.M. on a Tuesday morning, so I know for a fact he's already awake. Any girlfriend of Nathan's knows if she wants to see him at all that day, she has to wake up just as early as he does. Which is why

Satin-PJ-Kelsey is standing in the kitchen looking pissed off. No one appreciates the morning quite like Nathan. Well, except for me—I love it too. But we're sort of weirdos.

She turns her head slowly to me, hate burning in her delicate baby blues. "Yes. He's in the shower."

Before our run?

Kelsey looks at me like it grieves her deeply to have to expound. "I accidentally bumped into him when I came into the kitchen a few minutes ago. He had his protein shake in his hand and . . ." She makes an annoyed gesture, letting it finish the story for her: *I dumped Nathan's shake down the front of him.* I think it's killing her to admit she did something human, so I take pity on her and turn away to set the donut box down on the ridiculously large center island.

Nathan's kitchen is fantastic. It's designed in monochromatic tones of cream, black, and brass, and an expansive window wall overlooks the ocean. It's my favorite place in the world to cook, and exactly the opposite of my dumpy little garbage bin five blocks down the road. But that dumpy little garbage bin is affordable and close to my ballet studio, so all in all, I can't complain.

"I'm sure it wasn't a big deal. Nathan never gets upset about things like that," I say to Kelsey, waving my white flag one last time.

She takes out her samurai sword and slices it to shreds. "I already know that."

Alrighty then.

I take my first sip of coffee and let it warm me under Kelsey's frigid stare. Nothing to do but wait for Nathan to surface so we can get going with our Tuesday tradition. It dates all the way back to our junior year of high school. I was a sort of self-designated loner in those days, not because I didn't love people or socializing, but because I lived and breathed ballet. My mom used to encourage me to skip dance occasionally to go to a party and be with my friends. "*These days of getting to just be a kid and have fun won't last forever. Ballet isn't everything. It's important to build a life outside of it too,"* she said to me on more than one occasion. And of course, like most dutiful teenagers . . . I didn't listen.

Between dancing and my after-school job working in a restaurant, I didn't really have friends. But then *he* happened. I wanted to increase my endurance, so I started running at our school's track before school, and the only day I could make this happen schedule-wise was on Tuesdays. I showed up one morning and was shocked to see another student already running. Not just any student, but the captain of the football team. Mr. Hottie McHotterson. (Nathan didn't have an awkward phase. He looked like a twenty-five-year-old at sixteen. So unfair.)

Jocks were supposed to be rude. Chauvinistic. Full of themselves. *Not Nathan.* He saw me in my scuffed-up sneakers, curly hair piled on my head in the grossest bun anyone has ever seen, and he stopped running. He came over and introduced himself with his huge trademark smile and asked if I wanted to run with him. We talked the entire time, instant best friends with so much in common, despite our different upbringings.

Yeah, you guessed it—he comes from a wealthy family. His dad is the CEO of a tech company and has never shown much interest in Nathan unless he's showing him off on the golf course in front of his work friends, and his mom pretty much just hung around and badgered him to make it to the top and bring her into the limelight with him. They always had money, but what they didn't have until Nathan made it big was social standing. In case you can't tell, I'm not a huge fan of his parents.

So anyway, thus began our Tuesday tradition. And the exact moment I fell for Nathan? I can pinpoint it down to the second.

We were on our final lap of that very first run together when his hand caught mine. He tugged me to a stop then bent down in front of me and tied my shoe. He could have just told me it was untied, but no—Nathan's not like that. It doesn't matter who you are or how famous he is; if your shoe is untied, he's going to tie it for you. I've never met anyone else like that. I was so gone for him from day one.

We were both so determined to achieve success, despite how young we were. He always knew he'd end up in the NFL, and I knew I was headed to Juilliard and then to dance in a company after. One of those dreams became a reality, and one did not. Unfortunately, we lost touch during college (*fine,* I made us lose touch), but I serendipitously moved to LA after graduating when a friend told me about another friend who was looking to hire an assistant instructor at her dance studio just as Nathan signed with the LA Sharks and moved to town as well.

We bumped into each other at a coffee shop, he asked if I wanted to go for a jog on Tuesday for old time's sake, and the rest was history. Our friendship picked right back up as if no time had passed at all, and unfortunately, my heart still pined for him the same as it had back then too.

The funny thing is, Nathan was never projected to reach the heights in his career that he has. Nope, Nathan Donelson was drafted in the seventh round, and he effectively warmed the bench as a backup quarterback for two whole years. He never got discouraged, though. He worked harder, trained harder, and made sure he was ready if his time came to take the field, because that's how Nathan approaches everything in life: with nothing but 100 percent effort.

And then one day, it all paid off for him.

The previous starting quarterback, Daren, broke his femur on the field during a game and they had to put Nathan in. I can still close my eyes and see that moment. A stretcher carrying Daren off the field. The offensive coach running down the sidelines to Nathan. Nathan shooting up off the bench and listening to the coach's instructions. And then . . . just before he put his helmet on and entered the game for what would go down in history as his career-making start, Nathan looked up in the stands for me. (He didn't have a private box at that point.) I stood up, we made eye contact, and Nathan looked like he was going to hurl. I did the one thing I knew would help him relax: contorted my face like a ding-dong and stuck my tongue out the side of my mouth.

His face exploded in a smile, and then he led the team to play the best game of their season. Nathan stepped in as the starting quarterback for the rest of the year and carried the Sharks to the Super Bowl, where they took home a win. Those months were a whirlwind for him. Actually, they were for both of us, because that was the year I went from just being an instructor at a dance studio to *owning* the studio.

Today, I'm here for a run with Nathan, and since he didn't play his best last night, I know we'll be running extra hard today. His team still won the game (and they are officially in the playoffs, YAY), but he threw two interceptions, and since Nathan is a perfectionist when it comes to . . . well, anything, I know he'll be stomping around here like a bear with an empty honey pot.

Kelsey's shrill voice yanks me out of my nostalgia. "Yeah, so don't take this the wrong way . . . but what are you doing here?" By *Don't take this the wrong way,* she means, *Don't take this as anything nice because I fully intend for it to come out extra witchy.* I wish she'd act like this when Nathan is around. When he's watching, she's sweet as pie.

I give her my most sunny smile, refusing to let her steal my joy so early in the morning. "What does it look like I'm doing here?"

"Being a creepy stalker who's secretly in love with my boyfriend and breaks into his apartment to bring him breakfast."

See, here's the problem. She says the words *my boyfriend* like they should be trump cards. Like she just tossed them on the table and I'm supposed to gasp and close my hands over my mouth in shock. *My heavens! She won!*

Little does she know, her card is the equivalent of a lonesome five of clubs. Girlfriends come and go in Nathan's life like fad diets. Me, on the other hand—I was here *long* before two-faced Kelsey, and I'll be here long after, because I am Nathan's best friend. I'm the one who's been through it all with him, and he's been through it all with me: high school gangly phase (me, not him), college football signing day, the car accident that changed my entire future, every stomach bug of the past six years, the day I took ownership of the dance studio, and when the confetti was falling on him after his team won the Super Bowl.

But MOST important, I'm the only person in the entire world who knows how he got the two-inch scar right below his navel. I'll give you a hint: it's embarrassing and has to do with an at-home waxing kit. I'll give you another hint: I dared him to do it.

"Yep!" I say with an overly bright smile. "Sounds about right. Stalker who's secretly in love with Nathan. That's totally me."

Her eyes widen because she thought she'd really zing me with that one. *Can't burn me with the truth, Kels!* Well, except for the stalker part.

I turn away from Kelsey and wait for Nathan. There was a time in my life when I tried to befriend Nathan's girlfriends. Not anymore. None of them likes me. No matter what I do to earn their affection, they are predisposed to hate me. And I get it, I really do. They think I'm a major threat. But that's where the story gets sad.

I'm not.

They all get to have Nathan in a way I never will.

"You know," she says, trying to grab my attention again, "you could just go ahead and save yourself the embarrassment and leave. Because when Nathan comes out here, I fully intend to ask him to make you leave. I've been patient so far, but the way you act toward him is super weird. You hang around him like a clingy piece of toilet paper."

I try not to look too patronizing when I give her an over-the-top *Okay honey* turned-down smile and nod. Because here's what I forgot to mention before: I'm not a threat to these women . . . until they make him choose. Then, I'm more threatening than a glitter bomb. I might not get to sleep in Nathan's bed, but I do have his loyalty—and to Nathan, there's nothing more important than that.

Kelsey scoffs and folds her arms. We're deeply engaged in a battle of frightening expressions when Nathan's voice rumbles from the room behind me.

"Mmmm, do I smell coffee and donuts? That must mean Bree Cheese is here."

I flash Kelsey a not-so-subtle grin. A *winner's* grin.

2

BREE

Nathan turns the corner wearing a pair of black athletic shorts and no shirt. His chiseled, tan chest that could only belong to a professional athlete is on full display, and that Adonis V of his is winking and making everyone blush. His hair is damp and glistening, and the tops of his shoulders are slightly pink from the hot water. This is his fresh-from-the-shower look, and no matter how many times I've seen it, it never ceases to make me swallow my tongue.

He has a small towel in his hand, and it's getting rubbed all over his incredible chocolate brown hair. That lucky towel is giggling with glee. Nathan's hair is so wavy and delectable that he has a five-million-dollar endorsement deal with a men's luxury haircare brand because of it. After that first commercial went live—Nathan stepping out of the locker room shower with a towel wrapped around his waist, beads of moisture clinging to his taut muscles, and holding that bottle of shampoo—women everywhere flocked to the store to grab the same brand in hopes of it magically turning their man into Nathan. At the very least, they wanted their man to *smell* like Nathan. But here's another secret that only I know—Nathan's hair doesn't smell like that shampoo because he prefers a cheap generic brand in a green bottle that he's been using since he was eighteen.

"Thought you might need this," I say, handing Nathan a steaming cup of coffee from our favorite little shop a few blocks away. I open the donut box like a treasure chest. The donuts shine in the light. *Bing!*

Nathan groans and cocks his head to the side, a soft smile in the corner of his mouth as he tosses the towel onto the countertop. "I thought it was my day to get the coffee and donuts." He plucks a maple glazed out of the box and leans down to give me a quick peck on the cheek like he always does. Completely platonic. *Brotherly.*

"Yeah, but I woke up super early this morning with a charley horse in my calf and couldn't get back to sleep, so I went ahead and got it." I hope he buys my fib.

Truth is, I couldn't sleep because I broke up with my boyfriend last night and I'm dreading telling Nathan. Why? Because I know he'll prod me with questions until he finds out the truth behind the breakup. And he can't know that I broke up with Martin because Martin isn't Nathan.

Maybe if I'd squinted, plugged my ears, and wobbled my head side to side, I might have been able to trick myself into thinking it was him. But who wants to live like that? It's not fair to me or Martin. So now, the goal is to find a man who attracts me more than Nathan does. A real bug-zapper of a man is what I'm looking for. This time I won't settle for anything less than complete and total *smittenness.*

Nathan lifts one of his thick brows. "Probably should've eaten a banana before bed last night."

I roll my eyes. "Yeah, yeah, but my answer is still the same: I hate bananas. They're so squishy, and they taste like . . . bananas."

"Doesn't matter. Clearly your potassium is—"

Kelsey clears her throat, and that's when we notice her massive scowl. "Excuse me. Is it not odd to you that she is here at 6:30 in the morning with coffee and donuts when you have your *girlfriend* over?"

Again with that G word. And okay, yeah, maybe I should have realized Kelsey would be over this morning, and I should have waited for Nathan to meet me with the coffee and donuts. That's my bad. Sometimes I forget Nathan and I don't have a particularly normal friendship.

Nathan clears his throat lightly. "Sorry, Kelsey, I just thought you remembered Tuesdays are always my running days with Bree."

"Yup." She rolls her eyes and pops the p sound. "How could I forget when it happens EVERY SINGLE TUESDAY. Literally your only morning off during the season."

This feels like a private conversation I shouldn't be here for. Actually, I kinda agree with her. It's weird that Nathan and I are such good friends. I've tried to take myself out of the equation many times before so he could spend more time with his girlfriend, but he never allows it. If I were his girlfriend, though, I would be very territorial with free time.

Tuesdays in the NFL are off days for nearly every team. But here's the secret sauce that not all players realize: The best ones still go into the training facility on their off days. They use the extra time to focus on their weaknesses, meet with physical therapists, review old game tapes—anything that will help them excel above the rest. Nathan never sits Tuesdays out, *but* he does go in a little later so we can have our run together in the morning.

"Can't you take, like, this *one* morning off?" She is overexaggerating every single word, and I don't know how he handles her voice.

Nathan's brows dip, and he folds his arms. I want to slowly scoot out of the room because I know what's going to happen next.

"Not really. I need a good run to shake off that bad game before I go train today."

Kelsey's mouth falls open. "Bad game? Babe, you won! What are you even talking about?"

In unison, Nathan and I both say, "Two interceptions."

Yikes. Kelsey did not like that. Her eyes narrow down into scary little slits. "Cute. See what I mean? This is not a normal friendship. And you know what? I'm done competing with whatever this is. It's time you"—*Don't say it, Kelsey!*—"choose. It's either me or her."

She blinks several times, and I turn around to give Kelsey some privacy in this moment of loss. *Dearly beloved, we are gathered here today to mourn the insignificant, minuscule relationship that was Nathan and Kelsey.*

"Kelsey . . . I told you up front I wasn't looking for anything serious right now, and you said you were good with that . . ." Nathan pauses.

Gosh, I hate this for him, I really do. It kills him to deliver breakup lines, because he's a giant, rock-solid teddy bear. I wish I could do it for him, but I have a feeling I'd just get a cast-iron skillet to the face.

Kelsey squeals. "Are you kidding me right now?! Are you choosing *her* over *me*?"

Okay, I don't love her inflection.

"Yes," he says matter-of-factly.

Flames burst from the top of her head. "You cannot honestly tell me you're not sleeping with her then!"

"He's not, believe me," I say. Then I worry it came out sounding a little too bitter, so I add, "Really. Just friends. We'd be horrible together. We're more like brother and sister." Bleh, that tasted bad on my tongue.

His chin tilts down to me, and it takes him a second, but he smiles. "Yeah. We've never . . ." His voice trails off and I see him swallow because it's difficult for him to even picture us together in that way. "Been friends with benefits."

Never. Not once. Nada. Nothing. Zilch. A peck on the cheek is the closest I've gotten to any action with Nathan, which is why I know he's not into me. A man who is head over heels for a woman doesn't keep his hands to himself on movie night for six years straight. And Nathan and I always keep our hands to ourselves.

So now, I work as hard as I can to prove to him that I'm SO GOOD with this friend thing. Because, honestly, I am. Would I love to marry him and have his giant muscular babies? Yes. In a heartbeat. But it's not in the cards for us, and I'll be damned if I ruin our friendship by making things weird when he finds out I'm crushing on him while he already has the number of the next model he plans to date halfway dialed into his phone.

The bigger problem is that I know if I told him how I really feel, he'd humor me because he truly does care about me as a friend. He'd give it the old college try, might date me for a few weeks, but then he'd move on to someone he actually felt chemistry with, and I'd be out a best friend. Not worth it.

Yeah—I'm good like this.

I'll eventually find someone who is just as great as Nathan.

(Probably not.)

"Right. Well, then . . . enjoy your weird friendship. Because I'm leaving." Kelsey pauses a minute, but I don't hear footsteps. I think she's waiting for him to stop her. This is awkward for everyone. "I really am. Right now. I'm walking out that door for good, Nathan."

Noooo, don't go! I think with zero sincerity.

And then she storms off. Nathan follows her toward the door, saying something about how she's still in her pajamas and shouldn't she go get her stuff first? She tells him to have it sent over because she can't bear to look at him for another second. The drama is high.

I hear the door slam, and I kick the air. *Good riddance!*

I also whip out my phone and text my big sister.

ME: Another one bites the dust. Kelsey's outta here!

LILY: She lasted longer than I expected.

ME: Aka too long.

LILY: Be nice! He might be sad.

ME: Ummm I'm always nice, thank you very much.

LILY: I bet you have a creepy smile on your face.

When Nathan finally comes back into the kitchen, I train my face into a heartfelt frown, proving Lily wrong. "I'm sorry, friend."

"No, you're not," he says with a chuckle as he leans his bare hip against the counter.

I really wish he'd wear more clothes. It's painful having to look at something so beautiful and never touch it. Nathan's skin is like hot golden sand from an exotic beach, wrapped around a rippling form that makes you feel instantly dehydrated. His perfectly crafted physique is the reason he was named Sexiest Man Alive and made the cover of *Pro Sports Magazine*'s form issue where they highlight and celebrate all the different physical forms of pro athletes and what they have to do to keep their bodies in tip-top shape. It's a classy spread with well-placed hands and thighs to cover the most important bits. But yeah, Nathan was completely naked in that magazine. And although I own five copies, I've never been able to bring myself to look inside (the cover only shows him from the waist up). There are some boundaries you just can't cross as friends. Nakedness is one of them.

I pick up a donut and shove it in my mouth to keep from smiling. "No! I really mean it. Kelsey seemed . . . fun."

"You stuck your tongue out at her in the box last night."

"Geez! Do the Avengers know about you and your superhuman eyesight?"

He smiles and reaches out to tug on my messy ponytail. "Was Kelsey a jerk to you when I wasn't around? Be honest."

Nathan has black eyes. Not chocolate, not brown. Jet freaking black. And when they zero in on me like this, it feels like I'm suffocating. Like I couldn't get away from their intensity even if I tried.

I shrug a shoulder and take a drink of my coffee. "She wasn't the best, but it's no big deal."

"What'd she say?"

"Doesn't matter."

He inches closer. "*Bree.*"

"*Nathan.* See, I can do it too."

He's quiet . . . thoughtful, a mere five inches between our chests. "I'm sorry if she made you feel bad. I didn't realize she was like that toward you or I would have broken up with her a long time ago."

A corner of my heart aches. If he cares about me being in his life so much, why isn't he attracted to me? *No. Uh-uh. Not going there.* I refuse to be that girl. We're friends and I'm happy with that. Grateful for it. And maybe one day, life will toss me a man who loves me back as much as I love him. Either way, I'm good right now.

"Well, I didn't exactly help things. I probably shouldn't have come over here this early and let myself in." I take a big bite of my chocolate donut. "I should implement better boundaries."

"Probably," he says, sounding gravely serious. But when my eyes jump up to his, Nathan is grinning—right dimple popping and all.

I playfully shove his arm. "What! If that's the case, maybe I should take away your key to my apartment. Implement some boundaries there."

He takes the last bite of his donut, grin still in place. "Good luck. I'm never giving it back." His arm brushes against mine as he passes by me, and I wonder if it would be a breach of these boundaries if I plastered myself to his body like a barnacle.

I think I need this run more than he does, and for completely different reasons.

3

NATHAN

Sweating and worn out from our run, Bree and I dump ourselves onto the floor in front of my giant white couch. To my left is a floor-to-ceiling three-million-dollar view of the ocean, but to my right is the view I would give my soul to see every day for the rest of my life. Obviously, Bree doesn't know I feel this way about her.

I knock the back of my knuckle against her knee, right beside the jagged scar that changed the course of her entire life. "What are you doing later? You want to come meet me for lunch at CalFi?"

CalFi is my team's stadium. It has a recently added training facility where we practice and work out during the week, complete with a cafeteria catered by some of the best chefs in the business. And I, in case you are wondering, am an overeager puppy, begging for Bree to play with me—to always play with me.

She rolls her head so her soft brown eyes lock with mine. Bree is all honey-brown, long, wildly curly hair and a wide, gorgeous mouth with dimples the size of my thumb on either side. She has a Julia Roberts smile—one so unique and stunning that once you've seen it, no other smile even comes close. With our heads laid back against the couch, our foreheads almost touch. I want to lean in an extra inch. *Two inches.* I want to feel her lips.

"I can't. I have a toddler creative movement class at 11:00 today."

I frown. "You never teach on Tuesday mornings."

She shrugs. "Yeah, well, I had to add another class in the mornings twice a week to cover the studio's rent. My landlord contacted me last month and said property taxes went up again so he had to raise my rent by a couple hundred bucks."

Bree tries to stand, but I hook the T-back strap of her tank top and tug her back down beside me. It was borderline overly flirtatious, and I instantly know it was a bad move when she looks at me with wide eyes. I quickly continue the conversation to cover my tracks. "You're already teaching too many classes a week."

Bree employs one other instructor at her studio who teaches tap and jazz, but really, she needs to add another to help with the load. Her studio runs in more of a nonprofit capacity, but her overhead doesn't reflect it because every studio space in LA is enormously expensive. It's unfair because there's a large population of people in this city who are low income and under-resourced whose needs are overlooked. Bree's desire has always been to provide a place for kids who otherwise wouldn't be able to receive dance instruction, allowing them to attend her studio at minimal cost to their family.

Problem is, the tuition is too low for her current business model. She knows this but feels stuck, and I hate that her chosen solution to the problem is to teach more classes and trade more of herself to cover the deficit instead of accepting my money.

"I teach the normal amount of classes for the average instructor," she says with a clipped warning tone. Bree's warning tone, however, sounds as threatening as a cartoon baby bunny. Her eyes are big and sparkly and make me love her more.

I soften my own voice, preparing to go to a place I know is touchy. "I know you can handle it, and I know you're absolutely tough as nails, but as your friend, I hate having to watch you work through so much pain in your knee. And yes, I know your pain is flaring up because I saw you favoring your right leg during our jog today." Reflexively, I hold up my hands. "Don't pinch me, please. I'm only trying to make sure you take care of yourself while you're out there taking care of everyone else."

Her eyes dart away. "I'm fine."

"Are you? You'd tell me if you weren't fine?"

She narrows her eyes. "You're being overly dramatic about this, *Nathan*."

She says my name in a way that's meant to cause me pain but instead just makes me want to smile. Bree is one of the strongest human beings I know, but she's also somehow the softest. She can never fully bring herself to snap at me or anyone else in her life.

"My knee is not going to fall off if I use it too much, and I can push through a little pain. You know I don't control my rent, so if I want to be able to keep my tuition low for the kids, I have to add an extra class until I can find a different solution. End of story. And—AH!" She holds up her finger to press against my lips when she sees me about to argue. "I won't take money from you. We've been over this a thousand times, and I need to do this on my own."

My shoulders sink. The only consolation for continually losing this argument is the fact that her skin is pressed against my mouth right now. I'll stay silent forever if she will promise to never move. And with her finger pinned over my lips like this, I don't have to feel guilty about not telling her I've been secretly paying part of her studio's rent for years. (Not true—I still feel guilty about going behind her back.)

Bree's landlord raised the rent on her once before when she first took over the studio from the old owner. She cried on my couch that night because she wouldn't be able to afford it anymore (much like what's happening again) and thought she was going to have to find a cheaper location outside of the city, which would completely negate her purpose of providing a dance studio for the kids in the city.

Let's just say her landlord had a magical change of heart and called her the next day to say he'd moved things around and didn't need to raise the rent after all. We can also safely say that if Bree ever finds out I've been paying a few hundred dollars toward her rent each month, I will be relieved of my favorite dangly parts. I probably shouldn't have done it, but I couldn't bear to watch her lose her dream like that. Not again.

Bree was accepted to the dance program at The Juilliard School just before high school graduation, and I've still never seen a person more excited about anything in their life. I was the first person she told. I picked her up and spun her around as we both laughed—internally a little scared about what our separating lives would mean for our friendship. She would be moving to New York, and I would be off to UT on a football scholarship. I wasn't about to leave town without telling Bree how I felt about her, though, and hopefully making things official between us. We'd only ever been friends, but I was over it and ready to be more.

And then it happened.

She got T-boned by a guy running a stoplight one day after school. Thankfully, the crash did not take her life, but it did take away Bree's future as a professional ballerina. Her knee was shattered, and I'll never forget her words over the phone when she called from the hospital sobbing. *"It's all over for me, Nathan. I won't be able to come back from this."*

The reconstructive surgery was hard on her, but the physical therapy that summer was the most brutal. Her spark was gone, and there was nothing I could do to bring it back for her. I didn't want to leave her once fall rolled around—it didn't feel right to go on with my dreams when she was stuck at home without hers. Even more than that, I just wanted to be with her. Football didn't matter as much to me as she did.

But then, she pulled away. Or more like cut me off. She left me with no choice but to go to UT as planned—and then after I got there, she wouldn't return any of my calls or texts. It felt like the most painful breakup even though we'd never dated. We went four years without talking, and still to this day I have no idea why she did that. She's thriving in her new life now, so we don't revisit the past. I'm too scared to hear the answer to why she cut me out back then.

When I graduated, got signed by the Sharks, and moved to LA, Bree was here too. I believe it was cheesy, old-fashioned, honest-to-goodness fate that brought us back together. I walked into a local coffee shop, the bell chimed over my head, and she looked up from a book, eyes locking with mine from across the room. She was a defibrillator to my chest. *Bum.* My heart hasn't beat the same since.

That day, I found my old friend again. The friend I knew before the accident who was so full of life and energy, except even better. She was healthier, she had these incredible, soft, feminine curves that had not been there before, and her knee had healed up enough that she was able to work as an instructor at the studio she now owns. Unfortunately, she had a boyfriend then. Don't even remember his name, but he was the reason I didn't ask her out on the spot.

We picked back up with our Tuesday tradition, and I've been barrel-rolling into the vast, never-ending hellhole known as the friend zone ever since. I'm afraid I'll die in this friend zone because she's constantly reminding me that she's not interested in anything romantic. Almost every day she says a terrible phrase like:

"Just friends."

"Practically my brother."

"Incompatible."

"Two amigos."

Anyway, that's why I did it. I couldn't bear to stand back and watch her lose something important to her when I could easily fix it this time. So I've secretly been paying her rent, and she will be furious if she ever finds out.

I make a mental note to check in later with ol' Mr. Landlord just as Bree's finger falls away from my mouth. "Seriously, don't worry! I'll figure something out like I always do. But for now, I'll take some ibuprofen and ice it between classes. I'm okay. I promise."

Because I'm only her friend, I have no choice but to hold up my hands in surrender. "Okay, I'll let it go. I won't ask if I can give you money anymore."

She tips a cute, snooty chin. "Thank you."

"Hey, Bree?"

"Yes?" she asks suspiciously.

"Do you want to move in with me?"

She groans loudly and lets her head fall back against the couch cushion. "Nattthaaaannnn. Let it go!"

"Seriously, think about it. We both hate your apartment—"

"*You* hate my apartment."

"Because it's not fit for human habitation! I'm a thousand percent sure there's mold, the stairs are so sticky but no one knows why, and that SMELL! What even is that?"

She grimaces, knowing exactly what I'm talking about. "Someone suspects it's a raccoon that got in between the walls and died, but we can't be certain. Or . . ." Her eyes dart. ". . . itmightbeadeadhuman." She mumbles that last part, and I consider holding her hostage and forcing her to live in my clean, mold-free apartment against her will.

"Best of all, if you lived here, you wouldn't have to pay any rent, and then you wouldn't need to make as much from the studio." It's a loophole, a way for her to cut costs without accepting a single dime from me.

Bree holds my gaze for so long I think she's wavering. "No."

She's a needle, and I'm a full balloon. "Why? You already practically live here. You even have your own room."

She holds up a correcting finger. "Guest room! It's a *guest room*."

It's her room. She makes me call it the guest room, but she has spare clothes in there, some colorful throw pillows she added herself, and several items of makeup in the drawers. She sleeps here at least once a week when we stay up too late watching a movie and she's too tired to walk home. Yeah, that's the other thing—her apartment is only five blocks down the street (yes, five blocks makes a huge difference in a big city like LA), so we're practically already roommates, just separated by hundreds of other roommates. *Logic.*

"No, and I'm serious—drop it," she says in a tone that lets me know I'm inching up to pushy-asshole-best-friend territory and I need to cool it.

Some might be tempted to think my full-time job is pro athlete. Wrong. It's forcing myself to behave inside this gray area with Bree where I'm wild about her on the inside and nothing but a platonic guy-friend on the outside. It's a cruel form of torture. It's staring at the sun and not blinking even though it burns like hell.

Oh, and did I mention I accidentally saw her naked a few weeks ago? Yeah, that hasn't helped. Bree doesn't know, and I don't intend on telling her because she'd get super weird about it and avoid me for a whole week. We each have a key to the other's apartment, so I let myself in like I always do, but this time I had forgotten to tell her I was coming over. She walked out of the bathroom butt naked and then went back in without ever seeing me standing there in the hallway, jaw sweeping the floor. I turned around immediately and left, but that beautiful image is burned—no, something better than burned . . . engraved, transcribed, memorialized in my memory forever.

"Give me one valid reason why you don't want to live here, and I'll let it go for good. Scout's honor." I hold up my right hand.

Bree eyes it, tries not to smile, and then folds down my pinkie and thumb. "You're not a Boy Scout so your honor means nothing, but I can't move in with you because it would be too weird. There, I gave you an answer. Now you have to drop it." Bree hops up from the floor, and this time I let her go. Her curly ponytail swings behind her, loose wisps clinging to the sweat on her neck as she walks into the kitchen.

I follow behind, not ready to drop the topic of conversation quite yet because I think I finally found the real reason. "Who would it be weird for? You or *Martin*? Surely he knows he has nothing to worry about between us." I strongly dislike her boyfriend. He doesn't deserve her. I mean, I don't deserve her either, but that's beside the point. What kind of douchebag would be okay with his girlfriend living in a hazardous building and not offer for her to move in with him?

Bree's eyes leave mine, her mouth twisting to the side. She's debating something, and I lift my brows to encourage her. "Bree?"

She spins away, and her wrist full of ever-present, colorful braided bracelets dives into her monstrosity of a purse. "Did I mention I have something for you? It'll cheer you right up after your breakup with Screechy . . . I mean Kelsey." She chuckles to herself over her little quip, and I try not to let her see me smile. I couldn't care less about my breakup with Kelsey. I'm more concerned about why she's trying to change the subject right now.

She digs and digs and digs through her bag, and I know what's coming. Bree has a trinket obsession. If she sees something that reminds her of one of her friends or family members, she buys it and stuffs it in that Mary Poppins satchel to bestow upon us later. I have two whole shelves of items she's given me over the years. Her sister Lily has three shelves. We made a bet once to see who had more "Breenkets," as we call them, and I lost. Lily beat me by seven.

Finally, she finds what she's looking for, and out of her bottomless bag comes a miniature-sized Magic 8 Ball.

Her rainbow nails place it delicately in my upturned palm, and she quietly says, "Number eight. You know, because you're number eight on the team." I'll set it next to my number eight playing card, number eight shot glass, and number eight birthday candle. "Also, Martin and I broke up."

Wait, huh?

The world stops spinning. Crickets silence. Everyone, everywhere on the planet turns to look at us. I, however, have to try very hard to remain neutral. Somehow I instinctively know that my reaction right now is crucial if I want to keep the status quo of our friendship. *Don't mess things up, Nathan.*

"Since when?"

"Last night. We broke up after the game." Her answer comes out fast. "Well actually, I broke up with him after the game. He was fine with it though. It was pretty much mutual."

I can't believe this. "Why didn't you tell me before now?"

She shrugs, her attention focused on sliding her bracelets up and down her wrist one by one. "Just didn't think about it."

"Lie. No one conveniently forgets that they broke up with someone they've been dating for six months."

She grits her teeth and rolls her eyes at me. "Fine! I just didn't want to, okay? It wasn't a big deal. Martin and I barely saw each other, and . . . he was boring. We were boring together. No sparks. I just couldn't do it anymore." Bree says all of this looking completely nonchalant, while I have to remind myself to keep breathing—slowly, in and out, like a normal human and not like I'm short-circuiting on the inside.

Because this—right now—is the very first time we've both been single at the same time in the last six years. Somehow our relationships have staggered themselves out into an almost humorous cycle.

And now . . . we're both single.

At the same time.

And I've seen her naked. (That thought has nothing to do with anything, it just pops into my head randomly from time to time.)

If I leaned in right now and kissed her, would she let me? Would she cringe? Or would she melt into me and that would finally be the end of our platonic friendship? These are the questions that keep me awake at night.

I don't get to find out the answers, though, because Bree suddenly snatches her purse from the counter and throws it over her shoulder. "Okay, well, now you know. So, I'll see you . . . sometime," she says, backing away from me with a curiously flushed face.

I follow her to the door. "Tomorrow," I say, closing my fingers around the Magic 8 Ball. "I'm picking you up tomorrow for Jamal's birthday dinner, remember?" My teammates love Bree, call her the Sharks' little sister. I refuse to ever call her that.

She trips backward over a shoe and catches herself with a hand on the wall, her long honey-brown ponytail whipping her in the face. "Tomorrow? Oh yeah, I forgot. Sounds good!" She's being so strange. Or . . . more strange than normal, I should say. "Well . . . I'll see you tomorrow then!"

I grin as she tries to leave through the front door, but her purse gets caught on the handle, yanking her back a step. She yelps then frees herself and runs out the door.

With a sigh, I look down at my newest Breenket. "Well, Magic 8 Ball, what do you think? Should I tell my best friend I love her?"

I turn the ball over, and the message reads: *Reply hazy, try again.*

The next day during practice, it's clear that Bree's singledom announcement has taken up all the available space in my head. I can't focus on drills. I screw up too many passes. Jamal—the top running back on our team—has started calling me butterfingers, and it's catching on like wildfire. Everyone thinks it's hilarious because I'm never like this. Coach is concerned and thinks I have the flu. He sends for a team physician to check my temperature on the sidelines in front of everyone. I feel like an idiot.

"I just have something on my mind," I tell Jamal later when practice is over and he's badgering me with questions about why my game was so off today.

He grunts a laugh as he finishes buttoning his shirt. I'm already dressed and sitting on the bench in the middle of the locker room, waiting to go into the media room to answer questions with the press about our upcoming game.

"Does it have anything to do with you breaking up with Kelsey?"

My head flies up. "How'd you know about that? I only broke up with her yesterday morning."

His patronizing smile says, *You're an idiot.* "She announced it on her Instagram last night, along with a link to a gossip article on *In Touch Weekly* website."

"Dammit." I should have known better than to date her. Kelsey is a model who at first seemed nice but then, after closer examination, turned out to be a spotlight hunter. Though, honestly, I can't say I really care when a woman only wants to date me for the attention it brings her. I only date other women because Bree is always dating other men. But currently she's not . . . and since I can't seem to find a woman even remotely as amazing as Bree, I feel like it's time I quit looking anywhere else.

Plus, I'm sick of my girlfriends being rude to Bree. It's like watching someone try to swat a butterfly—cruel and depressing. Suddenly, I'm worried about that article for other reasons. Kelsey can talk shit about me all day, but if she mentioned Bree's name even once, I'll have my lawyers all over her faster than she can blink.

"Did you read the article?" I ask Jamal as he preens in the mirror.

He lets out a guttural laugh that tells me I'm not going to like his answer. "Oh yeah I did. And you're going to hate it."

My back goes straight. "Does it mention Bree?"

Jamal takes one look at my ready-to-fight demeanor and shakes his head. "No, but you're pathetic, you know that? Look at you, ready to ruin someone to avenge the woman you've never even kissed. Dude, you need to get a grip. Either go after Bree, or be done with her. Clearly you've got some pent-up frustration that's starting to affect your game, and that can't happen right now, because . . . playoffs, bro. PLAYOFFS." He's shaking his fists in a desperate attempt to make me understand. As if I didn't already know the playoffs are important.

I ignore Jamal. "Just to be clear, though, the article doesn't mention Bree?"

He gives me a flat look. "No. Your object of desire is safe from slander. You, however . . ." He laughs like friends do when they see a booger stuck to the side of your face but don't intend to tell you it's there.

Again, I ignore him. "I couldn't care less about the article, then." My *image* has never been important to me. All I care about is playing a good game. "Besides, we only dated for a few months. I doubt she could come up with that much dirt on me." Mostly because I'm boring. I don't party. I don't drink during the season. I go to bed early and wake up early.

Jamal looks like he's about to burst from jubilant anticipation. His smile is grinchy, his eyebrows are lifted, and now maybe I'm a little nervous about what Kelsey said. He claps me on the back on his way out of the locker room. "Come find me when you're ready to read it, okay? I don't want to miss seeing your face when you do."

As Jamal is leaving, another one of my teammates walks through the locker room and heads for the shower while laughing at whatever he's looking at on his phone.

"What's up, Price?" I ask with a head nod even though he's not looking at me.

He laughs bigger and passes by me. "Not you apparently!"

I have no idea what that's supposed to mean, but something tells me I'm not going to like it when I find out.

4

BREE

"OH MY GOSH, I'm drooling. Imani, grab me a mop so I can clean up this puddle."

"Shhhhh, she's gonna hear us. Keep it down, you dodo!"

"I don't care if she hears, she needs to know it's unbelievable she's not jumping that piece of—"

I clear my throat and fold my arms, tapping my foot like I remember my mom doing—although I refuse to think of myself as these girls' mom because I'm absolutely not old enough. I'm more like their big sister. Yeah, their supercool big sister who they'd be lucky to hang out with!

"Hand it over," I say, hand outstretched toward the group of sixteen-year-old ballet students hovering ominously around a phone. And yeah, now I feel like their mom.

"See, Hannah, you and your big mouth went and did it." Imani rises from their little huddle in the corner of the studio where they were waiting for class to begin and pads gracefully across the hardwood floor to me.

The pink and blue bejeweled phone case lands in my palm, and I look down to find a photo of Nathan in a sexy ad of some sort, wearing nothing but his uniform pants and a really awesome pair of black cleats. His abs are rippling under the studio lighting, and there's more than a little sheen reflecting off his taut skin from all the oil that's been rubbed on him. I'm not even sure what they are selling here, but I'm willing to spend all my savings on it.

I swipe out of the photo even though I want to copy and paste the URL and text it to myself. "First of all, you girls shouldn't be looking at this. He's almost twice your age!"

"So! Sexiness knows no age." Sierra—also sixteen—is the one to shout that little gem.

"Believe me, it does. Just ask the law." They all roll their eyes. Sixteen-year-olds are terrifying. "And second of all, this is 100 percent photoshopped. He doesn't look like this in real life." *He looks better.*

Hannah points aggressively at me. "Bite your tongue! He's the hottest man in the world and everyone knows it. And we want to know how you can be best friends with that god among men and not hit it."

I wrinkle my nose. "Ew, don't say *hit it*. Where did you learn to talk like that?"

"You're avoiding the question," says Hannah. She's the ringleader of sassiness in this class.

I cross the floor of the long slender studio to reach the sound system in the back corner. Remote in hand, I rise onto my toes and spin around to face the little fresh-faced jury now lined up by the floor-to-ceiling mirror, arms folded. These tiny babies mean business.

"I'm not avoiding the question. I'm just not dignifying it with an answer! Plus, it's an inappropriate class conversation. My business with my friend is my own, not yours." I want to bop each of them on the nose to drive the point home.

"But you love him, right?" asks Imani.

I put my hands on my hips. *Ugh,* more mom posing. “If I answer you, can we start class?”

“Yes,” the Spice Girls of ballet answer in unison.

“Then no, I do not love him, Sam I am. I do not love him in a car, I do not love him in a bar. I do not love him with a hat, I do not love him with a cat,” I chirp adorably while twirling and whimsically conveying this lie in a way I hope they’ll understand.

Their frowns are deep. They think I’m so uncool.

There is no way I’m giving these girls what they want: the truth. Telling them how I actually feel about Nathan would be like throwing thousands of Pixy Stix into a room of toddlers. They’d go nuts and I’d never have peace again. There’s also the very real possibility that they would find a way to contact him and tell him everything I say. Better to lie and pretend I don’t care about Nathan in that way.

“That’s so boring!” one of the girls moans. “What’s the point of even having a hot best friend if you’re not going to bang him?”

“OKAY EVERYONE GET INTO POSITION!” I yell and clap my hands together like a Parisian instructor whose only goal in life is to drive her students to the brink of death. Which is sort of what I plan to do today.

Just because this is an inexpensive ballet class, doesn’t mean they get a cheap education. I instruct these girls with the same precision and expectations I received in my fancy-shmancy-pricey-dicey studio growing up. I cringe thinking back to how my parents and I had to work our butts off to afford that place. Yes, you heard me correctly, my parents AND I had to work for it. Neither of my parents ever had jobs that paid particularly well, and because they were also taking care of my grandmother who fought an aggressive form of cancer for most of my childhood, my dad worked two jobs to make ends meet. Money was tight at all times.

My sister and I both worked during high school in order to pay for our cars, insurance, fun stuff like movie tickets, and even part of my ballet tuition. I wish a studio like the one I own now had existed near me when I was younger for many reasons.

1. We operate on income-based tuition. That means if your parents make less, your tuition is less and we make sure you can afford to come to ballet. Because dance shouldn't be available only to the wealthy. It should be something for everyone to enjoy. It shouldn't be a burden.
2. My studio focuses not only on technique and practice, but also on the whole person. I care about these girls. I care if they're eating. I care if they have clothes for school in the fall. I care if they are fighting with a friend and need a hug or a ride to class that day. I care more about what their eyes are telling me than the turnout of their feet. Because as I have learned firsthand, ballet can slip from your grasp in a blink, but your soul is with you forever. I'm finally taking my mom's advice and implementing it in my students' dance education.

But don't get me wrong, I also care about the turnout of their toes, and right now as we practice, I give them the kind of instruction they can be proud of. When they graduate from high school, I want them to feel like they received all the training they needed to go on to dance in a company or apply to Juilliard. During this one-hour class, I give these girls my all, and I expect the same in return from them.

However, some sacrifices have to be made in order to provide lower tuition. As far as ballet studios go, this one is minuscule. It's a mousehole—a mousehole situated in the upstairs portion of a pizza parlor where it has thrived for ten years. I took it over from the old owner, Ms. Katie, four years ago, and I've never looked back. This is my slice of heaven. It smells like yeast and pepperonis and sounds like classical music and laughter.

After class is over, I take up my usual position in front of the exit in the four-foot-wide hallway that extends the length of the studio. It's lined with dance bags, water bottles, and shoes, bookended by one single-stall bathroom on one side and my punctuation mark of an office on the opposite end.

The girls line up with their bags slung over their shoulders and go out the door one by one, pausing to listen to the inspirational message I tell them every time they leave. They want to pluck their ears off from having to hear it so often, but I will wax every hair from my body before I stop telling them, because I know they need to hear it. I hold out the basket of homemade oatmeal protein cookies I make each week for my classes.

"Imani, I'm proud of you. You're beautiful and worthy just the way you are. Take a cookie." She does and rolls her eyes with a grin. "Sierra, I'm proud of you. You're beautiful and worthy just the way you are. Take a cookie." She sticks her tongue out and wrinkles her nose. I stick mine out in return.

I go down the line of all eight dancers, looking in each of their eyes, noting if there's anything that seems off, making sure they look not too skinny, like they've been sleeping, like they are not losing their soul to dance like I wish my teachers would have done for me. Because here's the thing about dancers at this level: they will do anything to succeed, which usually translates to working themselves so hard their feet bleed, starving themselves so their bodies have leaner lines, constantly striving for perfection and spending more time dancing than living. That was me at one point, and I'm so thankful it's not me anymore. Now, I eat when I'm hungry, and I live life outside of dance.

That car accident saved my life, because if I had gone on to Juilliard with the unhealthy mentality toward my body and workaholic lifestyle I had at the time, I'm not sure what would have happened to me. Now, I will make sure my dancers feel seen, and loved, *and dammit,* FED!

Hannah is the last student in the line, and as she gets ready to take a cookie, my overprotective-teacher radar starts blaring because her eyes are cast down. Usually she makes a face at me like the other girls on her way out the door. I pull the basket of cookies away at the last second before her young-adult hand can grab one.

"Ah-ah-ah," I say like I'm reprimanding a puppy that's too cute to actually scold. I hold the basket far away. "No cookie for you unless you tell me what's up with the darty eyes."

Ooh, I forgot I was dealing with the worst kind of teenager, though—a level-four teen, aka a driving teen who now thinks she's a grown-ass adult.

She folds her arms. "Fine. I'm not hungry anyway." Her eyeballs cut purposely away from me, but I can still see *something* lurking.

Well, unlucky for her, I never fully grew up.

With her gaze turned away from me, I'm able to easily pluck the same little bejeweled cell phone that had Nathan's glorious picture on it from her hand. I hold it behind my back and convey with my eyes that she's never getting it back if she doesn't comply. She gasps indignantly, and I mimic it like an annoying parrot, widening my eyes mockingly.

"Oh, did you want this? Tell me what's wrong and I'll give it back."

"You can't take my phone! This isn't school."

"Uh—I think I just did." I'm ruthless, but I don't care if she's mad, because now I'm convinced something is going on that she's not telling me about, and I care too much about her to let it slide.

"Miss B!" She groans. "I need to go! My shift starts in forty-five minutes, and I need to go home to change. Please can I have my phone back?"

I make a thinking face. "Ummm . . . no. Tell me what's wrong."

Her slender shoulders slump as best as a perfectly refined ballerina's body will allow. "You're really not going to let me have it back?" I smile pleasantly and shake my head. She rolls her eyes. "Fine. My dad lost his job again. He said the company had to make budget cuts. I—I know my tuition is already low, but I still might have to quit coming. I can't work any more hours and still keep up my grades."

I extend the pink and blue jeweled phone back to her. "Thank you. Now, that wasn't so hard, was it?"

She gives me a death glare. "It was an invasion of privacy."

"Sure, sure, I see where you're coming from, but . . . I don't care." I grin and hand her a cookie. She smiles weakly, and I know I'm forgiven. "Forget about tuition until your dad gets back on his feet."

She looks stunned. "Are you serious? Miss B, I can't—"

"Of course you can! Now, quit worrying—it'll give you ulcers." I turn around to flick off the studio lights and pick up my duffel bag. "I want to see you in class on Thursday."

Once we're out the door, I lock up, and we both walk down the extremely steep and narrow stairs that lead to the parking lot. The smell of pizza dough punches me in the stomach, and I want to chuck these healthy cookies across the building and devour a supreme stuffed-crust pizza instead. You'd think after six years of smelling this haunting yeasty aroma, I'd be used to it, maybe even sick of it. Nope.

Hannah turns to me after we make it to the bottom of the stairs. She opens her mouth, but no words come out. I do see tears clinging to her long lashes though. She slowly lets her breath out and then nods. "Thanks, Miss B. I'll be here."

And that's all I want. Well, that and more money to rain down like manna from heaven somehow. I'm not sure how I'll make it work without Hannah's tuition and an already tight budget, but I refuse to turn away a girl who needs help.

The memory of an Instagram post I saw earlier this week suddenly pops into my mind. It was from The Good Factory saying that one of their incredible spaces is going to become available next month, and they are currently taking applications. I've dreamed of securing a place in The Good Factory ever since I learned about it a few years ago. It's a giant old renovated—you guessed it—factory that was endowed in some rich benefactor's will with the specific purpose of offering free rental spaces for nonprofit organizations. The only overhead costs organizations are required to cover are for any adjustments they need to make to the space (which for me would be adding mirrors and a ballet barre). There are only fifteen gigantic spaces available for use in the factory and they are ALWAYS occupied, because, *duh,* who wouldn't want to be in there?

Each space is lined with gorgeous windows, hardwood floors, and expansive exposed brick walls. I bet there's not a hint of a yeast scent anywhere in that building. I want to apply, because with the free rent, I would officially be able to convert my studio to a nonprofit and lower tuition prices to nearly free. But even as I think of applying, I roll my eyes. There's no way I'd get selected among the hundreds of other applicants. I've learned by now not to count too much on something in the future that's completely out of my hands. Best to make do with the resources I have available to me now.

I watch Hannah walk to her car and wait until she's safely inside to go to my own. I toss my bag on the opposite seat that's already piled high with sweaters and water bottles then check my phone. I'm not surprised to see a new voicemail from Nathan because we have become very good at a voicemail-and-text friendship. We tend to call and leave meaningless voicemails for no reason. Like cell phone pen pals.

"Hey, is it true that some caterpillars are poisonous? Somehow one made its way into my truck and then disappeared when I looked away. Now I'm wondering if I should buy a new vehicle and just give him this one? What do you think?"

I immediately call him back and leave a message when he doesn't answer. "I haven't had time to Google it yet, but better safe than sorry. Can you get a flashy sports car this time? Also, I'm really craving a cherry slushie. Does that mean I have a vitamin deficiency? That's all. K, bye."

After I hang up, I peruse the internet, trying to find that photo the girls were staring at before class.

5

BREE

I hear a loud knock on my apartment door followed by Nathan's voice. "Bree! You here?"

"Be out in a second!" I yell from my bathroom where I've just finished applying my face mask.

It's only 5:30 P.M. He's a little early to pick me up for Jamal's party, and I'm still in my strappy black leotard with my herringbone textured leggings overtop, but more important, bright green goo is currently hardening on my skin. I should probably worry about what Nathan will think of me in this thing, but honestly, he's seen me in worse. And this is one of the perks of never anticipating a relationship with your best friend—you can look like a dump and still hang out!

Welcome to the bright side, friends!

I leave the bathroom and head toward the kitchen where I see Nathan rummaging through my fridge. He's bent over when I walk in, and my stomach does a flip at the sight.

"Apples are in the bottom drawer," I say, forcing my gaze away from his derriere, because, *umm hello,* friends don't ogle friends' butts. Even when those butts look amazing in a pair of tight, gray chino pants.

"Ah—thank you." He stands up and shuts the fridge with his spoils in hand. When he turns to face me, the apple is already between his teeth and he freezes mid-crispy-bite. His eyes widen and his smile grows on either side of the red forbidden fruit.

"What?" I ask, leaning back against the counter like everything is perfectly normal. "Do I have something on my face?"

He lets out a guttural laugh, and the sound is so *him* it stirs me in ways a woman with her face painted like a frog shouldn't be feeling. In fact, I shouldn't be thinking sexy thoughts toward Nathan ever, but it's just . . . it's DIFFICULT, okay? I'm a woman with very opinionated ovaries, and let me tell you, they're real hussies. Currently, as Nathan rips the bite off that apple and tilts his head at me with a playful smile, they are down there waxing poetic about how his soft, white tee fits him so well it looks like a deity plucked him up by his feet and dipped him headfirst into a sensual cotton pond. In conclusion, I am deceased at the sight of him.

"Should I be worried about whatever is happening here?" He wiggles his big man fingers across the front of his face.

"Only because when I wash it off, I'll be so devastatingly gorgeous you might die on the spot."

It's a joke, clearly a 100 percent facetious statement, but Nathan swallows his bite of apple, and then his eyes do a very odd thing: they tiptoe down my body.

It only happens that one time and his gaze doesn't take the same path back up, but part of me wonders . . . *no! No wondering! Shut up down there, you little instigators.*

I register the wink of desire running through me and do the same thing I've always done over the last six years, what every good co-ed best friend dynamic has perfected. I dart around the kitchen like I have something very important to do, pretending like it never happened. At all costs, I NEVER acknowledge the feeling of desire.

I turn toward the counter at my back and find a cherry slushie in a Styrofoam cup. I gasp like it's a goblet full of stolen jewels. "YOU BROUGHT ME A SLUSHIE!?" I have to say this in a way that projects my voice and conveys excitement without cracking the mask on my face. It's an important skill to master in life.

I hear him chuckle and bite into the apple again. "You said you were craving one, right?"

"Yeah, but I didn't mean for you to go get me one," I say before putting the straw in my mouth and taking a long sip until my brain freezes deliciously.

Nathan is staring at me before looking grumpy and shooting his gaze down to his phone. "It's really not a big deal." He thumbs his screen then sets his phone down on the counter with a loud *thud*. "I'm so sick of this thing," he says, dashing an anxious hand through his hair. "I feel like it goes off nonstop. I can never get a break."

He leaves my little galley kitchen to move into the living room and plops down on my couch. I can't help but chuckle at the sight of him, limbs completely sprawled out and hanging off every surface of my teeny-weeny furniture. He looks like he just climbed down the beanstalk and decided to nap on Baby Bear's couch. His dark eyes close, and I sense how tired he is. Just looking at him and knowing the kind of schedule he has to keep makes me exhausted to my bones. I want to wrap him up in my bright yellow throw blanket, feed him soup, and make him watch cartoons all day.

"We could stay in and watch a movie, you know. I'm sure Jamal will understand if we miss his dinner."

Nathan doesn't open his eyes. "Nah, I want to go. It's important to him that I be there."

I sigh, knowing Nathan is as immovable on his reluctance to pass anything up in favor of resting as I am about taking money from him. I imagine a girlfriend would probably climb right on top of him and pin him down, giving him no choice but to stay in for the night.

But I'm not his girlfriend.

I shake myself from that fantasy. "Okay, well I need to go wash this goop off my face and then we can—"

I'm interrupted by the sound of Nathan's phone buzzing on the kitchen counter. I look over my shoulder, but he holds up his hand, signaling for me to leave it be. "Shhh, no one move and maybe they'll think I'm not home."

"I can answer it and pretend they have the wrong number."

"No one believed your French last time."

That's true. Tim, Nathan's manager, made me hand Nathan the phone right away.

Nathan grabs the lime green pillow resting under his head and pulls it up to bury his face in. There's an odd sense of satisfaction that hums through me because I get to see him like this, because he only lets his guard down with me. "I'm sure it's just Nicole or Tim wanting another piece of my soul."

The phone stops ringing.

"Someone is dramatic tonight."

Nathan peeks over the pillow and lifts a brow. "I'm dramatic every night."

His eyes shut again, and I let myself have one last good long look at him. He's lying on top of a pile of clean clothes that have lived in that spot for a week. There are nail polishes scattered all over my coffee table and bills open on the floor. The funny thing is, Nathan is the physical manifestation of order and tidiness, but he's never once tried to clean up my space. (And thank goodness because I know under the pile of leggings in the corner of my room is an open magazine with a red pen lying underneath, and if he ever moved that pile, I'd have no idea where the red pen is when I need it!) He's never made a negative remark about how I like to live messy or suggested order in my life. He just lies down on top of my clothes.

I mentally grab myself by the ponytail and pry myself away from Nathan to rinse the cracking mask off of my face. I change into some cute and casual party-going jeans and a T-shirt, and just as I'm exiting my room, I hear a loud series of quick buzzes erupt from Nathan's phone in the kitchen. It's a new voicemail alert. I'm down my short hallway and almost to the living room when Nathan yells, "Hey Siri, play that voicemail."

I love technology. Giving us these little servants.

The next voice I hear, though, stops me dead in my tracks.

It's my landlord.

"Hello, Mr. Donelson, this is Vance Herbert . . ."

I turn around and make eye contact with Nathan, who's now sitting up stiff as a board on the couch. We both stare at each other for exactly one second, and then we simultaneously bolt for the kitchen. I am closer, though, so I'm the one to get to the phone first.

I pick it up and make a break for my bedroom. Nathan is right on my heels and trying to catch my arms, but I zigzag and evade his grip. *Quick, someone put me in the NFL.* We sound like a pack of elephants stampeding the apartment building, all while Vance's voice continues on in a soft, monotone cadence. "I just wanted to let you know that all of the paperwork has been finalized—"

"BREE! GIVE ME THAT PHONE!"

"Not a chance!"

I make it into my bedroom and try to slam the door in his face, but his big hand catches it and thrusts it back open. I lunge to jump over my bed, hoping to make it to my bathroom where I can lock the door. But Nathan grabs my hips mid-jump and hauls me down onto my bed. I grew up with an older sister, though, so I'm practically CIA level when it comes to protecting my stuff.

I shove the phone down into my bra—the one place I know Nathan will never go.

Just as he flips me over so my shoulders hit the mattress and he's hovering over me, arms pinning me in on either side, we hear the final words from Vance. ". . . and you are the official owner of the building. I had my realtor pass the keys along to yours and will be calling Ms. Camden to let her know I've sold the building and she'll have a new landlord from now on—but as discussed, I will not mention your name. If you or your realtor could call me back and let me know which name and contact you would like me to give her, I'd much appreciate it. Have a nice day."

The room goes eerily silent, except for the sound of my heart pounding in my ears. I'm looking down at where the cell phone is silhouetted under my sports bra, and when I lift my gaze, Nathan's black eyes are staring at me. He looks like a man who just lost everything in a bad hand of poker.

"You . . . ?"

He doesn't need me to finish my sentence. "Yes."

Neither of us makes an effort to move, and for a moment the shock of it all leaves me frozen. My eyes trace the line from Nathan's shoulder down his bicep, to his elbow, over his tan forearm dusted lightly with hair, and to his hand pressed into my comforter.

"You bought the whole building?"

He sighs. "Yes."

"Wh—Why?"

The look on his face says he does not want to answer. "Because I've been wanting to invest in real estate?"

"*Nathan.*"

He swallows, and I watch his Adam's apple go up and down. I can feel his body heat all around me. "Because he kept changing the terms of the lease agreement and it was just easier to buy it outright than negotiate again. The guy is sleazy."

I blink a hundred times. "Wait . . . why did you say *the* lease agreement, and not *your* lease agreement?"

The fact that he takes several seconds to respond almost tells me everything I need to know before he even speaks. "Because technically for the last four years . . . it's been *our* lease agreement."

The reality of it crashes into me and I shoot out from under him to pace the room. "NATHAN! Have you been paying part of my rent all this time?!"

He swivels his legs so he's sitting on the edge of the bed, hands clasped between his knees in front of him, watching me walk back and forth. "Yes. I have."

I groan/whimper as dollar signs suddenly start rotating through my vision like a slot machine. Nathan has been helping me financially for FOUR YEARS when I have explicitly told him I don't want any of his money! This is one of my rules for being friends with him: *No accepting monetary gifts.* These rules are important to me because they help me keep our friendship in the right box. If I start letting him help financially, if I move in with him, if I attend fancy events and partake in all the perks girlfriends get, I'll get confused!

He might think it's nothing because he doesn't have feelings for me, but I will 100 percent get things mixed up in my head, and it will crush me when he never wants to be more than friends. Maybe I'm silly, but I'd prefer to not have my heart stuffed into a trash compactor if I can avoid it.

"So the first time . . . all those years ago when Vance told me he was going to raise the rent and then had a sudden change of heart . . . that was you? You called him and negotiated to pay the part of my rent I couldn't afford?"

Nathan's long lashes blink his answer in morse code. "Bree . . ."

I whip around to him so hard I'm sure I'll have a crick in my neck tomorrow. "*What?* Do you want to apologize now that you got caught? Now that you're in trouble?"

"No."

"No?!" Somehow that answer is even more infuriating.

"I can't apologize because I'm not sorry that I did it." He's so calm and collected. Mr. Cool Cucumber here to throw on his sunglasses and show us all up.

I, in comparison, feel like Ms. Erratic Woman Who Stuck Her Finger in a Light Socket. "How can you not be sorry? You went behind my back! You lied to me all these years. Oh gosh, I'm thousands of dollars in your debt!" My hands press into my cheeks.

"You owe me nothing. Not a single dime. You're not in my debt because I don't need anything from you."

"Yes, I do owe you!" My voice is screeching. "How can you not see that this is horribly uncomfortable for me, Nathan? I told you I didn't want to take your money, and I meant it."

Part of his cool and collected facade is cracking. He stands quickly. "Why? I've never understood! It makes no sense to me. You are my best friend, so why can't I help you when you need money? I have more than I know what to do with!"

"Because you won't always be here for me, Nathan!" Okay, whoa, that was way too loud. My statement cuts through the air like a foghorn in a bar fight. People are poised with chairs over their heads, ready to crack them down on their fellow outlaws and all blinking at me.

"Why the hell would you think that?"

"Because it's true." I can't meet his eyes while I say this. "We're just friends. What happens when I start relying on you financially and then one day you get married and your wife suddenly doesn't like it that you're paying for another woman's rent and all the other things you'd pay for if I let you?"

He shifts from one foot to the other. "I . . . I wouldn't marry someone who would be like that. I'll find someone who's comfortable with our friendship the way it is."

I laugh a short, sad laugh. "There is not a single woman who would ever be okay with it, Nathan! It's an inevitable fact that we have to face. One day we will not be able to be so close anymore. You will fall in love and marry a kickass woman who wants you all to herself—as she should—and you will want to give her your whole heart too. *That* is why I cannot rely on you financially." There's an uncomfortable twisting in my chest. It's only half of the truth, but it's all I can reveal.

I stare at him, hoping he will finally get it through his beautiful, benevolent head that I can't let him be my sugar daddy.

Finally, after a long, thoughtful pause, he says, "How come you're not also falling in love and getting married in this scenario?" His tone is nothing but playful. "Seems unfair that I get to find my fairy-tale love and you'll be over there penniless and lonely."

I growl and shake my fists in the air. "I'M PAYING YOU BACK!" I punctuate it with an indignant stomp. Ceiling drywall dust flits through the air like snow.

He shakes his head. "No you're not. I won't let you."

"Yes. I. Am." I blink furiously at him. "I don't know how and I don't know when, but I will find a way to pay you back. And I expect a normal lease agreement to be settled between us! No deals!"

"Can you stop yelling? Your whole ceiling is about to cave in. And seriously, Bree, that smell is getting worse. It might be more than one dead raccoon."

He's lost all reason! Cuckoo for Cocoa Puffs! I'm over here telling him our friendship has a ticking clock on it and negotiating a fair rent, while he's in la-la land talking about raccoons.

"You will not distract me." I jab a finger right in the center of his taut chest. "It's time for you to promise me you will stop meddling in my financial affairs. Promise me right now or I'm not going with you to Jamal's party tonight." I cross my arms and jut my hip out. There. *I'm in charge of this show, buddy.*

A dangerous glint slowly enters Nathan's eyes as he steps closer, forcing me to press my finger harder into his chest. "Sorry, but no." He steps a little closer. "Do you know what it's like to see your best friend care for every single person under the sun but herself? I watch you pour everything into those girls and their families, going above and beyond to not only give them incredible dance instruction but also make them feel loved in the process. And for some reason, you think that same kindness shouldn't be extended toward yourself."

His smile turns defiant now.

"Well, tough, *friend*. I have millions of dollars and I will spoil you with them if I want. You're going to have to throw me off a bridge if you don't want me meddling in your life, because that's what friends do. So get used to it. Oh, and you're getting a good deal on your damn rent from now on. So are the people in the pizza parlor below the studio."

I gasp. "Not fair! You don't get to go all soft-squishy-teddy-bear Nathan on me!"

"I just did. And if it helps you sleep at night, pretend I only did all of this as charity for your girls. It had nothing to do with you."

"That's it. I'm not going with you tonight. End of story. You need to be taught a lesson." I fold my arms. I am a solid, immovable stone. I will not be swayed!

Nathan's laugh is the last thing I hear before I'm scooped up and tossed over his shoulder, butt aimed up toward the sky.

6

BREE

"NATHAN! Put me down!" I screech as he carries me out of my room.

"There is nothing wrong with getting a little help in life. Friends help each other get ahead. In fact, I think my next project will be getting you out of this dump." He knocks a knuckle on the wall and paint chips fall.

"Don't you dare buy my apartment building and renovate it!"

"I might. I've got money to blow, baby."

Who is this man?!

"You're unhinged!" I yell at his butt.

"Yep. Feels good too. Now, come on, yell at me some more in the truck. I really don't want to go to the party tonight without you, and I know you don't want to miss it."

I kick and flail. "No way! I'm not going with you. We're fighting! You don't get to get your way right now, you big brute!" He gives my behind a single gentle pat after I say the word brute, which makes me gasp with outrage and also want to die laughing. UGHHHH I hate Nathan. Why can't we just fight like normal people?

"You can't touch my butt! That's against the rules," I say as he walks me back toward the front door, stopping to turn out lights as he goes. My hair dangles in the air below me like a weeping willow.

"I never did see a list written out anywhere."

"I'll make you one and laminate it! Why are you acting so weird tonight anyway?" It's freaking me out. Something about Nathan feels different. He's always been playful with me, but now he's . . . I refuse to let my brain finish that thought.

"I think I'm acting normal."

"No, you're not, and I'm not going with you to the party! PUT ME DOWN! Wait, can you grab my tennis shoes? They're down there beside the couch. And don't forget my sweater!"

With me still draped over his shoulder, Nathan sumo squats and retrieves my shoes before turning out the final light, picking up my sweater, and taking us into the hallway. He swings me around so he can lock the door behind us, and I find myself face-to-face with my sweet elderly neighbor Mrs. Dorthea. Her curlers are in her hair for the night, and her eyes are as wide as saucers.

I smile like everything is normal. "Hey, Mrs. Dorthea. Did you get that stack of coupons I slipped under your door this morning?"

Mrs. Dorthea is a widow, and I know she struggles financially. Since I also fall in the category of *struggling financially*, the most I can do is clip coupons for her and share my leftovers. More than once, however, she's thanked me for the hundred-dollar bill she found in her mailbox even though I never gave her one. I thought maybe her memory was just beginning to slip, but now I see the truth. *Nathan.* I need a paper bag to breathe into. In how many other areas of my life has this man secretly Mother Teresa-ed me?

"Well, yes, honey, I did . . . but . . ." She's at a loss for words since I'm casually thrown over Nathan's shoulder like this is a normal way for a woman to be carried around in the twenty-first century. Some part of me says I should be appalled to be hauled around by a man like this, but I can't hear her because the larger part of me is too busy yelling, *YES! Carry me back to your cave and make sweet, sweet love to me!*

Suddenly, I'm swung around the opposite way, and now my butt is aimed at my poor sweet neighbor.

"Hi, Mrs. Dorthea. Looking pretty as always. Do you have everything you need tonight?" Nathan asks—with a big charming smile, I'm sure. I bet all those pearly whites are completely dazzling her.

Yep. He totally smiled, because now Mrs. Dorthea is tripping all over her words trying to thank him for his compliment, assuring him she's as blessed as the Pope and congratulating him on another win this past weekend. I roll my eyes.

I'm then carried down three flights of disgusting stairs. I can hear Nathan's shoes peeling off the sticky floor with every step. *Yuck*. You'd think this apartment would come with super-low rent for how disgusting this building is, but NOPE. That's LA for you. I pay way too much to live in a building that smells like armpit.

Before we make it to the lobby, I decide that if Nathan can touch my butt, then I can touch his. I scrunch my nose then move my finger and thumb toward his butt cheek with the intent to pinch the daylights out of him so he'll put me down. The first attempt, however, is unsuccessful. He only laughs and flexes his rock-solid glute, making it so there's no padding I can grab to inflict damage.

"Do less squats," I tell him with a put-out tone and fold my arms, resigned to drape over him like a coat until he puts me down, wondering where I went so wrong in our fight tonight.

We make it to the truck and Nathan plops me into the front seat, shuts the door, and then gives me a *Stay* look through the window. I search my pockets and find a used gum wrapper to toss on the floorboard of his truck out of spite.

Nathan slides into the driver's side of his blacked-out truck—the windows so dark no one ever knows who's in here, which is lots of fun—and gives me a look that says, *Alright, let me have it.* So I do the opposite because I'm in a mood to make him pay for his good deeds. I raise my brows in a sassy mocking expression then pull out my phone and settle into my seat to ignore him for the entire drive.

He groans. "The silent treatment? Oh come on! Anything but that." I don't answer, just turn my gaze out the window like I can't be bothered by his distraction. "Fine. Make me pay. I deserve it." He leans over the center console and retrieves the gum wrapper. It goes in the tiny trash can he keeps in his driver's side door.

I'll be honest, though, it's tough to feel justified making a man pay for being *too kind*. I know it was underhanded and manipulative and deceptive, but *dammit* it was so sweet I could cry. It's so Nathan that the only thing he's guilty of is having too big of a heart. I wish he would stop making me love him more. It's annoying.

After scrolling through Twitter for a few minutes and trying to block out Nathan's ridiculous attempts to draw me in by rapping to '90s hip-hop songs about big booties, I come across a retweeted article with Nathan's face on it. Now, I've been friends with him long enough to know not to read any of the tabloids about him, but this one stands out for reasons I can't ignore.

"OH MY GOSH, I'LL MURDER HER!" I yell so loud I'm surprised Nathan's windows don't shatter.

"Who?!" he asks frantically while pulling his truck into the parking lot of the restaurant where we're meeting up with the guys.

I blink down at the article. "Kelsey! Your horrible ex! She wrote an article about you . . . and . . ." I look up at him. "Have you not seen it?"

"Oh." He's not concerned. "I heard something about it, but I haven't cared enough to check. I figured Tim would call me if it was that bad."

"Okay, well I guess you don't care that she's deemed you the lousiest lover in LA, then?"

"*What?*"

That got his attention.

Nathan takes the phone from my hand, his eyes scan down the article, and then he relaxes and tosses the phone back into my lap. "Eh, not so bad. Ready to go in?"

My mouth falls open and I peer down at the article that would have me burying myself alive. "Not so bad? Nathan, she shamed you for . . ." I let that sentence die off because Nathan and I have NEVER talked openly about our sex lives before. We treat the topic like it's a building on fire and give it a wide berth. Instead, I let my eyes drop to the forbidden area of his jeans and hope this conveys the words I'm too embarrassed to say. "Not being able to . . . well, you read it, so you know."

He's trying not to smile. "It's not a big deal." He reaches into the back seat and a crisp, white dress shirt materializes. He shrugs it on and buttons it up. Not a care in the world.

I don't understand his nonchalance right now.

"How are you not upset? I'm practically shaking with rage! I want to go put red ants in her underwear drawer! Put hot sauce in her coffee creamer! Duct-tape her car doors shut!"

"Ooh, how devious. Do the feds know about you?"

I lightly smack his shoulder. "Don't laugh! This is serious." For some reason, I'm blinking back tears right now. "She—she publicly shamed you for having erectile dysfunction, Nathan. That's a horrible thing to do! And humiliating. And you're the nicest guy in the whole world! And I HATE HER!"

Nathan barks out a laugh and his head tilts up to heaven like he's praying for wisdom. His big hand rakes through his hair then he turns his eyes on me again. "Bree, thank you for your concern, but I don't have erectile dysfunction. She blew the story out of proportion and was just trying to dig at me for not having sex with her . . . and probably for choosing you over her the day we broke up. But the joke is on her because, as you've pointed out, it's very insensitive to shame anyone for the condition." He gestures toward my phone. "Just look at the comments at the end of that article. She's getting terrible backlash, and men are saying they feel better knowing an athlete struggles with the same condition they have." He shrugs again. "All in all, not a terrible outcome."

Yeah, yeah, yeah, he's so noble. But my brain stopped listening after one very important key statement.

"Wait. Go back. Did you say for not . . ." Again I'm at a loss for words.

Nathan Donelson did not sleep with the underwear model he dated for two months? My brain is not computing. It's going to shut down, and fumes are about to puff out of my ears.

"You never had sex with her? Why?" I ask this question even though I shouldn't. But I need to know, because Nathan is . . . Nathan! Just look at him. He oozes sexuality, and every woman in the world wants him. Even Mrs. Dorthea probably has the hots for him!

His face is frighteningly serious. We're not joking around anymore. "Because I'm celibate."

"*What!*" I accidentally yell this so loud a woman walking beside the truck turns to try to peer through the darkened window. *Scram, lady.* I look back at Nathan and whisper, "You're a virgin?"

"No." His smirk is a little too indulgent if you ask me. "I guess I should say I've been celibate *lately*."

I shake my head, thinking of all the nights I wanted to cry myself to sleep thinking of him holding another woman in his arms. Holding Kelsey. Turns out, he wasn't. "I don't understand . . . she was there the morning I brought coffee over."

"You're at my house a lot in the mornings too. That doesn't mean we've done anything physical."

I suddenly can't swallow. Or feel my toes. What's happening?! Why am I reacting this way? It changes nothing really—except I feel like everything I knew has changed tonight. My foundation is shaking.

Nathan sees my wide eyes and rumbles out a short chuckle. "Why are you making this such a big deal?"

"*Because,*" I say emphatically like that's enough of an answer. "You could have anyone you wanted at the snap of your fingers. Why would you be celibate?" I NEED TO KNOW! There's something he's still not telling me, and it's bothering me. I didn't think he and I had any secrets, but now I'm learning he has two big ones! How many more are there?

His dark eyes stare back at me. "Not anyone I want."

My heart races up my throat. Those words mixed with the night and the fact that he bought my studio and we spend nearly every day together . . . it all suddenly holds so much implication, and . . . could this be it?! Could he mean—

He chuckles, a familiar playfulness washing over him again, and all hopeful thoughts halt. As they should.

"Look at your face," he says through a soft laugh. "You were so terrified there for a minute. Bree, don't worry. I'm only celibate during the season because it helps my game."

His game? He's celibate for the sake of football? *Oh. Right.* That's more realistic and yet another reason to remind myself not to think of Nathan as anything other than a friend. That's all we'll ever be, and that *has* to be enough for me. It has to! I need to sit my sad little heart down and give it a stern talking to.

I let the air out of my lungs in one big rush, pretending I'm relieved so I can maintain the status quo. "Oh! Oh my gosh! Yes. That makes perfect sense. I've read studies about that too! I was worried there for a minute that you meant . . ." It feels too uncomfortable to say it out loud, also maybe a little pathetic. "Never mind. Let's just go inside."

"Okay." He smiles inquisitively. I'm afraid my face is showing emotions it shouldn't. "Are you alright?" he asks after he's purchased a parking ticket (he refuses to use the valet because he says it only draws more attention to him) and we're walking toward the restaurant.

"Of course! I just—" I need a change of subject. So I come to a stop and Nathan does too. I wait until he turns to look at me. "Listen, I still hate that you went behind my back and paid my rent, but . . . completely off the record . . ." I smile. "Thank you for caring about me that much. You're . . . the best of friends."

He nods once, not looking as happy as I would have anticipated. "Anything for you, *friend*."

We stare at each other for a few beats.

"But I will pay you back," I say, breaking first.

He groans loudly and walks away.

7

BREE

The moment the restaurant doors open, several heads turn and do a double take. I feel like it would be easier if I just ran in front of Nathan with a megaphone and yelled, *Attention everyone! No, your eyes are not deceiving you. This truly is the great Nathan Donelson in the flesh!*

One head leans toward another. The restaurant is a giant cocktail of whispers and stares. Women are salivating now. We're going to need a mop on aisle two. They know him, they want him, and they will do anything to get him.

I do what I always do in situations like this and take two big steps away from him so I don't get in the way of his bachelor availability. But Nathan grasps my elbow lightly and tugs me close to his side. I look up at him with a scowl because my body is getting far too excited about our proximity right now. He knows not to do this, and yet here he is, breaking *another* rule tonight. His face is chiseled stone as he stares straight ahead, ignoring my glare.

The hostess finally notices us and rushes to her little podium. Her eyes rake over Nathan's body, and the sheer want displayed in her dilated pupils is uncomfortable for everyone. *Get in line, lady.* I sigh then inwardly growl as my jealousy rises up and tells me to pick apart this woman's looks to find a flaw that will make me feel better about myself. *Not cool, Bree.* If Nathan wants this beautiful woman, that's his prerogative.

"Mr. Donelson, you can follow me. Your party is right this way." But maybe I can be a little annoyed that she's practically purring?

He nods and gives her that polite smile that makes women drop like flies. But then he presses his hand to my lower back and pulls me with him. It's a possessive touch that he never uses. My skin boils, but I tell it to slow itself to a simmer because it doesn't mean anything. Based on the pace he's moving at, his hand is only pressing into me like this because he's trying to get me to move faster to get us away from all these prying eyes and not-so-subtle whispers. Maybe we should have called ahead and come in the back entrance?

I nearly trip over my tennis shoes as I try to keep pace with him. Also, tennis shoes?!

"Nathan!" I hiss as we walk not so discreetly through the upscale restaurant—I'm assuming this hostess was told to parade Nathan through the belly of the beast so everyone knows he is here—toward a hallway that leads to a VIP lounge. "Why did you have to kidnap me dressed like this? You should have told me to change! I thought we were going to a burger place or something." Which, I now realize, was a silly thought. The Sharks are officially in the playoffs, and Nathan and Jamal's celebrity status has skyrocketed. They have to be careful where they go right now, and I'm assuming most burger places wouldn't have a VIP lounge to give them privacy.

Nathan's brows dip and he scans his eyes over me as we walk. He takes in my yellow scrunchie, F.R.I.E.N.D.S. logo T-shirt, scuffed-up sneakers, and ankle-cropped jeans. He smiles. "You look great as always."

"No, I don't," I say, accidentally bumping into the back of his bicep when I look behind me at the women in tiny dresses lining the bar we just passed. "I look like your teenage little sister who you just picked up from school."

His hand presses firmer into my back so I don't trip again. "I don't think you're getting glares from those women because they assume you're my little sister."

I would refute that comment, but in the next moment we are swept inside the lounge. We're the only ones back here, so I'm assuming all the other celebrities decided to have their chefs cook for them at home tonight.

A velvet rope gets clasped behind us. We're led to a private little nook with drapes hanging around it for added privacy. Good thing, too, because a small crowd is beginning to form behind us, poised to receive autographs and photos the moment Nathan sits down.

"Here you are," says the woman I'm definitely not letting myself be jealous of. She gives a pretty little wink and walks off, cute hips swaying. It's not until I turn back to Nathan and see him staring at me and holding back a smile that I realize I was shooting laser beams at the hostess the whole time.

"If looks could kill," he says, giving in to his quiet grin.

I open my mouth to defend myself, but we get interrupted.

"Bree Cheese!" says Jamal Mericks, emerging from the draped nook wearing an incredible suit. I get tugged away from Nathan and wrapped up in an enormous, expensive-cologne-filled hug. "Quit hogging her, man. It's my birthday."

"Yeah, Nathan, quit being so stingy," I say sarcastically while digging around in my purse to find Jamal's present.

He rubs his hands together, and the gold watch on his wrist twinkles. "Ooh am I getting a Breenket?! Please say I am. It's been too long since you gave me that cat figurine." It was in honor of the time Jamal and I went to a cat café together to overcome his fear of felines. Unfortunately, the scratch he got from that particularly crabby tabby got super infected, and now he won't even go in the same room as a cat. Anyway, I got him the cat figurine so he can have one kitty that will never scratch him.

"Close your eyes and hold out your hands."

He grimaces, looking at Nathan. "She doesn't have a real cat stuffed in that bag, does she?"

"Wouldn't tell you if she did," says Nathan, earning ten brownie points from me.

Jamal sighs, shuts his eyes, and cups his hands in front of him. "Trusting you with my life."

So here's the story: Jamal likes to make sure he looks good at all times, so he slips off to look in the bathroom mirror a lot when we're out at a bar. Last time, while he was gone asking the mirror who was the fairest of them all, he missed a Nicole Kidman sighting. Nicole is Jamal's lifelong crush, and he was devastated to learn he'd missed his chance at seeing her in person. (It's important to note that this was the off-season and we were all several drinks in, and also that Nicole Kidman's friend called her Sally.)

I place a compact mirror in Jamal's hands. "So you never have to miss Nicole again!"

He squints an eye open and laughs, opening the little black circular mirror to peer at himself. "The perfect Breenket. Nathan, I hope you don't mind, but I'm officially stealing Bree as my best friend." He slips it into his pocket and wraps an arm around my shoulder at the same time that I put mine around his waist. Jamal turns me away from Nathan before I can get a look at his expression. I don't know why I want to see it. It's not like he'd be jealous.

But I do hear Nathan mumble, "Over my dead body." So that's sort of gratifying.

He parts the drapes, and all of my favorite guys in the world are already seated around a giant table. I'm once again struck by how wild it is that my best friend is the quarterback of the Sharks. These are Nathan's teammates, some of the sweetest men I've ever met.

Jamal Mericks is the starting running back, Derek Pender plays tight end, Jayon Price (we just call him Price) plays wide receiver, and Lawrence Hill plays left tackle. These men could all squash me between their thumb and forefinger, but they are all softies who honest-to-goodness treat me like their queen. They would carry me around on a chair lifted above their shoulders if I let them. I have no idea why—probably because I'm that girl who doesn't have an ounce of threat in my five-foot-four body. To these guys (Nathan included), I'm just Bree Cheese, the fun-loving, curly haired girl everyone loves with the dance studio above the pizza parlor.

"*Bree!*" All the guys cheer when they see me, and I give them a funny little curtsy. Next thing I know, these rowdy boys have all lifted and shifted me around the table to where I'm sandwiched in the middle of everyone. I look like a baby sitting between four bouncers. This is always how it goes. They're always very respectful, but they do like to move me around like I'm a hot potato.

"No ladies tonight?" I ask with a chuckle as everyone takes a turn kissing my cheek and then plopping a round of shots down in front of me. Jamal's arm goes behind me on the bench, and I can't help but notice Nathan's quiet grin as he watches from across the table.

"Nah—no one can compare to you. It's just us tonight," says Jamal with a smile nearly as devastating as Nathan's. Such flirts. "Also, Dad won't let us have more than one drink because of the playoffs. You good to party enough for all of us?"

The team refers to Nathan as *Dad* because he's always the respectable stick-in-the-mud. It's not because Nathan doesn't like to have fun, though. He can party with the best of them in the off-season, but in the regular season, Nathan puts his career first. He will do everything he can to win.

Lawrence picks up a shot and hands it to me with a mischievous glint in his eyes before he picks up his own. I eye it like it's a snake, because anyone who knows me knows I'm a lightweight. The guys can down one of these and never feel a thing. I, on the other hand, am a *jump on the table and karaoke Adele into my fork with a napkin on my head after only a few drinks* kind of girl. That's a completely hypothetical situation, of course. Didn't really happen a few months ago or anything . . .

Derek reaches over and plucks a shot for himself. "It's been too long since I've heard my favorite song."

Price and Lawrence tilt their foreheads together and sing into a single shot glass. *"Hello, it's Bree . . ."*

Yep. They change the lyrics and pester me with it as often as possible. So you can see how things go south for me real quick if I'm not careful. Considering that I haven't had anything to eat today since lunch and feel slightly unhinged after all the recent revelations from Nathan, I need to be extra careful with these innocent-looking beverages. I eye the shot then look back up at Nathan. What are the odds I'll tell him I want to have his babies if I drink more than one of these tonight? Usually, I'm pretty good at keeping my lips sealed. Well, karaoke songs aside.

Nathan and I make eye contact across the table, and I expect to see a note of warning to be careful in them (because he was the one who had to scoop me off the table and carry me home after my fabulous Adele performance), but his smile widens and he nods toward the shot.

"Go for it. I'll watch out for you tonight and get you home safe." He holds up his hand and closes his thumb over his pinkie, leaving the correct three fingers sticking up. "Scout's honor."

A familiar swirling sensation tiptoes around my stomach. He *will* keep me safe. He always does. I add that quality to my list of necessities for my future man: can trust him with my life.

I toss back the shot and let it burn my throat as the table bursts into shouts and cheers.

8

NATHAN

"Just go check on her so you'll quit obsessing," Jamal says, pulling my attention back to the table where I immediately stop tapping my finger. We've been here almost three hours now, and usually the guys would have run up an alcohol bill that could easily pay for a new car, but not tonight. We're all on strict diets to keep us in top shape, which means little to no alcohol, lean proteins, and lots of vegetables. We're not messing around.

Well, all of us except Bree. She's been knocking 'em back like a toddler with a juice box problem. I usually wouldn't mind, but tonight it's making me feel guilty, because I think I'm the reason she's drinking so much. When she found out I've been paying her rent and then on top of that found out I'm celibate, I think I basically flipped her life upside down and shook all the change out. I didn't mean to tell her I'm celibate, but I sort of had no choice when Kelsey's article was spreading lies. The honest truth is I'm celibate by choice. I don't know, one day I just woke up and realized I was done trying to trick myself into thinking I wanted anyone other than Bree. If it's not with her, I don't want it.

Geez. Now I'm realizing how absurd that sounds. Jamal is right—I've got to do something about this friendship or I'm going to die a lonely, pining, sexually frustrated man. I can't keep going like this forever, but I feel stuck. And the look on Bree's face when I hinted that she might be the reason for my celibacy . . . I'd rather be punched in the stomach than see it again.

"I'm not obsessing. I'm just . . ."

"Obsessing," the rest of the table states obnoxiously in unison.

I smirk and shake my head, looking down at my phone to see if Bree has sent me any rescue texts. None from her, but I have two missed calls from my agent followed by five texts updating my schedule for the week and adding more meetings to an already packed agenda. There's also a whole slew of messages from my mom with her own notes about how I could have played better in my last game.

MOM: I was just watching the highlights from Monday night's game, and you were looking a little sluggish.

MOM: I think you should fire your nutritionist and go with the woman I found for you.

MOM: And you're holding on to the ball too long.

Cool, now she's my offensive coach.

ME: I'm out with friends right now. I'll catch up with you tomorrow.

MOM: You're still out right now? It's late. This is not going to help you play better. You need to—

I stop reading there and pocket my phone. She lives in Malibu now, but somehow her expectations still reach me in Long Beach. They're nothing new though. She's been pushing me to play my best game since peewee football. I know I shouldn't complain too much because she helped get me to where I am, but it wears on me. Mostly because she *does* accurately point out my weak spots. It makes me feel like I should be up earlier tomorrow to watch the tapes and see if I am holding on to the ball too long.

I pull my thoughts back to Bree. "You guys know how she gets when she's been drinking."

Jamal laughs. "Yeah. She gets cute and talkative. You're the unbearable one."

"When I drink?"

"No. When *she* drinks. You hover around her like a bodyguard and just scowl at everyone who looks at her. So go on." He's pushing me out of the booth with the toe of his shiny dress shoe. "Go check on your woman before you bring this whole party down. We're already obnoxiously sober because of you. Don't make us all start biting our fingernails too."

"Agreed. Go find her," says Price.

Lawrence shrugs. "I think it's kinda nice how he's always looking out for her."

Jamal points at Lawrence. "Don't encourage him."

I shake my head and leave the lounge. Thankfully the bar is really dark and the VIP area is tucked back away from the main space, so I'm not immediately faced with fans wanting an autograph. I slip down the hallway and stop just outside the women's bathroom. I knock and open the door a crack to yell inside. "Bree Cheese, you good in there?"

I hear a drunken giggle immediately and relax. "That's me! Bree cheesy cheese," she says, probably to no one in particular in there.

But then a second later, the door opens fully and a tall, dark-haired woman appears. She's dressed professionally and wearing a smile that has a bite to it. I worry for a second that she's going to be an obsessive fan and get handsy in the hallway (it's happened several times), but then she opens the door to the bathroom wider and hitches her thumb over her shoulder. "I think your friend here needs a little help."

"Is she okay?" I'm already pushing my way in.

The woman follows closely behind me toward the closed stall. "Yeah . . . if you consider incredibly drunk okay. She was talking my ear off while trying to get that beer stain out of her shirt, and then all of a sudden she went white as a sheet and fled to the stall."

My heart tugs. Bree can't handle her liquor. I should have made sure she eased up earlier. I force-fed her a plate of fries (I say force because her attention span is the size of a gnat when she's drunk and I had to continually remind her to take bites), but I'm not sure it was enough to soak up everything she drank tonight.

I get to the closed stall and rap my knuckle against the door twice. "Bree? You okay? Can I come in?"

"NATHAN?! Hiiiii." Her voice is breathy but happy. At least I know she's not passed out in there or throwing up.

"Yeah, it's me. Can I open the door?"

I'm aware of the woman still hovering behind me. I want to ask her to go away. She doesn't need to be witnessing this, but that's the thing about fans—they don't believe in giving celebrities privacy. They seem to be under the impression that we "signed up for this" and our private lives should be an open, all-you-can-eat entertainment buffet. But Bree didn't "sign up" for this and I know she doesn't want anything to do with the spotlight, so I'm very protective of her in public situations. I'll be her bodyguard any day.

"Sure, QB! Mi casa es su casa." Bree is the friendliest drunk you'll ever meet. If at all possible, she gets more adorable with every shot she takes. I have to be careful with her, though, because one time she literally tried to give the keys of her apartment to a man experiencing homelessness and told him he should have it instead of her. She's generous to a fault—which is ironic considering that's what she says about me.

"Can you slide the lock open?" I ask her softly.

"OH!" She chuckles loudly, and I glance over my shoulder again. Brunette is still there, smiling tensely with a wicked gleam in her eyes that I don't trust. I adjust my body, trying to form a privacy wall with my back.

"Oops. That's the flusher. Hey Nathhaannn . . . where do I find the lockey thing? It's too dark to see anything in here." Oh geez. She's so far gone.

"Open your eyes, Bree." I tap the door. "The lock is over here."

She gasps loudly—probably when she realizes her eyes were shut. "You're right! There it is! Oh wow, that's a spinny room." I hear the click of the lock and get ready to open the door then remember the woman behind me again.

I look back at her with what I'm hoping looks like a soft smile. I have to be very careful when dealing with anyone in public not to do anything that could be misconstrued as aggressive or angry—basically anything that could go viral on Twitter and reflect badly on my career. Gossip is one thing, but a story about me yelling at a fan is another.

"Sorry, do you mind?" I ask, hoping she can read between the lines that I'm politely asking her to get lost.

She smiles wider and shakes her head. "No, not at all. Go right ahead."

Not what I meant.

It's fine. I'll just need to scoop Bree up and get her home. Well, to my home. No way am I sending her to her place like this. I don't trust her not to get up and go for a city adventure in the middle of the night.

I open the door of the stall to find Bree sitting on the toilet—thankfully with her pants on or she would be mortified tomorrow—slumped over against the stall wall. Her knees are pressed together but her feet are wide, arms dangling at her sides, a line of colorful woven bracelets drooping down her wrists. She looks like a kid who tried to stay up too late and couldn't handle the heat. The giant wet stain slashed across the front of her shirt adds to the effect. She's so cute, even like this. I wish I could lean forward and kiss her. Just a quick peck to let out a little of how I feel about her. It's been bottled up for so long it physically hurts, but I don't have permission to be that man in her life.

I squat down in front of her, taking one of her hands. "Hi pretty friend, how are you feeling?"

She smiles with her eyes closed again. "SO good. And my new friend Cheryl is reallllllly nice. Did you meet her?"

I look back at the woman, and she gives a wry smile. "It's Kara actually."

I turn back to Bree. "Yeah, I did. Kara told me to check on you."

"Good." Her eyes fly open. "And don't worry. She was really concerned about your problem"—her eyes widen and sink down to the vicinity of my crotch then shift back up to my eyes—"but I set her straight and told her not to believe that lying, shaming witch." She tries to bop me on the nose but taps my cheekbone instead. "Erfffectyle dips—" She pauses and frowns. "Dips—" She tries to get the word out two more times then gives up. "Your ding-a-ling is nobody's concern!"

Okayyyy, yep, time to go.

"Well, my ding-a-ling and I thank you for that. What do you say we go home now?"

She pouts. "Whaaatttt. But it's a party!" Her eyes belong to a puppy, and the side of her face is plastered to the stall wall. It's going to leave a textured print behind.

"I think the guys are all partied out. It's time for some sleep because we have practice in the morning." I stand up and extend my hand to Bree. "Come on, let's get out of here."

She takes my hand and stands, swaying dramatically as she goes vertical, and then promptly sits back down. "Ashhhhually, I'll stay here. It's too twisty up there," she says while swatting a lazy hand through the air.

"Come on, you got this." I bend down and help her up, wrapping her arm around my waist and making her lean into me. I'd just carry her out, but I have a feeling that would make a scene and end up on the cover of every gossip site tomorrow. So instead, I try to hold her up while we clumsily exit.

As we emerge from the stall, I find us face-to-face with Kara just as she's slipping her phone back into her purse. I don't have time to worry about that now though. "Thanks for . . ." Spying? Eavesdropping? Sticking your nose where it doesn't belong? "Checking up on her."

"Believe me, it was my pleasure," she says with a glint in her eyes that gives me a weird feeling. Sort of like when you're watching a movie and suddenly the camera zooms in with the slow, dramatic music and you think, *Oh damn! That person's bad!* Inevitably someone always tries to claim they knew it all along. *You knew nothing, Sandra.*

Kara turns and opens the door for us to walk through. Once out of the bathroom, I head to the VIP lounge, and thankfully Kara can't follow us.

Bree lays her head on my chest as we walk and breathes deep. "You smell sooooo good. Even your sweat smells good. How do you do that?"

I smile down at her, wishing she actually meant that compliment. "You're drunk. That's how."

The guys help me get Bree outside and away from prying eyes by creating a barrier around us as we walk. Jamal puffs up like a peacock, winking and flirting with everyone he passes. It's the perfect distraction from the droopy Bree hanging off my side.

In the parking lot, I'm getting ready to pour her into my truck when she whips around to the guys with a sudden alertness. It's her second wind, and I know what's coming. It happens every time, but usually I'm the only one around to witness it. "You guys are coming back to Nathan's place, right?! I have something soooo fun we can do!"

I give the guys a look that says, *Say no.* But of course they always give Bree everything she wants because she's impossible to say no to, and they all agree with gusto.

And that's how my running back, wide receiver, tight end, and left tackle all wind up at my place, getting our toenails painted in the team's colors by Bree. We're all lined up on the couch and armchairs, pants rolled up while Bree hovers over each of our feet in assembly-line fashion, painting our nails with the same meticulous attention someone would use while disarming a bomb. I imagine it's because focusing on toes is difficult when the room is spinning. Bree is nothing but joy and smiles the whole time though, telling us this will give us extra good luck and making each of us pinkie promise not to take it off before the next game.

When she comes over to lock our pinkies together, she leans over me then accidentally topples into my lap. My stomach dips with her face so close to mine. Her eyes look intently into mine. I've never had her in my lap before, and I can't believe how right it feels. Every inch of me tingles with awareness, and I begin mentally mapping out every way she fits perfectly in my arms. My mind growls. It's angry that now I have to know what she looks like naked and how she feels pressing against me. *Torture.*

Suddenly, all eyes in the room are on us, and I clear my throat. "Time to put you to bed, I think."

Bree's eyes are hazy, and instead of putting up a fight about me making her sleep here, she curls up against my chest, putting her head in the crook of my neck. "Can't walk. Too tired," she admits.

I stand with her in my arms and take her back to her room to the quiet snickers and chuckles of the guys around me like they are in junior high.

"Lovesick puppy," Jamal says as I pass by him, and I flip him the bird from behind Bree's back, hoping she didn't hear his comment, or at least won't remember it tomorrow.

After I get her in bed, I don't let myself linger. I tuck her in, turn off the lights, and shut the door behind me, not letting myself have one backward glance. The only way our friendship has been remotely successful in its platonic state is because of my acquired ability to keep moving. For instance, if I walk into the kitchen and see Bree leaning over the counter with her butt looking way too good, I don't linger and look. *Keep moving.* If I walk by Bree and we accidentally bump into each other, I don't stop and lock my arms around her. Nope. *Keep moving.* If we're up late at night and I'm tempted to tell her I worship the ground she walks on—*keep moving.*

So I don't look back tonight at the sight of her passed out against the pillow with her wild hair swirling around her. I *keep moving* back into the living room and straight into the sight of my friends, lined up on the couch, brows lifted and arms folded. It looks like an intervention.

"What's with the mom vibes?" I ask, frozen at the threshold. I'm not sure I want to go in there.

Lawrence is the first to speak. It's hard to take him seriously with his silver and black sparkle nail polish. "It's time, man."

My eyebrows rise. "That's cryptic and ominous."

Jamal smacks Lawrence in the chest. "This is why we didn't want you to be the one to deliver the opening line." He shakes his head. "He was supposed to say, *It's time to get your girl.* He said it all wrong. It was going to be great."

I try to hide my grin. "Do you want me to go out and come back in? We can start over."

"Nah, moment's over." Jamal pouts. He hates when someone ruins his special moments. And there are many.

I'm already turning around. "No, it's not. Come on, I'll run it again. Let's do it." I leave the room, coming back in a moment later like someone trying to pretend they don't know about the surprise party they accidentally learned about three weeks ago.

Lawrence is on his game this time. "It's time to get your girl, man."

A little bit of the spark has left Jamal's eye, but it's clear there's a part of him that still wants to play this out. "And we're gonna help you do it," he finally adds in his commercial voice. Honestly, the impression was made.

I puff out a breath. "That was worth it, guys. Well done. I have goosebumps." I appreciate what they're trying to do, I really do, but it's not gonna happen. "The problem is, Bree's not into me like that."

They all collectively shoot out a laugh. Price is the one to speak up first while dabbing his big toe to make sure the polish is dry before putting his sock back on. "Yeah. Women always curl up to me like a baby cub when they're not into me. Whatever man. Get your head out of your ass. That woman is in love with you."

I glance back toward Bree's room. I want to believe them, but it's too hard. We've had so many years to overcome the friend zone, and she's never done anything about it. Any time I get close, she puts up an extra firm force field that pushes me back. "I'm telling you—she doesn't want anything more than friendship."

"Or maybe she's just scared," says Jamal, standing from the couch and rolling his pant legs down.

"Scared of what?"

"Making the first move and it not being reciprocated. Y'all are stuck in a vortex of fear and miscommunication. Someone has to break through it first."

I know he's right on my part. I'm terrified to lose her again. I got a taste of it all those years ago when I went off to college and she dropped out of my life, and I never want a repeat. But is the same thing happening on her end? I don't have enough proof of that yet. "I don't know how to figure that out without straight-up asking her. It's too much of a risk. I don't want to lose her, because she's seriously the best friend I've ever had."

Jamal slides his jacket on. "First, ouch. And second, you just need an opportunity to test the waters without there being repercussions."

I'm all ears now. "How do I do that?"

He laughs and slaps my shoulder as he passes toward the door. "I don't know, man. We can't do all the work for you."

"I don't think you've done any work so far," I tell Jamal, and he waves double birds over his shoulders. "We'll have a whiteboard planning session soon."

Price passes by next. "Sorry, I'm too sober to come up with good ideas tonight."

"A little concerning to hear," I tell him.

Lawrence stops in front of me next. "I say just go for it. True love only comes once in a lifetime—don't let it pass you by." We all blink at our most aggressive left tackle. Turns out he is surprisingly romantic for a man who operates like a tank.

Derek is the last to step up and offer his sage advice on what I should do with Bree to get myself out of the friend zone. But it's not romantic or sweet, so I won't repeat it. *Although I will tuck it away for a rainy day.*

All night I'm lying awake thinking about what my friends said. Part of me thinks they've lost it and should be telling me to get over her instead of considering starting something up. But another part of me is left wondering what I can do to test the waters. And also maybe fantasizing a little too much about what Derek said . . .

9

BREE

Oh no.

I think someone has mistaken my head for a city road that needs repairing and is taking a jackhammer to it. Curse the guys for letting me drink so much last night! I must have been really far gone because without even opening my eyes, I know I'm in Nathan's apartment. Everything smells like him, and only in Nathan's guest bed are the sheets this soft. I had to have been out-of-my-mind drunk if he didn't even let me go home. *How embarrassing.*

Memories float through my head, and I give them attention with hesitation. Part of me is not sure I want to remember. What if I took my top off? No. Nathan would absolutely never let me do that. But we all know by now that serenading anyone who will listen is not out of the realm of possibility.

Thankfully, I don't have any memories of either of those events. I do, however, have a hazy recollection of spilling a drink on my shirt and running off to the bathroom to get it out. I think I remember talking some poor lady's ear off, and then . . . oh yeah, Nathan came in and rescued me. He's always doing that. That probably adds to his reasons for not being attracted to me—he wants a girl who doesn't ride the hot mess express on the regular.

I kick off the covers, much to the dismay of my screaming head, and look down: fully clothed in my outfit from last night and oddly disappointed by that. In the movies when the best friend gets drunk and the hero gets her home safely, he also helps her change into one of his oversize T-shirts (looking away the whole time with epic chivalry, of course) and she wakes up swaddled in his scent. I just smell like beer. And nail polish?

No time to lie here and wallow. I force myself to sit up and reach for my phone. The sun is out so I know Nathan is already gone. He has to keep a ridiculous schedule for the team and is usually at the training facility by six thirty or seven every morning. I'm grateful for it this morning, because I don't think I could face him after telling him he smells *soooo good*. Mm-hmm, I remember that part, and I regret it deeply. (Although it is true.)

Swiping open my phone, I see that it's eight A.M., and holy moly I have thirty-two emails?! Is that real? I also notice that my sister has tried to call me several times and texted me a million more. That's not normal, and a feeling of foreboding creeps over me.

I scroll down my contact list and press *call* next to her name.

It rings a few times, but I'm not worried she'll be asleep. One, because she called me enough times to make my cell phone provider want to give up and assume a new identity. Two, because Lily has three kids under the age of six so my poor big sister is always up with the sun. Someone give that woman an award.

"Hi babe!" she says in a loud sunshiny voice that rams into my skull. "NO, JOHNNY, PUT THAT KNIFE DOWN!"

I whimper and pull the phone away from my ear. *Ughhhhh* is my only response to Johnny's knife wielding.

"Uh-oh, are you okay?" says Lily. "Hang on, I'll—DOUG, WATCH THE KIDS, I'M GOING OUTSIDE TO TALK TO B!"

I hiss like an angry cat, and she just laughs. I hear shuffling and imagine her pulling on her puffy pink robe before opening the front door to go sit on the front stoop of her adorable cookie-cutter suburban home. It's white and has black shutters and a rose garden in the front. If I look out my apartment window, I see a convenience store with bars on the windows, some pretty horrific graffiti caked on the walls, and a tumbleweed of trash rolling down the sidewalk. LA is wild like that, because in a matter of five blocks toward Nathan's apartment on the beach, you go from my dehydrated-yellow apartment building with sticky floors to his three-million-dollar apartment with valet parking and perfectly manicured shrubbery.

So yeah, my sister and I are polar opposites. Where I have wild curly hair, she has straight, gorgeous, blonde locks that always look like she just left the salon. Where I was out drunk with a bunch of football players last night and tucked in by my best friend, she was probably rocking and singing one of my nephews to sleep before going downstairs to sit on the couch with Doug—her husband and the love of her life—to eat ice cream and watch TV. I'm sure he rubbed her feet.

Sometimes I'm tempted to be jealous of her, but a larger part of me also knows I'd never feel happy in her life. I love where I'm at. I also love that if you go look at that graffiti wall on the convenience store, you'll find my name spelled out in a really cool font, because I watched the guy while he sprayed the original art on the wall and told him it was awesome. He added my name as a tattoo on the dragon that's mauling the human. Really sweet stuff.

I don't want Lily's life; I mostly just want someone to love me like Doug loves her. That's the part I'm really jealous of.

"Does someone have a hangover?" she asks gently with a smile in her voice.

"Yes," I say on a groan. "It was Jamal's birthday last night and Nathan wouldn't let the guys have more than one drink—so let's just say I did all the drinking for everyone."

My sister laughs, and the sound is so sweet to my ears. I wish I was sitting with her and could lay my head on her puffy-pink-robed shoulder. "Poor B. That explains the video though."

I sit up with a jolt, and my brain knocks against my skull. "What video? Did Nathan send you an embarrassing video of me? I swear, I will—"

"Calm down, drunky. Do you really not know yet?"

"Know what?" I frantically start looking around the room like I'll find some sort of startling answer. An image of me on top of a table painted on the walls. A sound bite of my latest serenade playing through the overhead speakers. Nothing. Just the immaculate guest room and sprawling windows that overlook the lazy ocean.

"Oh gosh. Okay, I want you to take a deep breath."

"Lily, just spit it out!" I stand and ignore the churning of my stomach as I barrel into the kitchen, hoping to find any other clues that will point to my epic fail. There's nothing but an apple and a note in Nathan's handwriting that says, *Medicine. Drink. Eat. I'll check in with you on break. And don't worry, you didn't sing any Adele last night.* I smile to myself, feeling at least a little relieved.

That is, until my sister makes my stomach fall to my feet. "At some point last night, you sort of spilled your guts to a reporter in a bathroom."

"NO," I say on a long exhale, sinking my forearms down to the counter. "What do you mean I spilled my guts?"

"I think maybe you should just watch the video."

I whimper. "Where do I find it?"

Her sharp laugh doubles my worry. "Where can you *not* find it is the real question. It's viral, B. All over Instagram and Twitter. But the good news is, everyone loves you and thinks you're adorable. You've even started a hashtag!" She says it like I started a world-renowned charity.

"Oh my gosh, it better not include the word *boobs*."

"No, but I think after you watch the video, you'll wish you had flashed someone."

I haven't even seen it yet and I'm already contemplating possible relocation. How does one enter a witness protection program? Maybe I can just move abroad? Spain? I've always wanted to go there. I'll have to learn Spanish, and that could be a problem. DAMN MY YOUNGER SELF CHOOSING FRENCH INSTEAD OF SPANISH. Oh, wait, problem solved—I'll go to France. *Qui, I'll have une French fry, please.* Shoot, my French is rusty too.

"Just hang up and go to TMZ's website. Call me back when you're done." *TMZ! Are you kidding?!*

I feel like I drank an entire gallon of spoiled milk.

We hang up, and with trembling hands, I type in the web address on my phone. It doesn't take much digging to find the article . . . BECAUSE IT'S SPLASHED ACROSS THE HOME PAGE!!

And then it hits me.

Oh no. I *did* do something terrible last night . . . and it's staring back at me in the video under this very lengthy article. I blabbered. Apparently the new friend I met in the bar's bathroom last night was Kara Holden, gossip journalist for TMZ.

As my sober eyes focus on the bleary-eyed version of myself, a hand reaches into my chest and grabs my lungs. "Oh my gosh! NO NO NO."

The title of the article reads: STAR QUARTERBACK NATHAN DONELSON IN LOVE WITH BEST FRIEND AND OFF THE MARKET?

"Prepare yourselves, ladies. Longtime friend of Nathan Donelson hints that he may be officially off the market because of her. Local dance instructor Bree Camden claims she and Nathan have been harboring secret feelings for each other since high school. Watch my exclusive interview to hear the full story!"

I swallow down my queasiness then click play. Everything gets worse. Clearly, I'm drunk out of my mind in this video and wielding a Tide-To-Go pen in front of my body like it's a magical wand.

BREE: You know . . . Chherrryyll . . .

KARA: It's Kara.

BREE: Mm-hmm. Don't interrupt, izzz not nice. Anyway. I just wanted to tell you that there's nothing wrong with Nathan Donelson and his you-know-what. *winks aggressively* His meany ex was just tryin' to make him look bad because he didn't want to sleep with her.

KARA: Really? And why do you think he didn't want to sleep with her?

No, Bree. Don't do it.

BREE: He says isss because of his game. But I think it's 'cause he's pining after someone he can't have. *frantically rubbing shirt with Tide pen, looking like a sloppy child*

KARA: And who do you think that is?

BREE: *leveling pen at Kara* We sssspend every day together. We've been best of friends for *millions* of years. It has to be me! Whoelsewoulditbe?

KARA: Wow. That's exciting. And do you have feelings for Nathan?

BREE: *looks thoughtfully at the Tide pen* Chhhheryl, if I could . . . I'd use zisss pen to wipe away every other woman from Nathan's life. I'd be the only one left. *frowns* I need to lie down now.

And that's when I disappear into the stall and shut the door. The article doesn't end there though. The next video is captioned, *What do we think, friends? Does this look like a man in love? My vote is yes. Place your official vote in the poll below!*

The video is shot from behind Nathan, and clearly Kara was filming without his knowledge. My heart twists when I see him squat down in front of me and take my hand. He speaks so tenderly, rubbing his thumb across my knuckles. And I look . . . smitten. *What in the hell, Bree? Why do you have to look like that?* Anyone watching this video can see that I practically have glowing heart emojis in my eyes as I stare at him. And he's in love with me?! HA! No. He looks like a man taking care of a ten-year-old who lost her mommy. There is no way *that* Bree is attracting any part of Nathan.

I don't let the video finish playing. I can't take it anymore.

Nathan and I are the very best of friends, and we're going to be until we are ninety years old or he gets married and his wife excommunicates me. I never want to lose him, and this crap?! It's friendship ending. I've been so careful to never tiptoe anywhere close to revealing my feelings, but this absurd article is outing me! Now he's going to get weird on me.

I call Lily back.

"You see it?" she asks.

"Please run me over with your car."

"Awww, B. It's not so bad. So what if Nathan knows you like him? It's about time, don't you think?"

I want to pluck the hairs out of her arm one by one for saying that!

"It's the worst, Lily! You say *about time* and I say *too much time has passed*! It's been six years since we became friends again. That's so long to suddenly announce *Oh hey, by the way, I've loved you this whole time!* And he hasn't so much as hinted at attraction to me during that time. He never pushes the line. He happily dates other people and shows exactly zero signs that he wants me in any other capacity than friendship. So, YES, it's the worst!"

I turn the phone to speaker mode and set it down on the counter so I can rub my hands over my face. My hair spills all around me and I realize that, on top of everything, I've lost my favorite yellow scrunchie that I wore to the bar last night! COME ON, UNIVERSE!

"What if he sees this? No, who am I kidding—I'm sure he's already seen it. He's going to think I have feelings for him now!"

There's a long pause on the line before my sister speaks quietly. "Well . . . I still think it's a good thing to have everything aired out."

I growl. "Lily, you're not understanding. Do you know what Nathan will do if he finds out I have feelings for him?" I don't give her a chance to answer because I'm hysterical now. "HE'LL DATE ME! He'll date me out of pity, and then he'll get bored of pity-dating me, and we'll have a horrible, awkward breakup, and all these years of friendship will go up in flames."

"But you don't know that for sure!"

"I do! Have you seen the women he dates? They are gorgeous, stunning supermodels, and even they can't hold his attention for more than a few weeks. Nathan is waiting on some perfect woman out there that I don't think exists, and he's not going to settle until he finds her. Ask the poor girl he accidentally stood up a few months ago!"

"And how do you know he stood up a date?"

"Because I was with him! I saw it all firsthand! We were playing Mario and then she called and was furious, and he didn't even seem that sorry about it! I don't want to know that side of Nathan."

Lily lightly clears her throat in a way that almost sounds like she's laughing. "So . . . let me get this straight. He stood up that girl because he was hanging out with *you*. Tell me, Bree, how often does this happen?"

I narrow my eyes even though she can't see them. "I see what you're doing. Don't turn this into something it's not." I hate when people do this to me, when they try to plant an idea in my head about a future with Nathan. No. I won't allow it. If there is anything important I learned through my accident in high school and losing the only future I planned for, it's that everything works out better if I just live in the now and work with what I've got. No sense in relying on something I don't officially have in my hands at that moment. Life pulls the rug out from under us all the time, so if I can just be happy with what I have at this exact moment, I'll live a healthier life. Right now, I have a best friend I love to spend time with. If I start growing discontent and hoping for more with Nathan, that's when I'll lose him for good.

"I don't want a relationship with him, okay? Not unless he is the one to initiate it by declaring his undying love for me. Anything less will just end up as an epic failure, because no one—not even you—wants to be in a relationship where she's not loved as fervently as she loves."

"Okay, fiiiinnnneee. I see your point."

"Do you really?"

"No. But I want a present on my birthday, so I'll lie to you."

I groan and turn my back to lean against the counter. "Lily, what am I going to do? Also, I think I'm going to throw up." I eye the apple Nathan left out for me, and my stomach says, *Absolutely not.*

"Easy—you were drunk. You don't have to admit any feelings to him, and everything can go right back to normal if that's actually what you want."

"That *is* what I want."

Again she chuckles. I'll still get her a birthday present, but it's going to be a crappy one. "Okay, sure. Well, tell him it was the alcohol's fault, and then keep going with your boring, platonic, non-heated friendship."

"I don't like your tone."

"Deal with it."

I sigh and squeeze my eyes tight. "I need to hang up and call him."

"Okay. Good luck. Love you, B. And my guest bedroom is open if you need to come hide."

10

NATHAN

I'm just about to walk into a meeting with our offensive line coaches when my phone rings. I've been waiting on this call all morning—ever since I showed up at the practice facility today and was ambushed by dozens of reporters (mainly of the gossip column variety) wanting me to comment on the video of my best friend declaring her feelings for me.

My gym bag fell off my shoulder and hit the ground with a *thud*. I didn't bother checking social media this morning before practice, so I hadn't seen the video and article yet. I didn't comment on any of the reporters' questions, but I'm sure my face said it all.

I hurried inside, practically sprinted to the locker room where I ripped out my phone and immediately found a video of a very drunk Bree brandishing a Tide-To-Go pen and telling some reporter I was secretly pining for her. I almost threw up at that part. But then . . . THEN she said she wished she could wipe all other women from my life, leaving only herself, and a fire ignited under my hot-air-balloon heart and lifted me right off the ground. My manager called me shortly after and asked if I wanted to make an official comment. I told him we needed to wait until I had a chance to talk to Bree.

So all morning my mind has been racing. Wondering. Hoping. Could this be it? Could this be the moment everything changes for us? Because I'm ready.

I look down at my phone and then up at my teammates who are filing into the conference room. "You guys go ahead. I'll just be a minute."

They nod, and then I'm alone in the hallway. I take one steadying breath before answering. "Bree, hey." Did that sound normal?

"Hi! Nathan. Yep, it's me! Hey." Well, my response was definitely more normal than hers. It means she's seen the video.

There's no way on God's green earth I'm going to be the first one to bring it up, so I fish a little. "What's up? How are you feeling this morning?"

She groans. "Well, I was wondering if you knew of any places I could purchase a new head? I think this one is officially broken."

I laugh and lightly touch the toe of my shoe against the wall. "Sorry, I think you're out of luck."

She laughs, too, but it sounds nervous and stilted. And then there's silence. I know what's happening now. She's also fishing. Waiting. Neither of us wants to be the first to bring up Tequila-gate. Maybe we should just wait and try to have this conversation in person?

One of my coaches peeks his head out into the hallway. "Donelson, we're getting ready to start. You coming?"

"Yes, sorry. One minute." He doesn't look happy about that.

The NFL is very different from college. They don't babysit us here, but they sure as hell fine us for being late, bench us, or trade us off the team when there are too many strikes. Nothing less than complete competence is expected when you play at the pro level, and that pressure is always pushing in on me, some moments more than others.

Like now, I really need to talk to Bree, but I also need to go into that meeting. During the regular season, you forfeit your rights to a normal life. Everyone and everything other than football have to be put on the back burner. But I don't want to put Bree on a back burner. I want to give her 100 percent of my attention so she feels valued. I also need to give my career 100 percent of my focus or I'll fall behind. I just need to find a way to bring my capacity up to 200 percent.

I used to feel like I could balance it all so well. Lately . . . there's just this feeling I can't describe that follows me everywhere I go. It's like everything is swirling around me at all times. There's no way to make it settle down.

I don't know . . . I'll be fine. It's probably just playoff jitters.

I look toward the conference room, knowing I need to get in there before I'm officially late. "Listen, Bree—"

"I DIDN'T MEAN ANY OF IT," she shouts in a rush.

My lungs deflate, and I turn my back to the meeting I should be in. "Are we talking about the video?"

"Yes. And Nathan, I'm so sorry! You know how I get when I drink tequila. Drunk Bree is a territorial hussy, and I said a lot of crap about you having feelings for me and me stain-removing other women from your life, but it was the drink talking. It was all tequila's fault."

I can't speak, because I don't know what to say. A tumbleweed rolls across my thoughts.

I let myself dream too much this morning. I should have known better. Bree has been telling me for six years that she'd never want to date me. Why, after one drunken speech, did I think her feelings had changed?

"Right." I force a small chuckle because I will not get weird and lose her over this. "I thought so. Don't worry about it. It's forgotten."

"A-Are you sure? Do we need to talk more about this? Do you need more convincing? Because we're such good friends it would practically be incest if we dated! Can you even imagine?!" She laughs weakly.

My hand clenches at my side because, yes, I can imagine. And it looks nothing like incest to me.

I feel like I just stepped on a rusty nail while barefoot. I take in a deep breath and rub the back of my neck. "Seriously, we're good, Bree. I believe you. But I've got to get into this meeting."

"Oh right! Sure! So sorry to bug you. We can talk later."

"Definitely."

"Dinner tonight?"

"Yeah, I'll text you when practice is over. Probably around six thirty."

"Great!" she says in an overly peppy voice that grates on my shriveled nerves. "I'll make veggie lasagna."

I sigh at her obvious attempts to neutralize the situation. I'm so tired of neutral. I'm ready to provoke the hell out of something. "You don't have to do that. We can just order takeout and I'll pick it up on my way home."

"No! I want to! It's the least I can do after all of this. I'll make lasagna and we'll play Mario like normal and everything will be great!"

Yep. Completely normal.

Everything will be great.

I get home after practice to the smell of Bree's amazing veggie lasagna and the sight of her buzzing around my kitchen and dancing to "Do You Believe in Magic." Bree worked in the kitchen of a little diner after school from the time we met until she graduated from high school. I tried to get a job there to spend more time with her, but my parents found out and made me quit. They didn't want me focusing on anything besides my game, and since my parents were pretty well off, I never actually needed a job.

Bree's parents, however, worked hard for every dime they made, and so did Bree. I don't know how she did it all—school, dance, and work—but she did. Part of me was envious of her and the way she was able to work and save up to buy her own car. Oh man was it a beater, but it was *hers*. Everything was handed to me and even then usually spoon-fed. I drove a forty-thousand-dollar truck at age sixteen. Bree's bumper was held on with neon green duct tape.

I can't complain too much because my parents got me to where I am now, but something in me apparently hasn't completely forgiven them for how hard they drove me to success—any time I see one of their names on my caller ID, I have to take a deep breath before answering.

All I wanted was football *and* neon green duct tape, and I always got the feeling that my parents looked at me and saw nothing but a way to ensure their financial security and status for the rest of their lives. Football was the only life they wanted me to live.

But enough about my parents.

Bree is an incredible cook, but I also know she hates cooking, which is why I feel bad watching her try to make up for what happened last night. Although, I'll admit, she doesn't look like she's hating it currently with the way she's swaying her hips to the music.

She doesn't see me yet, so with a smile, I fold my arms and lean against the doorframe as I watch Bree lean over the island to drop a few dashes of parmesan in a salad bowl with a shimmy. Her hair bounces around her shoulders like it's just as peppy as she is.

Suddenly, she becomes aware of me and her head flies up. Her cheeks only turn pink for a fraction of a second before her dancing becomes even more dramatic.

"You're such a twerp standing there watching me!" she shouts over the loud music as she starts dancing her way over. She's throwing out a fishing line and reeling me in. She's taking me to the car wash. We're grocery shopping.

I don't say anything, just smile as Bree wiggles her arms like ocean waves all the way to stand in front of me. Bree is the most incredible ballerina, and to see her dance is truly magic, but oh boy, she's an adorably atrocious modern dancer. Her hair is twisting and twirling around her, and she's wearing a dark burgundy leotard with teeny-tiny crisscross straps all over the place. I don't know how she got into that thing. The back dips low, showing off a lot of skin as well as her black sports bra. Baggy gray joggers with the elastic band rolled down sit low on her hips. The leotard shows off each of her curves and athletic form, and I'm hoping my tongue is not hanging out the side of my mouth.

Bree has stepped straight out of my dreams, the sensation only increasing as her dance moves turn more modern and she twerks in front of me like we're in a club instead of listening to phrases like *if the music is groovy*. She's trying to make me laugh, and I'm just trying not to stare like a perv.

I can't hold it in anymore when she turns to face me, wiggling her hips dramatically and pretending to run her hands all over my body without touching me. Her expression is so over the top: scrunched nose, biting lip, and the most innocent song playing in the background. A laugh finally cracks from my chest, and I look to the side instead of letting myself put my hands on her hips and pull her up close to me so we can really touch.

Practically incest.

My expression must have changed because Bree stops dancing, a little out of breath, and reaches in her pocket to pull out the remote for the speakers. She cuts the music and the cheery sounds die. I realize my arms are crossed tightly.

She looks up at me and her smile fades. "Are you mad at me . . . for what I said in the video?"

Her face tears my heart in half. She thinks I'm mad about what she said?! I'm mad that it's not true! No, I'm not even mad. I'm just pouting. I'm being a big pouty baby and I need to get over it. The way she feels about me is not breaking news. It's always been this way.

I force my face to soften and form a smile. "Not mad in the least." I step forward, taking a deep breath as I pull her into my chest. She wraps her arms around my waist and squeezes.

Smashed up against my chest, she looks up to catch my eyes. Hers are the color of coffee with a splash of cream. Just the way I take mine. "You're sure?"

"I'm sure. How could I be mad knowing you were just trying to make everyone aware that my ding-a-ling is no one's business?"

She groans and buries her face in my shirt, gripping it dramatically like she wants to claw her way inside it and die. "I did call it that, didn't I? Pleeeease forget you ever heard that word come out of my mouth."

"Fat chance. It's so alluring, don't you think? Women will come running when I call it that."

It's good to feel her laugh against me. I've wanted her in this exact position all day. Every day. *Ughhhh just stop, Nathan.* I need a few minutes to gather up my fractured feelings before I'm ready to get back to our "normal" friendship.

I let go of her. "If you don't need any help, I want to change before we eat."

She rubs a hand on her arm, probably still feeling my weird energy. "Yeah. No problem. I'll scoop everything out onto plates."

I go back to my bedroom to lick my wounds. There's a giant canvas tote bag on my bed, stuffed with letters and packages. I'm just about to call out and ask Bree what it is when she appears in my doorway a little out of breath like she jogged back here.

"Oh! By the way! Your agent sent this over earlier. It's fan mail."

My eyebrows shoot up. I mean, I'm used to getting letters from fans, but not *this* many. "That's . . . a lot of mail."

She bites her bottom lip and grimaces. "Yeah. It's . . . sort of . . . well, maybe you should just open a few and see."

That's odd. I start sorting through the pile, and the number one thing I see are tons of Tide-To-Go pens with little notes attached. *"Wipe all the other women out and keep Bree!"* The next three I open say something similar. A few other letters go on and on about how much they adore Bree—and I agree, but clearly they are taking that drunken video a little too seriously.

I whistle when I look in the bag again and realize there have to be about 100 stain-removing pens in here. I'll never have an excuse for a stained shirt for the rest of my life.

"Are they all like this?" I sort through five more notes and toss them beside the canvas bag.

Bree walks up slowly behind me, like she's afraid I'm going to turn around and bite her head off. "Yeah." She whimpers. "I'm so, so, so sorry! I didn't realize Kara was a journalist. But even if I did . . . I was so far gone I'm afraid I still would have said all of that craziness." She groans again when she glances at the mountain of fan mail. "I've caused such a mess for you."

I take her hand and squeeze even though I know I shouldn't. "Hey, I said it's fine, and I meant it. I'll call Nicole and Tim later and get a statement together. I'm not worried about my image, I'm just a little worried about . . ." I look back toward the enormous pile of letters.

"The added work? Letting your fans down? Having to convince everyone we're not really together?"

"You." I look back at her. "I know you don't like being in the spotlight, and I'm sure this is uncomfortable for you. Also . . . you'll probably want to make your Instagram private now."

"Oh, I already have," she says, sounding weary in a way that makes my stomach twist painfully. She's never wanted this life. "I woke up to 10k new followers. And when I went downstairs this morning to walk home, there were reporters waiting for me outside. Your sweet doorman sneaked me out the back and gave me a lift home."

Dammit. I didn't even think about the fact that I drove Bree last night and she didn't have her car this morning. Geez, I'm failing all over the place.

This is not good. Not only because I'm freaked out about Bree's safety, but also because I'm terrified it means she's going to bolt out of my life. She's been stern from the beginning about what she'll allow in this friendship, and stardom was written in bold in the NOT ALLOWED section.

"How did this happen so quickly?" I ask while tossing a letter back into the pile.

"Kara's sneaky video of me in the bathroom has gone viral, and because she used my full name in the article, everyone easily tracked down my account. These all showed up because there was a post going around this morning encouraging people who live in the area to drop notes off at your agent's office so you'd get them. Can I just say that's super creepy?"

"Even creepier that so many did it. They had to actually go out and *buy* a Tide-To-Go pen too." I've never been able to get used to fandom. That's one part of this job I despise.

"I don't think it's going to stop any time soon either. They've been tagging us both in video reposts and using the hashtag #TideGirl.

Super flattering." She scrunches her nose. "It's a spin on something I said in the video."

"You mean when you said you wished you could use a Tide pen to wipe all the other women out of my life?" I regret bringing it up immediately. Clearly she doesn't want to revisit it.

Bree pulls her hand from mine so she can cover her cheeks. "Tequila, Nathan. Tequila made me say it!"

I laugh, hoping to ease her tension even though all I want to do is sink into a depressed ball on the floor. I'll be better tomorrow when I can reset my brain and wake up without the hope of a real relationship with Bree.

"Alright, listen, I want you to lay really low until I can call Nicole and get her to do some damage control. No walking home alone, and if you have to go to the grocery store or somewhere public, I'll send my bodyguard with you until all of this blows over."

"Damage control?! I damaged you! Oh my gosh, I'm the worst friend."

"Bree—the damage control is for *you*, not me." I'm not the one who despises the spotlight. Or the idea of a romantic relationship between us.

Her shoulders relax. "Oh. Okay. Well, that's a little better." She pauses and looks at the pile of fan mail like she's trying to harness magical abilities and send it all into another dimension. It doesn't work. Her powers aren't strong enough. "Can we just go eat and forget about all of this for a little bit?"

"Sure. I'm just going to change my shirt, because ironically, this one has a stain on it."

We both laugh, and it lifts a little of the tension in the air. I pull off my shirt and walk toward my dresser to grab a clean one. That's when I catch Bree's face in the mirror. She's still in here, staring at my back with her mouth slightly open. She's not looking away. Her eyes are glued to me, and I have to work so hard not to flex. Wait, should I flex? No. That would make it ridiculously obvious that I see her checking me out, right?

But she *is* checking me out. There's a spark in her eyes I haven't noticed before. I mean, she's seen me with my shirt off probably close to a hundred times, and I always thought she was indifferent to my body. Unimpressed. Now I'm wondering if she always looks at me like this when I'm not watching her . . .

Hope springs back up in my chest, and I decide to turn this into a little experiment of sorts.

I reach into a drawer and pull out a plain white T-shirt, stretching my neck side to side a few times like my muscles are just *oh so* tight. I lift the shirt over my head and tug it down in the sexy way I was made to do it in those Jockey commercials. I spread my shoulders wide and lift my arms, knowing full well it makes all my muscles bunch and ripple. Can someone get me some oil right quick? That would be great.

I'm not even sorry because this experiment is producing some very compelling results. Bree's eyes are fixed on me, and she's biting her lip almost to the point of drawing blood. Her eyelids are heavy in a way that says she likes what she sees.

That is not the look of a woman with sisterly feelings.

Not. One. Bit.

I turn around, and in that fraction of a moment, she's looking away like she's been an innocent little lamb the whole time. Her cheeks are pink though. Pretty ripe strawberries.

"Ready?" she asks in a high peppy voice. She can't meet my eyes, and suddenly I'm wondering if maybe the tequila didn't make her spout nonsense. Maybe it removed her filter. And maybe the guys were right.

Something inside me snaps. It's possible I didn't hydrate enough during practice today, or maybe I'm having an early midlife crisis, but suddenly, I feel like taking a big chance. Not thinking first, just jumping.

"Bree?" I ask, and my tone clearly says something big is about to go down.

Her eyes widen. "Yeah?"

I step closer. You'd think I would be at a loss for words, but I've rehearsed this in my head so many times that I know word for word what to say. "Listen, about what you said in the video—"

I'm interrupted by a loud knock on my front door.

Bree looks immediately relieved, and she practically bounces on her toes as she says, "Oh! Someone's at the door! I'll get it!"

Great. Just great.

11

BREE

I open the front door, and Nathan's agent, Nicole, sweeps in wearing a fabulous gray power suit, a large leather bag draped over her shoulder and a large foam board under her arm.

"Oh, good. You're already here," she says to me as she passes.

Her five-inch black stilettos click over the hardwood floor, and I have no idea how she manages to move so fast in those things. I would hardcore eat it on this slick surface if I tried to move like she does in those beauties. Not Nicole. She glides. Floats. A woman who dares you to mess with her. I think I have a girl crush.

Nicole has been Nathan's agent since the start of his career, and she's incredible. This woman is a no-nonsense powerhouse, and she's notorious for negotiating the most ruthless contracts in the NFL. Nicole has taken Nathan's career by the reins and steered it to incredible heights.

I want a Nicole. I've offered to pay her in lots of hugs and words of affirmation to guide my career in the right direction, too, but oddly, she said no then went back to scheduling stuff on her phone for

Nathan. *Loyal*—I can respect that. Besides, I'm doing okay on my own. Well, except for the part where Nathan has been monetarily floating me all this time without me knowing it. And I still can't bring myself to send in the application to The Good Factory that I've filled out five different times. Yep, doing good.

Just as Nicole is setting down what I can only imagine is a foam board presentation of some kind (I hope there is glitter involved), Nathan surfaces from his bedroom. I don't even want to think about whatever it was he was getting ready to say to me back there in his room. I've never been more thrilled about an interruption in all my life. The way it sounded, he was about to let me down easy. *Listen, Bree, about what you said in the video . . . I'm really flattered, but I just want to make sure we're on the same page and you know we will only ever be friends.*

I shiver and turn my attention to Nathan and Nicole.

"Hi Nathan, I'm sorry to bother you at night like this. I tried calling but you didn't answer. Clearly, you were busy." Her gray eyes shift mischievously toward me and then back to him.

We both start spouting babbling nonsense.

"Oh, we were just . . ."

"Lasagna!"

"And then a stain on my shirt."

"An apology meal, and then straight home for me!"

Nicole holds up a hand like she's silencing a kindergarten class. "Let me spare you both. I don't care." She then smiles and tightens her immaculate blonde high ponytail. It has that adorable flip at the end like Barbie. "I'm here because of a time-sensitive deal I need to discuss with both of you."

"Both of us?" Nathan and I say in unison, and I want to kick us for being so annoyingly in tune.

Nathan shifts closer to me as Nicole adjusts her foam board into an upright position on the coffee table then opens both of the flaps. This time, Nathan and I both gasp in horror. *Oh, Nicole.* Poor woman. Clearly the pressure of this job has taken a toll on her brain.

The presentation definitely has glitter. It also has lots of photos of me and Nathan, ripped from the deep pits of Google. They are mostly photos of us walking side by side to a coffee shop captured by paparazzi, or individual photos of us cut and pasted to look like we're standing together. So many are stolen from my Instagram. It's startling, but the worst part is the number of tacky hearts she's drawn around the photos . . . and the included list of baby names we can choose from for our nonexistent unborn child.

"Nicole . . ." Nathan starts, but he's at a loss for how to finish.

Her eyes shift between the two of us and observe our mutual horror. "Oh my gosh, you think I made this?! Insulting. No, this is why I'm here tonight. A fan made this for you two and dropped it off at the agency earlier. There are more like it too."

Well, that immediately changes things. Nathan has the same thought I do, and we both turn sharply at each other and yell, "I call it!"

I point at him. "I said it first!"

He rolls his eyes. "Not even close. It was a tie."

No way in hell am I losing out on this creepy board. "Why do you need it? Look around, buddy—it doesn't go with your decor in the least."

He lifts a brow. "And it goes with yours?"

"No . . ." I narrow my eyes and pretend to be a contractor, measuring it with my fingers. "But it is the perfect size to hide that big crack in my bedroom wall."

He shakes his head. "We'll settle this the right way: a thumb war."

I scoff. "Yeah right! I'm not falling for that again. Look at those gargantuan things you call thumbs. Not fair. What we'll do is—"

Nicole claps, and our shoulders jump. "I'm too busy for this. Figure out who gets the creepy shrine later. Let's go sit at the table and I'll bring the paperwork."

We follow Nicole to the kitchen table, and I can't help feeling a little like I'm headed to the principal's office. Nathan takes the seat beside me, and his hand goes to rest on the back of my chair. I'm hyperaware of it. Nothing else besides the presence of his arm at my back can hold my attention.

Nicole clasps her hands in front of her, elbows on the table. "Since everyone's time is precious, let's cut right to it. I'm not sure how much you've been on social media today. Nathan, I know you try to steer clear of it as much as possible, but I'm sure after seeing the foam board shrine and all the fan mail I had sent over earlier, you're able to grasp a bit of how viral Bree's video has become."

My stomach drops. This meeting is about me specifically! Oh gosh. Have I caused serious trouble for Nathan? Is she going to say he should get rid of me? I need to offer up a solution before things get out of hand.

"If I may," I say, rising from the table like I'm presenting a case in court. "Please allow me to say how terribly sorry I am, and I realize it's all my fault. I take full responsibility and will do whatever I need to in order to rectify the situation. My sister offered to let me come stay with her for a few days so all the gossip can die—"

Nicole interrupts me with a cackling laugh. I blink and look at Nathan. He shrugs, looking just as confused as I feel.

"You think I want you out of the picture?" She laughs again and shakes her head. "Sit down, Bree."

I comply quickly, bruising my tailbone when I sit down too hard.

"So what is it you think we should do?" Nathan asks, and half of my brain is still zoomed in on his hand clutching the back of my chair. When I take in a deep breath, the side of his thumb brushes against my shoulder blade. Is it just me or has he been casually touching me more often? Are these little touches accidental or . . .

Nope, never mind.

Nicole clears her throat—probably because it feels scratchy from all that laughing. "To put it simply, you two should date."

My jaw hits the floor so hard it makes the whole apartment building tremble. "I'm sorry, what? I didn't hear you correctly."

"You two should date."

I rub my ear violently. "HA! Sorry. Must have something in my ear. I keep hearing you say we should—"

"Date," Nathan finishes the sentence for me, and goosebumps chase that word all over my skin. "That *is* what she's saying. But why would we do that?" he asks Nicole.

She laughs again, and I want to steal her voice away like Ursula did to Ariel because it's really getting on my nerves now.

"Well . . ." She picks up some papers in front of her and taps them into a neat pile. "Major brands are finally beginning to catch on that social media is the number one way to reach the younger demographic. They've all begun to seek out influencers on Instagram and TikTok and utilize their platforms to sell more products in an organic way."

Which is why my Instagram feed constantly feels like a trip down a Target aisle.

Nicole continues, "Tide, as in the laundry detergent brand, caught wind of your viral video and loved it. Their account has had a thirty percent spike in engagement since the video went live last night, and to say they are impressed would be an understatement. They've offered you both a deal." Nicole picks up the pile of papers and lays them in front of us. It looks like a contract of some sort, and the letters are so tiny and packed together I'm not sure it's actually made for humans to read. "Tide already has a commercial ad spot scheduled during the Super Bowl, but given the massive hype around the stain-removing pen, they want you two to film a new one, playing off of what Bree said in the video everyone is going nuts for. It would be something cutesy and tongue in cheek with Nathan."

We're both quiet for a few beats, processing and reprocessing until we can make sense of this nonsensical information. All I can think is 1) I'm not in trouble, yay! 2) Nathan's thumb is still touching my skin. 3) An emphasis on number two.

Nathan regains consciousness faster than me. "So why would we need to date exactly? Why can't we just do the commercial together and that be it?"

"Couples in Hollywood do this sort of thing all the time as publicity for upcoming movies they're promoting. It's the same principle. They want you guys to become a couple—real or fake, depending on your preference—leading up to the commercial to continue building hype around the brand. Now, of course they know you're in the playoffs right now, Nathan, and your time is limited, so they're only asking for one public outing where you can be spotted and photographed looking couple-ish. There are some bullet points about posting on Instagram a certain number of times and the hashtags they would like for you to use, but it all seems doable in my opinion. Oh, and there is a nondisclosure agreement you both would have to sign."

"And after the commercial?" Nathan asks with one tiny sideways glance at me.

"Break up, get married, whatever . . . it's up to you." She shrugs again. No big deal. Just a casual conversation among friends where the word "marriage" is used in reference to me and Nathan. "You should know, if you decide to take the deal, the rate is a significant amount for both of you, but you will be under contract to uphold the terms. I've, of course, already looked at everything to make sure they're reasonable, and I wouldn't even be bringing it up to you if I didn't think it would be good for your career, Nathan. This kind of positive publicity is just the sort of thing we need to draw in more endorsement deals in the off-season." Nicole's bright, laser-beam eyes turn to me. "And Bree, like I said, it's really good money. This is the amount here."

I look down to where her manicured finger is pointing and HOLY CRAP! I would get all of those zeros from one commercial and a few dates with Nathan?!

I glance to my right, trying to catch a glimpse of him to see what his take on all of this is, but his face is impassive. He's waiting for me to decide first, but surely he wants to do it. I mean, this sort of thing would be amazing for his image, and pretending to date me for a few weeks would be no big deal for him because he doesn't have feelings for me. Also, it's a ton of money—the sort of money that could get me out of my nasty apartment and into something that probably doesn't have mold in the walls. I could get a new car! Or—no, duh! I can pay Nathan back for all the years of rent he has been paying on my behalf. This is huge.

I know Nathan would never hold the rent situation over my head, but it would make me feel better to have a clean slate nonetheless. The reason for wanting to pay him back is not pride or stubbornness. It's something more complicated. It's confidence in knowing I can provide for myself, and it's also a form of caring for my friend. I realize he doesn't need this money from me, but ever since we were in high school, Nathan's friends and family have always looked to him as their financial savior, like it's his sole responsibility to pull them out of their tight squeeze. I refuse to ever treat him like that. So, I may have to accept his friends-and-family discount on my studio rent until I figure out what my next step is, but I will pay him back for his kindness to me.

Unfortunately, it means I have to date my best friend. Could I handle crossing this friendship line and come back from it unscathed in the end? I'm skeptical.

My shoulders deflate, and Nathan notices. He looks at Nicole. "Can you give us a minute alone to talk it over?"

"Of course. I'll be out on the balcony making a few calls while you discuss it."

Nicole sets an innocent little pen by the papers before leaving the room. The door slams behind her, and I wince at the abrasive sound. I feel jumpy. My foot is vibrating. My knee is bouncing.

"Bree," Nathan says in a soothing tone, reaching down to still my foot. "We do not have to do this. Say the word and I'll tell Nicole to throw the papers in the trash."

I look from the stack of contracts to Nathan. He's so relaxed. Not a shaking foot or bouncing knee on him. Instead, his dark eyes look as peaceful as the dead of night, when you can't sleep and look out the window and everything is calm and still.

"So you're leaving the choice completely up to me?" I ask, uncomfortable with the weight of that realization.

"Of course. I'm used to this life already. It's you who would be affected the most by the sudden change."

"But . . . you're okay with . . . the dating part?"

Something flashes in his features. He looks away quickly and then back to me. "Well, I . . ." His thumb taps on the back of my chair, the movement brushes against my shoulder blade, and the hairs on my arm stand. They're all attentive listeners to the story his thumb is trying to tell. "I think we could work it out. But to be honest, the only reason I'd hesitate to do it is because I know exactly what you're planning to do with that money."

I lift my chin. "No you don't."

"It's written all over your face. See, right here across your forehead it says, PAY NATHAN BACK."

I laugh and give him a gentle shove. He doesn't budge because he's an ox. "I don't know. We'd have to be a *couple* for four whole weeks." A lot can happen in four weeks.

"A *fake* couple. It would just be acting."

Oh. Well, that's true . . .

"And besides," he continues, "you're always saying how much we're like brother and sister. So there shouldn't be any fear of feelings forming. Unless . . ."

My eyes widen to saucers and I cut him off. "You're totally right! It's actually not that big of a deal now that I think about it." The inflection in my voice is lighter. It's all starting to feel very practical and straightforward. Yeah. This is good. Nathan and I can totally do this. I can do this!

"And we're already comfortable around each other, so it wouldn't take much to sell it. If anything, we'll just get to go have some fun nights out together." Okay, now he sounds vaguely like the devil on my shoulder, but I'm just sold enough to not care. And maybe I'm just a tiny bit excited to see what it's like to date him in a way that will have absolutely no bad repercussions for me.

I smile and nod once. "You're right. Let's do it!"

His brows rise and the movement of his thumb stops. "Are you sure?"

"As long as you promise you'll accept the money when I pay you back."

He rolls his eyes and groans. "Breeeeeee, I don't need your money."

"Nathannnnnn, I don't care. Paying you back is the honorable thing to do. I don't mooch off of my rich friends. So promise me."

He holds my gaze for a beat then begrudgingly smiles. "Fine. I promise."

I swallow a sudden burst of butterflies. "Then, yeah! Let's do this thing. It'll be easy-peasy. Maybe even fun."

I watch with a sinking feeling as Nathan's head tilts ever so slightly and a grin tugs at the corner of his mouth. It's a look I've never seen before, like I just got duped by a card shark when I thought I was playing Go Fish against a toddler.

He hands me the pen. "Oh, it'll definitely be fun. I'll make sure of it."

12

NATHAN

"Not good enough!" I yell with my mouth full of popcorn and bare feet propped up on my kitchen table. It's late on Friday night and the guys have been here for hours.

Jamal looks at me over his shoulder, dry-erase marker frozen against the whiteboard I bought a few months ago for purposes exactly like this one. I keep it stored away in a spare closet and only pull it out for planning sessions. At the top of the board in bold letters is written **NO MORE FRIEND ZONE**. Not super catchy. We're still workshopping it.

The second I told Jamal about the meeting with Bree and Nicole last night, he group-texted the guys and told them to meet at my place after practice for a whiteboard planning session. This isn't the first time we've used this board. Last time it was to put a plan together for how to get Jamal's girlfriend to take him back after he acted like a peacocking ass at her sister's wedding. (The plan bombed. She didn't take him back.)

The time before that it was to figure out how to keep the girl Derek was seeing away from his mom on her extended visit to see him. Those women hated each other. Admittedly, that one also didn't go so well. Here's to hoping this third time will be the charm.

"What? Why? I'm telling you this will work." Jamal takes a step back and eyes the cornerback blitz play he just mapped out. He shrugs as he goes over it again. "Dude, do you seriously not know this? You just gotta time it right, come around her blind side, and *boom*, sack her. She'll never see it coming." I don't think he means "sack her" in the way it sounds. At least, he better not. The guys have learned the hard way not to talk about Bree or any other women like that around me.

I squint at the board like I don't understand the perfectly obvious play because it always makes for a good time to mess with Jamal. Although, how it applies in a metaphorical sense is still a little hazy. "But who is Bree in this play? QB or the ball?"

"QB, obviously."

"What's the ball represent then?" Price asks, leaning forward with his forearms resting on his knees, joining in on my game.

Jamal looks at us like we're missing brains. "The relationship."

"And Nate is . . ."

"He's the cornerback." He draws a heart around one of the Xs, and the new diamond bracelet he bought for himself glitters in the light. "Guys, this is super self-explanatory. I shouldn't have to spell it out like this."

Price skews up his face. It's a little overdramatic, but Jamal is still buying it. "I don't get it. Nate's a quarterback—he's not going to be able to play defense."

Jamal blinks approximately twenty times and then sighs. "It's just a metaphor!"

I shake my head. So defeated. "But he's right, I'm shit on defense. What if I'm no good metaphorically either?"

"It's not the same!" He's clutching that dry-erase marker like he's squeezing a lemon.

"Who are the other two linemen in the play?"

"That's me and Derek. Obviously, you're going to need our help on this one since we're the most sexually experienced of the group. No offense to Price and Lawrence."

"Offense taken," Lawrence says, standing up to his full six-foot-eight height. He walks over to Jamal and snatches the marker from his hand. "You're a sucker. They're messing with you." We *Three Stooges* boo Lawrence. "Alright, time to get serious. First of all, Nate doesn't need sexual experience in this situation. He needs *romantic* experience. And he definitely needs more than one very obscure play to show Bree there could be something between them besides just friendship. He needs a whole . . ." His words trail off as he finishes his sentence by writing ROMANCE CHEAT SHEET on the board.

"Ooh that's good," I say before tossing a piece of popcorn in the air and catching it in my mouth. I wear a cheat sheet full of plays on my wrist during every game; why shouldn't I do something similar in this situation so I can refer to it when I need a little inspiration? I like it. "Lawrence is officially in charge."

Lawrence is smug. Jamal crosses his arms and stalks over to the chair beside me to slump down into it. I offer him some popcorn, and he just gives me the stink eye.

"Don't pout," I say while crunching.

"I'm not pouting."

"You're pouting," we all say in unison.

Jamal rolls his eyes. "Just get on with it and tell us about your amazing *romance cheat sheet*." He says it like a dating cheat sheet is cheesier than what we've already been doing.

"I plan on it, thank you." Lawrence lifts his eyebrows in Jamal's direction before turning to the whiteboard and savagely erasing all of

Jamal's play. "This is romance, men. Not football. We can't use play fakes and little Xs and Os to portray an entire relationship. And no vague metaphors. What we need are *words*."

The guys all hiss. He just told them they have to dress up in suits and attend a cotillion.

Lawrence cracks his knuckles and stretches his neck from side to side. "Bree has always said she sees you like a brother (even though I don't believe it for one second), but over the next few weeks, you're going to show her a different side of you, all under the safety of this fake dating endorsement deal."

Okay, well I'm sold. I like the sound of that. I get a few weeks to finally show Bree the attraction I've always felt for her and see if she returns it. It's a lot of pressure to squeeze six years' worth of friend-zone-undoing into a short amount of time, but what's a little more stress added to my life? I can handle it.

"Sounds good. So what do I do, guru?"

Lawrence starts pacing and tapping the capped marker on his chin. "We've got to approach this carefully. Since you guys have barely touched over the last six years, you'll need to start slow. Small, gentle moves, building in intensity as the situation warrants, and only if she seems to be reciprocating." I think he missed his calling as Hitch, because he's exactly right. Bree is not one for sudden change. She's been wearing the same stack of bracelets for a year now and only added a new one to the mix after debating the merits of it with me for a week.

"If I've learned anything from Hallmark movies, it's that no woman likes a persistent man when she tells him no. So if Bree truly does only see you as a brother by the time this is all over, you're going to have to let her go and move on. Luckily, since you'll only be making moves in the name of the contract, you'll be able to go back to normal in the end without burning any bridges if she doesn't seem into you."

Yeah, normal. Unfortunately, there's a nagging feeling inside me that says I won't be able to go back to normal. I don't know if I'll be able to stand by after all of this and watch her date other guys again, or be near her and never touch. It's torture. I don't want to have to think about what I'll do if she doesn't want a relationship with me just yet.

"What's your first public date with Bree going to be?" Jamal asks, sitting forward now that he doesn't think Lawrence's idea is complete trash.

I get out my phone and look at the calendar Nicole keeps updated for me. "Wednesday we have to film the commercial. Oh, and by the way, it is a complete breach of contract for me to tell you guys we're going to be in a fake relationship, but I really needed help." They all agree to keep their mouths shut about it. "So yeah, not really a date, but we do have to pretend to be a couple in front of the crew that day."

"That's perfect," says Derek from where he's now raiding my fridge for the third time. "That'll be a good place to start exploring some light physical touch. See if any sparks start flying."

My stomach tightens at the words *physical touch,* and I immediately feel like a twelve-year-old scared to go on his first date. Even worse, I'm getting advice from possibly the most unqualified instructors. "What counts as light?"

Derek peeks over the fridge door and levels me with a gross smirk. "Depends on the woman."

I grimace. "Okay, never mind. I don't want to hear it."

Lawrence shakes his head at Derek. "I bet your mama's so proud of how you turned out."

"Holding hands!" Jamal shouts like he's on *The Price Is Right* and is tossing out his final bid.

"Hand-holding is good." Lawrence jots it down next to number one.

"Wink at her," Derek says while casually leaning back against the counter and peeling a banana.

I don't know about this one. Sounds kind of douchebaggy. "What do you mean? Just like wink randomly? I don't think I'm a winker."

"Yeah, you know, say something sexy first, and then just . . ." He gives me the most suave wink I've ever seen. I try to mirror it back at him and he grimaces. "Work on it."

"Forget his weird winking. You need to brush a stray hair away," says Price.

I look at him. "Expound."

"Don't you watch movies? You gotta wait until a piece of her hair falls into her face and then use your fingers to brush it back from her temple. Here, watch." He leans forward and demonstrates on me, looking deep into my eyes then slowly brushing an imaginary lock of hair behind my ear.

"Damn," says Lawrence. "I felt that all the way over here."

I point at the board. "Write it down."

He obeys, and we all get to work brainstorming the most romantic ideas we can think of, debating back and forth about what level of physical touch belongs to which week and whether a food fight would actually be as sexy in real life as it always plays out in the movies. There's also a sketchy idea of pretending the power gets knocked out so I have to fill the room with candles. I have no idea how I would make that one happen.

Finally, after our list is full, Lawrence writes "first real make-out" for item number 20. Derek wanted to write a different word on that line, but I wouldn't let him. That's not what this is about for me. I'm not trying to work my way into Bree's bed; I'm trying to show her that I want a relationship with her. I want to be committed to her in a way I've never been with anyone else.

Later that night, when our whiteboard is completely full of notes and ideas, I hear my front door handle jiggle. The only other person besides my housekeeper who has a key is Bree, and it's way too late for anyone to be coming to clean my place.

I shoot up out of my chair. "It's Bree. Hide the board!"

Everyone hops out of their chairs and starts scrambling around and bumping into each other like a classic cartoon. We hear the door shut behind her, and the whiteboard is still standing in the middle of the kitchen like a lit-up marquee. I hiss at Jamal, "Get rid of it!"

His eyes are wide orbs, head whipping around in all directions. "Where? In the utensil drawer? Up my shirt?! There's nowhere! That thing is huge!"

"LADY IN THE HOUSE!" Bree shouts from the entryway. The sound of her tennis shoes getting kicked off echoes around the room, and my heart races up my throat.

Her name is pasted all over that whiteboard along with phrases like "first kiss—keep it light" and "entwined hand-holding" and "dirty talk about her hair."

Yeah . . . I'm not sure about that last one, but we'll see. Basically, it's all laid out there—the most incriminating board in the world. If Bree sees this thing, it's all over for me.

"Erase it!" Price whispers frantically.

"No, we didn't write it down anywhere else! We'll lose all the ideas."

I can hear Bree's footsteps getting closer. "Nathan? Are you home?"

"Uh—yeah! In the kitchen."

Jamal tosses me a look like I'm an idiot for announcing our location, but what am I supposed to do? Stand very still and pretend we're not all huddled in here having a *Baby-Sitters Club* reenactment? She would find us, and that would look even worse after keeping quiet.

"Just flip it over!" I tell anyone who's not running in a circle chasing his tail.

As Lawrence flips the whiteboard, Price tells us all to act natural.

So of course, the second Bree rounds the corner, I hop up on the table, Jamal rests his elbow on the wall and leans his head on his hand, and Lawrence just plops down on the floor and pretends to stretch. Derek can't decide what to do so he's caught mid-circle. We all have fake smiles plastered on. Our acting is shit.

Bree freezes, blinking at the sight of each of us not acting at all natural. "Whatcha guys doing?"

Her hair is a cute messy bun of curls on the top of her head and she's wearing her favorite joggers with one of my old LA Sharks hoodies, which she stole from my closet a long time ago. It swallows her whole, but since she just came from the studio, I know there is a tight leotard under it. I can barely find her in all that material, and yet she's still the sexiest woman I've ever seen. Just her presence in this room feels like finally getting hooked up to oxygen after days of not being able to breathe deeply.

We all respond to Bree's question at the same time but with different answers. It's highly suspicious and likely what makes her eyes dart to the whiteboard. Sweat gathers on my spine.

"What's with the whiteboard?" she asks, taking a step toward it.

I hop off the table and get in her path. "Huh? Oh, it's . . . nothing."

She laughs and tries to look around me. I pretend to stretch so she can't see. "It doesn't look like nothing. What? Are you guys drawing boobies on that board or something? You look so guilty."

"Ah—you caught us! Lots of illustrated boobs drawn on that board. You don't want to see it."

She pauses, a fading smile hovering on her lips, and her eyes look up to meet mine. "For real—what's going on? Why can't I see it?" She doesn't believe my boob explanation. I guess we should take that as a compliment?

My eyes catch over Bree's shoulder as Price puts himself out of her line of sight and begins miming the action of getting his phone out and taking a picture of the whiteboard. This little show is directed at Derek, who is standing somewhere behind me.

Bree sees me watching Price and whips her head around to catch him. He freezes—hands extended looking like he's holding an imaginary camera. He then transforms that into a forearm stretch. "So tight after our workout today."

Her eyes narrow. "That's it. Let me see the other side of the board."

"No." I root myself in front of her.

"Why not? Is it something about me?" She tries to race around me, but I catch her abdomen with my forearm and twist her up to me until her back is pressed against my chest like we're doing some sort of salsa dance. She's scrappy though. Making her whole body go limp, she wiggles out of my arms like a fish. Faster than our top running back, Bree sprints past Price and darts into the living room. There's one small corner wall that holds the refrigerator separating the two rooms, and if she goes around it, she'll loop back around to the kitchen on the other side.

"She's going around the right side!"

Lawrence heads to the right, I head to the left. We both meet around the other side of the dividing wall, staring curiously at each other when we don't find Bree. A sudden flash of movement catches our eye as Bree jumps up from behind the couch and rushes behind my back, zipping her body around an oblivious Price and into the kitchen.

I make it around the corner just in time to see her face the whiteboard. Derek steps away from it. I'm out of breath and my palms are flooded with perspiration. This is it. Bree is staring wide-eyed at the damning evidence, and I want to jump out the window. How am I going to explain this? All this planning. All these years of patiently waiting, and *this* is how Bree finds out I have feelings for her.

"Bree . . . I can explain."

She laughs one loud, incredulous laugh, pointing a lazy finger at the board then letting her eyes pop up to meet mine. "Boobs."

My mouth opens, but I don't say anything, because suddenly I'm worried my brain just made that up. "What?"

Her eyebrows rise, and she looks both horrified and amused. "There really are boobs drawn all over this board. Just so many . . . boobs."

I swallow and discreetly look at Derek. He's giving me a thumbs-up from behind Bree's back. I'm a little frightened at how quickly he drew those.

I let out a heavy breath and shake my head, a relieved smile curving my lips. "Yep. Well, I tried to tell you."

She's laughing now. "Why are there boobs on here? Are you guys just a bunch of little boys?"

Derek offers himself up as sacrifice. "It was me. I was trying to describe to the guys—"

Bree cuts him off while throwing her hand in the air. "NOPE. LA-LA-LA! Don't want to hear whatever is about to come out of your mouth." She walks away looking like she wants to pluck her eyeballs out and heads toward me, pointing back at the board. "Erase it, Derek! That's gross."

"Yes, ma'am."

She stops in front of me and pushes her finger directly into my chest. "Something fishy is going on here, and I'm going to figure it out. But first . . . I need to use your washer because the one in my building smells like mustard again." Disturbing that this is not the first or the second time it has smelled like that.

An hour later, the guys are gone and I'm moving Bree's laundry from the washer to the dryer because she laid down on my couch and accidentally fell asleep. I won't wake her up. Instead, I'll carry her into the room she aggressively reminds me is only the guest room, and she'll stay the night. The guest room no one uses besides her. The room she'd be pissed to find an actual guest in because all the stuff she's left here over the years has really added up and formed a *real* bedroom.

Just before I go to bed, I get a text from Derek. It's the picture of the whiteboard from before he erased it.

DEREK: This is going to work.

I hope he's right . . .

13

NATHAN

The stadium is roaring.

It's game day and we're all suited up, shoulder to shoulder in the tunnel, gathered just out of sight, waiting for the go-ahead to take the field. This is a high-stakes game—every playoff game is—so the fans are extra rowdy. There's a heavy mixture of chanting and booing.

Jamal is buzzing beside me. He loves this. There's an energy meter above his head, and with every decibel increase from the crowd, it ticks up higher. Mine lowers. I have to tune it all out.

He accidentally nudges my arm while circling his shoulders, trying to get himself hyped up, and for some reason, that makes me irrationally annoyed. The rest of the team is behind us and bouncing on their toes, clenching and relaxing their fists, stretching their necks side to side. We're a bunch of bulls waiting to storm the arena.

Fog starts filling the air, and we'll be told to take the field any second now. I try to get my head clear, focus on this game alone and not worry about what it means for us. But it's hard not to feel the pressure.

I always feel it lately, and it's swirling around me in this moment. No matter how hard I try, I can't push it away.

I shut my eyes tight, trying to block everything out, but my pads feel tight. Tighter than normal. Constricting.

"Stand by!" a cameraman yells, lens pointed in our direction.

So much noise. The roar of the crowd, the music, the drumming of hands against the stadium seats—I used to love it, but lately I feel like running the opposite way. I can't figure out why. Something just feels off, and wrong, and I'm sweating even though it's only thirty degrees out.

I shake my head.

Jamal turns toward me and yells over the excessive noise, "You good, man? You look off."

My heart is beating in my ears. I feel like I'm going to pass out, but I know I can't. I have to stay on my feet. There's no time for whatever this feeling is creeping over me. I don't get nervous. I help get our team to Super Bowls, not pass out in the tunnel before a game. *But maybe I can just sit down on the floor real quick and take a breather?*

"Yeah, I'm good," I lie because Jamal can't know that I feel like I'm inside a tornado. He depends on me. They all do. Everyone does.

Trying to gain some sort of composure before we have to run out, I shut my eyes again and think of Bree. I see her wide smile and I hear her bubbling laugh. I tell myself that in roughly five hours, I'll be flying home and I'd bet my entire fortune she will be there waiting. She'll throw her arms around my waist and squeeze. It'll be quiet there.

My chest loosens a little.

"Okay, everyone get ready!" the cameraman yells again. The announcer comes over the speaker telling the jam-packed stadium we're about to take the field. The crowd sounds like an intense rainstorm slamming down on a tin roof. It's drowning me. Right now, the only thought grounding me is Bree. What would she say to me if she were here right now? It would be something perfect. She always says the perfect thing.

"Three, two, one! Go, go, go!"

We run out of the tunnel, through the heavy fog and directly into the chaos. The only way I keep myself from pulling a Forrest Gump and running all the way home is to picture Bree: nose scrunched, tongue sticking out of the side of her mouth with a big thumbs-up just like she did the very first time I took the field in Daren's place four years ago. I choose to hear her as a whisper in my ear instead of listening to the roar of the crowd. *You can do it, Nathan.*

BREE

Are you kidding me right now?! Only gigantically tall people keep their 9×13 baking dishes in the very tip-top of their cupboards. Nathan had his apartment renovated a year ago to fit his vertically blessed stature, which means taller-than-average countertops and cabinetry that touches the heavens. *We get it, Nathan, you're tall!*

Clearly, he didn't factor in his best friend breaking into his apartment and baking brownies for him while he's flying home from winning a playoff game! Yep, they won, but it was a tight one. I don't think I have any fingernails left. The score wasn't the only thing keeping me on edge though. Nathan seemed really off during the first quarter. He finally settled in and threw four touchdowns, but still, he didn't quite seem like himself.

I watched the game from his couch and screamed so loud through most of it that I won't be surprised if he tells me he could hear me at the stadium. There was one play where he got sacked, a really hard hit on a fourth down, and I held my breath until I saw him stand up and walk unassisted to the bench. Other than that moment, he played a solid game. I doubt anyone else was able to notice the difference in him, but I did. Any time the camera zoomed in on his face, I could see something lurking in his eyes that made me nervous. It was more than his usual focused look—he looked sad. Or maybe it was tired? Or worried?

I don't know, but I'm making him brownies to celebrate and cheer him up. He won't want to eat them because of his nutritional regimen, but I'm prepared to do whatever it takes to remind him that there is life and fun and sweet things outside of football and broccoli.

Honestly, I used to be just like him. I would do whatever it took to be the best, to perform my best. I didn't realize how burnt out I was until I had to take a year-long healing break, only doing basic physical therapy to regain the use of my knee after surgery. Not until I was forced to rest and seek out new ways to entertain myself in life was I able to see how I hadn't actually been enjoying ballet anymore. I had become a task-oriented robot who was obsessed with making it to the next level, no matter the cost.

Now, I try to not take life too seriously. I believe in working hard but taking breaks. Resting. Goofing off and eating yummy carbs occasionally. Yeah, they almost always go to my hips, but I choose to believe it only makes them more squeezable.

The oven beeps, telling me it's preheated, and the batter is mixed and waiting patiently on the counter. All I need now is that pretty little glass dish sitting wayyyyyy up there. *Hey, God, it's me, Bree—do you mind handing me that 9×13 baking dish right there by you?*

It's fine. I'll just climb up there like all of us short people learned to do when we stopped growing at the age of twelve. I hook my heel up on the counter then use every muscle in my body to hoist myself up there. Turns out, this was easier when I was twelve. I didn't snap, crackle, and pop as much back then.

I'm up here just about to grab the dish when I hear the front door open and close.

"NO!" I yell dramatically while quickly moving the smaller glass dishes out of the one I need, hoping I can scramble down with my loot before Nathan can see me up here and make fun of me.

I'm not fast enough.

He turns the corner and I peer at him over my shoulder, arms above my head, fingers clutching the baking dish. He's wearing black Nike joggers and a matching hoodie. A Sharks flat-billed hat sits backward on his fine, gorgeous head. Nathan always dresses in the finest tailored suits to arrive at games, but he goes for comfort on the flights home. And believe me, comfort looks good on him. There's something about a man not trying at all but still exuding confidence and strength that is undeniably sexy. It's in the way he casually drops his duffel bag in the middle of the floor. Tosses his keys onto the marble countertop with a lazy flick of his wrist. Looks up at me and tilts his head as his eyes drop to the small sliver of my exposed torso where my shirt has ridden up.

Oh geez, I'm feeling hotter than a widowed duchess in a bodice-ripping historical romance.

He lifts a brow and grins. "Hi. Whatcha doing up there?"

"Just some sightseeing."

His grin deepens. "Do you always stand on my counters while I'm gone?" He walks through the kitchen to stand behind me.

The air ripples like it always does when he gets near me. *Must ignore it!* The problem is, we haven't seen each other much since we agreed to the endorsement deal, so I've been able to block it out of my head that we're going to have to date for the next few weeks. But now, at the sight of him after a full weekend away, my thoughts are screaming HE'S BASICALLY YOUR BOYFRIEND NOW—JUMP HIM!!!

I turn back to my task of removing the baking dish. "Only when I'm trying to surprise you with brownies for winning a playoff game! But you're early! I was going to have these ready and smelling glorious by the time you walked in. I even prepared a whole song-and-dance celebration too. It was really going to be something." My tone is all pout.

He's standing behind me now. I hand him the dish and he sets it on the island behind him, right next to the batter. "I'm not early. It's nine o'clock."

My eyes bug out. "WHAT! That can't be true." I look at the clock and sure enough, it's nine at night. When did that happen?

He smirks up at me and leans back against the counter. I'm relieved to see that his face looks normal again—no weird *something* from the field still lurking in his eyes.

"Hmm," he rumbles with a mischievous smile. "Did someone perhaps take a little nap?"

"No!" *Yes.* I only meant to lie down for a few minutes, and then that somehow turned into four years and I woke up feeling like I had been teleported to another dimension. I think Nathan's couch is laced with NyQuil because this seems to happen to me a lot over here.

He peeks over his shoulder to the living room where the evidence is strewn all over the place, as apparent as a gruesome murder scene. A cozy blanket rumpled on the couch. A pillow from my—excuse me, THE GUEST—ROOM propped against the armrest. One of Nathan's phone chargers plugged in so the cord could reach beside my pillow.

I clap loudly. "Hey, look at me!"

My distraction doesn't work. He's already chuckling smugly and crossing those big arms. "You totally did. You napped hard and lost track of time because you were so comfy on my couch."

My hand goes to my hip. I feel powerful up here. Is this why tall people are always on power trips? I get it now.

"You don't know me," I say in my best reenactment of one of my sassy teenage dancers.

"You napped your ass off."

"Shut up." So I like to nap and they always get out of hand—what about it?

He steps forward so he's standing right in front of me. "And tell me . . . why is it that every single time I'm out of town, I come home to find out you've been spending all of your time here, napping and"—he peeks into the sink and notices the pan I used to scramble my eggs for breakfast this morning after sleeping a solid eight hours in the guest room—"living?"

I know what he wants from me. But he's not going to get it.

"Because I'm worried someone is going to break in and steal all your stuff while you're away and I need to protect it?"

He makes an obnoxious buzzer sound. "Wrong. Would you like to try again?"

I gasp when he wraps his arms around my thighs and easily lifts me off the counter. He pivots us away and slowly lets me slide to the ground. My power dissolves by the second. Every inch of me slides down every inch of him during this descent, and I think I might die. He's like a brick wall, this man. I've never been wrapped so tightly in his arms before, and my heart is stuttering. It's hurdling into my throat. It can't keep up.

This is my favorite trip in my history of trips. Along the way, I take mental pictures of all the sights. I pass his hair, flipping out adorably from under his hat. His jet-black eyes, as frightening as they are comforting. The full curve of his lower lip. The not-so-subtle suggestion of muscled shoulders under his hoodie. And I finally come in for a smooth landing at his wide, sturdy chest. I'll make a scrapbook with all of these gorgeous snapshots.

I want to take in a deep breath, add a sharp scent to these memories, but I'm afraid it will sound trembly if I do. I have to be careful. Because of Tequila-gate, I'm already on thin ice. If I want to keep everything normal between us, I *must* act normal.

I look up and meet his eyes.

BIG mistake.

We're standing so close, and his arms are still holding me. He smiles, and my stomach goes twisty. "You're always here because you hate living in your sucky apartment. Admit it—you want to move in here."

I raise my chin. "Never." Because it's not true. I stay here while he's gone because I miss him and everything in here smells like him. Well, and yeah, I want to live here, but only because he also lives here. I don't care about his fancy stuff or his soft sheets or the really deep soaking tub or . . . okay, fine, I like those things too. So the real reason I want to live here is because all of it combined is euphoria.

Speaking of euphoria, why are his arms still looped tightly around me? Should I try to wiggle away? My body will never comply. It has already curled up and made a new home here. Geez, his five o'clock shadow is hot. I bet it would tickle my neck.

Nathan's eyes dart over my shoulder, and his smile goes wicked. The next thing I know, his finger is covered in brownie mix and smearing across my cheekbones, slowly and with care. "Admit it," he says with that villainous grin.

I audibly inhale low and long, blinking like, *Oh no you did not just do that!*

He's so pleased with himself right now. "You look like a miniature football player."

Okay, well clearly brownies are off the table for tonight because he just started A WAR!

I reach behind me, dunk my fingers into the mix, and then stamp them onto the center of his face. Nice and slow.

"Never," I whisper in front of his lips like the bad guys always do in movies.

He blinks, brownie batter clinging to his lashes. I can't swallow as I watch him pull his lips in, nodding slowly. He lets go of me to put his hands on the counter in front of him, hunching over like a beast preparing his plan of attack.

I'm not an amateur, so I grab the mixing bowl full of brownie batter and make a break for it. Except . . . I'm not moving. My socked feet are gliding on the hardwood but going absolutely nowhere. Who put a treadmill in this floor?!

I look over my shoulder and see Nathan has the back of my shirt pinched between his fingers. And now I'm being slid backward, closer to him. That large hand reaches over my shoulder, and I watch it dip—his whole entire hand—into the bowl of brownie mix I'm clutching tightly in front of me. There's nothing for me to do but close my eyes as he slowly presses a blob of sticky batter onto the right side of my face. Hair and all. That's going to be fun to get out.

Can I just say, this is the weirdest, slowest food fight anyone has ever witnessed? And oddly, it's making me super hot and tingly.

I spin around to face him, and it's my turn now. I take a dip of batter then smear it across both of his eyebrows. He looks like Eugene Levy now, and I have to press my fist to my mouth to keep from laughing. With a subtle grin, he loads up his finger then uses the batter to paint brown lipstick across my lips—really . . . freaking . . . slowly.

Oh.

Okay, well my skin is on fire now. It's fine. I'm fine. Everything is fine. Except I'm not fine because I don't know what in the hell I'm supposed to make of this! Am I completely off my rocker or is the mood just a little bit sexy right now? I try not to acknowledge the way his finger is lingering on my mouth like he has nothing but time. Is he standing closer than he was a minute ago? His hand drops, and I look up. He's staring at my mouth. He's inching closer. His head is dropping.

My breath catches.

He leans down and says quietly in front of my lips, "Thanks for making me brownies. Too bad I didn't get to taste them."

Someone has clamped a clothespin over my windpipe. Did he really just say that? Am I still napping and imagining this whole thing? Because it feels a lot like some particularly wonderful dreams I've had about Nathan.

He and I have always been blatantly honest with each other (except for when I'm lying through my teeth about my feelings for him), so the question comes out of my mouth before I can stop it. "Nathan, are you flirting with me?"

He's not shocked by my candor. "Yeah. I am."

"Why?" I don't mean to sound so grossed out, but I think it came out that way. I'm just terrified. I've got my heart on a very tight leash. No exceptions.

"I'm . . . practicing."

"Practicing," I repeat, my eyes bouncing to the slash of his full lips and back up to his eyes in a moment of weakness. I wish the fact that he was covered in brownie mix was deterring. It's not. I love brownies.

"Don't you think it's a good idea?" He's talking so quiet, voice so gravelly. I feel lightheaded hearing his words this way. "We're going to have to flirt in public, so we've got to get used to it for it to be convincing."

I give that logical response the brilliant reply it deserves. "Uh-huh."

A small chuckle rumbles from his chest. "You okay, Bree?" He sounds extra flirty now. Amused. And his lips are dangerously close to my brownie lipstick. Ahh! His hand is on my hip! When did that happen?! Wait a minute—are we going to kiss right now? Are two friends about to make out in this kitchen covered in brownie batter?

That's when it hits me: this is an ego trip for him right now. He's on a high after winning another playoff game, and I'm nothing but a little mouse for the big cat to play with in the kitchen. We don't need to practice. He's just being a flirty jerk and messing with me during his macho ego high. NOPE. That's not going to happen. Just like I don't want a pity relationship with him, I don't want a well-she-was-there-and-it-was-convenient one-night fling either. Maybe he could handle something like that, but I couldn't. Friends with benefits will never be a part of our description, because it would kill me for him to walk away from me after it's all said and done. It's all or nothing for me.

Nathan continues his game. "So let's pretend we're in public right now, and everyone is watching." He's still staring at my lips. "We've really got to sell it. If I said, *Too bad I didn't get to taste them*, what would you say to that?"

I have the strongest willpower in all the land. I have a free pass to let Nathan Donelson taste the brownies right off my lips, and instead, I stick my hand in the batter, pull out a whole scoop, and smear it around his entire face until it completely hides his features. There. He's Mud Man now.

I step back, wipe my hands on a kitchen towel, and smile proudly. "I'd say, *Now you've got plenty to sample! Enjoy!*"

I think he's frowning under all that batter, but it's hard to tell.

I turn away and flee the kitchen, calling over my shoulder, "I'm staying in the guest room tonight because it's too late to walk home and no other reason!"

Boom. Status quo re-established. Friendship saved.

14

BREE

Completely normal. Everything is absolutely and completely normal. Just my normal friend Nathan and normal me hanging out on a normal day where everything is fine.

Except news flash: IT'S NOT FINE.

"Are you going to get in?" Nathan asks, standing outside the open door of the giant blacked-out SUV we're going to ride in to get to the set of the commercial today. I've never ridden in it with him. Nathan only takes it to special events and places where he might need more privacy and security, places I refuse to go with him because those are things *girlfriends* do with him, not best friends.

Along with the nice man who's going to drive me around like I'm the Queen of England, Nathan's hulking bodyguard is sitting in the passenger seat waiting to jump out and . . . I don't know, peel a rabid fan off of Nathan's body if need be? This is an aspect of Nathan's life I'm not used to.

I'm trying to convince myself this is an average sunny day and I'm simply taking a drive with my BFF, but this pumpkin feels an awful lot like a carriage, and it's making me want to run for the hills. I can practically see the giant pencil in my mind flipping over and smudging its eraser across those beautifully drawn lines that define our friendship.

"Bree?" Nathan prompts again, his brows knitting together in a confused smile. "Are you okay?"

"Hmm?" I blink. "Yeah! Oh yeah. Totally good. Of course I'm going to get in. I was just wondering if they clean those bench seats or not."

He chuckles, looking at me like I've lost my marbles. "Yeah, I assume they do occasionally. Why?"

I shrug. "Just . . . didn't want to get in there without knowing for sure. Because they're so spacious, and people could have done goodness knows what back there, and—"

Nathan steps forward now and starts pushing me by my lower back into the SUV. "This is my personal vehicle, Bree. I own it. There's nothing funky on those seats, don't worry. Now, please get in or we're going to be late. And smile, there's a paparazzi over on that corner catching every bit of your indecision."

I smile really big and scary up at Nathan to make him laugh and show him just how much I care about paparazzi.

He gives me his full-teeth, cheek-dimples laugh that inflates my heart ten sizes and shakes his head. "You're all fun and games now until you realize that photographer will have zoomed in dangerously close on your silly face and will splash it all over newsstands tomorrow declaring, *Bree Camden cracking under the pressures of newfound fame!*"

"I don't think they would be all that wrong," I say before I hop into the SUV, slide over to the far side, and suction myself to the window. Oh my gosh there is nothing normal about this vehicle. The leather is butter soft, and there's an adjacent bench seat that faces this side with a flatscreen TV behind it. My fingers glide over a panel of buttons on my armrest, and after I press one, warm lights fill the space (mood lights) and my seat starts to recline with a footrest popping out.

I turn wide eyes to Nathan, and he's laughing silently. "You're like a kid in here."

"I *feel* like a kid in here! I'm not supposed to be allowed in fancy places like this. Nathan, I'll spill something on these million-dollar seats." I set my seat upright again and cross my hands primly in my lap.

"You don't have a drink."

"Doesn't matter. It'll happen somehow. You know me—I can't be trusted with luxurious things."

"It's only stuff, Bree. I couldn't care less. Spill anything you want in here." His eyes are crinkled in the corners, but what I notice most are the dark circles hovering under those jet-black pools.

I tilt my head and reach up to softly tap a finger under each of his eyes. "You're tired."

His hair is still slightly damp because he's fresh from practice. Nathan had to wake up at five A.M., work a full day of his usual practice and meetings, putting his body through a complete beating, and now at the end of the day is going to film a commercial for several hours when he should be resting and recuperating.

He takes my wrist and softly wraps his fingers around it. I feel his touch like it's wrapping around my heart. "I'm okay."

"You're overextending yourself. We didn't have to say yes to this commercial."

The SUV starts moving. Nathan looks down at my wrist and lowers it but doesn't let it go. We're one position shift away from holding hands. "I wanted to do the commercial. It'll be good for both of us."

For me. It will be good for *me* is what he means. Because yes, it's good for Nathan's image, but let's be real, he doesn't need the money. I do. I want this money so I can pay him back.

But then another thought pops into my head. *What then?* What is my next step after paying Nathan back? Something about him buying the studio and me realizing he's been paying part of my rent all these years has shaken up a restlessness in me. It's made me a little antsy and craving more for my studio. Which completely terrifies me. I don't like craving more, because I don't like who I was back when all I did was strive for more. Contentment is what I need. If I had possessed even just an ounce more contentment back in high school, I wouldn't have spent all of my time and energy trying to get into Juilliard. I would have gone to parties. Made friends. Maybe even had a hobby or desires outside of dance that would have kept me from spiraling into such a dark place when my one and only dream got snatched away.

I should be grateful for the help my friend has given me and find tangible ways to make the studio I currently have better. But instead, when trying to find new ways to not have to completely rely on his generosity, I accidentally stumbled across a new dream. One where my studio is not scented with pepperonis, and where it could officially function as a nonprofit, able to accept more students who normally couldn't afford dance classes.

The only way any of this would be possible is if I was granted the space in The Good Factory. The problem is, I've put all my eggs in one basket before, and it did not turn out in my favor. I'm terrified to want something just as much again.

Nathan's phone rings, and he lets go of me so he can answer. "It's my mom," he says, looking a little weary before pasting on a tight smile and answering. "Hey Mom, what's—" There's a pause as he listens, followed by several mm-hmms and sures. His eyes shut tight for a moment like he's in pain, and then he opens them again. I can only imagine she's asking for something that takes too much from him.

Nathan has a problem saying no—especially to his parents. They've always expected a lot of him and have never been hesitant to ask for a lot too (and give nothing in return besides criticism). They always commit him for their charity events without truly asking him, manipulate him into dropping by their holiday parties just so he can be seen and sign autographs, and even ask him to float their lavish vacations because they know when something is paid for on the famous NFL quarterback's black card, it gets them into a whole other sphere of luxury than even their padded bank accounts can achieve. They parade him around like a tiger at the circus and then whip him when he gets tired so he'll perform better and keep that social status coming in for them. Yet another reason I never want Nathan to feel like he has to take care of me financially or carry me on his arm to special events. That's not what he is to me.

I want to rip the phone out of his hand and tell this woman, *Sorry, Nathan is no longer available for your constant soul sucking. Try taking up embroidery instead.* But it's not my place to protect him from his mom.

After a minute, he hangs up and sighs.

"Fun conversation?" I ask sarcastically.

He shrugs. "Not a big deal. She just wanted to see if I could fly home shortly after the season to show up to some charity event for them at their country club."

"And you told her you'll be taking some time off to reenergize?" I ask, even though I already know the answer.

He looks down at his fidgeting hands. "I told her yes. I have to see them at some point anyway, so might as well do something for a good cause while I'm there."

I hate that he does this. Nathan is convinced he's Superman, and . . . well, I'm not completely convinced otherwise, but I know he has flesh and blood like the rest of us, and the load he's carrying can't be sustained for long. I don't want to see him crash and burn. I want to strap him down and make him rest.

"How's work life?" he asks softly.

"Don't think I don't know that you're sidestepping my concern."

He grins and leans his head back against the headrest to stare at me. "Hoping to. So what's new at the studio? How are the girls?"

I settle back against the seat, thankful that some of our normalcy has permeated the strangeness of this luxurious environment. This feels more like us. If I close my eyes, I can almost imagine we're on his couch at home.

"It's all been good. Imani has a new boyfriend who everyone and their brother can tell Sierra is jealous of, and . . ." I'm momentarily breathless at the sight of his soft genuine smile. He truly cares what's happening with the girls in my class just like I do, and it makes my heart twist. ". . . Hannah's dad got laid off again, but I was able to waive her tuition fees so she can still attend class because a certain generous benefactor bought the building and lowered my rent."

I look out the window and see a car full of teenage girls riding beside us, keeping their car at the same speed as ours. The one in the passenger seat is telling us to roll down the window so they can see who's in here. Gutsy. For all they know, it's an old balding senator. My eyes slip to Nathan. *Not* an old balding senator.

"Because of you, these girls are able to continue to pursue their dreams. And knowing what I know now about how you've been helping with my rent all along, I realize I never would have been able to keep the doors open for them without you. So thank you."

He's frowning now. Not the look I was expecting after that speech. "You kill me, you know that?"

"With my devastating good looks?" I flash him an over-the-top debutante smile.

He doesn't laugh at my quip. "You kill me when you don't see your own worth. Bree, those doors are only open because of you. Those girls are achieving their dreams 100 percent because of you and the work you put into their lives. If I hadn't bought the building, I know without a doubt you would have found a different way on your own. Probably would have worked a second job just so you could continue doing your first job! So no, don't give me that credit. All I did was use money that would have been sitting around collecting dust."

I swallow and clear my throat, not enjoying the sudden seriousness of this conversation. Even more, I don't like that his words settle a pack of hot coals in my heart. It's glowing and warm. Nathan makes me feel seen in a way no one else does.

But still, this conversation feels too intimate for our normal vibes, so I chuckle lightly and deflect. "You're my best friend. It's your job to say stuff like that."

"Bree—"

I cut him off. "Hey, I have something I need to give you before we get to the set."

"Now who's sidestepping?"

I ignore him, dig the piece of paper out of my purse, and hand it to him. He looks at the folded slip of paper like maybe I've wiped a thousand boogers on it. I shake it in front of him with a laugh. "Here! Just open it."

"What is it?"

"It's a list."

He gives me a look then takes the sheet of paper. It's minuscule in his big hand. Nathan gingerly unfolds it like it's a snowflake but then scoffs before he reads it aloud. "*Rules for survival*." His eyes are annoyed as they slide to me. "A little dramatic, don't you think?"

I nod toward the paper. "Keep reading! It's important. If we're going to make it out of this fake relationship with our friendship intact, we have to have some ground rules." I scribbled this list after Nathan's little *practice* exercise the other night. I can't handle more situations like that, so it's time to put some parameters in place to ensure it doesn't happen again.

I watch closely as Nathan's dark eyes scan over what I wrote. His jaw flexes and he clears his throat. "*No kissing. No touching when not in public. Absolutely no snuggling ever.*" I'm silently mouthing the words as he reads. "*No flirting when alone. No . . .*" His words trail off on this last one, and he tucks his lips into his mouth to lick them before continuing. "*No hanky-panky.*" His gaze swings to me, and I can tell he's trying to school his expression so he doesn't smile. "What exactly is hanky-panky?"

I roll my eyes. "You know what that means. Even my grandma knows what that means."

He shrugs lightly. So innocent. "Is it a game? Or . . . I don't know . . . a dance move? You'll have to fill me in here. And please be as specific as possible."

I slap his hard bicep. "Stop! You know what it means." My cheeks are turning pink for some reason.

He raises an eyebrow. "Well, I have an idea, but you know, it leaves a lot open for interpretation. Hanky panky is very vague. I might think it means old-fashioned sex, but then if that's true . . . it means second base is totally up for grabs. Maybe even—"

"NATHAN!" My stomach barrel-rolls right out of this SUV because I do not want to hear what's about to come out of his mouth next. We *do not* talk like this. *Ever*. Suddenly it doesn't feel like we're on his couch anymore, and I need to bring us back down to level ground. "No . . . sexual . . . *anything*!" I struggle saying each of those words. "And don't be such a jokester about all of this. I'm serious."

Don't get me wrong—I'd love nothing more than hanky-panky with Nathan, but I know it wouldn't mean the same things to us. I would never be able to separate my feelings from the act.

He hears the sharpness in my tone, and his amusement dies a little. "I know. I'm just playing. No hanky-panky . . . I got it. But the rest of this . . ." He scans the paper one more time before shaking his head and RIPPING IT UP! My rules are nothing but confetti falling to the floor now.

My mouth falls open. "Why did you do that?!"

"Because it's ridiculous. We're going to touch. We're going to kiss, Bree."

My heart stops. He said those words so matter-of-factly. Without hesitation or question. Just like, *These lips will be touching those lips, no big deal.* It would be a big deal for me.

"No. No kissing."

"Couples kiss. If we're going to sell this relationship, we're going to need to kiss in public at some point."

I sigh, a part of me knowing he's right. "Okay, only if the absolute need arises, we can share a closed-mouth kiss. Just a quick peck for the cameras." I'm not sure what would happen to our contract if the fake part of our relationship is discovered, and I don't want to find out. I need that money.

He doesn't agree, just picks up the shreds of my peace of mind and tosses them into a cup holder. He pulls out his phone. "Actually, all of this reminds me—we need to take a picture together and post it. An official 'we're a couple' photo for social media to ooh and aah over."

Oh right. That was in the contract—abundant social media lovey-dovey-ness. He turns the camera around to selfie mode and aims it in front of our faces. I lean toward him so our heads are almost together and cheese it up.

"Why aren't you taking the photo?" I say through my smiling teeth.

"Because this pose makes us look like best friends."

Duh. That's what we are.

I drop my smile and turn my face to his. "Okayyyy. Well, what should we do then?"

He bites the side of his lip as he contemplates something and then unbuckles my seatbelt.

"Hey! Unsafe!"

Nathan loops his arm around my middle and, before I can protest, hauls me up onto his lap. HIS LAP! I guess that throws my *no touching when not in public* rule out the window. I can feel his solid chest against my back and his strong thighs under mine. He leans in and his breath warms my neck. My body doesn't know how to react to this, so it just bursts into flames. "Wh-What's happening right now?"

"Just relax. Pretend you like me." *Oh the irony.*

His nose presses into the side of my jaw and I can feel his eyelashes brush against my skin as his eyes close. He holds the camera up in front of us, and my terrified expression is mirrored back at me. Eyes wide. I'm a deer in the headlights. But Nathan looks so natural, so like a man enjoying the feel of a woman—*not* his best friend. I hear him breathe in deep, and the hint of a smile touches the corner of his mouth. He's a good actor. Before I realize it, my head is tilting into his, my eyes are closing, and my lips are curving up on their own.

He smells good.

So damn good.

I want to fill a pool with his scent so I can swim around in it all day long while sipping a margarita.

Sitting on his lap, I feel tiny. Like he could wrap his arms around me and shield me from a hurricane. So many sensations flit through my body as Nathan's breath fans against my skin and his arm tightens around my waist. His lips don't make any attempts at contact. He's just hovering here in this nearness we've never had before, forehead and nose pressing into me like an affectionate nuzzle.

My skin is singed, and before I have time to worry that I'm letting myself enjoy his touch too much, the SUV crawls to a stop. Nathan pulls his face away from mine and cold air rushes over me. Acting complete.

"I think we got a few good ones. What do you think?" he asks with almost no emotion in his tone. Zero hints that he was feeling anything close to what I was feeling.

Still perched on his lap like this is my new throne, I take his phone and look closely at the photos. I can't form any words because I almost can't believe what I'm looking at. That's not me and Nathan in this picture. This is a couple who's head over heels for each other.

I know why I see that blissful look on my face, but why is it on his too?

I clear my throat. "Yeah. This works."

I slide off his lap and tug at the bottom hem of my shirt, trying to put myself back in order before we leave the SUV.

The driver comes around to open our door, and just as Nathan is sliding out, my phone pings with an alert. It's a new tagged photo notification from Instagram. Opening it, I see that Nathan already posted the photo along with a caption that reads: *The only woman I want.*

Nathan hops out first and holds his hand out for me to take. I look up into his eyes, trying desperately to not read too much into all of this, but already I feel my heart try to take liberties I swore I'd never allow it.

"Still with me, Bree Cheese?"

I don't know . . . am I?

15

BREE

Nathan is holding my hand.

He's. Holding. My. Hand.

Fingers intertwined, carry-my-backpack-on-the-way-to-science-level hand-holding. I feel a giggle bubbling in my stomach as my feet try to match his long strides into the soundstage where we are filming the commercial. It's ridiculous. His skin is so calloused and hot. Is this what every football feels when Nathan holds it? Wonderful, now I'll compare future men and their less-than-adequate hands to Nathan and his big primal mitts.

It's time to get a grip on reality. That was a disorienting drive with Nathan's face smooshed up next to mine, so naturally I'm a little off-kilter. But it's time to center myself and prepare to be Nathan's *fake* girlfriend. Emphasis on the fake, Bree. I can do this. I can hold his hand all day and not let it go to my head. Plus, I'll probably hate being in the spotlight with him today. I'll let the experience serve as a perfect example of why we will never be a real couple.

"You okay?" Nathan asks, feeling my spiral telepathically.

"Soooo okay."

He smirks. He knows I'm full of crap. He turns to face me. "It might be overwhelming in there. There will be a lot of directions to follow and people who will want your attention. Just remember that they are all here for you."

"You mean they are all here for *you*."

He shakes his head slowly. "I'm not the one who broke the internet. They wanted me to date *you*. That's why we're here, because the world fell in love with Bree Camden. None of this would be happening if it were anyone else."

Goodness. When he puts it like that, this whole situation sort of hits differently. I'm not sure I like it. I try to brush off the parts of me that are grabbing on to his words for dear life. My heart feels like vanilla ice cream melting over a hot chocolate brownie at the thought of people wanting me and Nathan together. I want to ring Kelsey up really quick and yell something obnoxious at her like, YOU SNOOZE, YOU LOSE.

The doors to the soundstage open and Nathan's tall and gangly manager, Tim, steps out looking frantic. Then again, he sort of always looks this way. "Oh, you're both here! Good." He looks down at his watch then waves us through the door. "They're almost finished setting up lighting, so you have just enough time to get into hair and makeup."

We're following him down a cold hallway now as he continues to talk a mile a minute. Nathan squeezes my hand.

"I explained to the crew that you're on an incredibly tight schedule and they have three hours with you tops. Not a minute more because you have practice in the morning. Also, there's a seared salmon and kale salad dinner for you in the dressing room, Nathan. I've already told hair and makeup you have to eat while they're working on you."

No dinner for me? See, it's already happening—I'm seeing how miserable it would be to date Nathan. Everyone will fawn over him and I'll fade into the shadows. This is good. Keep it up, world.

Tim barely takes a breath before he continues. "The full script is in your dressing rooms, but the gist of it is simple. You two are walking through a restaurant and women are rushing up and writing their names and numbers on Nathan's shirt. He tugs you into a hallway to escape them, pulls a Tide-To-Go pen from his back pocket, and hands it to you. You guys exchange flirty looks and then Bree erases the names with the wave of her pen—in the style of *I Dream of Jeannie*."

Oh man. That's cheesy, but I can see how fans would eat it up. It's the perfect nod to my drunken speech. The speech that will haunt me for the rest of my life.

A moment later, Tim drops us at a dressing room that has Nathan's name on the outside. We're still holding hands, and I realize I'm clinging to Nathan like he's a buoy in the middle of the ocean.

"Smile," Tim says, snapping a quick picture of us with his phone. "I'll post this to your stories, Nathan."

The door opens to a cute smiling blonde with a tight top and overflowing cleavage that I admittedly am 100 percent jealous of.

Tim looks bored, bless him. "Nathan, this is Aubrey. She'll be doing your hair and makeup."

"Hey Aubrey," Nathan says with a grin and a nod that I know is fake but Aubrey clearly eats up because her pores start emitting sunbeams. And really, I get it. He's so huge and ridiculously hot, and his deep growly voice is intoxicating if you're into all that kinda stuff, but seriously, Aubrey, pick your heart up off the floor and get to work. *He's mine!* Uh, wait, what? No.

He's fake mine.

Fake fake fake fake fake. Not real. If our relationship was a purse, it would be a Proda and sold to someone out of the trunk of a car.

Aubrey bounces lightly on her feet. She can't wait to get her hands on Nathan. "If you want to come on in and take a seat, we can get started." That sparkle in her eye makes me think she's going to get started on her lap dance rather than hair and makeup, and I consider jutting my foot out and tripping her. Yeah, I'm the jealous type. Poor thing hasn't even done anything wrong and I'm plotting her demise. I feel like I should apologize to this professional woman for degrading her actions. My inner territorial cavewoman is getting out of control lately, and I need to get a grip.

Tim pulls me from my stormy attitude. "Bree? Let's keep walking. You're down this way."

The moment I have to drop Nathan's hand, my stomach twists. I did not anticipate being this nervous to leave his side. It's just that I have no idea what I'm doing, and I'm not even given a chance to look back at Nathan before Tim has us practically jogging down the hallway.

"I know you don't have a manager, so Nathan has me acting as yours today, if that's okay with you?" He doesn't give me a chance to actually answer. "Your dinner is also in your dressing room, but Nathan had me order you chicken tacos from Chipotle, extra guac. Was that right?" He flings open a dressing room door and the smell of delicious tacos slaps me in the face. A little smile curls my lips because . . . *I wasn't forgotten.* Nathan thought ahead to have them cater my favorite meal.

"That's perfect."

"Great. This is Dylan"—he points toward a smiling guy who looks about my age and is laying out makeup brushes on the beauty counter—"and he's going to be doing your hair and makeup. Joy will be by in a bit to drop off your wardrobe. Eat fast—we have an hour until you're needed on set. Harrison, the director, and Cindy, the producer, will be by at some point to talk to you about the script. Don't post any photos of anything happening today, leave that up to me. And if you need something, ask me and no one else. Do you need anything?"

I shake my head quickly, feeling a little shell-shocked from that tornado of a speech.

"Good. I'll be back in twenty. She's yours now, Dylan." Before he fully walks out of the room, Tim stops and turns back to me. "Oh, and Bree? I'm glad you and Nathan are together. He's better with you." I guess Tim hasn't been filled in on the actual terms of our relationship and the fact that we are Proda.

Tim disappears through the door, and I let out a deep breath.

Dylan chuckles. "Are you ready for your name quiz now? List everyone he just mentioned in perfect order or you're kicked off the set." The sparkle in his eyes gives him away.

"Umm, was it Sam, Brittney, and Tina?" I answer incorrectly on purpose.

He laughs again and steps forward to extend his hand. "Ding-ding-ding! Correct. And now you win a delicious taco dinner!"

"I was sort of hoping for a car," I say with a bummed face as he guides me to the makeup chair.

"Well, you're in luck! This extra guac your boyfriend requested for you has the same value as a car. Maybe you could pawn it for extra cash or something?"

I love him. The surest way to my heart is to play along with bad jokes. He's almost helping me forget I'm on a set right now and my whole world as I know it is turning upside down.

"I'm Bree, by the way," I say as he plops a glorious-smelling Chipotle box in my hands.

"Oh, I know. Even if your name wasn't plastered outside the door and I hadn't been given a photo of you ahead of time, I'd still know those dimples anywhere. You've been all over my Instagram and Twitter feeds lately." He immediately starts sliding his fingers through my hair in an inspecting and appreciating sort of way. "I won't even pretend I'm not slightly obsessed with you and your curls and dimples. I almost died when they hired me to do your hair and makeup. When I told my boyfriend, he was so jealous his skin actually turned green."

I laugh and make a weird face because A) I don't know how to take compliments, and B) He can't be serious. I'm the most average person who's ever walked the face of the earth.

"These?" I bat my hand at my curls. "Bleh. They're ridiculously hard to tame."

He looks offended as he claps a hand over his heart. "Who said anything about taming?! Why would anyone want to subdue these gorgeous curls? No, I'm planning to put even more pep in their step." Dylan moves behind me, eyeing my curls from all angles in that intense way only hairstylists do when they are imagining what could be. It's a little terrifying.

He narrows his gaze and tilts his head as I take a huge bite of my taco.

"You know? I think we'll lean into the whole girl-next-door look. America loves you so we'll keep you looking sweet as apple pie." He leans in close, eyes twinkling. "Although, if you're dating Nathan Donelson, I don't think anyone expects you to be too innocent."

I almost spit my taco out. Instead, I suck it into my windpipe and settle for a life-threatening coughing fit. Dylan pats my back, and my face turns bright red.

He smiles like the Cheshire cat once my coughing is under control. "I knew it," he says, going to work on my hair and spritzing it with water then pulling some products out of his gigantic travel kit. "That ex of his tried to make him look bad with the article, but no one believed it. There's too much gossip that suggests otherwise. So, be honest, no use lying to me because I can read a poker face from a mile away—he's a freak in the sheets, isn't he?"

My stomach jumps out of an airplane. I know nothing about Nathan in that capacity. We are not even the kind of friends who joke around about it. We keep that conversation zipped up tight because I think subconsciously we both know there are just some boats you can't rock in a friendship. Therefore, I have no idea how much Nathan's boat rocks at night.

But I'm his "girlfriend" and I'm expected to know.

I widen my eyes and put on what I hope is a sultry sort of a smile. Like I'm picturing a memory of Nathan's muscley, tan body wrapped up in white bedsheets with the sun shining over his shoulders. Actually . . . I am picturing it pretty easily. "Oh yeah, total freak in the sheets. A real tiger. Earned his stripes for sure. No one has ever blown my mind like Nathan Donelson."

"Well, that's good to know."

NO! That voice did not come from Dylan. It came from my best friend leaning against the open dressing room door looking like a smug devil.

I inhale my taco on a gasp again, and suddenly, Dylan has my hands over my head trying to make sure I don't die in this dressing room. But I want to. *Just let me go, Dylan! I can see the light!*

Nathan swoops in beside me, crouching down and chuckling while patting my back. "You okay? Sorry, I didn't mean to startle you."

I give my throat one last epic clearing then force myself to meet Nathan's eyes. His hair is now tousled and shining to perfection, and he's wearing black dress pants and a white button-down tucked in. The top few buttons are undone, and I'm going to choke again.

"Yep! Good to go. Dylan is taking good care of me."

Nathan's dark eyes glint. "Not too good, I hope. That's my job—and according to what I just heard, I'm doing it really well."

Dylan makes a strangled squealing sound then turns away to give us some privacy while he goes to dig around in his travel kit again.

I take the opportunity to point a stern finger at Nathan. "Don't ever bring this up again! I panicked, okay? He was digging for gossip and I didn't want him to find out the truth. Would you rather me say you're a lousy lover like Kelsey did and WHAT is that face about?"

He shrugs. "Nothing. You're just awfully defensive."

I feel my cheeks heating and refuse to let them grow rosy. I REFUSE. "Why are you in here anyway? Aren't you supposed to be in there with *Aubrey* getting made up or enjoying a lap dance or something?"

He tips a brow. "Now we're jealous?"

I groan. "Of course not. Don't be ridiculous."

"Well, good. Because the lap dance really wasn't anything to write home about anyway."

I punch him in the shoulder just as Dylan comes to stand behind me again to finish his work. He has the face of a man who is trying to look like he's not eavesdropping but is very clearly memorizing every word we say so he can repeat it later. Oddly, I don't mind. I kind of hope he does.

"Kidding." Nathan glances up at Dylan and then back to me. His eyes aren't joking anymore. They are just Nathan looking back at me. His eyes shift to one of the curls hanging beside my face, and he tugs it gently. "Tim whisked you off so quickly, and I was just coming to make sure everything is good with you. Do you need anything?"

I swallow, realizing how differently this feels than I predicted. His eyes aren't distant like I've seen him look with previous girlfriends when they're in public. He's not too busy to check on me. He's twirling my curl between his finger and thumb. *Don't freak out—it's probably all for show.*

"Yeah, I'm okay. I'm a little disoriented, but I'll get used to it." I regret those words as soon as I say them. I won't get used to it, because I won't let myself. No getting comfortable in this life. No enjoying it.

Nathan smiles wider, and he leans in slowly to brush a kiss on my cheek.

Once he goes back to his dressing room, Dylan shakes his head at me in the mirror. "Where's that manager of yours? I need a bucket of ice to dip my face in."

I laugh softly and turn my attention back to my tacos, trying to ignore the tugging sensation in my heart.

Later that night, after we pull up in front of my apartment and I sprint out of the SUV, leaving Nathan in my dust by telling him I'm not feeling good, I immediately call the one person I know will help me sort out my ricocheting feelings, the one person I never hide anything from.

"Hello?"

"Lily, something's wrong!" I say, shutting my front door and leaning my back against it.

"What! What's wrong?!"

"I had a fantastic day."

She growls. "I'm going to kill you when I see you next. You gave me a heart attack."

"I'M THE ONE HAVING A HEART ATTACK!" I say, pressing my hand firmly over my chest like she can see my dramatic performance.

In the words of Mrs. Bennet, *she has no compassion on my poor nerves!*

"Okay, hang on. I need to get some ice cream and then you can tell me what happened. DOUG, I'M GOING OUT ON THE PORCH TO TALK TO B."

Once Lily is settled, I tell her all about filming the commercial. I explain how I was supposed to hate it, feel like a fish out of water, and be counting down the minutes until I could get home and put on my PJs. But none of that happened. I loved every second of it. Once I got used to it, I loved how hectic it was. I loved how all the important people there made me feel like I actually belonged. I thought Nathan's world was supposed to be like *Mean Girls* and I wouldn't be allowed to sit at the cool table because I wasn't one of them, but everyone was incredibly nice and helpful, and the crew was hilarious. Everyone was joking and playing around in between takes, and it felt so natural to me.

But being next to Nathan through all of it . . . that was something I can barely explain with words. I've seen him in his element countless times, but it's always from the sidelines wayyyyy far away from where he is. Today, I was with him in the center of it all, and we were focused on each other.

"I don't know, Lily, but while we were filming, everything was easy. We worked seamlessly together, and even the director commented on how smooth each take went. It all just felt oddly . . . normal. And fun."

"And the problem?"

"The problem is that at some point during all of this, I forgot we were pretending to be a couple! I forgot, Lily! And Nathan was . . ." I sigh remembering the feel of all the little touches he constantly gave me. Remembering the way his hand splayed out firmly on my lower back. Remembering how my whole nervous system hummed to life when he smiled at me like I was the only woman in the world for him. "It was nothing like I expected it to be. I don't know . . . it was almost like he was feeling what I was feeling."

She's dead silent for a beat before she bursts out laughing. So loud.

So over the top I have to pull my phone away from my ear. "OF COURSE HE WAS, YOU LOONY TUNE, BECAUSE HE LIKES YOU TOO!"

"Okay, well name-calling is not nice."

"Bree, I want to shake you right now. Have you truly never thought Nathan has feelings for you?"

"Never! But can you stop being so intense for a second, because I'm freaking out and you're not helping."

She sighs deeply. "Can't we just skip this freak-out, you can run back over to his place and get it on, and then you can call me in the morning to tell me I'm right and you'll listen to me from now on?"

"No," I say firmly. "I'm not going over to his place and there will not be any *getting it on*. I won't do a fling with Nathan."

"Umm, I hate to break it to you, but you're kind of in one now."

"THE FAKE KIND!"

"Now you're yelling. Just shush a little. So you don't want a fling? Fine. But that doesn't mean you have to freak out just because you think he might have feelings for you too. Maybe you can use this opportunity with Nathan to explore some of the boundaries you've put up in the past. Treat it like a real relationship starting from ground zero and see if something new develops between you two naturally."

I sigh, mentally reciting a thousand reasons why that could go wrong. "Then I'll be opening my heart up to hope, and that's what I promised myself I wouldn't let it have during all of this. It might end badly, and then I'll be friendless."

"Bree, hope is healthy. Even if you prepare yourself for the worst in life, it will never make the fall hurt less. So why not let yourself really and truly want this instead? And then, if things end badly, I'll help you eat your feelings."

I think back to Nathan today, and my skin lights up like a circuit board, zinging with energy in every single place he touched me. I want to give in to that hope Lily is talking about, but I'm too scared. I'd rather just wait until it's a sure thing. You know, until he drops down on his knee and has a ring kind of sure thing?

"I think I need to do the opposite. I need to implement MORE rules until this is all over."

She groans, deeply discouraged by me. "Why do you even call me about stuff like this? Next time just talk to your wall if you're not going to listen to my advice."

"Grumpy much?"

"Yes! Because you think you're in such a good place right now. You tell me all the time how happy you are that the course of your life changed and you're working in the studio now instead of dancing in a company, but you don't see what I see." I don't like this shift. Lily is not teasing now.

"I *am* happy, Lily. I love being an instructor, and my life *is* more full than it used to be."

"I know you're happy at the studio and you're making the most of how things turned out, but I also see something else. After the accident, you stopped letting yourself dream completely." She pokes an old wound I didn't know was still there. "You went to therapy, and you learned to grieve the future you planned for and that was all great and helpful, but then it's like you learned to cope so well you completely stopped hoping for anything. You're seriously the queen of making the most of what you have now, but I'm not sure that's completely healthy. Not if it means never dreaming or striving for more."

My instant reaction is to defend myself. After the car accident and my surgery, I shut down. Depression and anxiety were heavy, and even just getting out of bed in the morning was difficult. I pushed Nathan away completely, and then after he went off to college and everything felt even harder, my mom and dad got me into therapy. It was the best thing they could have done for me. I learned how to properly grieve ballet as I knew it, and little by little, my life got brighter. One day, I realized I was feeling happy again. I was doing the emotional work and the physical work to get my body moving again in a new way. Sure, I had limits, but I learned to work within them and appreciate what my body could do instead of focusing on what it couldn't.

Bottom line, until ten seconds ago when my sister just dropped a bomb on my heart, I thought the wounds from my accident were healed. I thought my mental work was done. But is she right? Do I not let myself hope for more out of life?

My mind races not just to Nathan, but to the studio. I've been so unwilling to work toward making any dreams come true concerning it. Now that Lily has pointed it out, it's almost as if I can hear my hope screaming from a locked closet in my heart. I want that nonprofit space more than anything, but I've been terrified to hope for it. I want Nathan, but I'm petrified of losing him.

I can see that my sister is right, but I don't know how to snap my fingers and change the way I feel. My scars remind me of that crushing disappointment I felt at seventeen and how hard it was to piece myself back together afterward. I don't want to go through that again. So yeah, maybe I'm missing a little bit of hope, but to me, it's a small price to pay to avoid shattering again.

As far as Nathan and I are concerned, I just need to hold on and get through this fake relationship until we go back to BFFs who don't touch. Then, after that, I'll be open to starting a new relationship with someone else where I won't have so much to lose.

16

NATHAN

"Mr. Donelson!" A voice calls out to me when I get out of my truck. I turn toward Bree's dance studio and see a teenage boy standing outside the door that leads to the pizza parlor's kitchen below the studio.

"Who is that? Who's yelling your name?" my mom asks from my phone, which I've been on for fifteen minutes now. I wouldn't mind talking to her if she wanted to actually *talk* with me. Instead, it's a long droning speech about all the ways she thinks I could enhance my image (I'll give you a hint, a children's golf day at her country club was mentioned) and then nitpicking every move of my last game. On the rare occasions when she does ask to hear about my week, I always get the feeling she's really only fishing for ways she can comment on what I'm doing wrong. Bottom line, I've learned to keep my mouth shut about my private life, and I'll give her about ten more seconds before I end the call and avoid her other attempts at communication for another week.

"Just a fan I think," I tell her, squinting toward the teen about twenty yards away.

"There's a fan in the training facility?" Her voice is getting annoyingly high. She's winding up to release a critical comment.

I shut my truck door, raise my hand, and give the kid a quick wave. "No, I'm not at the facility right now. Practice ended a little early today because of a meeting our coaches had to attend, so I'm dropping by Bree's studio."

There's silence followed by her lightly clearing her throat. "Do you really think it's wise to be taking extra time away from your training when you're so close to another playoff game this weekend? Maybe you should have spent that extra time with your physical therapist, or—"

"I'm a grown man as well as a professional athlete. I can handle my own training schedule." *Wow*, that felt good to say. Also, it feels like something I shouldn't have to voice out loud.

She lets out an offended scoff. "Well, excuse me for trying to help you succeed."

"Cutting out an hour early one day out of the season to spend time with Bree is hardly going to interfere with my success." Ever since Bree and I started "dating" (she doesn't know it's fake), my mom has been making lots of passive-aggressive comments about Bree. She can make digs about my game or nutrition or looking pudgy in a magazine spread all she wants, but I won't put up with a single word against Bree.

"Oh honey, don't fool yourself. That girl has been interfering with your success since you were in high school. I saw you almost throw it all away for her back then, and I won't watch you do it a second time."

I stop walking and turn away from the teen—who is currently poised to intercept me with a napkin and a pen—so he doesn't get to hear what I say to my mom next. "First, she's a woman, not a girl. Second, yeah, if she would have let me, I would have stayed home for her in a heartbeat back then. I still would. Football will never be as important to me as she is, so you can either support my relationship with Bree or forfeit a relationship with me. Your call, but just know I won't budge on this."

My mom makes a few sounds of disbelief, and then . . . hangs up. Yep, she ends the call without another word because Vivian Donelson doesn't know how to react when someone puts her in her place. I'm sure I'll get a call from my dad in about an hour demanding I apologize to my mom and telling me how she hasn't come out of her room since we spoke because she was so hurt. *She birthed me after all! Did everything she could to make my dreams come true! How dare I not let her micromanage my entire life!* It's why I usually avoid conflict with them. It's just easier to go along with her and let her stampede over me than get into something with them that will eat up all my energy. But where Bree is concerned, it's a fight I'll take on every day.

I turn back toward the studio and find the teen baring all of his teeth in my direction. The pen is shaking in his hand. I train my face into a pleasant smile even though pleasant is the least thing I feel. This mask I have to wear is just part of the job. Can't let the fans down. Can't let the team down. Can't let anyone down.

"Hey man," I say, walking closer. "Sorry about that. Do you want an autograph?"

He shakes like a leaf the entire time as I sign the napkin, thanks me profusely, tucks it back inside his canvas apron, and darts back into the pizza kitchen. I hurry up the steep stairs of the studio before the kid can tell anyone else inside that I'm out here.

The moment I open the studio door, I hear Bree's voice counting out beats in the main room. It's hot up here due to the heat the pizza stoves give off, and it smells like yeast and dancer's sweat. Not a great combo. Immediately my mind starts racing to all the ways I could improve this space for her, but even in my imagination, Bree won't let me get away with anything. I feel a phantom pinch on my side and picture her leveling me with a glare. *Don't you even think about it, Donelson!*

The studio is laid out like one long horizontal box. After stepping through the front door, I'm standing in the four-foot-wide hallway that runs the length of the entire studio. If I keep walking straight, the next door goes right into the actual studio. To my left is eight feet of hallway that ends in a single-room bathroom, and to my right is eight more feet of hallway that ends with Bree's office.

I follow the music and sounds of dancers' feet thumping the floor until my head is peeking into the studio. I find twelve teenage dancers doing some sort of hop-jump-foot-crisscross thing with Bree standing in front of them, back to me. She's wearing my favorite strappy leotard today, the one that shows miles and miles of her toned back. Just as my eyes are dropping to my favorite curvy backside on the planet, the dancers begin to notice me one by one. Like a row of dominoes tumbling, the girls stumble into each other and hit the floor.

Bree yelps at the sight and turns the music off with a remote. "Imani! Hannah! Are you girls, al—"

She's cut off when one of the girls points aggressively in my direction. "It's HIM!"

I swear the sound of Bree's head turning in my direction makes a wind-tunnel noise. Her eyes land on me and BAM, her attention kicks me in the heart. Her look of shock slowly slides off and a smile unfurls. I want to wrap my arms around her waist. I want to drop my mouth to her neck and kiss my way up and down it. She looks dangerously sexy in her leotard and dance shorts. I love when she wears that tidy ballet bun, because there's something so satisfying about knowing what her hair looks like when it's not wrapped up tight like that.

There's always a moment at the end of the day when she takes the pins out and all those wild curls fall down around her shoulders—kills me every time.

Yesterday on set, I felt something between us. It wasn't one-sided. Bree was reacting to me, and every time I touched her, she blushed or leaned in a little closer. Although it was in the name of fake dating, there was some serious mutual flirting that didn't *feel* fake. It was perfect.

Until she bolted.

The SUV was barely parked before she jumped out and told me not to follow her because she didn't feel good. "What's wrong?" I asked her. "It's . . . MY PERIOD!" she said and then ran out like that was an actual answer. Except, apparently she forgot she's a notorious over-sharer and had already told me a week and a half ago she was on her period.

So, yeah, obviously she was freaked out after our first day as a couple. I'm here today to make sure everything is okay between us, and also fulfill number 18 on the cheat sheet. *Surprise her at work to show her you care about her.*

"Nathan? What are you doing here? Is everything okay?" Bree asks, looking a little nervous as she glances back and forth between me and the girls all lined up gawking at me. I rarely get the chance to visit her at the studio, so I can see why she'd be concerned.

One of the dancers throws her forearm over her eyes dramatically. "Quick, someone get me some sunglasses—that man is so hot he's burning my pupils off."

The whole class giggles at their obvious ringleader, and Bree glares at her. "Cut it out, you! And don't say pupils like that again. It's weird." Naturally they all start chanting the word pupils, and I'm struggling to not laugh.

Bree sees my smirk and walks slowly toward me, her lean lines looking as graceful and deadly as a panther's. She stops right in front of me and narrows her big brown eyes up at me. "Something funny about interrupting my class and sending these hormonal teens into a fit of hysterics?"

I grin down at her. "No, absolutely not."

She lifts a brow and hums. "I don't think I believe you."

Her gaze snags on my mouth and my smile slowly fades. We stand here like this for a few seconds, balancing on this tightrope of tension, unsure what to say or do next.

"OOH," squeals one of the students. "Call the fire department! These two are about to make this studio burst into flames!"

Bree whips around. "Not another word out of you girls! I need to go talk to Mr. Donelson in my office for a minute. Continue your jumps while I'm gone."

I look at Bree with an antagonizing smile and lifted brows while silently mouthing, *Mr. Donelson?*

She rolls her eyes then whispers, "Don't egg them on. These girls are ruthless. They've been nagging me to date you for months now, and I continually remind them we're only friends. Since news finally broke about our . . . relationship, their taunting has become nearly unmanageable."

They've been trying to convince Bree to date me? This news only validates my instinct that Bree and I would be perfect together, making me feel even flirtier. "So I shouldn't pinch your butt in front of them?"

"NATHAN!" I love the way her cheeks go pink lately. Bree flashes me a *Behave* look before turning to address the class again. "Okay, line up and get into position. I better hear the sound of graceful jumps the entire time I'm talking with Mr. Donelson."

"Mm-hmm, she's going to go *talk* to Mr. Donelson," says another girl, addressing the class with air quotes bracketing the word talk.

These girls are trouble, and I totally see now why Bree loves them so much. They're just like her.

"Jumps!" Bree barks while clicking the classical music back on.

Collectively, the girls all bat their eyelashes and singsong, "Bye, Mr. Donelson." Okay, that makes me feel creepy.

Note to self: Maybe surprising Bree at work when she has a room full of teen girls is not the best idea.

Bree reads my thoughts. "Yep. And you should stop posing in so many shirtless ads! You should see all the photos they have saved of you on their phones." That's disturbing and also something I could have gone without knowing.

Bree suddenly catches my hand and pulls me with her into the hallway. I wasn't prepared for this skin-to-skin contact, and it triggers my whole body to zero in on that one point of contact. Bree stops when we are on the other side of the studio wall just outside of eyeshot. She lets go of my hand to face me, and I want to take it back again. I stuff my hands in my pockets to keep from acting on the impulse.

"So what's up?" she asks as classical music swirls around us.

I swallow, suddenly feeling nervous to admit that I came all this way just to see her. That's what the guys said to do, but . . . I don't know that I can go that far out on a limb. I've never said anything like that to her before, and I'm not sure how she's going to react.

I shift from one foot to the other. "I, uh—had something I wanted to . . ."

"Oh my gosh, is that giant man stuttering?! He's so adorable."

Bree looks over my shoulder to where that whispered comment came from. "Back in the studio or you're all doing ten minutes of push-ups before class is over!" Such a drill sergeant. I wonder if these girls find her threatening. I just want to kiss her.

Bree turns away and motions for me to follow. Looks like we're going to squeeze into her tiny office now. I'm so used to Bree not wanting to be in any sort of close quarters with me that as I eye the two feet of available standing room, I accidentally give her a look of hesitation.

Her eyes widen with impatience and she waves me in. "Come on, hurry up. This is the only place we can talk privately, and I need to get back in there soon."

As I step into her packing-box-of-an-office, I'm reminded of the finally legal sensation. You know? It's that feeling when you order your first beer on your twenty-first birthday, the bartender studies your ID, and for a split second, you break out in a sweat because you're so used to always having to sell the fake one. But this one is real, he slides a beer across the table, and you get to drink it without fear of punishment. That's what being invited to stand in this minuscule room with Bree feels like.

Her desk takes up most of the space, the backs of her legs pressed up against it to make room for me to shut the door. I can't get it to close behind my back though; I have no choice but to step closer to Bree until we are touching. NO CHOICE, I TELL YOU! My chin is resting above her head. Now the sweet scent of coconut overpowers all the others. When we're chest to chest, I'm able to scoot the door shut behind me. It scrapes my back as it passes, and I hope it leaves a mark so I can always remember this moment.

The door latches, and for some reason, I don't move away. Bree doesn't push me back either. Instead, she looks up, eyes searching mine. A hair has fallen loose from her bun and is dangling by the side of her face. Without a second thought, my hand rises and I brush my fingertips across her cheekbone, tucking the hair gently behind her ear. She sucks in a quick breath, her lips parting. She's so damn pretty. Soft and sweet, but also vibrant and sharp. Is that how kissing her would taste?

I drop my hand from her ear to skim down the side of her arm. Her lashes fall to watch the path my hand takes until it lands right beside hers, knuckles touching lightly. Her deep brown eyes pop back up to mine, and it's like time stands still. We're frozen together. Something about the way she's looking at me tells me if I bent down to kiss her right now, she'd let me. I don't know who initiates it first, but our fingers shift and climb toward the other's until they're loosely intertwined.

My heart is in my throat. No, it's in my hands. I'm holding it out here for her to take.

Suddenly, the air fills with the opening notes of "Let's Get It On" by Marvin Gaye, and giggles erupt beyond the wall.

Bree lets out a high-pitched growl and steps to the side so she can bang the side of her fist against the wall. Our hands unlink. "Hey! Turn that off!"

They don't obey. More giggles.

I bite my lip to keep from smiling, and Bree doesn't appreciate it.

"It's not funny!" she says in a sad, defeated tone.

"Come on? It's *so* funny," I say, giving in to a full smile.

Bree relents with a smile of her own and shakes her head. "Fine, it's a little funny."

I'm not willing to let our moment end quite yet. And if these girls are going to help me out, I'm not going to turn up my nose at the gesture. I stretch out my hand toward Bree. "C'mere, let's dance."

Her brows twitch together and she eyes my hand like it's moldy. "What?" She lets out a nervous, breathy laugh and looks around like she's expecting to find hidden cameras. "In here? No way. That's silly."

I take her hand and tug her up to me. *Get over here, woman.* She doesn't fight it. Instead, she snaps into my arms, and I pull her up close—one hand on her lower back, the other holding her hand beside me, palm to palm, chest to chest. She blinks a few times and tentatively slides her free hand up onto my shoulder.

"You're being weird," she says, even though her thumb is brushing a tender movement up and down the base of my neck.

"Yeah. Really weird." I put a little more pressure on her back and sway us side to side. Being this close, I'm steeped in her shampoo, and thanks to the way her leotard dips in the back, I can feel the soft, velvety texture of her skin against my hand. She is heaven in my arms. Nothing exists outside these walls for me.

"Nathan, why are you here right now? I have a class I need to be teaching." She says this while snuggling a little closer. A strong revelation is growing as I see her words and her actions are in direct conflict with each other. Which one is fake?

"I wanted to ask you if you're free tomorrow night."

"You could have done that over text," she says, fishing for more of an answer.

"I could have."

She casts her eyes down briefly, like she doesn't want me to see her expression, her soft grin, and the side of her face skims across my chest. "Yeah, I'm free."

"Great. *Pro Sports Magazine* is having their big ten-year birthday bash. It's a red carpet event, and I was hoping you'd go with me." In the past, Bree has always said no to attending any career-related event with me. She always tells me to take a date instead. *Friends don't go with friends to fancy events like that.*

She keeps her gaze low. "Well, I guess I sort of have to go, right? As your official-fake-girlfriend."

"No. If you don't want to go, I'll plan something else a little more low-key for one of our contract-mandated outings."

"Oh," she says, and I hear a little disappointment in her voice. I think she wants me to tell her she has to come with me. She wants me to take the choice away from her, but I need to see if she's willing to come with me on her own or not.

"So what do you think?" I ask, stopping our swaying so she'll look up at me. I dance my thumb in a circle against the skin of her back.

"Okay," she says, her lashes lifting. "I'll go with you. But I don't have anything to wear."

My heart rams into my sternum. I want to wrap my arms all the way around her and squeeze. Instead, I settle for a subtle press of my fingers. "Leave it up to me, and be home by five tomorrow."

"I'm nervous about what that means."

I reach back and open the door, reluctant to let her out of my arms but knowing she needs to return to her class of hellions. As I step away, I try to check one more item off my cheat sheet.

Looking at her over my shoulder, I smile and wink. "You should be."

She's frozen for a second and I think, *Derek, you magnificent devil, it worked.* But then her eyes widen and she bursts out laughing. "Did you just WINK at me?!"

Okay, so apparently winking goes into the non-sexy category for Bree. She roasts me all the way out the door, and I will murder Derek at practice tomorrow.

17

BREE

It's a little after five and I'm rushing up the sticky stairs of my apartment building, out of breath and maybe wheezing a little bit. Probably the effects of living in a moldy apartment for too long.

When I make it to my floor, I stop and frown at the sight in front of me. Dylan is sitting on the floor surrounded by what looks like enough luggage for a weeklong cruise. Five suitcases stand around him along with a pile of garment bags draped over the top. How did he get all of these up here? I look behind me wondering if there's a secret elevator everyone's been keeping from me. But when I see that his chest is heaving just as much as mine, I realize he hauled all this up himself. *Poor thing.*

"Dylan?" I ask, stepping closer, wondering if I'm going to have to resuscitate him.

His head shoots up and he smiles wide despite his labored breathing. "Hi Dimples! You're late!"

"I'm sorry," I say, still in a daze at seeing him here. I guess this is what Nathan meant by *Leave it up to me*. "Traffic was nuts today.

Here, let me help you up. Also, I don't want to alarm you, but there's a good chance you caught an STD sitting on that floor."

He shrieks and jumps up without my help. "Am I going to have to burn these clothes?"

"It's probably for the best if you do."

"Oh my gosh. Why do you live here?" He looks around like cockroaches might be crawling all around him. Actually, it wouldn't be that much of a surprise if they were.

I laugh and turn to unlock my apartment. "It's a little thing called money. You see, I don't have much of it."

"Umm, you're basically dating a bank. He probably has more money than a bank actually. Go move in with him! Here, I'll help you. We'll pack your things and move right now."

It's on the tip of my tongue to tell Dylan that Nathan is just my friend and I don't want his financial help when I'm cut off by the sight of my apartment. Dylan steps in behind me, pulling two of his suitcases, and gasps.

"Holy flowers, Batman! I'm assuming, Ms. I-don't-have-any-money, that you didn't go out and buy yourself all of these magical bouquets?"

I shake my head slowly, speechless. There are dozens of bouquets filling my living room. Big glorious pink and green blooms everywhere. I don't have a favorite flower because it's too hard to narrow it down to one, but I do have a favorite flower color combination. Apparently, I've told Nathan this at some point. And he remembered. *Pink and green.* My stomach clenches tight.

"You've got a note over here." Dylan is already picking it up and opening the card like we've been besties for twenty years and don't keep secrets from each other. I snatch it out of his nosy hand with a reprimanding look and turn away to read it privately.

I hope you don't mind, but I found a way to make your apartment smell better. Be by at seven to pick you up.

—Nathan

My heartbeat is fierce, and it's all I can do to not squeal like an excited little piggy in my living room. What is happening to me? What is happening to us? Nathan and I have been friends for a million years and he's never once bought me flowers . . . and definitely never bought me a whole flower shop before. My mind races wondering what this is. What does this mean? That *hope* Lily was talking about blooms in my chest unbidden.

But I'm too scared to fully dive into it. He's probably just trying to get me in the mood to fake a date tonight. Put hearts in my eyes. Unfortunately, they were already there even before any of this—and it's making it much harder to not allow those feelings to escalate. And yesterday in my office . . .

"Lock it down, Bree."

"Did you say something?" Dylan asks.

"Nothing. Never mind."

He gasps suddenly. "There's some sort of sticky goop on my butt! What do you think it is? Actually, no, I don't want to guess. I want you to move apartments. Right now."

I laugh and tug him with me to my bedroom where I pull out a pair of sweatpants and toss them at him. "Here, you can wear these."

"Ugh, thank you!"

I leave the room so Dylan can get changed, and when he comes back in the living room in my light gray jogger sweatpants, he points to his rear end. "Umm, ma'am, these say *Juicy* on the booty."

I strangle a laugh with a flower pressed to my nose where I was snorting it like an addict. "I know."

"You didn't have anything else that would fit me?"

"Oh, I definitely did."

He crinkles his nose and steals a pillow from my couch to toss at me. "And to think I shopped all morning to find you the perfect dress. I should have just found you a T-shirt that had SKANK written across it."

"You shopped for me?" I ask with big round puppy dog eyes.

He tosses me a look over his shoulder as he goes to unzip the bag draped over my couch that holds several GORGEOUS dresses. "What did you think these were? Body bags? Like I just carry around my victims wherever I go?"

"Should I be scared that you thought of that so quickly?"

His only answer is pulling out a long floor-length gown and holding it up with proud eyes. "Okay, so I didn't know your exact size, and I was a little skeptical to trust your man to accurately know it . . . but it looks like he was right! This is going to fit you like a glove."

I take the dress from Dylan and look at the tag. Sure enough, it's the right size. I'm terrified that Nathan knew that, because I've definitely never told him. Another thing I find is a price tag that makes me choke. "Please tell me this is not the real price of this gown!"

He shrugs and busies himself with unpacking those suitcases that, turns out, are full of designer hair and makeup products. Sephora has exploded in my living room, and it's a beautiful sight. Lily would be so jealous. I text her a picture like the annoying, gloating little sister that I am.

"Whatever you want to believe. All I know is Nathan had me buy you fifteen dresses to pick from, all totaling up to the price of my house. On top of all that, he paid me my full on-set day rate, andwhydoyoulooklikethat?"

I put my face in my hands because this is bad. This is really, *really* bad. Everything I've ever avoided with Nathan is all happening in one rushing avalanche. Fancy public date. Big gestures. My own entourage. High-priced gifts. It's too much, and it's all going to end just as quickly for me as it does for all of his other girlfriends. Except unlike those other women, I won't miss all of this—I'll miss him.

Dylan comes over and puts his hand on my back, rubbing a circle just like Lily would. "What's wrong? This is not the reaction I thought I'd get when I told you your boyfriend bought you thousands of dollars' worth of dresses and hired the best in the business to style you tonight." He says that last bit with a grin.

I want to tell Dylan the truth, want to tell him none of this is real, we're faking it, and I've been avoiding jumping into this life with Nathan for six years because I never wanted to experience it—never wanted to enjoy it or get used to it because it will hurt so much more when it's just a memory. And yes, I do enjoy this side of him too. I'm a living, breathing human, so of course I like to be spoiled by a celebrity. Who wouldn't? But I can't tell Dylan any of that because I signed a very scary looking nondisclosure agreement promising I wouldn't tell a soul. I've already told Lily, so I can't afford any more slipups.

I settle for part of the truth. "I have trouble receiving things like this from Nathan. It feels like a lot."

"Well don't! He clearly has enough money to spare and wants to dote on you a little. Let him. And if it makes you feel better, I'll return all the dresses you don't want."

I lower my hands. "That does make me feel better, actually. Thank you."

"Good. Now, just try to let yourself enjoy this moment! Come admire my incredible styling skills and pick a dress for tonight. It's not like you're going to have to live in it for the rest of your life or turn into a real housewife of Long Beach. It's just a fun little night. Just put one glittering high heel in front of the other."

I take a deep breath. He's right. It's just a night. I'm getting ahead of myself. Nothing has to change; I just need to think of this as a fun game of make-believe. Pretend. It's okay to enjoy something when you know it's nothing but a game. Easy-peasy. I can do this.

For the next ten minutes, Dylan and I go through each of the dresses he selected, and it's seriously hard to choose my favorite because they are all so beautiful. In the end, I pick one that reminds me of bubbling champagne. Tonight is not quite as fancy as an award show, but it's also not casual enough for my Juicy sweatpants. My dress is a tea-length bodycon with long sleeves, a sheer glittering overlay, and a champagne-colored silk lining. The most glorious part is the back. The silk lining scoops low down my spine, and the sheer overlay dotted with fine diamond-looking sequins spans across my back. It's sexy and classy at the same time. My mom won't gasp in horror if she sees it in the tabloids tomorrow, which is always a perk.

For my hair, Dylan wants to leave it down. He adds all sorts of products until my curls are sleek, shining, and springy. He parts my hair far on the right side and pins the other half away from my face with a diamond-studded clip. *I'm really hoping those diamonds are fake.* He gives me a soft eye shadow look with fierce cat-eye eyeliner and a nude pink lip.

When I look in the mirror, decked out in a glamorous gown, designer makeup, and hair styled within an inch of its life, I still see me, and it makes my heart swell. At least I don't feel like I'm putting on a whole different skin to go with Nathan to this event. Everything else might be fake, but not me.

Dylan pops up over my shoulder, and a big cheesy smile stretches across his face. "I stuffed the lipstick tube in your purse, so when Nathan ruins it, you'll have more."

"Nathan is not going to—" I stop myself, because yeah, any boyfriend who saw me like this would definitely ruin my lipstick. ". . . be able to keep his hands off me. Good call."

"Just don't let him touch your hair! It's perfect and if he messes it up, I will destroy him."

An image of slender Dylan in my Juicy sweatpants challenging mountainous Nathan to a boxing match pops into my head, and honestly it's exactly the kind of distraction I need right now. My hands are shaking and I feel like I'm going to puke.

"Thank you for all of this, Dylan. You did an incredible job."

He waves me off. "You're an easy canvas. And I should be the one thanking you. Your boyfriend is paying me more than I should allow. In fact, I feel a little dirty accepting it." He pooches his lips out in thought before a mischievous smile curves them. "Okay, I'm over it. I'm going to get out of here before he arrives so you two can have a moment by yourselves before the craziness of tonight. Text me later and tell me how it goes!" He kisses my cheek and disappears to grab his bags and leave.

I'm still standing at the mirror staring and trying not to have a panic attack when I hear the door shut behind Dylan. And then a moment later it opens again. My heart beats double time because I know who just stepped inside. He doesn't call out for me, but I hear his dress shoes clicking across the hardwood floor as he approaches my room. I can't bring myself to look away from the mirror. It's not fight or flight—it's freezing. I so desperately want to see someone reflecting back at me who feels out of place and all wrong, but no. Everything feels right, and lovely, and exciting. *I'm scared.*

I'm scared because I want to go more than anything.

I'm scared because I'm so looking forward to walking beside Nathan tonight and holding his hand.

I'm scared because all these feelings I've kept at bay for so long are pelting me like a hailstorm.

The clicking grows closer, and I can see Nathan in my peripheral now, standing outside my bathroom door, staring at me. He doesn't speak, and neither do I.

The air gets hot and thick as he steps into the bathroom and fills the space behind me. Now, he's reflecting back at me, too, wearing a light gray suit that fits snugly around his biceps and shoulders. His square jaw is clean shaven, and I want to drink whatever cologne he's wearing. His black eyes hold mine in the mirror, and I can feel his heat radiating through the sheer back of my dress.

He smiles.

I smile.

And then he leans down to softly kiss my cheek. Just like always—but completely different this time. His hands remain at his sides, but his eyes slide over every inch of me. I stay so still, trying to keep breathing despite the lack of oxygen in the room.

"Beautiful," he whispers against my ear, and a shiver runs sweet prickles up my spine. "You still with me?"

I nod.

18

NATHAN

I've been on the phone the entire ride to the magazine party. All I want is to focus on Bree, but my agent needed to discuss an endorsement deal she's negotiating for the off-season, and then that turned into listening to Tim blabber on about who all I need to kiss up to tonight after we get through the doors. It's been one phone call after another.

Although Bree has known me long enough that seeing me on the phone for an extended period of time is not a shock to her anymore, I still hate it. It's rude to spend an entire car ride with a phone glued to my ear. Most women can't handle this part of my life, and it contributes to our early breakups. Some days I can tell my manager and agent to back off and give me some space, but on days like today where I've been moving from one scheduled meeting, practice, and physical therapy session to another, I have to catch up with the people who run my life in my free moments.

"So Paul will definitely be there tonight, and you'll want to make sure you seek him out and have a public conversation with him," Tim says, like maybe I don't already know from years of experience that I need to be friendly with our team's owner.

"Yep. Got it."

"Also, Jacob Nelson might try to corner you. He contacted me about scheduling an interview with you, and I told him no. I've yet to see a positive article come from him, and I don't want you anywhere near the guy. Smile and remind him that you leave all scheduling up to your manager."

"Mm-hmm . . . sounds good."

"Are you even listening to me?" Tim asks in an annoyed tone.

No. Nope. Not a bit. I'm staring at Bree's long bare legs.

I don't mean to be, but damn, she looks killer tonight. She looks killer every single night, but right now, she's making herself stand out in this skintight sparkling dress, hair long and wild but also somehow perfectly styled. And her eyes . . . wow. I don't think I've ever seen her wear eyeliner before, and it makes her already vibrant eyes practically grab me by the collar of my suit and demand that I empty my pockets and give her everything I've got. *You can take it all, Bree.* She has no idea my eyes are glued to her because her attention is completely locked on her phone. I don't think I've seen her blink in two minutes.

"No, I'm not listening anymore, Tim. Can you just text me a list of people you want me to schmooze and who I need to avoid?"

He sighs, knowing he's lost me. Honestly, even if Bree wasn't stealing my attention, I still think I'd only be halfway listening to Tim. I'm tired. No, I'm exhausted. If I closed my eyes right now, I'd pass out. And even though Bree looks like a literal golden goddess, I still would rather be home on the couch with her in our sweatpants watching something funny on TV.

"Okay, last thing and I'll let you go," Tim says.

"You have fifteen seconds."

"Nicole told me to tell you to kiss Bree on the red carpet tonight.

Just something chaste and sweet for the news outlets to keep your relationship in the spotlight and trending."

My eyes sweep to Bree and my pulse picks up. I am getting official permission to kiss Bree. Actually, I'm being told I have no choice but to kiss her. Our lips will meet in only a few short minutes, and my mind can't wrap itself around the idea. Suddenly, I'm sweating. I feel out of practice. So much rides on this kiss. What if I screw it up? I've generally gotten positive reports in that area, but this is Bree. I have to give her my best so the word *brother* never surfaces in her mind in reference to me again.

"Noted. We'll get it done." And then I hang up before Tim can give me any more assignments.

Bree must notice the grit to my voice because her head rises from her phone for the first time, haunting eyes knocking into me. "What will we get done?"

I'm not ready to tell her yet so I sidestep. "Hey, I'm sorry I've been on the phone so much. It's not always like this, but being in the middle of playoffs means my time is—"

She laughs and holds up a hand. "Nathan, please. It's me you don't have to explain to me how busy you are in the playoffs. I've actually been thankful for the time to myself on this ride."

"Yeah?" I smile and nod toward her phone. "What've you been doing?"

She bites her full bottom lip, and I wonder if it would be too much if I did that during our first kiss.

"Nothing." Her cheeks go pink.

I laugh at the way she immediately tilts her phone so I can't see the screen. "That pretty much means you're absolutely up to something then. Come on, hand it over."

"No!" Her long dark eyelashes practically touch her eyebrows with how wide she opens her eyes. "You'll laugh at me."

"Of course I will," I say with a grin. "But that's nothing new, so let me see it."

She lets out a disgruntled sigh then hands her phone over. I'm now looking at a Google search page full of images of "celebrities on the red carpet."

I don't laugh because I can see she's genuinely embarrassed. "Why are you looking at this?"

"Because! I need to get ideas for how to pose. You're so used to all of this, but . . . I'm over here trying not to have a freak-out because in like two minutes I'm going to be ON A RED CARPET FOR THE FIRST TIME IN MY LIFE!"

I feel bad now. I completely forgot to run her through what the red carpet is like. Of course she's nervous. I remember feeling totally sure I would faceplant during my first photo op, and I wasn't even wearing four-inch heels like she is. Probably not the best time to tell her we also have to publicly kiss for the first time on that same red carpet.

"You have nothing to worry about. I'll be there the whole time, and I'll make sure you don't trip or fall. As for posing, you want everyone to have a chance at a good angle. Keep your shoulders back and chest proud, and then pretend you're trying to set up facial recognition on your iPhone."

She sputters a laugh and her shoulders relax. "What does that mean?"

"You know, when it makes you turn your face every which way so it can learn every detail of your face to unlock it. Do that with the cameras. Look left, right, tilt your chin up slightly in one direction, and then repeat on the other side."

She nods, focusing on my instructions. "Okay, and what do I do with my hands?"

"You'll be holding my hand with your left, and the other hand can go to your hip. Don't worry about knowing when to walk and when to stop. I'll guide you the whole way."

She takes in a deep breath, and I don't let my eyes fall to the part of her cleavage that's showing under that sheer piece of sparkly fabric. But I want to.

"Thank you. Is it . . . is it bad that I'm looking forward to this a little?"

Something about those words eases the constriction in my chest. She's excited? Bree has always made it a point to tell me how much she would hate to be involved in this part of my life. I lick my lips in lieu of pouncing on her statement. "I'm happy you are. Because I like you here with me."

Her bright eyes shift to me, and suddenly, this SUV feels small. Like a gloriously teeny-tiny box.

"We need to kiss," I state with zero tact.

Her expression falls. "Excuse me?"

I clear my throat and mentally punch myself for being the furthest thing from smooth. "On the red carpet. That's what Tim was telling me on the phone. Nicole thinks it would be good for our 'couple image' to kiss briefly while they're taking pictures."

Bree's eyes are so wide I'm afraid they're going to fall out of her head. She twists her hands in her lap. If she were standing, she'd be pacing. "I can't kiss you out there! I'm worried about just smiling as it is! Kissing is going to . . . Nathan . . . oh my gosh. Our first kiss can't be in front of paparazzi!"

My stomach flips at her words: *first kiss*. Like she knows for sure there will be more.

"Do you—Do you want me to kiss you now?" I HATE how nervous I feel right now. *Don't let your voice quiver like a damn fool.*

"No! Absolutely not!" She pauses, looks out the window for a few seconds, and then pivots her gaze back to me. "Well, maybe. Actually, yes." Another pause with a definitive headshake. "Wait, no. It's better to only kiss in public so we don't feel like it's real."

"It will be real."

She glares at me. "No. It. Won't."

"My very real lips will be on your very real lips, Bree. That's the very definition of real. It will not be in our heads."

She gets ready to put her hands over her face but pauses when she remembers she can't mess up her makeup. She whimpers instead. "Ugh. Nathan." Her eyes slide to me, and she looks scared. "It's . . . a lot. All of this. Me and you."

"I know." I want to rest my hand on her thigh to comfort her, but I know that would make it worse. Instead, I feel like I should sit on my hands so they don't get any ideas. I'm supposed to be inching Bree into this shift in our relationship, not tossing her over the front of the boat without a life jacket. "Look at me, Bree."

She does, and her eyes are filled with so many emotions I can't read.

"It's just me. Me and you. Nathan and Bree Cheese. Kissing won't change that." It'll make all those things better.

The heaviness in her expression lightens, and she smiles. "You're right. It's just a kiss. No big deal."

Well, that's not exactly what I meant.

I don't get a chance to expound, and we don't have time to practice our kiss even if we wanted to. The SUV slows to a stop, and Bree's frantic, terrified eyes fly to me. Oh no. She looks like she's going to puke. Now, I do reach over and squeeze her thigh. Her skin is warm and smooth beneath my fingertips. I don't let my brain register how good she feels. I can't right now or I'll lose my mind.

She swallows, and then the door opens. There's immediately an explosion of cheers from fans lurking beyond the rope and flashes of cameras wanting to catch the exact moment we step onto the red carpet.

I give Bree one quick nod. She nods back, and we're really doing this. Together. It's my dream come true, and I only hope this doesn't end up being Bree's nightmare.

Immediately this night is different from all the other events I've had to endure without her by my side. The whole energy is different with Bree gripping my hand and sticking to me like a June bug as we stride down the red carpet. I keep glancing back at her to make sure she's not puking while walking, but after about ten steps, her smile changes from tight and terrified to softer and more confident.

I know that feeling. It's the same as when you jump off a diving board for the first time. That first second after you jump is the worst, and then from there, it's easy. There's nothing to do but enjoy the free fall.

Bree's hand squeezes mine, and I look back to see her crinkle her nose at me in her signature cute smile. It's her *Can you even believe it?* look. My heart bursts. It's wide open, completely hers for the taking. Always has been.

"Nathan! Over here!"

"Nathan!! Bree!"

The paparazzi are loud and the flashes are bright, but I barely register them as Bree and I come to a stop in front of the backdrop with *Pro Sports Magazine*'s logo printed all over it. Because it's time to kiss Bree.

I let go of her hand to wrap mine around her hip and angle myself a little more toward her, making sure to keep the majority of our bodies facing the photographers. Suddenly, I hate that this has to be our first kiss. It's the worst. It feels stiff. Calculated. So far from romantic we might as well be in a garbage dump with a rotten banana peel lying over my head. There's no way this is going to make her knees weak, and I don't want to settle for anything less.

I feel Bree take in a deep breath as she angles her smile up toward me. More photographers are shouting. One yells, "Give us a kiss!" Bree widens her eyes in a *Go ahead* look. And now that's what they are all chanting. Nicole was right—everyone is dying for this. I'm dying for this. I just want it in the privacy of my own home where I can give Bree the attention she deserves. Where I can pin her against the wall. Where I can worship her mouth like I've been dreaming about for years.

This is my one shot, and I'm going to ruin it. Should I just take her lips in a harsh kiss? Should I let it roll low and slow? Should it be a peck? Damn. I can't. Now my heart is pounding painfully, my hands are sweating, and we've been in this spot too long. The woman with a clipboard and a walkie-talkie is telling us we need to keep moving. We're monopolizing the red carpet and she wants us to get lost so the next SUV that just pulled up can unload. But I can't move. My hands are feeling pinchy and tingly, and my face is hot. The flashing lights are painful and the abrasive shouts are closing in around me. What's happening? It's the same sensation I felt in the tunnel before the last game. I think I'm going to pass out.

Bree's smile slips for only a second. She must see something in my face that I don't mean to be showing. Her delicate hand comes up to my jaw, and she smiles for real. It's soft. A blanket. A Bree and Nathan smile.

"You still with me?" she asks quietly, making me focus on only her. I let myself drown in her, and my pulse calms a little.

I nod and swallow. She rises up on her tiptoes and places a soft, quick kiss on my lips. I squeeze her hip, wanting to keep her here, wanting to soak up every moment of her mouth pressed against mine, but all too quickly, she pulls away. She faces the photographers again and angles her face in two more directions like she's been doing this her whole life. Apparently satisfied with the amount of photos taken, she crosses in front of me, takes my hand, and pulls me along *behind her,* smiling like a seductive queen back at me. Everyone should bow down to her as she passes. I follow along, her lost puppy. She squeezes my fingers a few times as we walk like I did for her on the way in. I'm still in a daze, not quite registering everything around us, but I'm sure that later when I'm alone, I'm going to kick myself for ruining our first kiss.

19

BREE

I get Nathan into the tent and pull him off to the side quickly. He is not the kind of man who's easy to hide though. I'm basically sneaking a hulking bear into a tea party. *Here, grizzly, wear this cute little hat and no one will notice!* Everyone still notices. Heads everywhere are turning as we walk in, which means we have about thirty seconds before someone decides they need to be obnoxious and monopolize his time. So many people are already gathered here, professional athletes and celebrities galore. It's an all-you-can-eat-buffet of people I like to stalk on social media. Can't focus on that now though.

I link my arm through Nathan's and guide him ten steps to the side of the tent entrance before pivoting us so his back is to the crowd and his chest is facing me. I'm hoping I'll be able to give him at least a few seconds away from prying eyes. His gaze still looks sort of glassy, and those dark circles I noticed the other day have worsened. I can't help but feel like we shouldn't be here tonight. Nathan is exhausted.

"Hey." I step closer and rest my hand on his chest so everyone knows this is an intimate conversation they shouldn't interrupt. And also because, *hello,* I like touching him. He feels so solid beneath my touch. "Are you okay? Should we go home? It's okay if you say yes."

His eyes drop to my palm pressing against his firm chest, and he covers it with his hand. The contact is a jolt through my veins. It reminds me that I just kissed him. On the red carpet. In front of everyone.

It was so brief and full of onlookers that I barely registered it. And then, the second I pulled away, I felt disappointed. Not because it lacked sparks, but because I didn't get a chance to pay attention to the sparks. I was too worried about the panic attack I think Nathan was having out there and focused on getting us off that red carpet before every photo in tomorrow's gossip magazines showed Nathan looking like a deer in headlights. The tabloids would have had a field day coming up with lies to explain his expression: *Nathan Donelson losing the fight against narcotic pills!*

He breathes deep, and I feel his chest expand against my palm. "Sorry about that back there. I'm okay now."

It's so like Nathan to breeze over this. "Are you sure? It looked like you were having a panic attack."

He grimaces and looks left, the sharp, strong corner of his jaw emphasized. "Nah—I don't get those."

I laugh because the man is dead serious. Like he's some super breed of human that just doesn't have mental health issues from time to time. *Look out, science, we've found a man who never feels stressed!*

"You don't have to have an anxiety disorder to get a panic attack. Sometimes they can come on from too much stress, or overextending yourself, or—"

"Bree, I'm telling you, I'm fine." Nathan cuts me off with a pleading voice. He really does not want to talk about this right now, and judging by the way his face has gone pink, I think he's embarrassed. "C'mon. Let's go have a good time."

I nod, taking pity on him and his embarrassment. We can talk about all of this later when we're in private. "Okay, let's do this thing."

Nathan takes my hand and turns us toward the room. That's when I really look at the crowd for the first time, and now it's my turn to freeze. This glitzy, glamorous party tent is stuffed with important famous people. Athletes from every sport. Actors and singers. I doubt there is a single normal person here. Correction: There is exactly ONE normal person, and it's me.

"Changed my mind, I want to go home." I let go of Nathan's arm and take five retreating steps backward right into a giant standing poster.

I wish I could say I just bump it lightly and everything is okay. But no. It happens in slow motion. I feel the thin paper at my back, but my high heel gets stuck on the stand that's propping it up. I feel myself falling backward and see Nathan's eyes go wide and his mouth forms my name. His hands shoot out to grab me, but he's not fast enough. I careen backward right though the poster and hear it rip right down the middle. On the bright side, I don't fall to the ground. I somehow manage to stumble on my feet. On the dark side, I now stand in the middle of a nine-foot-tall ripped poster, and every eye in the event is on me.

Yep, I'm going to throw up. I turn around to quickly grab each side of the torn poster and stick it back together. And now I realize belatedly that this poster I have torn is a Goliath-sized image of a naked Nathan Donelson, and my hands are directly holding his hands . . . aka his hands that are holding the football that's perfectly positioned in front of him to keep this photo PG-13. Realization dawns on me as I look around and find many similar posters of other athletes, all featuring one of their photos from the form issue. I then see a photo op station in the corner with a backdrop that reads "FORM ISSUE'S 10TH

BIRTHDAY CELEBRATION!" There are fake illustrated muscles you can use as props. *Cute.*

Right. I'm face to thighs with Nathan's blown-up naked form, looking like the biggest pervert in the room. Time speeds back up. I yelp and drop the poster. Naked Nathan floats in the wind as he separates and falls limply open, showing how I've completely ruined what was probably a couple-hundred-dollar poster. I hear several laughs behind me and a few *oh no's*, but mainly it's heavy silence. My face is so hot it's going to melt off my bones.

Nathan steps up beside me, wraps his hand around my bicep, and presses his chest to my back so he can lean down and whisper, "Are you okay?"

I shake my head in a few quick movements. "How quickly can you get me to a new continent?"

Nathan is still laughing at me during the elevator ride up to his apartment. He's been chuckling ever since we left the party, and any time I think he's going to speak, I hold my finger up at him. *Don't you dare.*

All in all, the poster shredding wasn't that big of a deal. Nathan—the enigmatic, sexy, life of the party that he is—easily turned the whole situation around to be framed in an endearing light. He faced the crowd and let his voice carry across the room with one of his trademark smiles. "So . . . I think my girlfriend wants to box this one up and take it home—can we get a little help with that?"

Everyone exploded with laughter and I did a little stage bow, and somehow, that made us the hit of the event. Nathan and I even posed beside the torn photo, and when I posted it, I added a caption that read: *If only Tide pens could wipe out embarrassing situations.* It got four thousand likes in the first hour.

The whole night we barely got a moment to ourselves because absolutely everyone and their mother wanted to speak with Nathan and wish him luck in the playoffs. I didn't mind. It felt good to hold his hand and be introduced to so many people as his *girlfriend*. There was also something deeply satisfying about seeing Nathan give everyone his business smile. It never reaches his eyes, and only I would know that, because now, he's giving me *his* smile. The one I've seen since high school.

Nathan rips his tie from his neck and loosens the top button of his shirt as we walk through the foyer of his apartment. I kick off my heels and he tosses his coat and tie onto the entry table, and now it's just us and the waves outside his window crashing onto the shore. I can breathe. A thrill trickles through me when I realize this time I'm the one walking through the door with Nathan after an event. *Me*. I was out with him in front of everyone, and . . . I loved it. Which is bad. Very bad.

How do I stuff this jack back in the box?

I freeze by the door, and Nathan keeps walking. It takes him a few seconds to realize I'm not with him anymore, and then he looks back over his shoulder with a fading smile. "What's wrong?"

Oh, nothing much. Just having an internal freak-out because I'm realizing the full extent of how much I've wanted this life with you. No big deal.

"Nothing's wrong." My bare feet are backing up.

Nathan gives me a skeptical side-glance. "*Bree . . .*"

My shoes are in the corner by the door, but I don't have time to grab them. If I'm going to make a break for it, I've got to move fast. I turn around to bolt, but Nathan is on me in two seconds flat, taking my legs out from under me and scooping me up in his arms.

"No way. You're not getting out of here that fast." He carries me to the couch and deposits me on a cushion. He points a stern finger at me. "Stay. Nothing is different. We are completely normal." Then he disappears into the kitchen to grab something.

The lights are still low when he returns, and I need someone to kick the high beams on because he looks too suave, too James Bond-ish in this romantic lighting with the dark ocean roaring in the background. And the way he looks at me, I feel like our friendship is a ticking time bomb. I just know I'm going to lose my best friend somehow.

Nathan's shirt is untucked now and hanging loose. He stops right in front of me and tosses an unopened Starburst log into my lap. "I keep this for emergencies. I think this moment constitutes one."

I smile down at my favorite candy, and my shoulders relax a little. How does he always know the exact right thing to do to take care of me?

"I'm going to run to the bathroom real quick. Please be here when I come back." His words are gentle and sweet, and for some reason, this shifts my mind back to the feel of his lips against mine.

While Nathan is gone, I close my eyes and try to remember every detail, but it's too hazy. Like a delicious dream you wake up from and feel slipping through your fingers. Did that kiss even happen? Nathan hasn't mentioned it once, so it must not have meant much to him. But really, how could it have? It lasted maybe two seconds.

It meant something to me.

Nathan comes back into the room just as I shove a pink square into my mouth. He looks incredible in his suit pants and loosened dress shirt. My mouth waters, but not from the candy.

He sits down on the far end of the couch and smiles. "Better?"

I nod and shift the soft taffy to my right cheek. I'm a chipmunk who hoards pink Starburst. "Better."

"Do you want to watch some TV? Pick up where we left off in that comedy special?" He's already reaching for the remote and my gaze snags on his exposed, muscled forearm. I'm hyperaware of him in ways I've never let myself dwell on before.

The TV turns on and a comedian spouts off a joke about pancakes. Then, as if nothing in the world is different, Nathan's hand wraps around my bare foot and pivots my whole body so he can pull my feet into his lap. I stare with my mouth hanging loose as his thumbs push in and glide up my arches. His strong, calloused fingers knead my sore feet with expert care, even going so far as to dip past my ankle and press into my calves. For as hot as my skin feels, his hands are somehow hotter. Like stones, fresh from a fire and melting my skin away.

All I can do is stare, blink, savor. He's touching me in an intimate way that has never happened as friends before. But for how much of a living, breathing hot tamale I am right now, Nathan is not even focusing on the life-changing massage he's giving me. He's watching the comedy special, loose-limbed and relaxed. Yeah, no big deal. Are we just those kinds of friends now? Friends who occasionally date? Friends who snuggle? Friends who . . .

"Nathan, we kissed tonight," I blurt. *Cool, Bree. Cool. Nice and smooth.*

Nathan's hands freeze on my skin, and his brows fly up. He pauses the TV then swivels his gaze to me. I kind of wish he'd left it going so it would fill the uncomfortable silence, but now we're alone with my statement and it's flicking us both between the eyes.

"I'm surprised you want to acknowledge it," he says, confusing me with that answer.

"Do you not want to?"

The corner of his mouth tilts up. "I'll talk about anything you want, anytime you want. We can even talk about how you destroyed my naked photo because you were so jealous of anyone else seeing it."

I gasp and throw an orange Starburst at him. He laughs as it bounces off his bicep. "Not true! I did not destroy that poster on purpose! I didn't even see it before my butt sliced through it! In fact, you could have warned me that we were headed to celebrate the birthday of the FORM ISSUE!"

He chuckles with his head falling back against the couch and lightly swats my shin twice like he does his thigh when he laughs too hard. "Your face was so priceless! Red as a stoplight."

I put my hands over my cheeks, afraid they're still glowing. "STOP! You're so mean."

He's still laughing—shoulders shaking, stomach clenching. "I had no idea my nakedness would affect you so much. It's not like you haven't seen that image before. And it's nothing compared to the rest of them from that spread."

I give him a meaningful look, feeling like we're tiptoeing toward something we shouldn't but also desperately wanting to. "I . . . wouldn't know." I busy myself by trying to yank down the hem of my short dress to add some class to this setting.

When I look up, Nathan's smile is curious. "What do you mean you wouldn't know?"

I raise one shoulder. "I've never looked inside."

"You haven't?"

"Okay, well, you don't need to sound so disbelieving. It's true, some women *can* resist looking at nudie photos of you." Just barely though.

"You haven't even been the least bit curious?" His voice is doing something new. Something growly. Something that makes my stomach bunch and twist.

"*No.*" It's a bald-faced lie. "Friends don't see friends naked. It's the most basic rule of humanity."

Nathan's long legs are sitting at 90-degree angles in front of him.

Solid tree trunks taking root. He moves his arm to drape over the back of the couch, his fingertips ever-so-slightly brushing my shoulder as his other hand moves to rest on my ankle. His thumb moves up and down. Up and down. Up and down. But the most curious thing is the way his gaze shoots forward and he's biting down on his lips.

"What?" I ask, feeling the earth shift beneath me. "What's that face for?" I poke him in the cheek.

"Hmm? Nothing."

"You're the *worst* liar, Nathan. Seriously, I hope you never play poker or you'll lose all your money. Spill it."

His dark eyes slide to me. "You'll wish I hadn't if I tell you."

My heart races. "Okay, well now you really have to tell me. In fact, I demand it."

He lets out a deflating puff of air from his cheeks while rolling his head from side to side like he's getting up the courage. "I've . . . I've seen you naked. There, I said it."

For some reason, my natural instinct when hearing those words is to shoot to my feet and throw a couch pillow at him. "No you have not!"

Nathan's laugh feels surreal. Like I'm dreaming. "I really have. It was an accident. You were getting out of the shower, and—whoa! Are you okay? Bree, sit down. You look like you're going to pass out."

I am. I am one hundred percent going to pass out. Nathan Donelson has seen me naked and I had no idea! This is not okay. What was I doing? Oh gosh, please tell me I wasn't dancing or something horrible. Maybe this is why he's never made a move on me. He saw me naked and felt nothing!

Nathan takes my arm and tugs me down beside him on the couch. And here's the problem with this whole situation: He's my best friend who I always turn to in situations like this, so even though he's the one I'm embarrassed around, he's also the one whose chest I bury my face in for comfort. His long arms engulf me and he secures me to him. I'm anchored. His cologne washes over me, and now I know this was a mistake. He's not going to let me go.

"See, this is exactly why I didn't tell you. I knew you'd freak out, and I was afraid you'd take your key away from me."

"Good idea. I want my key back!"

"Not a chance. Bree, we can be adults about this."

"No we can't! We're not adults about anything—why would you expect that now? I'm so humiliated. Did you linger? Did you stare? How much of a look did you get? And . . . what . . . angle?" I don't want to know any of this, but I'm also desperate to know. Like a train derailing. You can't look away from something like that.

Nathan sort of growls, and I feel his head tilt back like he's looking at the ceiling. "Okay. No, I didn't linger, because I'm not a perv. And . . . it was sort of a 360-degree angle because you walked out of your bathroom and then . . . I don't know, forgot something you needed in there and spun around to go back in."

Well, let's call it, folks. *Bree Camden's time of death: 10:30 P.M. Died of humiliation overdose.*

I groan and whimper in succession, burying my face harder into his chest. I will burrow in here and never come back out. Sure, I'll be attached to him forever, but at least he'll never get to look at me again.

His hand lightly strokes down the back of my hair. "I gotta say, I don't take you for a walk-around-naked kind of a girl. You don't even wear bikinis to the pool."

"I was probably waiting for self-tanning lotion to dry."

Nathan is quiet for so long I think he fell asleep. I peek up at him and see his glazed-over eyes staring into the distance. And then I realize what's happening.

I clap loudly in front of his face. "Oh no you don't! You don't get to picture me naked!"

"Sorry." He blinks, looking sheepish. "You mentioned the self-tanner and then . . . never mind."

I clench my teeth. "This is completely unacceptable."

His smile turns compassionate. "Bree, I'm so sorry. What can I do to make it better? Stop talking about it? Tell you what I thought when I saw you?"

"NO! HELL NO!" I push out of Nathan's arms and stand. I'm pacing like a panther in a cage at the zoo. An idea immediately strikes me, and I don't give it a second thought before blurting it out. "You can take off your clothes and even the score."

Nathan blinks up at me. Stunned.

I mean, I get it. I didn't expect myself to say that either. But it's a solid idea! He got to see me naked in a less-than-favorable situation, and now I get to see him naked in the same sort of situation.

He swallows. "Or you could just go grab one of those magazines and finally take a look."

"No." I shake my head, a defiant toddler. "You're perfectly lit in those, oiled, and—let's be real—probably airbrushed. You'll look like a god among men, and that's not fair because you saw me in harsh light and bobbing around."

He tries to stifle a smile. It makes me more angry. I do one quick *up, up, up* motion, telling him to get his smug ass off the couch. He groans, hangs his head down, and then slowly rises to his full height. Good gracious he's like a tower. Jet-black eyes meet mine from where he's standing three feet away, and he arches his brow. "Are you sure this is a good idea?"

"It's a great idea! Get to it." My eyes probably look feral. Like a rabid squirrel you don't want to run into at the park.

Nathan doesn't blush like I hope. He doesn't look insecure or scared about what I'm going to find under his clothes. He just begins unbuttoning his shirt. His hands are steady as he works, and my legs are shaking like those of a newly birthed fawn. With every undone button, I question my sanity in requesting this, but I don't tell him to stop.

Three buttons down, and I see a triangle of tanned flesh. Four buttons. *Five,* and now there's a slight sprinkle of hair.

He pauses with a teasing glint. "You want a cigar or something? Maybe put your feet up?"

"Shush. This is fair." That's the only reason I'm doing this. *The only reason.*

Nathan's fingers reach the last button, and then he slides his shirt down off his shoulders and tosses it on the couch. I've seen him without his shirt so many times before, but this is . . . different. His shoulders are cut granite, and his collarbones are like two crowbars pressing against his golden velvety skin. Shadows paint around the ridges of his abs and obliques, making them look like stepping-stones down to a perfectly tapered waist. His Adonis V disappears into nicely pressed suit pants held up by a matte black belt. He is muscles, tendons, veins, and aching handsomeness. Gorgeous in a way no human should be. Magnetic and electric at once. He draws me in and will electrocute me if I touch him.

Who was I freaking kidding? Lighting doesn't matter one bit for a body like Nathan's. He could be under sharp fluorescent doctor's office lighting, and my tongue would still be lolling out the side of my mouth.

His black eyes flare as he undoes his belt, and now I'm feeling woozy. I didn't think this through. What happens after he's naked? My mind fills in that blank for me, and the sound of his belt sliding out of his pant loops sounds sharp to my ears. My pulse hammers in my neck, and I watch every detail of his sinewy flesh moving as he throws the belt next to his discarded shirt. I'm suddenly aware that I want this too much. That my hands are gripping the fabric of my dress. This is going to change everything, and I WANT that. I want Nathan like *this*. Not friendly. A little dangerous. A little taunting. A lot sexy.

I want to take a step closer and run my hands down his abdomen. Wrap my arms around his neck and let him hold me against his masculine form.

Nathan pauses with his hand on the button of his pants, and then when he flicks it open and I can see the band of his black briefs, reality crashes into me. He's really going to do it. He's going to get naked right here in the living room, enacting the fantasy of every woman in America (including me). The air around me is burning, and before he can make another move, I shoot my hands out in front of me.

"Stop!"

He freezes, eyes slicing up to me, lips parted in surprise and pecs flexing from how I startled him. He doesn't say anything, and my breath comes out in a tremble. I shake my head. What was I thinking? I can't do this. It would be jumping-out-of-a-plane-without-a-parachute-level life-changing.

I've got to backtrack.

"Kidding!" I blurt out like this was a gigantic prank the whole time. *Ha-ha! You totally fell for it!* I laugh and turn away from Nathan just so I can let out a big puff of air. I have 2.1 seconds to salvage this before it becomes weird for everyone. I let this night get the best of me and am starting to lose sight of the plan.

Stay strong, Bree. You're dazzled by the fake relationship.

With my back to Nathan, I mentally repeat my secret rules for a successful friendship.

1. Keep those feelings wrapped up like an egg salad at a church potluck—they're not actually good for anyone.

2. Nathan is a natural-born flirt. Don't embarrass yourself by misinterpreting his personality for flirting.
3. Don't look at his bare skin or you will burn alive.

I halfway broke that last rule, and I'll suffer the consequences from now on. I gather all of these feelings buzzing around my body like a hornet's nest and put them in a jar. I screw on the lid. Seal it with Loctite just to be certain no stragglers get away. And then I turn around. Oh my gosh, I need to hold my hand in front of me so I can't see his body.

"So . . . kidding?" he asks, and the boyish uncertainty on his face nearly kills me.

"Yeah!" I laugh a little too loud. "Oh my gosh, no way would I actually let you get those pants off. I don't need to see all that. Just wanted to mess with you and see how far you'd go."

"Pretty far," he says with an amused tick of his lips. It makes my stomach turn inside out like a reversible jacket.

I stare one more moment at all that he is and then clear my throat and head for the door like a woman who still has all of her faculties intact. I need to start carrying around smelling salts.

"Okay, well this has been fun! But whew, look at the time. I've got to be up early in the morning to bake cookies for the week! Early bird catches the worm!"

"Bree?" Nathan asks with a drawn-out amused tone. "Are you okay over there?"

I stop just briefly to flash gloriously wide eyes at him. HOLY MOLY his body . . . it's sculpted clay—soft, taut lines cut over every muscle to perfection. "Moi?" My hand covers my heart. "So okay! Why do you ask?"

I'm now performing the flight of the bumblebee, buzzing around the room and collecting my things. *Shoes. WHERE ARE MY SHOES?!* I turn three circles and look like I'm chasing my tail.

Suddenly, Nathan's big hand covers my shoulder. I drop away from his touch like I'm in *The Matrix* avoiding bullets. He looks completely shocked as he silently holds my heels out to me. "Well, glad you're okay." His tone conveys that I'm fooling absolutely no one.

I take my heels and quickly slip one on while hopping on one foot. Nathan's hand shoots out to wrap around my forearm to steady me. I want to whimper/cry/laugh because I feel extra sensitive to his touch. Once my heels are on, I start wobbling away. Wobbling because I have put my heels on the wrong feet. I'm a little girl who sneaked into her mom's closet and tried to sneak off with her best heels. No time to stop and fix them though. I gotta get out of here.

"It's been so nice to see you as always, bestie!" That was a strange thing to say. "Good luck with the game this weekend! I'll call you to—"

I feel his hand slide into mine and he tugs me back. I yelp as Nathan spins me around, a dangerous playful glint in his eyes. "Just a minute, *bestie*."

I hold my breath, only three—maybe four—inches from his bare chest. My palms ache to flatten against his pecs. But then his chest disappears from view as Nathan drops down to one knee. OH MY GOSH IS HE PROPO—

His hand wraps around my ankle and lifts it slightly off the ground. Then my heel gets slipped off—the tale of Cinderella played backward. "You'll sprain your ankle like this." He lowers my bare foot to the ground then lifts the other ankle. That heel gets peeled off, and then the correct one gets slipped on. This time his hand lightly taps the back of my calf, signaling for me to lift my other foot again—and if you're guessing I'm deceased at this point, you're right.

Nathan finishes putting my heels on the correct feet, and I notice something odd before he stands back up—he stares at my legs for two breaths. In those two breaths, WILD ideas I have no business imagining race through my head. He looks down again and then stands, but by the time he rises to his full height, I'm already turned toward the door and racing out, promising him I'll call tomorrow, and maybe also that I'll bake him a cake? I don't know what that was about, but clearly my ovaries feel like they owe him something.

20

BREE

I move like a zombie all the way down to the lobby. My eyes are unfocused, and I'm sure the lady working the front desk assumes I'm on something. My heels echo loudly across the empty expansive lobby, and I'm aware of every sound. Like maybe when I look back on this day, that will be the thing I remember most—the sharp clicks.

I'm not letting myself think about what happened back in that apartment yet. I absolutely will not poke it, or prod it, or dissect it in any way. Instead, I'm floating out of the main entrance's sliding doors. Chilly air-conditioning collides with a balmy ocean breeze, and I'm still floating. Choosing to hyperfocus on how I feel and what I see just so I don't let my thoughts tiptoe back to that moment upstairs.

Outside on the sidewalk, I find the SUV Nathan and I rode in earlier pulling up, and that's when I remember that he asked his driver to remain on standby in the parking garage until I was ready to go home. Thankfully, I haven't had too many issues with intrusive paparazzi or obsessive fans, but I've also not been taking my chances by walking alone too often. Tonight though, I need the walk to clear my head.

Robert, our same driver from earlier tonight, cuts the engine and dashes from the driver seat like a NASCAR driver at a pit stop.

"Ms. Camden, wait! Mr. Donelson asked for me to drive you home."

I look from the driver to five blocks down Cherry Avenue to where I can literally see my apartment building. Sure, it's nighttime, but it's well lit and the road is pretty empty. It seems a little overkill to drive two inches home.

"That's okay. Thank you, but I'd like to walk."

I don't need to get in Nathan's fancy SUV and be full of every single reminder of the night. I'm afraid I'll short-circuit. I need to walk off my nerves and get my head on straight, because something definitely almost just happened between us and I have no idea how to feel about it. Not sure I *want* to feel anything about it.

I keep walking, and Robert hops into the SUV and starts crawling along beside me. I cut my eyes sideways, trying to figure out if he's following me or not. I speed up and he does too. I abruptly stop and so does he.

I turn to him with my hands on my hips. "Robert! Roll down the window." He complies, and now I can see his sweet smiling face. It's hard to be mad at Robert in his cute driver's hat. "What are you doing?"

"Seeing you home. Mr. Donelson was very specific that I need to make sure you get home safely."

I groan. "So you're going to follow me like a stalker all the way to my building?"

"I prefer bodyguard. And yes." He gives me an apologetic smile. He knows he's being annoying, but his boss pays him too well to not obey. "Unless there's somewhere else you'd like to have me take you?"

I think about this for a moment, and then realize, *Why yes!* There is somewhere I'd like him to take me. To the only person who always makes everything better.

"Okay, but I'm riding shotgun because there's way too much I need to talk about to be stuffed in the back like a snooty politician."

I throw a rock at the window. Nothing. So I throw another little pebble. It makes a really bad cracking sound, and I'm scared that maybe I broke it. That never happens in the movies! I thought those things were supposed to be indestructible!

I'm just about to turn tail and run when the curtains flutter open and my sister glares down at me from her second-story window. I can see the shock register on her face. I gesture wildly for her to open the window like maybe she wouldn't think of doing it on her own.

She slides it open and I quietly yell, "Rapunzel, let down your hair!"

"Bree?! What the heck are you doing here?" Lily's so cute. She never cusses.

I point aggressively toward her front door. "Come down!"

"This is so weird! I feel like I'm dreaming."

"Itt'sss noooot a dreeeammm," I say in a spooky voice. "I am the ghost of Christmas—"

"Oh my gosh, I'll be down in a second."

Two minutes later, I'm sitting on the front porch with my big sister and laying my head on the shoulder of her fuzzy pink robe.

She nods toward the curb. "Who's that?"

"Bob. My driver." Only his true friends call him Bob. I sat in the front with him all the way here and we shared a bag of convenience store candy while he told me the story of how he met his wife, Miriam, forty years ago. So yeah, best friends.

"Why do you have a Bob?"

"Because Nathan wouldn't let me walk home alone."

"Sure. Sounds logical." We're quiet for a minute. "Not that I don't love having you here with me, but can you please tell me why in the world you drove two hours in the night to throw rocks at my window and sit on my porch?"

"I thought the rocks would be cute. Just like in the movies. But I think I might have cracked your windowpane."

"Are you serious?" she asks in a heightened tone that tells me she doesn't find it nearly as cute as I do.

I grimace. "No. Just kidding." Okay, I might have to call in a favor with Nathan and have his magic worker bees get that window replaced before my sister finds out.

"Oh." She sighs with relief. I really hope she doesn't check it later. "Do you want me to go put on some water for tea?"

"No, thanks. I've got to get Bob back home soon or Miriam is going to hunt me down."

Lily laughs incredulously. "Okay, come on. Seriously—you didn't drive all this way for a hug. What's going on? Did something happen?"

I whimper and snuggle deeper into my sister's softness, letting the reality I've been avoiding finally crash over me. "I think Nathan and I almost got freaky tonight."

"WHAT! I—"

I whip my head up to level her with a stern look. "If you say the words *I told you so,* I will steal this pink robe right off your back and go throw it in a muddy puddle."

"Rude! But fine. I won't say it. Just know I'm thinking it." She grins at me, and I feel a little bit of the weight on my shoulders lessen. "So, I'm guessing since you're here instead of there with him this means you didn't *get freaky,* as you so immaturely put it?"

"Right. I was completely in control of my emotions and able to calmly put a stop to it before it went too far."

She coughs. "You panicked." And coughs again.

I bump her shoulder. "Yes, fine, okay?! I completely spiraled. I tripped my way out of his apartment and promised I'd bake him a cake. I'm a complete mess."

"A little bit, but that's why we love you. So tell me what happened from beginning to end."

I do. I tell her about tearing the poster (she laughs like a hyena and I don't appreciate it at all) and then I tell her about going back to his apartment and how he's seen me naked (oh gosh, I totally forgot about that part until just now) and then I tell her about the stripping and how I cut it off. At that point, she pinches me hard under the arm.

"OW! What was that for?!"

"For running out on him mid-striptease!" Her cheeks are seriously red. She's so mad at me.

"Don't say striptease like that. You make it sound like there was gyrating and helicoptering of clothing."

She shakes her head. "Next time there should be. Oh my gosh, a man like Nathan Donelson giving you a striptease! And you stopped him! How are you my sister?"

"I'm going to go wake up Doug and tell on you if you don't stop being so creepy."

"Doug would back me up! I'm genuinely mad at you. I need a minute."

I raise my eyebrows and fold my arms, waiting for my sister to calm down from her conniption fit. Finally, she takes in a deep breath and releases it. "Okay. I'm ready."

"You good?"

"Mm-hmm."

"Great, now can we stop making this about you, please? Because I'm on the brink of a big life decision here and sort of need your support."

"Fine, yes, I'm sorry. Proceed." She tightens the pink tie of her robe primly like she wasn't just encouraging me to turn Nathan into a Chippendales dancer.

"I think . . . I think I want to rip up my rules and see what happens between me and Nathan. You know, what do the hip kids say nowadays? *Go with the flow*? I'm sick of being just friends with him. I'm ready to hope for more."

Lily raises her hands like she's sitting in church and the Holy Spirit really spoke to her. "Praise be. We've all been waiting long enough!"

I close my eyes and finally let my mind race back to that moment in his living room. It's time to dissect every tiny feature of his face to make sure I'm making the right decision. I use this memory to track the movements of his body, not out of desire (though that's there too), but like I'm studying a new language, trying to decipher its meaning.

In this recollection, Nathan doesn't hesitate. He doesn't look away from me once when I ask him to remove everything protecting him and stand in front of me exposed. There's trust in his eyes. I use the fancy CIA-level surveillance system in my brain to zoom in on his skin. ENHANCE! Goosebumps line his arms. But then, lastly, when he looks up at me while helping with my heels, his hand wraps around my ankle—*there,* I pause the image and point to the screen—in his face is the look of a man with *feelings*. I'm not sure how big those feelings are, but they are right there on the surface.

I open my eyes, courage filling me up like a balloon. I can't hide from risk anymore or I'm going to be sitting all by myself inside these protective walls—lonely and disappointed—for the rest of my life.

I look at Lily, squaring my shoulders. "You know what I've realized? It's time to hope for more with Nathan, because hope is healthy. Even if I prepare myself for the worst in life, it will never make the fall hurt less."

Her mouth falls open in shock, and then she smacks my arm. "I'M THE ONE WHO TOLD YOU THAT."

I scrunch up my nose. "I don't think so."

"Yes. It was me."

"I think it was an inspirational graphic on Instagram."

"IT WAS YOUR GENIUS BIG SISTER!"

I laugh, wrap my arm around her fuzzy-pinkness, and kiss her on the cheek. "Thank you, big sister. You are a genius."

"And don't you forget it."

We sit like this for a little while longer, talking about life and her boys and Doug's recent promotion and the upcoming birthday party she's throwing for my oldest nephew (of course I'll be there). Lily is truly happy, and that fills me with joy to no end.

Finally, she asks, "So what's next? Are you going to call Nathan tomorrow and tell him you have feelings for him?"

"Call him?! I might have had an epiphany tonight, but I'm not ready to place my heart on the chopping block completely yet. I'm going to lay it on thick under the protection of our fake relationship and see how he responds first. I'll hope privately in my heart."

Lily looks horrified. "What does '*lay it on thick*' mean?"

I gawk at her. "You know, flirting! Being sexy." I shimmy my shoulders on *sexy*.

"I'm concerned that you don't know how to do either of those based on the phrase you just used and the thing you just did with your shoulders."

"Oh stop. It's so sexy. Hey, Bob! Does Miriam ever lay it on thick?!" My new BFF will back me up.

He rolls down his window with a beaming smile. "Oh yeah! She never skimps on the mayo for my ham sandwiches."

I grimace, and Lily gloats. Fine. My sensual phrases need some work.

Just before I stand to leave, I remember something. "Oh! Wait, I have something for you!" I tell Lily while digging in my purse.

"Is it a Breenket?! Please say it is. Nathan is starting to collect more than me and I want to squash him next time we compare."

I pull out a tiny little Barbie. It's wearing a—

"Pink robe!" Lily says with a huge smile as she runs her fingers over the tiny little plush garment.

"I saw it in the grocery store the other day when I got distracted on the knickknacks aisle, and I was missing you so much I had to buy it."

Lily's arms wrap around my shoulders and squeeze. "Thank you, I love it. And now I'm going to own your man."

"Not *my man* yet."

She laughs. "Bree, darling, he's been your man for years."

21

NATHAN

"Food fight? You actually did it?" Jamal asks, looking up from a sheet of paper I printed off with all of our line items on it. I've crossed out the things I've already tried. I put a check mark next to things that went well and an X by the ones that were a no-go. "How was it?"

I nod toward the sheet. "What do you think that X means?"

Derek slaps Jamal in the chest with the back of his hand. "Told you it wouldn't work."

"You have nothing to gloat about," I say, sitting forward so I can see Derek. "Your wink tanked *big* time."

Lawrence leans around Derek so he can snatch the paper out of Jamal's hands. "Let me see this." He runs his finger down the list, and I know what he's hunting for. His face splits into a victorious smile when he finds it. "I knew randomly slow dancing would work. You can trust everything that happens in *The Notebook* to be romantic as shit. You guys need to listen to me more often."

"I liked you better when you were the quiet, sullen one," Jamal says to Lawrence, tapping his fingers on the armrest primly.

Price chimes in from my left. "Why? Because he's stealing your thunder?"

Jamal narrows his eyes with a mocking smile. "Keep it up and I'll come over there and smudge your toenail polish."

"Definitely not a threat I ever expected to hear in my lifetime."

I look down at my own feet, propped up on a folded towel so my black and silver toenails can dry. Yeah, we came to a nail salon today because after Bree painted our nails for the first playoff game and we won, we got pretty superstitious about it. As long as we continue winning, we'll continue painting. I would have asked her to paint them again today, but I also needed to brainstorm with the guys. So here we are, just five big dudes destroying stereotypes, getting our toenails painted in our team's colors, and enjoying the hell out of ourselves. Did you know they serve champagne at these places? I'm honestly hooked. I need to bring Bree back here.

Jamal somehow wrestles the list back from Lawrence. He wants to reclaim his thunder. "Okay, so judging by this list, it's time to step up the physical touch a notch. You've held hands. Touched her arm while talking." He's ticking these off on his fingers. "Brushed a strand of hair back from her face. Rubbed her feet . . . yeah, I'd say it's time to make out a little if she seems up for it."

Item number 20. Yes, I have them memorized. And yes, I've been looking forward to this one more than the rest. Mainly I've just been hoping I'd make it to this one without Bree shutting down on me and having to abort the whole plan. So far, all signs have pointed toward: *Yeah, she's feeling it too.* I've never been full of so much hope. Or dread for if this all goes well and I have to tell her I've been working from a cheat sheet this whole time. But we can cross that bridge when we get to it.

"How though? I can't exactly make out with her on my couch at home and use the fake relationship excuse. And we don't have any events coming up."

"I'll throw a party," Derek says from his end. "After the game tomorrow. If we win, we'll call it a victory party. If we lose, it's a consolation. Parties are the perfect excuse to make out. Everyone's always slipping off to a dark corner."

I grimace, feeling sort of gross to be premeditating a make-out with Bree. "Actually, I don't want to plan that one. If it happens naturally, it happens. I'm not going to force it."

Derek rolls his eyes. He thinks I'm such a prude. "Fine. But it's still a good place to act as a springboard for a few of these other ideas."

"You just want an excuse to party," says Jamal with a tattletale grin.

Derek is the resident playboy/troublemaker/media magnet. He's always getting into trouble, which is why during the regular season, I keep the guys on a short leash. There's nothing I can actually do to stop them if they want to party, but for some reason, they look up to me. They want my approval. Which is why Derek has been champing at the bit to get into a little trouble.

He clasps his hands below his chin like a pleading toddler. "Pllleeeasseee let me throw a party, *Dad*."

"I actually think Derek is right," Jamal says, thumping the back of his knuckle against the sheet of paper. "A party is a great place to unexpectedly short-circuit a fuse and have to light a bunch of candles."

I look at each of the hopeful puppy dog faces lined up around me. "Fine. A small one. But you guys better not end up on the news the next morning."

Derek is already ripping his phone from his pocket and his thumbs fly across his screen. Jamal chuckles under his breath beside me and starts reading down the list again.

"Wait—did you really get stuck in an elevator?"

I tip my shoulder. "I paid my apartment's security guard to stop it while we were inside it."

Jamal's eyes glimmer. This was another one of his ideas. "And? Did you get cozy?"

"She had to pee and started obsessing about possibly having to urinate in the corner of the elevator. I texted the guard and told him to get it running again after two minutes."

He groans. "Don't tell Lawrence."

It's Sunday night, and Bree and I are on our way to Derek's *victory* party. That's right, we won the game. Only one more to win to secure a spot in the Super Bowl. More important, whether we win or lose this next game, the Super Bowl will still happen, which means the commercial will still air, and this fake relationship will have no reason to continue on. No reason, unless . . . it's not fake anymore.

Currently, Bree is sitting in the passenger seat of my truck reading me all the outrageous DMs she's been getting from prying fans while on our way to the party. I only have a few weeks left to convince Bree of how great we could be as a couple, and I need to attend every public event I can so I have excuses to woo her.

". . . and THEN she asks if I would snap a picture of you in the shower and send it to her! Can you even believe that?! Naturally, I asked how much she'd be willing to pay for it."

I cut her a glance, and she just laughs and continues reading. We go on like this for twenty more minutes because Derek lives in a ritzy suburban community full of mansions a little outside of Long Beach. I'm exhausted from playing earlier today and wish we were headed back to my place instead of a party where I still have to be *on,* but this is important. *Item number 20 important.* Which, I'm still not planning. Only open to the possibility should it arise.

You might be wondering if I'm nervous about tonight and the prospect of finally making out with the woman I've loved since I was seventeen. Nah, I've gone out with so many women, and—YES I'M FREAKING OUT. My palms are so sweaty I can barely turn the steering wheel. My heart is hitting my ribs so hard they're cracking. I'm sure she can hear it. Probably thinks it sounds like I'm crinkling candy wrappers, but nope, it's just my bones disintegrating.

I'm hoping to cross some major lines with my best friend tonight, and if she doesn't reciprocate, if she still sees me as a brother after this, I'm throwing in the towel. I won't force something between us, and I won't ruin our friendship in the process. If I make a move on her and she shuts it down and runs off like she did after my cameo as Sir Strips-a-lot the other night, I'll officially make myself get over her.

But first, I've got to get a grip. How am I supposed to touch her with these sweaty palms? I'll leave greasy streaks behind on the sexy black dress she's wearing. *No, Nathan, don't think about the dress. Don't look at the dress. Don't slide your gaze to the tight fabric hugging her thighs—* I looked. I've been looking all night and it's doing nothing to help me keep my cool. I'm so far away from cool I'm an active volcano.

"So what sort of party is this going to be?" Bree asks, a touch of nervousness tinging her voice. At least I know I'm not alone, even if our nerves are for different reasons.

"It'll be more like a low-key get-together. Nothing big." Derek promised me it wouldn't be over the top, nothing that could stir up any trouble for the guys on the team.

But apparently his word means nothing, because as we pull through the security gate that leads to his property, I see what looks like hundreds of cars. It's a freaking carnival. His mansion is lit up like the Fourth of July, colored lights shining through the windows and the pulse of music hitting me as soon as I step out of the truck.

"Orrrr maybe it'll be a rager," I say after coming around the truck to open the door for Bree and help her down.

Bree is dressed to kill tonight. An assassin on the run in her jet-black dress. It's tight and cuts off midway up her thighs. Curls twist and spill over one of her shoulders, and I'm in awe of her. Those wide, brown eyes stare at the scene ahead of us, and I feel her hand slowly slide into mine. Our fingers lace. I can't help but smile when I realize her palms are a little sweaty too.

She swallows audibly. "Stay with me, please."

I grin. "Always."

The crowd is thick in here. The lights are low and the music is loud. Unless someone is right in front of you, it's hard to tell who anyone is. I don't like that.

Bree has my hand in a death grip and keeps shooting me looks that say, *I don't belong here!*

I squeeze her hand. *Yes you do.*

"Do you want a drink?" I have to lean down and ask in her ear so she can hear. It feels more like a club in here than a home. I'm going to kill Derek.

She frantically nods yes, and her hair tickles my lips. I maneuver us into the kitchen where we find Derek and Jamal along with the largest selection of liquor I've ever seen. Enough to get our whole damn team in trouble.

Jamal spots me first—whiskey in hand, mid-pour into his red cup. He promptly sets it down and takes one extra-large step backward then points an accusing finger at Derek. "Told him not to."

I swing my gaze to Derek, who is shooting a *look* at Jamal. "I thought you said it would be low-key."

Derek flashes a mischievous grin and stretches his arms out side to side. "I tried, but the people overpowered me."

Jamal laughs. "Nope. He's lying. I saw the guest list, and he definitely invited all these people on purpose."

I scan the party and am able to make out several of the single guys from our team. All drinking, all encircled by women I don't recognize. Sure, they're not really doing anything wrong yet, but the night is still young, and we have practice in the morning. My blood pressure hits the ceiling. Why are they all acting like this? Does no one else care that we're in the playoffs? What if one of our starters gets drunk and ends up in a fight? What if the cops get called? What if that leads to a suspension? I was okay with Derek throwing a small, chill party, but this feels negligent. Downright reckless.

"We have practice in the morning, Derek. If you overserve everyone—"

"Nathan." Bree interrupts me with a light hand to my chest. My brain registers this touch like a trigger sensor on the game Operation. My skin buzzes where her hand is resting, and I'm afraid my nose is going to light up red. I look down, and her soft smile immediately wraps around my racing heart and soothes it. "Let's just relax for a little bit. Don't worry about the guys. They can make their own choices and deal with their own consequences if they get into trouble. Tonight, just let yourself have fun."

Wait, is that an option? For four years, I've been the level-headed guy. The one who makes sure everyone is doing exactly what they should be. I'll admit, it's tiring.

Bree pats my chest lightly. "Let's grab a drink and then maybe you could show me around?"

I stare down at her wondering how in the hell she just did that. I could feel that tightness starting to grip my chest, that smothering sensation settling down on me again. An out-of-control panic was tiptoeing up to me, then one touch and a few soft words from her pulled me back to my body. I feel safe with her. My thoughts feel quieter.

Jamal hands her the drink he just made and mouths *Thank you* like she just saved him from a fire-breathing dragon. Derek runs away like a coward. *Yeah, you better run, fool.* I spot a guy over Bree's shoulder looking her up and down and backing up again in a way I don't like one bit. His eyes say disgusting things, and it's natural instinct for me to bottle up my rage and clench my fist at my side, unable to do anything about it because I'm just Bree's friend. But then I realize—we're in public! For all intents and purposes, Bree is my girlfriend right now, and all bets are off.

I slip my hand around her waist and feel the crease of her hip against my palm. I make eye contact with the guy and make sure he knows this possessive touch is a middle finger to his face. *Not tonight, buddy. Eyes off.* Habit has me waiting for Bree to shoot a glare up at me for touching her like this. When I see her eyelashes lower, registering the touch, and then she cozies in closer instead of pulling away, my pulse doubles.

She finally looks up at me, and there's something there. Something new. Something sparking and inviting, and I'm not just imagining it, right? I dare to find out what it is.

"This is okay?" I ask.

She lifts a coy shoulder with a small grin—flirtatious. *ALSO NEW!* "I mean, sure. But just know that if you're going to act possessive in public, I will too." She goes up on her toes to kiss my jaw.

My heart stops.

In that tiny little kiss, there was a country-sized amount of meaning. The way her eyes look, the way her body feels against mine . . . it all adds to the implication. That small kiss was a checkered flag, and not once tonight has Bree made a single move to remind me of the friend zone. No *brother*, *amigo*, *BFF*, or *incest* references.

No, right now, her eyes have fire in them, and there's no way I'm going to pretend it's not there. I won't *keep moving* and ignore the signs tonight. Item number 20 is underway. I'm going to harness the flames in her eyes to burn our platonic friendship to the ground.

I squeeze her hip tighter and steer us out of the kitchen. "In that case, come with me."

22

BREE

Nathan's hand presses into my side as he takes me with him out of the kitchen, drinks forgotten, weaving us through a crowded dance floor in the living room. The couches have all been moved to the perimeter and so many people are packed into the center, cups in hand and dancing like they belong in an underground club. My first feeling is relief. *Dancing! Yes!* That sounds great. Nathan saying "In that case" had my mind racing to other outcomes. Outcomes I definitely want but am also a little terrified to embrace. So, let's dance!

Oh, we're passing the dance floor now. A woman backs into me, and her sequined dress scratches over my bare arm. Nathan tucks me in closer to his side and steers us toward a hallway. A dark hallway. That's fine. I'm good. Everything is good.

"Umm, should we be going this way? Looks sort of . . . dark." I try to persuade him, but he just quietly grins and keeps moving us toward that forbidden hallway. I don't know that it's forbidden, but no one else is in it, so it sure feels forbidden.

This is what I get for talking a big game with Lily! I thought I could *lay it on thick*, but now I just want to lie down and pass out because I can feel change in the air. I can feel it transmitting from Nathan's fingertips through the fabric of my dress and seeping into my veins.

We step into the hallway, and I know we're not coming back out the same people as before. It's also important to note that Nathan is the only man in the world I would trust to take me down a creepy, dark passage like this—and if that doesn't say something about his character and the way I feel for him, I don't know what will.

With every step, I feel more excited, thrilled, and terrified.

"What a lovely hallway. It's so . . . dark . . . and . . . hallwayish."

We don't go to the end of it like I think we will. We don't open any of the closed bedroom doors. We stop in the middle where the colored lights from the party still reach, and yet it's private enough to not be watched. I suck in a breath when Nathan abruptly spins me around so my shoulder blades touch the wall. He smiles down at me, still not saying a word, and then really confuses me by taking a step away. Two steps. Three. His back hits the opposite wall, and we look like two kids who got in trouble at school for calling each other names. Definitely not the direction I thought this was going . . .

Maybe I misread him the other night. Maybe he doesn't have feelings for me. Maybe—

"I'm giving you ample warning," he says in a deep tone that crawls up my neck in the most pleasant way. Like someone trailing their finger across your skin to make your hairs stand up. His eyes glitter in the darkness. "I know change scares you, so I'm going to tell you what's about to happen, make sure you approve first."

Did anyone else just hear me gulp?

I try to say *okay*, but nothing comes out. My lips are only moving for show.

"I'm going to take three steps back to you and put my hands on your hips." His eyes rove over me, and he squints just below my chin.

"Maybe your jaw, maybe the back of your neck. We'll see. And then I'm going to kiss you."

I. Can't. Feel. My. Toes.

When my voice finds its way out, it sounds like a croak. "Why?"

His head tilts rakishly, and he smiles but doesn't answer me.

This is where habit tells me to END IT. The little hall monitor that enforces my self-preservation blows a whistle and says, *Stop this right now!* But things are changing around here, and I want them to change, so I shove her into a locker. (But then I feel bad about that so I take her back out, thank her for her service, give her a chocolate bar, and tell her to take a vacation to the beach. She deserves it for all her hard work.)

Would I have liked for Nathan to admit his undying love for me and THEN kiss me? Yes. But I'm going to make myself do something new and hope for the best. He's taken the utmost care of me over the past six years, and deep down, I know I can trust him now.

"Still with me, Bree Cheese?" he asks.

I nod.

Just as promised, Nathan takes one, two, three steps, and now he's in front of me. I have to tilt my chin back so far to see him that my head rests against the wall. One hand moves forward and rests on my hip. It feels like a match striking a box. I have been forcing all of my attraction for this man away since high school, and now that I can let it out . . . I'm giggling.

Oh gosh, I'm giggling! No! This is no time to pull a Rachel Green!

Nathan freezes and frowns down at my bubbling laughter. I'm terrified I'm going to sabotage us again, so I clasp a hand over my mouth. At first, he looks uncertain and defeated, but then his frown clears and he smiles.

"Rachel Green?" he asks, because of COURSE he'd know what's happening to me. We've watched the whole F.R.I.E.N.D.S. series together multiple times, so he knows when Ross Geller finally gets with his longtime friend Rachel Green, she can't help but giggle every time he touches her. And I can't believe it's happening to me now. Is this an actual condition?

"I'm sorry," I say from behind my hand. "I'm ruining this."

"Ruining what?" he asks savagely, trying to get me to admit there's a *this* between us to ruin.

I don't take the bait. "The facade. Anyone watching right now will be able to see that this is totally foreign for us. The jig will be up." Total crap. No one can see us right now, and no one at this party gives a flying monkey what we're doing.

Nathan hums a deep sound and inches closer, taking my other hip in his free hand. He pushes me flush against the wall and drops his head to my neck. His breath grazes my skin and he whispers, "You'll just have to pretend it's nothing new."

I hold my breath as his soft, warm lips press against the side of my neck. Tingles erupt across my skin.

"Pretend I've kissed you here a thousand times already." His hands leave my hips to skate up my sides and land on either side of my jaw. He tilts my head and moves to the other side of my throat. "Pretend I have every inch of you mapped out like the back of my hand." His hand slides around my back and drops low to just above my rear end. "Pretend I know you have a two-inch birthmark right here." Reality is colliding with fantasy because I *do* have a birthmark right there. I'm on the brink of spiraling, remembering he's seen me naked, but he moves on quickly.

His lips lose contact and he takes a handful of my curls in between his fingers, raising them to his nose to breathe in. "Pretend I was the one who washed your hair with this coconut shampoo before we came here tonight."

Oh my gosh. I can't breathe or swallow or think or move or *live* any longer. My soul has reached nirvana and I'm not coming back. Nathan is overwhelming. He's powerful and yet *oh so* gentle. How has it taken me so long to experience this side of him? And if he's truly pretending, his acting is next level.

"Pretend," he says in a gravelly tone, quiet enough for only me to hear as he drags his thumb across my lower lip. "I am *off my face* for you, and all you want right now is for me to kiss you." He lowers his head so his lips are hovering just a fraction over mine. I'm aching for him. Dying for his mouth to land on mine and BE DONE WITH IT. I close my eyes and part my lips and feel his barely brush against mine as he points out, "You're not giggling anymore."

I drag in a deep breath then whisper, "No. I'm not."

Finally, Nathan's lips press into mine. It's the softness of a rose unfurling. It's velvet brushing over silk. Dipping your toes in a hot bath and languidly inching your body into the water so you don't get burned.

I've dreamed of this kiss for years, but in my imagination, I was never able to accurately conjure the rich, taut texture of his skin, or the strength he's trembling to restrain behind his powerful hands.

All of the space between us closes as Nathan pulls me in tighter. Our hips meet and I'm in his arms fully now, dragging a deep inhale of him into my lungs. Into my veins. Into my soul. I can't get enough of him.

Can this really be happening?

Yes, his lips say as they press into mine over and over. Searching. Exploring. Coaxing. My palms slide up over his chest to lock around his neck. While I'm here, I might as well take some liberties. I get my paws in the back of his hair, right at the nape of his neck where it curls deliciously. He makes a quiet groan of appreciation and everything speeds up. It's a kick drum now with a rising tempo. He parts my lips. I taste him and he tastes me.

It's no surprise to me that Nathan is completely controlled in his movements. He's precise and meticulous on the field, and that translates here too. He's disciplined. But I sense there's another side to him, one where he lets go and surrenders. I crave that recklessness in him, so I lightly bite his lower lip and tug. A gentle reminder that I'm not as fragile as he thinks.

He responds immediately, hands wrapping fully around my ribs. My feet leave the floor. He hoists me up easily, and I wrap my legs around his waist, holding on for dear life. *Him. Nathan. My sweet friend* is hungrily devouring my mouth like I am everything he needs in this world and he will take it all.

I press my fingers into his shoulders, relishing the muscles flexing beneath my touch. His body is devastating. Glorious. And it's attached to his soul so I adore it even more. I cling tighter because our kiss is so intense I'm dizzy. Yearning and desire pulse through both of us until it feels like a tangible current. Years of holding back combust.

"*Bree . . .*" Nathan breaks the kiss to whisper reverently against my throat. He kisses it, bites gently, soothes it with another kiss.

Shivers race through my body and I burn everywhere he touches me. How is this reality? How are we here?

I catch his lips again, and my blood hammers through my veins. Now that I've tasted his kiss, I'm addicted. I'll be chasing this sensation for the rest of my life.

We're plucked out of the hallway and transported into another reality among the stars. Up here, there are no sounds other than our hearts beating and breaths curling between us like tidal waves. Heat and Nathan's calloused touch are my only guides in the dark, and everything is *right,* and safe, and as it should be. Our bodies were made for each other—that has to be the answer to how this can be so good.

Suddenly, everything goes dark and startlingly silent, quickly followed by squeals and curses. The power is out.

Nathan's lips peel off of mine, and it physically hurts to have to say goodbye to them. I think I whimper, and he chuckles pleasantly and kisses my cheek.

"What do you think happened?" I ask him, clutching the front of his shirt in case it was a serial killer who cut the lights and the music and is about to have his way with us.

Nathan lets out a grumpy sigh and slowly lowers me to the ground. Through his teeth, he says, "Seems like the house blew a fuse."

What terrible timing. It feels like someone tossed us into freezing cold water. Our magical moment is over.

In the next moment, we hear Jamal's voice boom through the house. Something about it sounds oddly monotone, robotic, and almost . . . rehearsed. "Oh no. Looks like we blew a fuse! I guess we'll have to light some candles. Nathan, you around here? Need a candle, buddy?"

Nathan mutters something under his breath, and it sounds oddly like, "Thunder-seeking jackass."

He's still holding me. His fingers are still clamped onto me like the prongs of a bear trap. There's a desperation in his hold that matches the one in my heart. I want to ask him a million and two questions. I want to bombard him with declarations. But my mouth won't open and reality sinks back in around us.

My soul is shaking.

I know a whole new side of Nathan now, and I don't ever want to go back to what we were.

23

NATHAN

"Wake up, sleeping beauty!"

I crack open my eyes to Bree hovering over the side of my bed. Her curls are tied up in a high ponytail and draping over the side of her face. The apples of her cheeks are splotched with pink, and I wonder if I'm still dreaming. I have to be. Why would Bree be in my room right now? The sun isn't out. She's a figment of my imagination.

I stare at her. What's Dream Bree going to do?

She smiles, and I mirror her. If she raises her hand, I'll raise mine too. Her soft brows crinkle together, and so do my bushier ones. This makes her laugh. "You're being weird. Come on, get up! It's Tuesday."

I really hope this dream ends with us not going on a run. I glance at the clock on my bedside table and it says 5:00 A.M. Now I know I'm still asleep. Bree is always trying to get me to sleep in, so she wouldn't wake me up before 5:30.

It's best if I just settle in and see what happens. I put my arms behind my head and watch her as she crosses my room to paw through my chest of drawers. She selects a black Nike T-shirt and gray athletic shorts. A balled-up pair of socks hits me in the face. I don't flinch. Bree moves to stand at the foot of my bed, her eyes roaming over me. All that's showing is my chest and abdomen, but Dream Bree likes what she sees. The pink splotches turn to red apples. Variety: *Delicious*. She's wearing my favorite pair of short turquoise running shorts and a black tank top, neon yellow sports bra underneath. She puts her hands on her fantastic curvy hips.

I love dreaming. Because in here, there are no boundaries. No friend zones. Just me and Bree as we should be.

"You look like someone should be fanning you and feeding you grapes. What are you waiting for?" she asks curiously.

"Come around here and find out." I'm sexy in my dreams.

Those brown eyes widen, but she complies. Her sneakers squeak a little with every step. Then she's standing beside me, and I reach out and take her hand. *Warm skin.*

Oh no.

THAT'S REAL SKIN, PEOPLE!

This is not Dream Bree. This is real-life, actual-consequences-if-I-pull-her-under-the-covers-with-me Bree. And I need to quickly backtrack.

I look up and see her swallow her nerves. I feel her hand trembling in mine. We might have kissed the other night, but this is different. This is alone. In my room. I have no excuses here for talking dirty or holding her hand and what I had planned just now is definitely not on the romance cheat sheet.

I tug her down a little so her shoulders hunch toward me, and then I pretend to flick something off. "I thought you had a spider on you. It was a piece of lint."

"And you were just going to wait all day for it to bite me?" She slaps my bare shoulder. Crisis averted. "Some friend you are."

Okay, time to switch gears. My brain is in a fog, but I force myself to clear it out. I sit up straighter and throw the covers off, swinging my legs over the edge of the bed so I can rub my hands over my face. My breath is rank. That should have been clue number one that this is real life.

"What are you doing here this early?" I ask her, digging the heels of my palms into my eyes. I stand up and stretch.

"I couldn't sleep. So I thoughtwecouldgoonarunearly . . ." All of her words end in a pileup.

Turning to her, I see her unblinking gaze locked on my body. *Right.* I sleep in boxer briefs. Kinda forgot about that when I stood up. Bree looks like she's in some sort of pain. Her mouth is still open, unfinished words dangling off her tongue.

I step toward her, trying not to smile. "Bree?"

She's that famous painting now. She doesn't move, but her eyes follow me around the room. "I shouldn't be seeing you like this."

"Probably not." I don't normally feel embarrassed in my underwear. I'm pretty used to my own nudity at this point. I've done ads for Jockey underwear, and also, you know, that whole *form issue* thing where I was completely naked. But this is Bree, the woman of my dreams, staring me down in an intimate way I don't think anyone else ever has before. It's like she's matching puzzle pieces together to finally see the whole picture. *Nathan loves strawberry Twizzlers + ah, that's where his tan lines live.* It's unnerving.

"You're . . ." Her words end there. She's yet to look at my face.

Before I can stop it, embarrassment slides over me. I feel my face heating. "Can I have my clothes?" I extend my hand toward the bundle she's clutching, but she holds it up and away from me.

"Not yet."

I sputter a laugh because I don't know what else to do. She's ogling me. Very openly. This is new—and I'm not sure how to proceed. This is not on the list. "Do you think I'll get them any time soon?"

"I suspect so, but the jury is still out." She sounds like someone hit her with a tranquilizing dart.

"Okay, enough." I step forward to take my clothes, but she holds them behind her back. She's not going to let me have them. "What are you doing?" I ask, sounding just as amused and confused as I am.

"I don't know." Her eyes are bright. Excited. Fearful.

Our kiss the other night is humming intensely between us.

"Can I . . ." Her words hesitate again, and she sounds like she's trying to keep all the air in her lungs. "I just want to . . ."

I suck in a noisy breath when Bree steps closer, raises her hand, and presses it onto my pectoral muscle. The palm of her warm hand is directly over my heart, and I know she can feel it knocking against her skin. I raise a brow and tell everything in my body NOT TO REACT. She swallows, staring at the place her hand is touching me, and then she abruptly breaks contact, foists my clothes into my arms, and dashes through the room toward the door.

"GREAT. MEET YOU DOWNSTAIRS." My bedroom door gets slammed shut.

The front door slams next.

I blink and look down at my crumpled running clothes. "What. The. Hell. Was. That?"

24

BREE

I'm pacing the sidewalk outside Nathan's apartment. Up and down I go, back and forth. I'm contemplating just taking off running and never coming back, because . . . I just touched him. *Nathan*. Nathan's bare body. I reached my greedy little hand right out and felt the man up. What was I thinking?! (I was thinking he was ripped, that's what!) It was so forward of me! I might as well have taken spray paint to his wall and written I LOVE YOU NATHAN with a big heart around it!

The sun is peeking over the horizon just as Nathan exits his apartment building. I whip my head away from him. I can't meet his eyes yet. I know I should be mature and apologize for what I did back there, but I prefer being childish and pretending it never happened instead.

"Ready?" I ask, bobbing my gaze anywhere and everywhere besides in the direction of his face. "Let's go!"

I take off at a brisk jog and he has no choice but to catch up. In two seconds flat he's beside me. His gaze is heavy on the side of my face, I can feel it, and I want to scream I DON'T KNOW, OKAY?! I don't know what I was doing back there! I'm in love with my best friend, and I've been hiding it from him for ten zillion years, and now all of a sudden I'm deciding to not hide it and see what happens, but I'm too scared to own it, and what if he doesn't love me back! *insert giant inhale here*

See? I'm losing it! I've lost too many fries from my Happy Meal!

"Hey, might want to slow down," says Nathan, taking my forearm to tug me lightly. "We'll burn out if we start in a sprint." But his touch feels like positive and negative connectors to my dead battery—it jolts me to life and now I want to take off like Speedy Gonzales. "Seriously, Bree. Slow up. We haven't even had our coffee yet. Why are we running before coffee and donuts, anyway?"

Good question. Answer: because I'm everything all wrong and backward today. I woke up this morning like it was Christmas. TUESDAY! It's been two whole sleeps since our kiss in the hallway, which was also the last time I saw Nathan. I've been busy with dance and he's been busy with practice and a photo shoot after practice yesterday, so basically, I've been dying. (Not to be dramatic.) But when my eyes popped open this morning (at 4:30 A.M.), I couldn't wait any longer—I had to see him. I had to see if all the heat and zings I experienced during that kiss were still there or if he was faking it for the dating facade. I highly doubt it though. He's a terrible liar—also so fun to play poker with—so I'm thinking he's into me.

Now, before, this would have sent me screaming in a frenzy and overanalyzing every move he makes. Not the new Bree. The new Bree isn't worried that Nathan is only into me as a passing fancy. The new Bree isn't even thinking about that (yes, I am). The new Bree is going with the flow! Seeing where this *sexy little fling* takes me. LAYING IT ON THICK!

I force myself to slow down so I can toss him a normal smile. He frowns, so it probably wasn't so normal. "Just wasn't in the mood for donuts."

"You're unwell," he states flatly, so shocked. I couldn't have told a worse fib. "Come on, let's take it easy today and go down to the beach." He veers left, and I have no choice but to follow.

We jog together down a boardwalk and kick off our running shoes when we reach the sand. It's so early in the morning that the air is still chilly, and the beach is relatively empty. No one is here to watch us or take photos—which makes it all the more startling when Nathan intertwines our fingers and pulls me with him down toward the water. We both stand so that the tide can wash over our feet and ankles. The icy water prickles my skin, but it's nothing compared to the sensation of holding Nathan's strong hand.

He audibly sighs, making me look up at him. His wavy brown hair flutters around his brow, and the salty air makes the strands at his nape flip up with an extra ounce of rebellion. The wind catches his T-shirt, pushing and pulling it around his abdomen, once again drawing my attention to his perfectly sculpted form. A soft smile curls the side of his mouth as he stares out over the water where the sun is just starting its day.

"I miss the ocean," he says quietly, and then he looks down at me. "We don't come down here enough." His dark features are a direct contrast to the soft blue sky behind him, and yet they somehow complement each other perfectly.

"Life is busy."

Well, truthfully, *his* life is busy. Mine is, too, but it's a different sort. I have built-in breaks and days where I kick back and watch TV for no good reason in the middle of the afternoon. I don't work myself to the bone like he does.

I blink back toward the water. "Confession . . . I was down here yesterday morning."

"You were?"

I shrug.

"Why didn't you tell me?" His voice sounds sad.

I point up at his face. "That's why! You turn into a sad puppy when you find out I've done fun things without you. I don't like to rub it in when I know it's not something you can swing."

His hand squeezes mine and he pivots slightly to look down at me. "That's very sweet on your part—and super pathetic on mine."

I chuckle. "You don't like to be left out. Nothing wrong with that." I stare up into his eyes, feeling the space between us close a fraction. The same magnets that pulled us together in that hallway are working now. His thumb glides up and down my hand. I ache to tell him how perfect this feels between us.

"You're not annoyed by my faults?" he asks, sounding perfectly serious.

"I don't see it as a fault. It's just you. Sort of how you never tell me to sort the piles of random crap in my apartment."

He grins softly. "Who am I to mess up your system?"

"See, that's why we work so well together. Best f—" I cut myself off and clamp my mouth shut. No more constant reminders of our friendship. I want more. And I'm pretty sure the first step is not claiming an old label.

He hums in suspicious amusement at my cutoff sentence. Then his eyes crinkle in the corners. "Well, you're right. I don't like missing out on fun with you. So let's go swimming now."

I shriek at that thought. "No way! It's going to be so cold, and—AH!"

Nathan scoops me up in his arms and runs full steam ahead into the water. I scream and kick and think he'll stop at the last moment and tell me he's only kidding then take me back up to the beach. Nope. He dunks us both under the frigid water. The temperature can't be more than sixty degrees, and I'm going to murder him! But when we resurface and he flashes me his sunshine smile, I lose my rage. He is happiness embodied. He is also sexiness embodied. His dark, wet shirt molds to him, and water droplets slide from his hair down that square jaw.

I bet I just look like a wet cat.

Nathan eyes me and my shivering body, and my suspicions are confirmed about how I look when he chuckles. "Are you cold?"

I glare at him. "No, I'm incredibly w-w-w-warm, you jerk!"

"Awww, I'm sorry. Come here." He stretches out his long corded arm and pulls me up close to him, wrapping both arms around me as we are swayed by the water. I'm pressed against the hard planes of his body, and now I don't feel so cold anymore. It's a miracle!

I swallow, wondering for the hundredth time in the span of a few days what this is, what it means . . .

"Hey," Nathan says, breaking through my thoughts and pushing my sticky wet hairs back from my face. "Are you happy, Bree?" His eyes trace the line of my mouth. I don't know what this moment is exactly, but it feels important. My heart trembles.

"Very. Are you?" My gaze darts to his mouth and back up.

"Right now? Yes. I'm always happy when I'm with you."

My lips part on an inhale. We're going to kiss again. I can see it in his eyes, can feel it in his fingertips pressing me closer to him. The waves splash against our sides, and I wrap my arms around his neck, rising up on tiptoe to reach him. Our lips are just about to meet when Nathan's head turns abruptly to the side.

For one terrible second, I think he just rejected me. I'm ready to slip away from him and swim into the ocean, never to return again, when he pivots both of our bodies so his back is to the shore. His eyes are stormy now when they look down at me.

"Paparazzi found us. A guy with a long lens is hunched down by the boardwalk snapping photos."

"Oh!" I say in a relieved rush, happy to know I don't have to become queen of the crustaceans. "That's . . . bad? I thought we wanted paparazzi to see us being *couple-y*?"

Nathan shifts me behind him, ducking his head and shielding me as much as he can as we make our way out of the water. Which I'm beyond grateful for since my clothes are practically painted on my body right now and that's really not the image I want my dad to see when he's shopping for milk at the grocery store tomorrow.

When Nathan's voice reaches me, low and quiet, I almost think I've heard him wrong. "Yeah, but that was when it was just fake."

Nathan and I are soaking wet and jogging back to the apartment. The paparazzo was relentless, following behind us all the way down the boardwalk, snapping away even when Nathan asked him to stop. Nathan's jaw was flexing in a way that made me worried for his teeth, and he kept his arm tucked protectively around me until we were back to the main sidewalk and could head back to his place.

This time, he seems determined to run at the breakneck speed I was encouraging earlier to get us back to privacy. Only problem, I'm now wearing sloshing clothes that I'm sure are going to leave a terrible chafe on my inner thighs. I feel like I'm running in weights. Sure, Thor over there runs in weighted vests all the time. Not this gal, though, so I am horribly unprepared for this level of physical endurance. It also doesn't help that my mind keeps wandering back to what Nathan said in the water. *That was when it was just fake.*

Because it's not now?

The next thing I know, I'm tripping over my own feet and hitting the pavement *hard*. Instinct has me protecting my bad knee by landing mostly on my good one, my hands, and my elbows. Everything stings—but nothing as bad as my pride.

I curl up in a ball and wrap my arms around my smarting knee as Nathan crumples down beside me. "Bree! Are you okay?" He's fussing over every inch of me. "You're bleeding. How's your other knee?" He immediately assesses it like he's a doctor and knows what he's looking for.

"It's okay. I didn't land on it." Tears fill my eyes, making me feel like an idiot. I don't want to cry in public over a few scrapes, but my body seems to have other plans. "I'm fine, Nathan! Just look away for a second!"

"Why?" His voice is tender, which only heightens my emotional state.

I cover my face with my hands. "So I can cry like a little baby."

He doesn't laugh, but he does smile softly. He takes my face in his hands and forces my leaking eyes to meet his. "Bree, you can always cry with me."

Later, back at the apartment, I'm lying on the couch like Cleopatra (if she were sweaty, bleeding, and tearful). My knee was really bleeding and stung too bad to walk, so after Nathan whipped off his shirt and used it as my new favorite bandage, he piggybacked me all the way to his place where I was laid like a delicate porcelain doll on the sofa despite my protests of soaked clothing and bloody limbs ruining his furniture.

"I'll buy a new one. Don't move," he said gruffly. I didn't argue or point out the wastefulness of his statement because I've seen this look on Nathan before, and it's the one he gets when he's worried down to his bones. I won't tease him when he's like that.

A few minutes later, he's walking back into the living room carrying a first aid kit and an ice pack. He's put on a clean white T-shirt, and I could swear I hear a choir of women around the world collectively groaning in annoyance. We all despise that opaque material.

Nathan sits down beside me on the edge of the cushion and twists his hips to face me. He takes my leg and gently pulls it into his lap. It stings as he doctors up my three-inch road burn, but I barely notice because I'm too busy staring at him. Occasionally, his fingers glide over the healthy skin of my legs, and it sparks everywhere in my body. My elbows get fixed up next, and now I look and feel like a clumsy, awkward child, wearing three ugly brown bandages with frizzy curls swelling rapidly around my head as they dry. I'm sure I have tear stains. *She's looked cuter, folks.*

Once I'm completely bandaged, Nathan sits back and positions the ice pack over my wounded knee. He's frowning down at it.

"What is it?" I ask cautiously, afraid I'm bleeding out or something and I just can't see it.

With my leg still in his lap, his index finger traces a soft line around the bandage. I can feel the reverence in his touch. "Nothing. It's just . . . seeing your knee bandaged brings back memories."

"Of my accident?"

He nods, still not looking at me. "I've never felt more terrified or helpless than I did that week." His eyes snap to me. Heavy. Serious. Aching.

We rarely ever talk about that time in life—though I'm not sure why. It's just something we avoid for reasons I don't think either of us really knows.

"I wanted to . . . I don't know. When you told me ballet was over for you and you cried over the phone . . ." He sounds anguished. "Bree, I would have sold my soul to be able to get your dreams back for you in that moment."

I smile at the hard edges of his jaw. The stern set of his brows hanging over his black eyes. His shoulders are rigid like he could plow through a mountain and knock it down, but the pressure of his finger lazily moving over my skin is a feather. A tender kiss.

It makes me want to reciprocate. To be just as vulnerable as his touch.

I lightly flick the lock of hair at the nape of his neck. "I'm glad you didn't. Because . . . I like your soul."

His finger stills and he looks up at me. Our eyes collide for two twisting, drawn-out breaths. I am scorching. My skin prickles from my head to the tips of my toes. Does he know how much his nearness affects me? Does he know I'm dying to dive through those beautiful eyes and see all his hidden thoughts? I need to know if there's a chance he will ever love me like I love him.

Are we friends?

Or are we more?

My heart pounds more and more aggressively the longer we sit staring at each other. He doesn't say anything. WHY?! Why won't he speak? *Do you like my soul too?* I'd settle for a compliment on my shirt. A casual, *That's nice, your shorts are cute.* Anything! Just say something please!

But the longer he takes, the more I wonder if he's trying to formulate the perfect response to let me down easy. *Your soul is okay, I guess. I've seen better.*

I don't give him a chance to answer—I panic. "Instagram!"

He frowns. "Huh?"

I scramble out of his lap, feeling my cuts all sting angrily when I bend my knees and retrieve my phone off the coffee table. "We haven't posted a cutesy photo in a while, and that was part of the contract agreement, right? They wanted us to post couple stuff with their curated hashtags?"

"Yeah . . ."

"Let's get to posting, then! We could stage a photo of us playing checkers or something? Do you own a checkerboard? Or cards? We could play cards . . . I'll let you win. Why are you smiling like that?"

He chuckles almost under his breath. "Why are you blabbering?"

I stare right at him and blurt my truth in one long word vomit. "Because I told you I like your soul and you didn't respond."

Half of his mouth tilts into a smile. "I was going to, but you didn't give me a chance."

"You were taking too long. If we were on *Jeopardy!*, the buzzer would have sounded way before I interjected."

"I didn't realize there was a time limit."

"There is. There's always a time limit. And now I know you hate my soul."

He takes my phone from my hand, fiddles with it, and sets it carefully back onto the coffee table. "Some people need more time to get their answer right. It's not fair to give a time limit."

"Sorry, but that's life, buddy. You can't wait forever." I realize now that he's angled the phone on the coffee table, setting it up so that it's facing us.

He looks at me again. "I disagree. I think some things are worth waiting for, no matter how long it takes."

Nathan leans over and punches the button on the side of my phone, and a light starts flashing for the ten-second timer. Before I have a moment to grasp what's happening, he puts a hand on my shoulder and gently pushes me over so that my back falls flush with the couch cushion. *This is new.* Nathan hovers over me, pinning me in as the subtle countdown flashes continue to spark beside us.

"Bree, I want to kiss you. Is that okay?"

All I can do is nod.

He bends down, slowly, and drops one soft lingering kiss to my mouth. Fire explodes in my belly. We are not in public. And the camera is still counting down. This kiss isn't for anyone but me and him. *That was when it was just fake.* His lips are warm, soft, vulnerable caresses. They end far too soon.

"Your soul is my favorite in this entire world," he replies quietly, just as the camera sends the final bright flash signaling the photo.

I'm shocked. So scared I'm dreaming I could cry. It wasn't exactly a declaration, but it felt like it. My heart beats: *Hope. Hope. Hope.*

I take his jaw in my hand. "Hold still."

"Why?" Nathan says on a chuckle, because if I can be counted on for anything, it's making a moment weird.

"Because you don't have a good poker face, and I want to see if I can find the answer to something."

His smile fades into something more serious, and as I tilt his face slightly to the side, he complies easily. His jaw is scratchy beneath my fingers. I tilt his head the opposite way, sizing him up from all angles. He indulges me like he has every day of our friendship. No squirming or averting his eyes. He lets me swim through those deep, dark irises, and just when I'm almost to the glowing answer at the end of the tunnel, his phone blares an alarm.

He expels a breath and drops his head into my neck, and I'm able to register his full glorious weight pressing down on me before he pushes off the couch to get his phone. The alarm is silenced. He looks at his phone like he'd enjoy crushing it in his palm and tossing the debris out the window. "That's my alarm telling me it's time to go to work."

"Okay," I say, my breathy voice barely punctuating the air. But seriously, how am I supposed to respond after a moment like the one we just shared? We're on the brink of everything changing, but we're not able to jump quite yet.

He and I stare at each other for one long moment, and then he groans and shakes his head. "I'm sorry. I have to go. Can we talk later? About . . . everything?"

I smile. "Yes."

25

BREE

You know what's strange about being a normal person and not living inside a Netflix movie? After significant moments, you don't get a scene jump. After your best friend whom you've been secretly pining after for years and years *maybe-sort-of-did-he?* admits to liking you, too, you don't get to flash forward.

Nope. My life goes on, painfully slow and full of uncertainty. I get to live in the gray for three whole days. You'd think with how often I wear gray, I'd like living in it, but NO! I don't. I want to take everything gray I own and burn it in a pile in the parking lot. I'll do some sort of ritual dance around it to cleanse myself of its hold on my life. I'll lift signs and chant, "WHAT DO WE WANT? NO MORE GRAY!"

So anyway, Tuesday was rough. After Nathan left for practice, I had to go teach my new toddler class with a banged-up knee and elbows that felt like someone was scraping shards of glass over them every time they bent. And guess what? You bend a lot in ballet. It's practically all we do. Bend all over the place.

I taught the rest of my classes that day and then was hoping I'd get to see Nathan that evening, but he had an event at the children's hospital and I wasn't about to be that girl who asked him to skip making tiny children's dreams come true, so we texted a little (texting inside the gray is super awkward, in case you were wondering), and then I went to bed early.

Wednesday, my scrapes were scabs and I could remove my bandages. Why am I telling you this piece of unimportant information? Because it was the only interesting thing that happened that day. Oh, and I found the match to my favorite leg warmers that I'd been looking for for months. It was somehow behind a jug of milk in my fridge. Woohoo for buried treasure!

Nathan's practice ran long that day and then he had another meeting about another thing that I can't keep up with. Life during the playoffs is incredibly hectic, and it seems like somehow, Nathan's days are only getting MORE full. I'm not sure how it's possible when they were already stuffed to the brim to begin with. I'm worried about him. When I ask if he's tired or if he's slept at all, he just brushes it off. *I'm fine. Don't worry about me.* Right, sure, I'll just turn that switch off then. Easy-peasy.

This morning (Thursday), I finally did a big thing! I submitted my application to The Good Factory. It's done and out of my hands, and that thought is as thrilling as it is terrifying. I still find myself trying to temper my expectations, but for the most part, I'm forcing myself to hope. To think about how wonderful it will be if my studio is granted the space. I even went by the factory and toured it just so I could be able to more accurately dream of how I would arrange everything—which wall I would have the mirror installed on, which one would get the barre. I took pictures for Nathan of every nook and cranny in the place, and he dreamed with me through text. It has felt unbelievably freeing.

It's 9:30 P.M. now, and just as I'm crawling into bed for the night, I see Nathan's name lighting up my screen. I lunge across my bed to grab it so hard I pull a muscle and accidentally fly over the edge and crumple on the floor.

"HI! HEY! I've missed you!" I say, rubbing my sore neck and completely forgetting that I'm supposed to be playing it cool.

His low chuckle races across the line and tickles the little receptors in my ears. "Hi, I've missed you too," he says, not bothering to play it cool either. Goosebumps flood my arms. I wish I were there with him right now more than anything.

I climb back up into my bed and scoot against my headboard, pressing my phone between my ear and shoulder so I can pull my comforter up. It's worth noting that I have a disgustingly dreamy smile on my face as well. I've completely sunk into la-la land where everything is beautiful and sadness is only a mythical idea. "Yeah?"

"Yeah." He sighs heavily, and somehow I know he's also lying in his bed. I hear him take a deep breath and imagine his hand resting above his head. If I were there, I'd run my fingers across his scalp until his eyes shut and he groaned with delight.

"I'm sorry I've been so busy." He doesn't say this in the way most people do—where it's sort of flippant and really you hear, *I'm not actually sorry and I haven't thought about you once before now.* He says it in a pained and guttural way, and I know he means it. He's spread thinner than butter on toast, and my worry for him ratchets up again.

"No, Nathan, it's okay! I understand what the playoffs are like."

"But I don't want to be too busy for you."

My fragile little paper airplane heart gets launched into the sky. "I'll still be here when playoffs are done."

I hear rustling on his end and imagine he's turning over onto his side. "I know we need to talk about the other day on the couch . . . I haven't meant to leave it this long. I've just barely had time to even look at my phone for the last few days. Do you want to talk about it now?"

Imagine the Michael Scott gif of him yelling NOOO. That's what my brain says. In no way do I want to potentially have a DTR with my best friend over the phone when he's half asleep. Or . . . oh gosh, even worse, what if he's had time to think it over and realizes he never should have hinted at anything? He doesn't like me like that. He doesn't.

"Bree?" Nathan's voice cuts into my terrified thoughts.

Let yourself hope.

"Sorry, I'm here. But no, I'd rather talk about it in person."

"Good. That's how I feel too. So we agree to stick a pin in it for now?"

"That sounds painful."

"It will be for me."

My smile stretches so wide the corners of my mouth touch my earlobes. If ever there was a reason to let myself hope for something, that statement was it.

"What are you doing tomorrow night? Maybe I can slip out of practice a little early and we can have dinner?"

"Yeah! That will be—" I grimace, suddenly remembering the plans I already have. "Ah, shoot. I can't. I forgot I have my nephew's birthday party tomorrow night. He's turning six. I got him a new harmonica just to really drive Lily over the edge."

"You're going to a family thing tomorrow night?" His voice is doing that thing where it's filled with longing mixed with disappointment. Not because he's disappointed I'm going, but because he loves my family and wants to go too.

"Yeah . . . I know you're busy though."

"What time?"

I don't know why he could possibly be asking me this. "It starts at six, I think. They're having dinner and an outdoor movie. My parents will be coming in for it too!"

I'm really looking forward to it. I love my family, and since my parents retired, I haven't seen much of them. They're RVers now and spend most of the year traveling around the US. When we all get together, things get rowdy in the best of ways. My mom is also super into TikTok dances and is always begging me and Lily to do one with her. I'm not sure I'll ever recover from seeing her dance to Cardi B though. Watching my dad dance to it was even worse.

But it's good. After seeing them work so hard for most of their life, the day they were able to retire felt like a burst of sunlight to all of our souls. I miss them, and I can't wait to hug their necks tomorrow.

"I'll be there," Nathan says, followed by the sound of a click. Must have turned off his light.

Listen, there's nothing more I want in this world than for Nathan to come with me to a family event. My parents adore him and it's always fun to see my mom try to mother him like she does the rest of us even though he's eight miles taller than her, but I hear the exhaustion in his voice. In fact, I've heard it for the last month.

"Nathan, if you have the night off tomorrow, you should take that time at home to rest. Watch that documentary you've been wanting to see. Drink some hot tea in a bubble bath!"

He's quiet for a second.

"Do you take bubble baths?" he asks, his tone changing ever so slightly.

"I do when I'm at my sister's house. I only have a walk-in shower here."

He makes a thinking sound. "I have a bathtub here. A big one."

I swallow. "I know . . . I've seen it."

"You can use it any time you want."

I laugh, feeling slightly nervous and zingy all of a sudden. "Okkaayyy, but we're not talking about me. We're talking about you and how you should use tomorrow night to rest. I think you'd love a bubble bath!" If Chandler Bing loves them, anyone will.

"I think the only way you could get me in a bubble bath is if . . ." His words trail off, and I'm left to fill in the blanks all by myself. My heart thumps again: *Hope. Hope. Hope.* "Never mind." He clears his throat. "I'm good though. I have plenty of energy," he says, sounding like a dehydrated man having to be carried across the finish line of a triathlon. "Let me come with you. *Please.*"

I can never say no to his pleases. They are made of tiny little strings that wrap around my heart and squeeze.

"Fiiiine, you can come with me. But fair warning, there's going to be a lot of chaos. Screaming, dancing, cake flying everywhere, and that's all just coming from *me*."

He chuckles, and an image of his dimples pops into my mind. I remember the way he looked lying in his bed before I woke him up the other morning. In my mind, I go to him there in his room like I have a hundred times before, except now, I have a perfect image to accompany me. I tiptoe in quietly and gently lift the covers back. I slide in and it's like a sauna in there because Nathan always runs at a thousand degrees. He feels me move beside him and hums a sleepy sound before wrapping his big arm around me and pulling me in tight. His breath tickles my hair and his skin is hot all around me.

"I've been warned," Nathan says, puncturing my fantasy.

"Good night, Nathan."

"Night, Bree."

Nathan was supposed to pick me up after practice, and we were going to go together to the birthday party. Unfortunately, he wasn't able to slip out early like he hoped and texted me this afternoon saying I should go on ahead without him and he would catch up as soon as he could. The thing is, Lily's house is not just down the street. It's a two-hour drive, and my nephew's sixth birthday party is a completely ridiculous reason for Nathan to drive two hours out of the way after a long day of practice. I tell him this over text with lots and lots of exclamation marks, but he just responds the same way he did last night: *I'll be there.*

I make it to Lily's house about half an hour before the party. Good thing, too, because my entrance is so epic it would show everyone else up and make them feel terrible for their mediocre existence in life. I am The Fun Aunt. Aka, I don't have any kids yet and therefore still enjoy running wild around the house, screaming and flailing my arms like a monster on the hunt for little boys while my sister hides in the bathroom with the glass of wine I've poured her.

I throw open the front door and hold my hands up in the air, showing off my bling. "Holla! Aunt Bree is in the house!" I'm decked out with Ring Pops on every finger. Three candy necklaces adorn my neck, and a superhero cape is draped over my shoulders. Gift bags full of LEGOs, water guns, and bubblegum (because what kid doesn't like bubblegum) are cutting off the circulation of my forearms.

I hear the stampede of nephews before I see them. I brace for impact as they run down the stairs, scream my praises, and hug my legs, and then one by one, I'm robbed of my loot. They don't even leave me with a single Ring Pop! The little footpads run off, and all I see is a haze of birthday bags as they brush past my sister, who is now approaching in the hallway with a scary smirk.

She levels me with a frosty glare. "You brought sugar into my house when I already had CAKE AND ICE CREAM?!"

"No." I shake my head aggressively. "You misunderstood what you saw. Those were broccoli pops."

"And the candy necklaces?"

"Vitamins."

At this, she cracks a gorgeous smile and opens her arms. "Get over here and hug me you terrible, *terrible* sister."

Mid-hug, I hear the door open behind me and my mom's voice trill through the air. "My babies are hugging!! HAROLD, GRAB THE BAGS YOURSELF! MY GIRLIES ARE HUGGING!"

Mom barrels into us next and squeezes with all her motherly might. She fusses over Lily first and smacks her right butt cheek. "You haven't been eating enough. Don't worry, I'll fix it while I'm here." She looks over her shoulder and calls to our dad, who we've yet to see. "HAROLD, BRING IN THE CASSEROLE!" Of course Mom made a casserole.

Next, her sharp blue eyes turn to me, and I wonder what lecture I'll receive. She gets close—closer than close—and narrows her eyes like she's looking into a crystal ball.

"You've been kissing Nathan."

I gasp. "How did you know that?!"

She waves me off. "I'm a mom, honey. I've always known everything, and I always will. It's called motherly intuition."

Lily cackles and then yells, "Baloney! It's called Twitter! She signed up for a dummy account a few weeks ago and didn't tell us. She saw your red carpet kiss." Mom looks affronted. "Yeah, thought I didn't notice, didn't ya? Well I did, *Mrs. Brightstone*!"

"You *didn't*," I say, looking at my guilty mother. Mrs. Brightstone was the name she'd always use when we played dress-up growing up. She was a very wealthy woman—always going to balls in her mink coats. (Don't throw paint, they were really only scratchy wool blankets.)

"I didn't think you'd remember! And I had to! I knew you'd start filtering your content if you knew I was following you."

"What? No way, Mom. You're cool, and we've always known it."

She smiles and turns with her oversize purse whipping against her hip as she saunters into the kitchen, at which point Lily and I both show each other our wide eyes and crossed fingers.

Mom yells from the kitchen like some sort of supernatural being, "Uncross those fingers, ladies, and gather the boys! It's time to TikTok!"

At that moment, Dad emerges through the front door, loaded down like a pack mule with enough luggage to last them a month, beads of sweat trailing down his forehead, and a casserole tin clamped under his arm. "Please tell me Nathan is here too. He's the only one who will be able to talk your mother out of the costumes she brought for the dance video she wants to do."

I highly doubt that, but still, I throw my dad some hope. "He said he'll be here."

26

NATHAN

I'm almost to Bree's sister's house and I'm two hours late. After practice, I was already set to be an hour late, but then I sat on I-605 in traffic for another hour. I'm exhausted. Frazzled. And really wanting to bump the minivan in front of me to get it to go faster even though I think the stick family wearing mouse ears on the back windshield is supposed to deter me. *It doesn't.*

Probably should have had my car service bring me, but . . . I don't know. Sometimes when I'm tired and I think it would be great to take a nap, I feel the need to push myself harder. Plus I hate taking the SUV to personal events. It feels like I'm showing up with a blinking sign that says, LOOK AT ME I'M SPECIAL!

I let go of the steering wheel to rub my chest. It's tight, and my heart rate is still high from practice. Bree was probably right—I should have gone home tonight. I couldn't though. Things finally seem to be happening for us, and I want to demonstrate to her that I can be there for her and have a career in the NFL. I don't want her to feel overlooked or put aside. I know she values family and events like this, so I want to show up for her. Maybe it's just because I'm feeling deliriously tired, but during that brief kiss on the couch the other day (and definitely the one in the hallway that I'm still thinking about), I could have sworn she wanted it just as much as I did. Wanted *me*.

My wooing is working, and I can't believe it. All this idiotic stuff the guys told me to do is freaking working. Bree and I are . . . I can't even let myself think about it yet. Until I hear the words "Nathan, I don't see you as just a friend anymore" come straight from her mouth, I'm not going to be able to accept it.

Finally, around eight P.M., I pull into Lily's driveway. It's dark, but the lights in the house are illuminating the windows, and occasionally a little shadow darts past. After opening my truck door, I can hear absolute mayhem inside. I smile to myself because growing up as an only child, my house was always quiet. I *love* this. I want this.

My knocks on the front door go unanswered, so I let myself in. Chaos hits me like a tsunami.

Kids. Are. Everywhere.

So many of them in all different shapes and sizes. They are cackling and screaming, running through the halls with little NERF guns and pelting foam pellets at each other. I've met Lily's boys a few times and Bree has brought their entire family to a few games, so the nephews know me right away. The birthday boy, Levi, sees me first and sprints toward me. I'm braced for impact, but he stops right in front of me and flashes me his toothless smile. "Nathan! Look at my new NERF gun!" He's pumped, and I act as though I've never seen anything greater in my entire life.

I didn't know what to get him, so I pulled a few strings and had most of the guys on the team sign a football for him. When he pulls it out of the bag, it's clear I've epically failed, but he tries his best to look impressed.

"Oh. A football. Cool! Thanks." It's garbage. He hates it. I sort of love it, though, that some grown men would sell their kidney for that ball, and this kid savagely tosses it onto the couch. Old news.

And then they yell, "Quarterback sack!"

I immediately have ten little leeches on me, and I can't shake them off. Even though I'm not feeling it right now, I decide to just run through the narrow main hallway like a growling bear all the way back to the kitchen, because I know play and fun are how this family does things.

In the kitchen, I find all the adults. Too many adults actually. It's suddenly clear this is not just a family party, but a massive birthday gathering where the parents were all invited to stay too. Cool, cool, cool. It's somehow even louder in here, everyone laughing at a higher than normal volume. *Chill, Nathan, it's a party—of course they're going to laugh loudly.*

One guy sitting on a barstool at the counter spots me first. He does a double take. "Uh—is that . . . Nathan Donelson?" He's wearing an LA Sharks shirt, so I know this can't be good. I'm really not in the right frame of mind to deal with fans tonight.

I raise my hand in a small wave and look around the room for Bree. She's standing by the sink filling a pitcher with water. At the mention of my name, her head of long gorgeous curls swivels in my direction. She's wearing a yellow cotton dress with a long line of wooden buttons down the front. Bree looks like a literal ray of sunshine, and man is she a sight for sore eyes after this long, grueling week. I want to run my hands down her bare arms and soak up all of her attention. I want to steal her out of here and keep her all to myself.

Our gazes connect, and for one glorious moment, everything else falls away. It's just me and her here. Her smile splits across her face, and my favorite dimples punctuate her cheeks.

And then I'm punched hard in the stomach by a random kid, and

I double over with a curse not suitable for said kid's ears. There's more chaos now.

"Nathan! Oh my gosh, I'm so sorry. Kids, OFF!" I'm not even sure who said that. Parents are fussing around me, peeling each of their relentless sugar-fueled offspring off of me. It's a swarm of adults and children all invading my personal space in this narrow portion of the kitchen that connects to the main hallway. Bree is trying to make her way through the crowd, but I'm trapped, and she can't get to me.

Lily's head pops into the mix out of nowhere and acts like this scene of pandemonium is completely normal. "Hi, Nathan! It's good to see you!" She squeezes under my arm to slide her way through the people and into the kitchen.

"Nathan's here?!" That's Bree's mom. I'd know her voice anywhere, but I can't see her because three dudes are pressing in, reaching over their wives who are corralling the kids. *Really? You want a handshake right now, man?* Bree is outside of everyone still just trying to make her way through. Someone hands her a baby and she's trying to hand it back.

Doug comes up behind me and slaps me on the back. "Good to see you, man! Hell of a game last week."

I'm smiling—I think?—and trying to answer everyone's congratulations and introductions while a kid is pickpocketing my wallet. (Did I say I want a big family? I changed my mind.)

Everything. Is. Swirling.

I'm aware of my jaw tightening, teeth clenching painfully. I haven't even made it fully into the kitchen yet. I'm still stuck in this damn hallway, surrounded by people. An urge to wave my arms around frantically and yell GET BACK! nearly overtakes me. I want to throw my elbows side to side until they all scatter. But I can't—I know I can't. I have to stand here like I always do and take it all with a winning smile.

I need to focus on the voices, but they're all slowed down, mixed together—muted. I can't follow them. I can't swallow. My heart is racing and I feel like I've been plunged in icy water. *Where is Bree?* I can't find her.

Why do my limbs feel heavy and numb? There's a falling sensation, and the fact that I know I'm not really falling only makes my heart pound faster. Something is *wrong*. I can't breathe. My *chest*. My *fingers*. My *breath*. What's happening to me?

I have to . . .

I can't . . .

I just . . .

27

BREE

Oh no. Something is wrong.

I watch as everyone clamors for Nathan's attention and suddenly, his face goes pale. His eyes look distant and glazed. His shoulders are rounding in on themselves and he takes a step away from everyone. It's so noisy in this tiny hallway that I'm barely able to hear him say, "I'm sorry, I've got to . . ."

He turns away from everyone and dashes down the hallway. There are about twelve bodies between me and Nathan and I push through them with the gusto of a Black Friday shopper fighting for the last doorbuster TV. "Excuse me. Just let me—ugh, MOVE, Doug!"

I emerge from the mob and stare down an empty entryway. He's nowhere to be found. I run into the living room, but I don't see him. He's not in the dining room. I check outside. His truck is still parked, but he's not out here. I'm frantic now, like I've lost my child in the mall. Nathan looked terrible right before he disappeared, and I've got to find him.

I decide to look up the stairs and peek in all the rooms. Finally, I see the door to the laundry room cracked with the light off. Inside, I find my mountainous best friend curled up in the corner, shaking. Nathan—my unflappable Nathan—has his knees up to his chest, big arms wrapped around his legs, head dropped between them. I can hear his gasping breaths from here.

I rush over and drop down beside him, resting my hand heavily on his back. "Nathan, hey, shhh it's okay. I'm here."

"I can't—" He tries to drag in a breath again. His shoulders are heaving. I put my hand on his chest and feel his heart pounding as if he just outran a bear. "I can't breathe. I feel like I'm going to pass out." All of this comes out in a frantic rush, like he's desperate. "Am I dying?" he asks, completely genuine and terrified, and now I know for sure what's happening.

I scrunch in closer and stretch out my legs around him so I can pull his back against my chest. Winding my arms around him, I hold him tight. "No, you're not dying, I promise. You're having a panic attack." He's shaking from head to toe, and my heart twists painfully. I know what he's feeling right now. "Just listen to my voice, okay? I'm here. You're safe. It feels like you're dying, but you're not. Now, all I want you to focus on is how my arms feel around you. Are they tight or loose?"

He expels a shaky breath and, after a long pause, answers, "Tight."

"Right. I'm not letting go. Now, what do you smell?" I wait for his answer, and when he doesn't reply, I gently ask again. "Nathan? Tell me what you smell."

"Umm . . . cake," he finally murmurs, voice raspy.

"Yeah, it smells so good. It's vanilla with sprinkles. My favorite. Do you have any tastes in your mouth?"

I can feel his breath evening out a little and the tightness in his body loosening. I resituate one of my arms so I can run my hand tenderly up and down his arm.

"Mint," he says quietly. "I had gum in my mouth, but I think I swallowed it." He sounds so defeated and embarrassed by that. I know the fear and mortification of having someone experience my panic attack, of being seen so out of control and frantic. I want him to know I will never view him differently or see him as less just because I've seen him undone.

"That's okay. I've done that before. I mean, I've only ever been able to taste watermelon-mint ever since then, but it's not so bad."

I get a minuscule chuckle from him so I know he must be coming back down to me. I lean my head against his shoulder blade and kiss him there. He sinks back against me a little more, his limbs loosening slightly.

We sit like this for a few minutes, and I talk to him until his breathing sounds normal again and his weight is heavy against me. My palm is pressing against his chest, and when his hand covers mine, I know he's feeling more like himself. He squeezes.

"How did you know what was happening to me and what to do?" he asks, his voice hoarse and broken.

"Because after my accident, I used to get them all the time. Any time I got in a car for the first few weeks, the panic would settle in. It's the worst feeling. Like everything is closing in and you can't escape it. Like you would be willing to claw out of your skin just to get a minute of relief."

"Yeah," he says weakly. "Exactly."

Silence stretches between us. Shirts are hanging above our heads on the drying rack, and the tile floor beneath my legs is cold. Nathan's hand falls to my shin, and he squeezes. A silent show of gratitude.

"Are you feeling better now?" I peek over his shoulder to see his face, but he turns it away.

"Yeah," he says, though his voice shakes.

"Nathan?" I crane my neck around his shoulder, but he won't look at me.

His shoulders begin to shake again, but it's not the frantic sort of tremor from before. "Please, don't . . . just don't look at me right now." He raises his hand to press his thumb and index finger into his eyes.

"Why not?"

There's a pause followed by a broken inhale. "Because . . . I'm going to cry like a baby," he says, echoing my sentiment after my spill on the sidewalk a few days ago. "You can go back out there. I'm okay now. Just go." He's not trying to be mean. He's desperately trying to preserve his dignity.

I hold on tighter. "You can always cry with me, Nathan. We're safe with each other."

This breaks him wide open.

He drops his head into his hands and a sob racks his frame. I hold on to him, pressing my palms into his chest so he can feel that I'm here, that I'm not going anywhere, that he could cry enough tears to fill the ocean and I would still think he's the strongest person I know.

Suddenly, he twists, wraps his arms around my waist, and pulls me onto his lap. My legs are on either side of his, but there's absolutely nothing sensual about this moment. I am his anchor. He wraps his arms tightly around me and buries his head in my neck, crying in a way I'm sure he never has before.

I run my hands through the back of his hair. "Nathan, talk to me."

It takes him a moment, but finally he answers. "I'm so tired. I've had this tightness in my chest for weeks, and this is the first time it's lessened at all. I feel broken. I used to be able to handle everything, but . . ."

"But now not so much?"

He nods against me.

"You're not broken. Having a panic attack or anxiety does not reflect your wholeness. You're burned out, and that's completely understandable. You push yourself more than anyone I've ever seen before, and it's only natural for you to reach this point."

He shakes his head. "No . . . I can't. I should be able to handle it. I *have* to be able to handle it."

"Says who?"

He doesn't answer me. I pull away and frame his jaw with my hands to make him look at me. Even in the dark I can see his eyes are red and puffy, and he's deeply embarrassed. He tries to turn his face away, but I don't let him because I need him to know I'm not ashamed of this part of him. He's probably never cried in front of anyone in his entire life, largely due to the culture he's steeped in day in and day out that tells him his maleness is defined by his ability to remain impenetrable to emotions.

"Why do you have to handle it all, Nathan? Why won't you let yourself rest?" I ask, looking deep into his eyes.

He squeezes them shut and tears roll out. "Because I don't deserve to."

"*What?*" I ask on an exhale.

"Bree, I've never had to work for anything in my life. Nothing! It's all been handed to me. Catered to me. I wanted to work in high school, but my parents actually wouldn't let me. Even my current position on the team is because it was handed to me. Daren, the man who rightfully earned his spot, got injured, and I took over after sitting on the bench for two years. Do you see? I've been *given* all of this success—so what do I have to complain about? What right do I have to be exhausted? None. I'm just a rich kid who was provided everything he ever needed and handed more money and more success on a silver platter."

I had no idea he felt this way.

"So this is the reason you work yourself to death? Why you never say no to people? You're trying to prove your worth?"

His eyes turn down again. "When I work hard, when I feel tired, it's the only time I feel a little bit of the guilt in my chest lessen." I want to speak to this, but he keeps going, new tears shaking his voice. "I've never had to go through hard things in my life. I've never known anything close to poverty or struggle or even just budgeting, for that matter. I have a chef, a driver, a manager, an agent—everything I could ever need, so tell me . . . what reason do I have to complain about any of it?"

Tears are streaming down his face, and the look in his eyes is anger mixed with defeat.

"What right do I have to resent it? To want to escape any part of it ever? No. I don't deserve to get help for the anxiety I can't escape. I don't get to feel overworked. I need to keep my shit together and give as much of myself as I can, because otherwise everyone will see that I don't deserve to be where I am."

Nathan lets go of me to press his face into his hands. For a moment, I sit, stunned. I stare at this man I thought I knew better than anyone in the world and realize all along he's been bottling up his feelings, his hurts, his anxiety and stress because he feels like he has to wear a cape to be a hero.

If he can bare all of this to me right now, I can do the same for him.

I pull his hands down from his eyes so I can look in them. "Listen to me. It is not the things you do that make you worthy, it's that you have a beating heart in your chest. You have a soul, which means you are allowed to feel hurt, tired, stressed, sad, angry. All of those things—you are allowed to feel them. Everyone is." I gather all of my strength for my next words. "Your ability to shoulder everything, to give 200 percent of yourself all the time, to be perfect at everything you attempt . . . these are not the attributes that make you a valuable human being." I pause. "And they are not why I fell in love with you."

His black eyes shoot up to me.

I smile. The weight of these heavy secrets falls off of me, and I feel relieved to continue. "I fell in love with you because you're goofy. You're fun. Your heart is so big I don't know how it fits in here," I say, pressing my hand to his chest. "You're a terrible singer. You make me soup when I'm sick. You bought me tampons that time I was laid out on the couch with cramps and couldn't move. You didn't even send someone else for them. You went yourself!"

He chuckles lightly, and I wish there was more light so I could see his smile clearer.

"Look, Nathan, I don't care if you never pick up another football a day in your life, or if no one in the world attaches the word *successful* to your name ever again." Now I'm the one dumping tears, and Nathan's hands have moved to cradle my face. His thumbs dash across my cheekbones.

I shake my head lightly and try to swallow down my sob enough to finish speaking. "So don't say you're not worthy or deserving, because you are to me. You always will be."

Nathan pulls me closer and crushes me against his chest. His strong forearms are pressing into my shoulder blades, his face buried in my hair.

"I love you too," he whispers over and over again. "I love you, Bree. I love you. I always have."

28

BREE

I talk Nathan into letting me drive him home in his truck, and he arranges for someone from his entourage to go get my car and drive it back for me tonight. *Hello, celebrity perks.* We leave almost immediately even though Nathan is severely worried this is going to upset everyone.

"Let me take care of you," I say, looking up into his hesitant eyes. "Please?"

He relents and hands me his keys. "Thank you."

I get a kiss on the cheek, but I sort of want to do the move where you turn your face really quick and get a kiss on the mouth instead. Not the time.

On the drive home, we're both physically and emotionally exhausted. Nathan turns on some mellow music, takes my hand, and laces our fingers. He kisses my knuckles with an aching tenderness that tears right through me. We drive for two hours, not saying a word, just listening to the music in comfortable silence.

"Will you stay at my place tonight?" he asks, finally breaking the silence as I pull into the parking garage of his building.

I've stayed at his apartment a hundred times, so that question shouldn't feel heavy or important. But it is, because I've never been asked it while he holds my hand and the words "I love you" hang between us. It feels easy to say yes though. Natural.

When we finally walk into his apartment, he tosses his keys on the entry table. I toe off my shoes and go into the kitchen to get us both a glass of water. It's all so normal, but also lightly scented with *different*. Neither of us speaks, because we're not sure what words would be adequate enough to follow the emotional roller coaster we just rode together. So we carry our waters down the long hallway that leads to our rooms. I get ready to part from him and go into mine for the night like I always do, but he catches my hand, tugging me back around. A bit of water sloshes onto the floor.

"Stay with me?" He says those three words not as a demand, but as a defenseless question. A need. A desperate hope. Tonight has peeled back everything I thought I knew about Nathan, and now I see a man who's just as scared as me. I love him more.

I nod and step into his expansive room. Nathan gently closes the door behind us, and my heart gallops when I hear it quietly latch. The floor-to-ceiling window is ten steps away, and I take each of them with a measured calm then look out over the most incredible view of the ocean, nothing obstructing the dark expanse of water and white crests of the waves breaking against the sand. It looks peaceful yet dangerous out there. That's exactly how it feels in here too.

"Bree?" Nathan asks from behind me, and I whirl around like a tornado that's suddenly directionless.

"I'm nervous," I blurt.

Nathan's eyebrows rise, and then he lets out a long breath and a tiny smile. "Same."

"Really? Okay, good. Because logically, I know it's me and you." I sputter a humorless laugh. "It's a dream come true, in fact! I shouldn't be nervous—I should be tackling you."

"It's harder to accomplish than you think," he says, cracking a joke that instantly eases the prickling in my lungs.

"But what I'm nervous about—or afraid of, really—is that I said I love you back there and you said it too only to humor me." I have big cartoon eyes now—I can feel it.

Nathan smiles in a way that shows barely contained amusement. "Humor you?" He takes a nervous step away and runs an awkward hand through his hair. "You thought I could have been humoring you by telling you I love you?"

"Yes. You don't have to keep repeating it."

"I do. Because if you were in my head, you'd see how difficult the concept is to comprehend. Bree, I . . ." His voice trails off and then he freezes. He deflates with a sharp breath. "Sit down," he commands, and then he disappears into his giant walk-in closet.

I perch on the bed and bounce my knee. Then I realize I'm sitting on Nathan's bed—something I've never done before—and I jump up like it just burned my butt cheeks. I force myself to sit back down and process this like an adult. I'm in Nathan's bed. In his room. He loves me. Nope, see? None of these abstract ideas will permeate. I've spent too long believing he has not a care in the world for me outside of friendship. It's all I've known. How am I supposed to retrain my thoughts?

Nathan steps back into the room, and if he notices that I'm barely letting my cheeks rest on his mattress, he doesn't show it. His attention is fixed on the shoebox in his hands. He looks nervous, maybe even a little sick as he extends it toward me. When I try to take it, it doesn't budge. He's white-knuckling this thing so hard.

I grunt. "Nathan, do you want me to look in here or not?"

"Not," he says, dead serious. "I mean, yes. But no."

I shift back a little. "Well now I'm terrified. What do you have in here? Bones? Endless pictures of earlobes? Am I going to be scared of you after I lift that lid?"

"Probably." He winces lightly and then relinquishes the box.

I set it down on the bed carefully (because who knows what's in here or how fragile thousand-year-old bones are) and gingerly lift the lid. I steel my spine for something to jump out, because he's prepared me zero percent for what's actually in here. Lizards? Maybe he keeps a box of moths in his closet and when I open it, they'll rush out and choke my airway.

It's neither.

After the lid is off, it takes me a second to realize what I'm looking at. Nathan paces away from me with a tight hand on the back of his neck. I dip my fingers inside and pull out . . . *my scrunchie*. The sunshine yellow scrunchie I thought I lost after Tequila-gate several weeks ago. I look up and make eye contact with Nathan. He looks like he's going to barf. His fist is pressed to his mouth, and his eyes are crinkled. Poor thing is really going through the vulnerability wringer tonight.

"This is my scrunchie," I say, holding it up for his confirmation that what I think I'm seeing is actually true.

He gives me a tight nod. "You took it off and left it on the table that night. I kept it." He gestures toward the box with his eyes. "Keep going."

Nathan resumes pacing, looking at me every so often like someone might watch a surgical operation they have been forced to attend. Next, I find a cocktail napkin with my lipstick imprint from the epic poster-ripping night. Then the orange Starburst I threw at him on the couch.

The deeper I go into the box, the more I recognize things I haven't seen in years. A concert ticket from a Bruno Mars show he took me to for my birthday (and got us backstage passes to, which he pretended to randomly find on the sidewalk because I never allow him to buy me extravagant things). Toward the bottom, I find a gum wrapper with my phone number scribbled on it from high school. I remember this day like it was yesterday. We had run together for the first time that morning before classes. That afternoon in homeroom, he asked me if I'd want to run together again sometime. Of course I said yes, and we exchanged numbers. I didn't save the slip of paper he gave me with his number, though, and now I feel like a horribly unromantic monster!

Once I've gone through every single item in this box and spread it all out on the bed around me, I meet his gaze. He finally comes near me and plucks the scrunchie I'm clutching like it's a million-dollar bill out of my hands. "This smelled exactly like your hair. *Coconut*. I should have given it back to you, but I couldn't." He tosses it in the box. I'm never getting that scrunchie back. Next, he grabs my hands to tug me up to stand with him. "Do you see now? You're always giving me things that remind you of me, but I'm over here stealing things that remind me of *you*. I'm not humoring you, Bree. I'm not taking this lightly. I'm so devastatingly in love with you, it hurts sometimes—and I have been since high school."

Hope, hope, hope. I hear it beating in my ears.

"I've been dying for you to love me back—but I never thought you would. Remember when you found out I'm celibate and I told you it was to help my game? That was a complete lie. I've been celibate because I am so gone for you I couldn't even stomach the thought of another woman anywhere near my bed. She would never be you." He cradles my face. "I love you with everything I am, and that's never going to change for me. I think I should be the one making sure you're not just humoring me."

I can't take the space between us anymore. I rise up on my toes to lay one soft kiss on his lips, feeling like this *has* to be a dream and I can do anything I want in my dreams. "I've loved you since the day you tied my shoe on the track. You didn't tell me it was untied, you just tied it."

The muscles in his jaw jump like he's swallowing back tears. "Bree, that was the first day we met." His tone says, *Don't toy with me, woman.*

"I know. That's the day it all started for me."

His massive shoulders rise and fall in one huge breath, and then his eyes shut like he's in pain. "Do you mean to tell me . . . we've both loved each other all this time and never said anything?"

I laugh even though it's not funny at all. I run a finger over one of his eyebrows. "Yes. I think so."

"But what about college? You completely pushed me away then. I thought I did something wrong."

Oh. That.

I smooth a hand down the front of his shirt, suddenly very concerned about wrinkles. I guess while we're emptying our emotional tanks, I might as well go ahead and squeeze a little more out. "I'm so sorry, Nathan. I pushed you away because I was terrified. I could see the way you were thinking of turning down your UT scholarship to stay home with me, and although I never told you, I was really depressed after the car accident. I was afraid you were about to completely give up your dreams for me, and after hanging around me in my mopey, angry, defeated state, you'd realize I wasn't worth your time anymore and resent me. I was scared you'd see me low and heartbroken and not want me like that. So I pushed you away. I'm sorry, Nathan. I Old-Yellered you."

His hand tenderly cradles my face. "I never would have felt that way. I've always just wanted to be the one to take care of you."

"I know that now. But back then, depression told its own story, and it was hard to hear the truth through it."

He dips his head and sighs against my throat. "Well, hear me now: I adore you, Bree. When you're happy or sad, I love you." Nathan lays a slow, open-mouthed kiss on my neck and climbs up to my mouth.

Heat swirls in my belly, and my head tips back to receive his lips. Softly, they sweep over mine. He gently tastes the corner of my mouth, and I part my lips to reciprocate. I am a puddle. So melted he has to hold me up. Kisses by themselves are nice; kisses after a declaration of love are life-changing.

I'm lifted off the floor and tossed playfully onto his bed. A laugh rips through me until Nathan grabs the back of his shirt and tugs it over his head. His eyes are as dark as the sky at his back. I swallow thickly as he moves to hover over me. His weight. *GAH.* Golden taut skin. *OOF.* That ripped abdomen I finally get to dance my fingers across. *MMM.*

Nathan smiles down at me as I explore every inch of his exposed skin. I rise up and kiss one pec. Then the other. I lightly bite his bicep, and he laughs. "So that's how it's going to be?"

I innocently bat my lashes at him, and he dips his head to crush his mouth against mine. This one is not soft or tender. It's years and years and *years* of waiting. It's a desperate breath at the surface of the water when you're rescued from drowning. I cling to him for dear life. He kisses me deeply, thoroughly, lavishly. His hand slides under the back of my shirt, and that calloused skin scrapes delicious fire over mine. I feel branded.

Nathan is everywhere. And I am full of need. I have fallen for this man so completely, and now we're finally here together, twisting in his sheets, kissing like it might be ripped away from us at any moment.

Kissing like we love each other. He whispers soft declarations over my skin that I won't repeat. They are for me and me alone.

Suddenly, Nathan pulls away, a drugged look in his eyes when he smooths the hairs away from my face. Breathless, he lets out a guttural groan, coming to some sort of unvoiced conclusion in his head. He adjusts onto his elbow beside me. "Bree, I want everything with you right now more than anything, but . . . dammit. I can't believe I'm going to say this. I think we should wait."

Shocked doesn't begin to describe how I feel hearing those words, especially since he's been celibate for so long. But I won't lie, part of me is sort of grateful. I'm a girl who likes to be prepared for these kinds of things, mentally and physically, and tonight was so unexpected; I know I'm not in the right headspace for it yet. I need a little digesting time.

But then Nathan shocks me in a less-than-pleasant way when he continues, "Actually, I . . . I sort of want to wait until we're married."

WHAT!? My brain screeches to a halt. Did he say *married*?! Did he propose at some point tonight and I missed it?

My eyes must convey my thoughts because Nathan's smile widens and he trails his finger down my neck to dance lightly over my collarbone. *Conflicting body language there, buddy.* "Don't worry, I'm not proposing yet. But I know you don't like to be surprised by stuff, so this is me saying I *will* propose to you at some point. And I'm hoping you're okay with that time being pretty soon, because I feel like we've already been dating for six years, just not officially."

He's right, and I tell him so. I've never known another human more intimately than I know Nathan, and best friends like us don't casually date. It was an unspoken agreement that by declaring our feelings, we were saying, *I'm all in. You're it for me.*

"I agree," I say in between his teasing kisses and light nips at my bottom lip. "But why wait until we're married? That seems so . . ."

"Old fashioned?" he asks, his fingers feathering down my arm to trace my bare ring finger. He presses a firm kiss against my temple. "I know. I won't lie, that's part of the appeal. If I've learned anything over the past few weeks, it's that I've never really had to pursue romance before. You know? Savor the little touches"—his knuckles brush against my belly, and it tightens—"instead of just going for it right away."

A jealous little troll rises up inside me that he's *gone for it right away* with so many women before, but I tell it to get lost. Because I'm the one who's with him now, and hopefully forever.

He gazes into my eyes with a longing smile. "I just want to do things differently with you, Bree."

I breathe in his scent and let my heart steep in it. "Okay. We'll wait." I grin up at him and poke him in the cheek. "You're such a big softy."

"With you, yes."

He kisses me again, this time softly, sweetly, gratefully. He rises up onto one muscled arm to lean over me and turn off the light. That powerful image of muscles and tendons and masculine flesh is the last one I'll see tonight, and it does nothing to cool me off.

Nathan drops down beside me and pulls me onto his chest. I kiss it. "Just don't spread it around that I'm a marshmallow," he says in a teasing tone. "It'll kill my image."

"Which image? The one of you secretly sneaking hundred-dollar bills into my widowed neighbor's mailbox? Or you buying an entire building so little ballerinas can continue to afford their training?"

He kisses the top of my head, and I don't miss the moment he breathes in the scent of my hair. We're home in each other's arms. I nuzzle into his strong chest like a little cat. It is a done deal. I'd marry him in five minutes if that were an option.

"It's all for you, Bree."

29

NATHAN

Saturday, Bree and I sleep in until ten o'clock. I can't remember the last time I did that. High school, maybe? I wake up a few times and never once feel the urge to get up and get my day going. Everything I want is right here in my arms. Drooling.

Eventually, I'm going to have to leave Bree for a few meetings and then get to the airport for my flight to Houston where we'll play our last playoff game.

Saturdays are the closest thing I have to an off day during the season because I don't step foot in the weight room on these days, so it usually gets packed full of meetings. Which . . . now that I think about it, makes it *not* an off day. This morning, though, I blew off an early meeting in favor of staring creepily at Bree while she sleeps. I'll have to deal with Nicole's wrath, but it's worth it. I think that's considered progress.

One of Bree's hairs gets sucked into her mouth, and when I try to carefully extract it, she jolts awake. Like a jack-in-the-box, she bolts upright in bed, hair eight sizes larger than normal. She whips around to me with wide eyes looking like she just woke from a cryogenic sleep.

“I TEACH A CLASS AT TEN THIRTY!”

A bit yell-y in the mornings. It’s okay, I’ll still keep her.

Throwing the covers off, she sprints from the bed and out of the room. I stare at the empty doorway until two seconds later I hear footsteps racing back. A flash of octopus hair and limbs is all I see before she tackles me on the bed. Hovering over me, her dimples pop and she kisses me with a punctuated POP. “Good morning. I love you.”

I smile and lean up to kiss her more fully, but she tucks her chin.

“UH, no. Neither of us brushed our teeth last night, and morning breath is rank. You get a closed-mouth pucker and NATHANSTOP-ITRIGHTNOW!” She’s scream-laughing because I’m tickling her ruthlessly.

“You’re saying my breath is bad?! You’ll pay.”

“Let me go! I have class!” She can barely talk, she’s laughing so hard.

“You shouldn’t have come back. That was your first mistake, and now you’re caught.” I stop tickling her long enough to reach into my bedside table, grab my Listerine spray, and take a hit. Her jaw drops at my audacity to keep something like that at my bedside, but what can I say, I’m no amateur here. With her mouth open like a fish, I’m able to give her a spritz.

She cackles laughing, and then I kiss her like I want to. I take my time.

Bree texts me later that she’s late for class and it’s all my fault. I’ll gladly take that fall.

I lean back in the giant, porcelain, clawfoot tub and FaceTime Bree. The call connects just as a bubble pops by my shoulder. Her smiling face fills my screen, harsh studio lights hovering above her head. She squints, and then a smile bursts across her mouth.

"You're in the bath!!!"

"A *bubble* bath." I hold up a handful of suds.

I've never seen her look more pleased. I can see the light pink spaghetti straps of her leotard, and the hairs on her neck are matted down with sweat. When she takes the phone with her to sit down with her back leaning against the mirror, I can tell in the reflection that she's alone. She's breathing heavily. "And? Completely wonderful, right?"

"I had no idea what I was missing." Truthfully, I'm pretty bored, but I'll sit in here every night for the rest of my life if it makes her smile like that. Also, after my talk with Bree last night, I'm ready to start doing some things to take care of my mental health. I also scheduled an appointment with a therapist for next week. Nervous about that one, not gonna lie.

"Only way it could be better is if you were in here—"

"NNOOOPPEEE," Jamal yells from the other side of the bathroom door.

Our flight got into Houston a few hours ago, and because of the strict curfew the team enforces the night before each game, I'm already in my hotel room for the night. Every player is assigned a suitemate when we travel, and Jamal is usually mine.

"Don't you start all that. No one wants to hear your bubble bath dirty talk," he says from the other side of the door where I'm sure he's lying on the silk pillowcase he brought from home.

"Hi Jamal!" Bree yells into the phone.

"Just put your headphones on," I tell him.

"No. I'll still know what's going on in there, and I'm not okay with that."

I roll my eyes. "You're just mad I stole the bathtub before you."

"YES, I'M MAD!" he says in an indignant tone. "For years I've been taking a nightly bubble bath and enjoying the hell out of it, and all of a sudden, your new girlfriend tells you how glorious it is and you usurp my self-care time. Not cool, man."

Bree looks delighted.

"He wears one of those crackly green masks like yours too," I tell Bree, not bothering to keep my voice down.

"Yes, I do, and I don't appreciate your condescending tone. Men can appreciate having good skin too. In fact, you could stand for a pore treatment or two, Nathan. I can see your blackheads through the door."

My pores are just fine.

"Ignore him," I tell Bree, sinking a little lower into the water. "So what are you doing at the studio?"

"Oh, I'm just working on the choreography for one of the recital dances coming up."

"Yeah? Can I see?"

Her cheeks turn pink. Other than when I've peeked in on her teaching a class or two over the years, I haven't seen her *really* dance since high school, since before the accident. For some reason, it's always something she keeps to herself. I'm hoping now that things are changing between us, she'll let me back into that part of her life as well.

She wrinkles her nose. "I don't know. It's still rough. There's not much to see." Her shoulders are twitching and her head keeps shaking, making her look like an alien trying to do an impression of a Normal Human Being.

"Breeee." I cut off her blabbering, and she shoots me a look.

"Natthhaannn."

"Come on. Let me watch you dance. I'll even put on a bubble beard the whole time to make you feel less embarrassed."

Jamal interjects again. "UGH, Y'ALL ARE GROSS!"

"Mind your own business!" I say, throwing a bar of soap at the door. I focus my attention on Bree again. "Why don't you want to dance in front of me?"

Her eyes dart around the room and her teeth sink into her bottom lip. Damn, I wish I was there to kiss her. We didn't have enough time last night or this morning. I need weeks with her—no, *years* to make up for lost time.

"I'm not as good as you remember."

"You're in luck—I don't remember anything. What even is ballet? Is that the thing where you make all the noises with your shoes?" She laughs and gives me a look that says, *Nice try*. "Bree, take a good look at me. I'm FaceTiming you from a bubble bath right now. Doesn't get much more vulnerable for me than that."

"Fiiiiiine. Okay, you win." The phone gets placed on the floor and angled up so I can see the entire studio. Bree leans down toward the screen and points a finger at me. "But just know, I'm not as fluent or graceful as I used to be. And the choreography needs a lot of work. That's the whole point of me staying late tonight."

I hold a bubbly hand up in the air. "It'll be like I'm not even here."

Her smile slants. "Mm-hmm. Sure."

The sound of soft piano fills the air, and Bree stands in the center of the floor. Her bubblegum pink leotard is painted to her body, making her look soft and delicate, but then her favorite oversize gray joggers swallow up her lower half, contrasting with her prim and proper upper half. It's a perfect representation of her personality. She's wearing them as she always does: rolled down at the waist and cinched up over her calves. Pointe shoes are tied around her ankles, a rainbow of bracelets stacks up one of her arms, and her hair is in a wispy French braid dangling down her back.

Those long lean arms stretch at her sides and glide above her head. She goes up onto her toes like it's nothing and begins a soft walk that turns into a series of impressive turns. I sit in awe, watching Bree's powerful, graceful body twirl, jump, and completely captivate me until my water turns to ice. I don't care though, because I don't ever want to look away.

We don't talk at all during this time. It's clear she is hyperfocused on her movements, and I wouldn't dare ruin this glimpse into heaven for the world. Quiet confidence pulses through her veins as she leaps. The angles of her body are sharp glass and soft velvet at the same time. She creates the illusion that she's as delicate as lace, but when she leaps off the ground with her legs flawlessly extended in opposite directions and then lands—barely making a sound—you realize she is not to be underestimated. She is strong and fierce in her delicate skin. Life tried to hold her down, but she gave it the middle finger and stood up again.

Bree is everything I aspire to be, everything I love, everything I desire. She holds my heart, and, with all that I am, I hope she never gives it back.

30

BREE

It's Super Bowl Sunday, baby! And, yes, the Sharks made it! They won the NFC Championship two weeks ago, and now we're all here in Las Vegas where the Sharks (aka the greatest team on earth) will be playing the Donkeys (just kidding, they're really called the Stallions, but no one cares about them, and we want them to eat dirt). Lily left her kiddos with Doug so she could be my plus-one. Nathan paid to fly us out first-class last night, and I let him because my bank account has about two bucks and a piece of gum in it but there was no way I was missing the freaking Super Bowl. Also, now that we are officially together, I've had to get better at letting him pay for things. Turns out, it sparks joy for him when I let him spoil me, so I'm trying to say yes more often.

Like, for instance, when I received the email that my dance studio had been chosen for the available space at The Good Factory (I'm trying to play it cool, but just know I'm jumping up and down), Nathan immediately asked if I would let him pay for the renovations we'd have to do to turn the space into a dance studio, and we made a compromise. Instead of paying him back with the money I earned doing the commercial like I had planned, I'm going to use it for the renovations. *See, growth.*

I haven't seen him since we got to Vegas because he's been ridiculously busy with the team and media events, like he has been the last few weeks after winning the NFC Championship. I completely understand, though, and have stolen every moment with him that I can. Soon, it will all be over and we can finally spend a few months together in the off-season, free of his rigorous schedule.

There's been nonstop, next-level texting though. Always flirty little numbers like this conversation we had shortly after landing last night.

ME: Hi hot stuff. We're in Vegas!

NATHAN: I thought the day suddenly seemed brighter.

ME: Stoooopppppp jk it's so gross and I love it. Keep doing it.

NATHAN: :) Miss you. Please don't get drunk and elope with any strange dudes tonight.

ME: Gosh you're so picky.

NATHAN: Damn straight. Only man you can elope with in Vegas is me.

ME: Oh good. Because you're the only one I want to elope with. How about tonight?

NATHAN: Can't tonight. I'm busy. How about tomorrow night? I have a little thing from like 6:30–10:30 but after that I'm free.

ME: Sure! Sounds good!

Now, Lily and I are walking to our provided box at the stadium, strapped into painful high heels and Saran-wrapped in fashionable designer dresses *à la Marshalls.*

Except, because I'm me and can't be counted on to completely conform to societal fashion norms, I've also paired my cute, white, bodycon dress with a black jersey (with Nathan's number 8, of course) cinched with a little knot in the front.

Something I learned early on in Nathan's career: NFL wives and girlfriends live by a strict fashion code, and that code is fancy AF at all times. As his friend only, I was free to go to the games in sneakers and a T-shirt. As his girlfriend . . . actually, who cares. I'll still come to the games in whatever I want. Today, I wanted to wear heels and dress up. Next game, it might be a onesie with a hood. No one can ever really predict what's going to happen with my sartorial choices.

After being shown to the box, we step inside and find Vivian, Nathan's mom, already here and sucking up all the oxygen with her big ego. She's swirling the olives in her martini glass, looking like she's got at least ten snooty comments on the tip of her tongue.

"Hi, Mrs. Donelson, it's good to see you again." I smile and hold out my hand like a car salesman. *Wanna buy this load of crap?* Normal people hug in situations like this. But let's all remember that Vivian Donelson is far from normal, and she's always seen me as a threat to Nathan's career. In other words, she hates me.

Those dark eyes—similar to Nathan's but in a haunting way that makes you think they never shut— slither down to my extended hand. "Next time, you'll do well to get a manicure before a big game like the other players' wives and girlfriends. And leave the tacky bracelets at home. They don't fit in this world." Those eyes slide back up. Hand: unshook. "No one likes a hippie sitting in the NFL wives' section."

Lily steps forward like she's going to rip her earrings out of her ears and pummel this woman *Wreck-It Ralph* style. I grab her forearm and stop her, because I don't need her to fight this battle for me. I'm not even stung by her words. All I feel right now is sadness for Nathan. To have grown up with such an exacting, demanding mother would have been excruciating. No wonder he feels swamped by pressure and expectations. I'm also in awe of him for overcoming this woman's influence and becoming such a generous, kind person in spite of her. It just proves that money is not what defines a person; it only enhances their nature.

Well, it's time Mrs. Donelson is enlightened about her nature and what sort of effect it has on the people around her. Nathan has really stepped away from his parents over the last few weeks as per the suggestion of his therapist and has been committed to implementing new boundaries. He's opened up to me about things from his childhood that I had no idea about and also talked frankly about his mom's attitude toward me specifically. He was clear from the beginning of our new relationship that I never have to wear a gag around his mom. I'm free to speak my mind and stand up for myself with his full, unwavering support.

So everyone, stand back—I'm about to become this woman's worst nightmare.

"Mrs. Donelson," I begin with a measured smile. "First, it's well past time for you to stop saying rude things like that to me."

I think she is frowning, but her face is always set in a scowl so it's hard to tell.

I continue, "As I think you already know, I am here to stay. And you can be completely sure that if you continue to speak to me or my boyfriend like you have in the past, your days in this box with us will be over. Just because you birthed him and pushed him toward success, does not guarantee your place in our lives."

As I've said before, I'm no threat to women in Nathan's life—until they make him choose. He will choose me every single time, and now that I know why, I fully intend to let that power go to my head. I will protect him just as fiercely as he protects me.

"I won't speak on Nathan's behalf even though I have a list as long as my arm of issues I would love to comment on, but as for how you treat me, you are condescending and rude, and I won't put up with it."

Lily's eyes go wide and she presses her lips together to keep from openly smiling. Mrs. Donelson's left eye twitches ever so slightly. Her chin rises in the air, and I'm prepared for her slashing words. Actually, I'm prepared for a literal slap across the face.

Neither of those things happens.

"This drink is horrible. I'm going to see if what they have out there is any better." She brushes past us, and a chill sweeps through the air along with her. I thank my lucky stars Nathan is not close with that woman and I don't have to endure her but a few times a year.

Once she's gone and the door closes behind her, Lily turns to me. "I have never been more proud of you in my life." Well, good, because I'm literally shaking now that it's all over. "All that woman needed was a fur coat and she'd be a Disney villain. Also, where is Nathan's dad?"

"He has a big meeting tomorrow that he wants to be rested for. He told Nathan he'd catch part of the game on TV."

Lily blinks. "You're kidding me."

"I wish."

Nathan has worked so hard to please his parents, and here he is, at the Super Bowl for the second time, and his dad doesn't even bother to show because he needs to wash his hair and get his beauty sleep.

Lily and I walk down the three little stairs that lead from the entertaining area of the box to the leather seats in front of the glass. The stadium is rapidly filling with fans all decked out in conflicting colors of black and silver, orange and navy. Energy sparks through the stadium like fireworks. My own anticipation is bubbling through me, fancy champagne style.

Nathan (and his team, but seriously who cares about them) will run through that tunnel shortly, and this stadium will go wild. They hold signs with his name on them, wear jerseys printed with his number, and the opposing fans fear him and what he will do today. His name will be on the tongues of thousands. Chanted and screamed. Everyone speculates, *What is Nathan Donelson like in real life?*

But I know.

I know about the green bottle of shampoo, and that he's scared of flying. I know he can keep a secret better than Lily the summer a bottle of wine mysteriously went missing from my parents' wine fridge, and I know Nathan's sheets feel butter soft against my skin. He is mine, and my heart fist-pumps at the thought.

Mrs. Donelson returns a little later with a fresh drink, and we all sit in terribly awkward silence. She taps her long manicured nails against the plastic armrest, and we're all dying for this game to begin. The long point of her high heel vibrates back and forth. Lily and I keep making discreet tortured faces back and forth behind her back.

Finally, the announcers boom over the speakers. "Ladies and gentlemen, it's time to welcome the NFC Champions, the LA Sharks!"

The stadium flares with screams, and camera crews swarm. It's showtime. I'm on the edge of my seat as the dense fog and bright lights fill the front of the Sharks' tunnel.

And there they are.

Nathan emerges first with the team on his heels. They sprint through the fog with a self-confidence that shivers over everyone's skin. In this moment, I don't care what you think about the sport—you want to *be* these athletes.

Jamal flexes both arms and gladiator-yells. Other men are fist-pumping and air-kicking their way across the field to their bench. Nathan is quietly Nathan. He runs out with steel in his veins, unflappable as always. When he's on the fifty-yard line, he stops and his helmet tilts up. I can feel his eyes on me as if his fingers were trailing across my skin. He smiles for the first time and lifts his arm to wave at me. And then he points. The universal gesture of *This is for you, love.* I make a goofy face then blow him a kiss. He catches it. Fans turn and zero their laser-beam eyes on me—but all I care about is Nathan.

During halftime, Lily and Mrs. Donelson are attempting to chitchat, but since Lily is talking through clenched teeth, I'm assuming it's probably not going well. I've slipped away into the snack bar area of the box to stare at my phone just in case Nathan gets a minute to text me.

". . . it's because he's been . . . *distracted* lately," says Mrs. Donelson in a not-so-veiled attempt to blame the fact that the Sharks are down by a touchdown on me. I select a cookie from the table and take a large bite. Mmm, chocolate chips.

Lily feels the need to go to bat for me and Nathan—which is adorable and hilarious to me because I don't waste one feeling on Vivian. "Distractions are good for humans. I think his distractions are what helped him evade that sack in the second quarter." A bit of a reach, Lil, but the gesture is sweet.

Mrs. Donelson huffs. I continue to eat my cookie. "Not likely. He looks sluggish today. I don't think he's been spending enough time training."

"I don't think you've been spending enough time telling him he is doing a great job!!"

Whoa, that escalated quickly. Lily stands. Mrs. Donelson stands. These women are about to throw down, and I'm just back here enjoying my cookie.

My phone buzzes so I turn away and get lost in conversation with my favorite person.

NATHAN: Hi. How's your day going?

ME: Oh, fine. How's yours?

NATHAN: Pretty boring. Nothing's really happening. I miss you.

Mrs. Donelson's voice cuts through my thoughts briefly. "I push him because I love him!"

ME: Same. Same.

NATHAN: Are we still on for our plans later?

"THAT IS NOT LOVE," Lily shouts.

"And just how long have you been a mom, missy?"

"Don't missy me!"

ME: Our elopement? Oh yeah, I totally forgot about that. Sounds good though.

I love that we're joking like this. Behind me a daytime soap opera is unfolding, and Nathan and I are pretending we're going to elope.

NATHAN: Perfect. Well, my boss says I gotta get back to work. Love you.

ME: Love you!! Go kick your fellow employees' asses!

NATHAN: *shark emoji*

I turn around to the sight of Mrs. Donelson and Lily hugging. What the hell did I miss?!

We've all been holding our breath for the last ten minutes. This game is so tight. Currently, the score is 21–17, Sharks down by four. There are only thirty seconds left on the clock, and it's fourth down. They need to get a first down in order to have a chance at winning, and they have no time-outs left. The stress in this stadium is palpable, and I honestly can't imagine the pressure Nathan has on his shoulders right now as he sees the clock running out.

Both teams get into formation quickly, and then the ball is snapped to Nathan. He shuffles on his feet a few times, looking for an open receiver, but there's not one. My heart hammers as I watch him tuck the ball under his arm and run. He has no choice but to try to get the first down himself.

At first, things look promising, but then, as if I'm seeing it all in slow motion, a defensive player busts through the line and plows into Nathan, laying him flat on his back.

The ball is knocked loose. Fumbled. *Game over.*

A collective gasp tremors through the stadium, and all of our shoulders sink. The player who tackled Nathan stands and extends his hand to help him up. I sigh with audible relief when Nathan takes it and stands unharmed.

I realize at that moment that I'm stuck to the glass wall like a bug on a windshield. Peeling myself free, I turn to face my sister and Nathan's mom. Somehow, we've all managed to bond over this second half of the game. Lily really gave Vivian something to think about during their verbal spar, and she's been more pliable ever since. Oh, don't get me wrong, she's still a major pill, but I think in that moment when Lily helped Vivian see that she had somehow become an exact replica of her own mother whom she despised, it stunned her.

We've gone through a lot, the three of us during this Super Bowl game.

And now it's over.

The Stallions take a knee on the next snap, ending the game officially. I don't give myself even a moment to search for Nathan's face on the sidelines, because all I want to do is wrap my arms around him as soon as possible. So I use this time to hustle my booty down the elevator and to the media entrance. Security guards check my badge at the gate, and then I'm herded with the rest of the players' family members through a dark tunnel that leads to the field.

Oops. I just realized I moved so fast out of the box that I accidentally left Lily and Mrs. Donelson in my dust. Too bad. Got to hustle, ladies.

I emerge from the tunnel just in time to see Nathan in the middle of the field, sharing a quick hug with the quarterback of the winning team. He's classy, that Nathan. The man manages to look genuinely happy for his opponent, even though I know he's devastated.

He has worked so hard to get to this moment, only to be the one who delivered the losing play in the end. I hope the media doesn't harp on that one fault, because that man played a hell of a game before that moment and it deserves to be noted. But somehow, I know they will. That one clip of Nathan fumbling the ball will get shown on repeat *over and over*.

Cameras are all over the two quarterbacks exchanging words. Confetti rains down from above as players congratulate each other and show good sportsmanship that I know they are not feeling. Jamal is across the field, and he presses his finger and thumb into his eyes to stop tears from falling. Derek is on the bench with his head hanging low. I can't find Price and Lawrence, but I'm sure their vibes are similar.

It's a kaleidoscope of emotions on this field. Where one man is elated and chest-bumping his teammate or kissing his wife, and another's eyes are cast down and he's choking back disappointment.

I lose sight of Nathan and feel slightly panicky. How is he holding up? My steel teddy bear of a perfectionist is on this field somewhere, and I know he's crushed. I need to get to him.

Standing on my toes in the end zone, I crane my neck to see, but it's difficult with so many other bodies on the field. I consider asking one of these giants in pads to lift me on their shoulders, but I'm saved when I finally spot Nathan on the sidelines exchanging words with one of his coaches. The man hands him something then points in my direction. I throw my arms open wide, ready to hold Nathan while he cries into my bosom.

When he turns, his gaze hits me like a heavyweight champion in the ring. I'm breathless. He doesn't need to cry into my bosom. That man is smiling.

He walks toward me, confetti raining down on him, people hugging, celebrating, and crying all around him, and he parts the emotions like the Red Sea. He is sweaty and glistening. Sinewy arms are pumped and veiny from playing a long, exhausting game. Camera crews see his smile and swarm him. (I understand their curiosity.) Maybe he's having a mental breakdown at this very moment? Maybe he threw the game on purpose? Because this is not the look of a person who just lost everything he's ever wanted.

No. He gets close to me, and his bright white teeth glint under the field lights. He drops his helmet at his feet, and then his knee follows suit. All the chaos around us disappears. It's me and my best friend. And he's proposing.

"Hi, pretty friend," he tells me, taking my hand in his, which is rough with new calluses and wrapped in medical tape. "I know we already planned it last night, but I thought you might like to hear it from my mouth rather than over text." Nathan squeezes my hand, and I'm already crying. "Bree, my best friend, I love you. We haven't been together very long, but we've also been together for years. Will you marry me? Will you let me love you every day from now on? Will you finally move out of your shitty apartment and into mine?"

I laugh. "This is all just a ploy to get me away from the mold, isn't it?"

"It's the only way you'll allow it."

"You're so good at loopholes."

He blinks up at me, and I see moisture on his lashes too. "Is that a yes?"

I nod my head frantically, laughing and crying and nearly peeing myself in the process. "Yes!"

Nathan shoots up from his feet and picks me up, spinning me as confetti lands around us like fresh snowfall. Can this really be happening?

"Tonight?" he whispers against my ear. "Will you elope with me?"

At this point, the camera crew gets bored with our Hallmark moment and wanders back to the winning team to hear them declare they are going to Disneyland.

Still in his arms with my feet dangling two feet above the ground, everything feels surreal. "Are you sure? I don't know if you realize this or not, but this was sort of a big day for you. And . . . you do realize your team lost just now, right?" I don't want to ask it, but the way he's acting you would think the man was celebrating instead of mourning. And although eloping with Nathan is legitimately the stuff of my dreams, I need to know he's sure. Need to be certain he's not acting rashly because he's disappointed.

He chuckles, and his arms tighten around my lower back. "Yes, I know we lost. And yeah, I'm disappointed, but mainly I'm just relieved it's all finally *over*. I feel like this huge weight has dropped off of me. Now, I'm just ready to breathe beside you for a while. Preferably on a beach somewhere. With you in the skimpiest bikini I can find."

I would poke him in the sides, but he's wearing full pads—hardly fair. Instead, I lean forward and take his lips in one bruising kiss. *There, you're punished.*

"Bree, the whole answer is that I don't want to wait another second without being 100 percent truly and completely yours. But if you want to wait and have a big wedding, I will. Don't feel like you have to marry me tonight to make me feel better for losing. Because that's not what this is for me."

I lean in and kiss him again, taking my time to peruse his lips as if thousands of strangers are not watching. He tastes like sweat and hope, and there's no way I'm passing this opportunity up. We can have a giant party when we get home.

"I'll be mad if you don't marry me tonight," I tell Nathan, completely serious.

His cheeks crease with a smile and he sets me down. "Oh, I completely forgot to give you this—should we start over?" He holds up the ring box then pops it open.

I'm swimming in its beauty. This ring is punch-me-in-the-gut pretty, but most of all, it looks like me. It's not gaudy or massive. I won't have to drag my hand on the ground as I walk. It's a simple, beautiful, princess cut diamond. Exactly what I would have picked out myself.

Just as I slip the ring on, Jamal, Derek, Price, and Lawrence all crowd around us. It's a commotion of congratulations and sweaty hugs. It doesn't get to last long because the guys have to go shower then Nathan has to be available for a post-game interview. He has just enough time to kiss me once on the cheek, twice on the neck, and once more on the mouth before he grunts in aggravation and forces himself to back away.

He points at me like he's getting ready to toss me the winning catch. "Bree Cheese. Still with me?"

Cupping my hands around my mouth, I yell, "Always!"

I find Lily back in the box ten minutes later. Mrs. Donelson has already left, thank goodness, so I don't have to explain anything to her right now.

"HURRY!" I say, pulling her up out of her chair. "GET YOUR BOOTY MOVING—WE GOTTA GET ME READY FOR MY WEDDING!"

31

BREE

"I'm getting married, I'm getting married, I'm getting married." I repeat this to myself fifteen more times in the hotel bathroom mirror. Lucky for me, I was already wearing a white dress at the game. I shed the jersey and voilà, instant bride! That sort of makes me sound like a soup. I tilt my head at my reflection in the mirror. I hope I don't look like soup.

Lily stands behind me and puts her hands on my upper arms. "Are you having second thoughts? I will have a car ready to whisk you out of here in five minutes if that's what you want."

"I will put you in that car and have you driven to the airport and shipped off to Australia if you try to talk me out of this! I'm so ready to marry Nathan it's painful."

Lily smiles. "I know you are. I'm so happy I get to be here for it."

We've already called my mom and dad, and although they were not thrilled about missing their baby's wedding, they are both completely addicted to Hallmark and can appreciate a romantic whirlwind when they see one. They'll be at the wedding via FaceTime, as will Nathan's parents, I'm assuming.

The next thirty minutes are spent primping, but since neither Lily nor I is very experienced with an eye shadow palette and bobby pins, we FaceTime the master.

"Sweep the right side back like a gorgeous wave rolling onto the beach at sunset," Dylan says from the screen of my phone.

Lily grimaces, and her clunky hand pulls my hair back too tight. My scalp burns. "What does that even mean, Dylan?"

"A GORGEOUS WAVE AT SUNSET, LILY! I did not say a tight-fisted old granny at Christmas."

My sister deflates and whispers, "I don't know what any of this means!"

"Neither do I. Do your best."

Lily eventually pleases the master, and we move on to eye shadow. The brush trembles in her fingers as it advances toward my lid, and she repeats Dylan's instructions. "*A bird flying over the canyon with gold dust on its wings* . . . got it." His eyeball is taking up most of the screen he's sitting so close to it.

Once my makeover is complete, I look in the mirror. Both Dylan and Lily swoon at the sight of me, which brings tears to my eyes. "I can't believe this is real. I get to marry my best friend tonight."

Lily sniffles and lays her head on my shoulder.

Dylan swipes a misty tear from his cheek and nods. "Yes, girl, you do. Now, stick that hand in your bra and bob those little duckies toward the surface."

Nice. A much needed tear eraser.

Nathan texts Lily his minute-by-minute agenda, saying it's our wedding day so I shouldn't be bothered with logistics. It's 11:00 P.M. now, about an hour after the game, and Lily is ushering me through the hotel lobby and out into the night. The cold air sweeps over my arms, and like the most well-executed kidnapping, a blacked-out SUV pulls up to the curb. Lily opens the door and thrusts me into it. It slams shut behind me, and I'm worried for a minute that she didn't make it in with me. *Whew.* She did. Everything is okay.

I look around the interior and feel a tug of sadness that Nathan's not in here. I haven't seen him all weekend minus that brief moment when he asked me to spend the rest of my life with him. No big deal.

Lily must see my expression. "He's already at the chapel. He wanted everything to feel as much like a real wedding day for you as he could. You're not going to believe the things he pulled together in this short time."

I can believe it, because that's just Nathan. Now, with clear eyes, I can see that there's no length he wouldn't cross for me—it's how it's always been with him.

Which reminds me how deeply unromantic I am. "Oh no!" I pat my sides like pockets might suddenly appear. "His ring!"

Turns out, in Vegas, there are hundreds of places to buy a wedding ring at the drop of a hat. We bought Nathan's on our way back to the hotel. (Well, technically Nathan bought it since he made me use his credit card. I accepted his money, because, remember? Two dollars and a piece of gum.)

Lily smiles and digs in her purse for the ring box, holding it up triumphantly. "Yep, I got it. Just so you know, your head would fall off if it wasn't attached."

"Awww, you make me feel so good on my wedding day."

"And then you'd use that head as a ball and get distracted with a bunch of kids in a field, starting up a new after-school program where they use your head as the soccer ball."

I grimace. "Morbid. Just really dark humor."

She shrugs like, *It is what it is.* Just some casual wedding day cheer.

After a few minutes of my leg bouncing and my fingers tapping my knee, Lily slides over to take the seat closer to me. She puts her hand on my knee. "You know, I just realized, with Mom not here, I have a very important job."

"And what's that?"

Her smile goes wicked. "Explaining the wedding night bliss to you."

"Oh my gosh. Don't you da—"

"So honey, you might have noticed some interesting sensations when you and Nathan have kissed before. Don't feel frightened—"

I talk right over her, trying to cup my hand over her mouth. "This is not my first time, Lily. I know what I'm doing! Ew, stop saying that word—"

". . . and that's what happens when everything is done." She shimmies her shoulders, undeterred by my aggressive paw swiping at her mouth. "Now, a few fun tricks I've learned, and you can text me a thank-you later."

I'm laughing so hard I can barely hear her. I cover my ears to muffle the sound of her voice and drop my head between my knees. "I don't want to hear about your weird sex with Doug! *La-la-la.* OH MY YOU DID NOT JUST SAY THAT WORD TO YOUR BABY SISTER."

She torments me with her sexual tips the rest of the drive, and this will surely go down in history as one of my favorite days.

Did I say one of my favorite days? I mean my ABSOLUTE favorite day of my entire existence.

We pull up to the chapel and I'm whisked out by an entourage of people I've never met before. A woman carrying a clipboard drags me quickly inside the small white Vegas chapel, and I'm surprised that on the inside it doesn't smell like liquor and strippers. I barely have time to register anything as she tugs me into a little room off to the side of the main double doors. Lily holds my hand the whole way.

The woman whips around, out of breath, clutching her clipboard like it holds the codes to Area 51. "Hi. Hello. Happy wedding day! I'm here to assist you into your dress."

"My dress?" I look down. Am I naked? "Oh, I'm already wearing one. See?" I gesture to the fabric in case she's skeptical.

She laughs. "No, your wedding dress."

"I didn't . . ." My tongue stops moving when I see she's stepped aside to reveal a whole garment rack full of sparkly, lacy, white, and even some champagne and light pink gowns. There are at least twenty hanging there.

My words tumble out. "Are these . . . do these come with the chapel? Is this like a dress-up corner?"

She laughs. "No. I believe they are a gift from your husband-to-be."

I clutch my chest and look back at Lily. She's trying her best to keep her crap together, but it's no use. Tears are streaming, and she looks like she already knew all of this was going to happen. I step forward and find a little envelope attached to the garment rack. Inside is a note from none other than Dylan.

Hello, Dimples. Once again, your man came through for you. I hand-selected all of these for you a week ago, and I made sure to only pick what I think you'd absolutely adore (even though I reallllyyy wanted to get you the Cinderella-fell-into-an-orange-creamsicle gown). Love you boo. You've got yourself a good man. Hugs and kisses from your second favorite man in the world,

Dylan

A week ago? That can't be right. That would mean . . .

"What are you waiting for?!" Lily says, muscling me out of the way so she can start sorting. "We've got a wedding to get to!"

Twenty minutes later, I'm clad in a dress that should be illegal it's so beautiful. The long sleeves are made of delicate, fragile lace that extends into a stiff-lace bodice. It has exactly thirty-one pearl buttons down the back. It poufs at the waist and then cascades into a multi-tiered, luxurious, tulle skirt with an understated train in the back. My skin shows through the lace sleeves, the bodice tapers into a deep V at the neckline, and when I walk, it swishes. I am a princess, a ballerina, and a powerhouse badass woman all swaddled in one intricate package. I have never felt more lovely or cherished than I do walking into this chapel.

And then, I have to amend that thought when I realize NOW I have never felt more cherished. My breath catches at the threshold. It's not at all what I thought it would be. Where's Elvis? Where's the smell of gin and bad decisions? No, I'm hallucinating.

This chapel was purchased in heaven and overnighted to Earth. Vaulted ceilings sweep over my head up into the clouds. An enormous crystal chandelier glitters in the middle of the intimate space. White wooden planks make up the ceiling, and gorgeous beams reinforce them. Dark oak floors allow my heels to *click-clack* over the surface, and the swish of my skirt sounds like kisses from the ocean. Enormous green and pink flower bouquets fill the room.

But that's not what has me contemplating my consciousness. This chapel is *full* of people. My people. Nathan's people. My family, friends, and even his mom. This is no elopement. This is my wedding—a wedding Nathan has clearly been planning since before yesterday.

My dad—my dad who supposedly was going to watch the ceremony from his cell phone—is approaching me via the center aisle. His eyes glitter with unshed tears, and he looks dapper in his suit. He holds out his arm. "Hello, sweet girl. Are you ready to get married tonight?"

Well, now I'm sobbing. Too bad Lily worked so hard on my makeup since I'm going to ruin it in two seconds. Dylan would be horrified. *Wait!* Speaking of Dylan, there he is! Third row back making a heart shape with his hands and blowing me imaginary bubble kisses through it. I look back at Lily with question marks in my eyes. She's smiling and nodding. *She knew the whole time.*

Then my dad starts walking me down the aisle and *I see him.* Nathan. My Nathan, my best friend and the love of my life, standing in his black tux, fantastic hair waving artfully away from his face, a tear running down his cheek, and a dazzling smile stretching across his mouth. He is mine. He loves me. He loves me enough to plan an entire surprise wedding of my dreams. How did I get this lucky?

I float all the way to the altar.

My dad hands me off to Nathan, and now I'm in a dream. Jamal is standing behind Nathan, and Lily is behind me. The rest of the guys are all lined up in the front row, each tossing me a thumbs-up. My mom does the same thing from the other side. Nathan's mom settles for a subdued smile and wave.

Nathan takes my hand, and tingles swirl through me. I look up into his jet-black eyes and drown in lavish, luxurious, ardent love.

"Still with me?" he asks with a soft, unsure grin.

I swallow and try to speak through my tears. "You did all of this for me?"

"I'd do anything for you. Do you like it?"

I take a moment to look around again. All the smiling faces. There is no oxygen left in this room, everyone is running on emotional fumes. We're all sobbing messes, and I can't see straight from joy. I squeeze his hand and meet his gaze again. "I love it. I love you. How long have you been planning this?"

"Since I warned you I was going to propose. I hired a wedding planner the next day. Are you sure you like it? Because if not, we can call it all off right now."

I search for the best words to adequately express how I feel and come up severely lacking. "Nathan—I . . . you . . . and all of this!" I shake my head. "Thank you. I love it all so much." As I take in Nathan's eyes, his clean-shaven jaw, his wide shoulders, the sleek black tie knotted at the base of his throat, and his strong hands holding mine so tenderly, a feeling of impatience sweeps over me. "So what now?"

His smile stretches, he nods toward the officiant standing off to the side, and then he looks back at me. "If you're up for it, we can get married."

I let out a short laugh through my tears. "Yes, please."

32

BREE

My hand is wrapped in Nathan's as we walk silently down the carpeted hotel hallway. We're on the twenty-eighth floor, headed to what I have no doubt is the best suite in the whole building. We stop outside the door and Nathan kisses my knuckles. Neither of us can believe this is real. He keeps touching me, kissing me, sliding his hand over my skin at every turn—and I think it's because he's trying to convince himself this is real in the same way I am. We're in a fairy tale. We're puppet shadows on the wall.

He slides the keycard into the lock, and the light flashes green. His forearm hits the back of my knees as he scoops me up into his arms to carry me over the threshold. My heart is in my throat, and we're both laughing at the cheesy love that's been echoing back and forth between us all night. I've been calling him *husband*. He's been calling me *wife*. Everyone has cringed. But not us—not tonight.

Nathan carries me inside, and it's dark. With me still draped in his arms, he reaches for the light switch, but I stop him. The moonlight is spilling in, steeping the room in romance and soothing my nerves.

I swallow, and Nathan looks sharply down at me. His eyes are black, velvet blankets. His gaze wraps me up tight. "Don't be nervous," he says, plucking my thoughts right out of my head.

"I am though. I've wanted it for too long, and you might be disappointed. I might not be enough."

His smile is only a hint. A whisper on his mouth. He leans down and nuzzles his face against my neck, five o'clock shadow a murmur of delight. "You will always be enough."

A trembling sigh falls out of my mouth, and I'm carried to the bed in his strong arms. He stops short and lets me slide down gently until my feet hit the floor. I look up and my breath is strangled. He is perfect. Moonlight casts over his strong jaw and sharp cheekbones, sketching out a profile that should be captured by da Vinci. I rise up onto my toes and kiss his full lips. He responds with patience. It's so soft and tender. My hip is grasped. I slide my hands under the lapels of his tux and *up, up, up* his strong chest until they clasp in the soft hair at the nape of his neck.

I'm pulled in tight, pressed into him and grasped as if he's planning to never release me. I'll live in his embrace from now on. Our mouths explore. His hand splays out firmly at my back, and the other comes up to my neck. Our lips dance: soft, firm, back and forth.

My senses tip like a canoe going over a waterfall as Nathan's mouth trails down my neck to my collarbone. His tongue lightly tastes my skin, and he groans in pleasure. This is it. *Mine, mine, mine,* my heart says now. I push his tux jacket off of his shoulders and feel the taut muscle beneath his shirt. I'm shaking. My stomach is tight. I need him. He helps me with the buttons, and then it's tossed aside.

I hover my hands in front of his body, and he grins. I try to breathe, but someone has sat on my lungs. He chuckles, and impatience finally overtakes him. He grabs my hands and presses them firmly on his chest. *Skin. Warm. Firm.* Still grasping my wrists, he tugs me with him toward the bed. He sits, letting me stand. Those big hands go to rest behind him on the bed, propping him up.

"You lead," he says softly, handing me all the power.

I wish more than anything I didn't feel timid right now. I wish I could show him how sexy I can be. Powerful. Not this trembling girl standing here in her fancy gown. But when my eyes glide up and meet his eyes, I see only tender adoration. He wants me as I am—always and forever.

As I step forward between his legs, the fabric of my skirt brushes against his pants. It's jet black against pure white. A moon in the night sky. A white page speckled with ink. Starkly different, but together, a perfect complement.

I run my finger across his collarbone. Down his arm. Over his fingers. They flex, and I repeat on the opposite side. His entire body responds. Those muscles bunch and I paint my fingers down his abs. They are . . . *glorious*. There's a faint bruise forming on the side of his bicep from when he got tackled in the game. I bend down and press my lips to it. Heat swirls in my stomach. Fire crackles in my heart. Nathan takes my hips and pulls me onto his lap.

We stare into each other's eyes, and silence stretches in the most comfortable, soft cocoon. He pushes a wisp of my hair behind my ear, and I shiver.

"I've loved you for so long," he says quietly, as if to himself. "You're really here right now?"

I lean in and lay warm kisses up his neck to his jaw. He holds me like I'm spun glass. I will break if he squeezes too tight. "We're both dreaming," I say against his velvet skin.

"Thought so."

He turns his face and catches my mouth. This time, it's not such a quiet kiss. His lips are ardent. His tongue exploring. His heart is a hammer. It's going to break through his chest and attack me.

Those hands grip my waist again, and he easily lifts me off his lap. I stand beside the bed, and he spins me away from him. I feel his fingers at my back, working the tiny buttons. I imagine what they look like between his big fingers and thumbs. Like a giant reaching into the sky and rearranging stars.

With every button that pops open, Nathan trades it for a kiss against every newly freed inch of skin. Romance curls around us. It winds through my bones like a taut string and connects to his touch. He kisses me like I'm hallowed. I hear his breath tremble, and I know he's feeling the weightiness of this moment too. This pressure building, this intensity we've been carrying since that day on the high school track all those years ago. It's all been building to this. Us.

Pop, pop, pop. Kiss. Kiss. Kiss.

"I will cherish you until my last breath," he whispers against my bare shoulder, and the sound of my dress falling is like wind through luscious green trees.

His arms slide around my waist, and he pulls me back against his chest. Skin to skin. Holy and sacred. I tip my head back, and he kisses my throat.

"My beautiful, lovely, *wife*."

We spend hours in our own world. Our love story tangible. Our hopes bared. Our souls light. Our fears set aside for this brief moment in time where nothing can touch us. In this place—in those arms—I am safe and free. I open my arms and dance in the rain. I twirl in the current. I lie back in the meadow as dark eyes sparkle above me.

EPILOGUE

BREE

The next morning, while Nathan and I are still snuggling under a giant fluffy comforter and completely unwilling to leave the bed, he strokes his hand across my hair and mumbles, "Bree. I have a confession."

I'm still in happy la-la land, so he could tell me he's an axe murderer and I'd still probably just hum. *That's nice, honey.*

He chuckles and twists me around so I'm facing him. "I'm serious. I think I might have accidentally tricked you into marrying me. I forgot to tell you something really important before we said 'I do.'"

Fine. Just ruin my happy vibes, why don't you?

"Okay, just say it!"

He shuts his eyes and inhales. "It's more like something I have to show you."

I give him a sultry look. "Nathan. I've already seen *everything*."

He grunts a laugh and rolls his eyes before reaching toward the bedside table to retrieve his wallet. He sits up to rest his back against the headboard and starts tugging me by my armpits to sit up too.

"Okay, okay, I'm coming! Sheesh."

The man is serious about whatever this is. From his wallet, Nathan pulls out a folded sheet of paper and hands it to me. He nods for me to take it. This is feeling like the Shoebox of Potential Horror all over again.

I unfold it and find an itemized list of sorts with lots of scribbles in the margins. Some items, like *food fight,* have an X beside them, and others, such as *foot rub,* have a check mark. Nathan looks prepared for me to throw my wedding ring in his face.

"What am I looking at?" I ask, not feeling nearly as murderous as he seems to suspect I should.

"It's . . . a romance cheat sheet. The guys helped me make it when we first agreed to fake date. It was to help me get out of the friend zone."

I shift my eyes from his pained look back to the paper and read it with enlightened realization. While reading the list, so many memories stick out to me. *Dancing in my office. The Starburst log. The stopped elevator.*

"Bree, I'm so sorry! I fully meant to show you this when you first came into the chapel last night, but after I saw you, it completely slipped my mind." He's babbling and running his hands through his hair. "Are you upset? Do you feel betrayed?"

I stare at him slack-jawed. Mainly because his bicep is really spectacular when he runs his hand through his hair.

"I can't believe you," I say, my voice hard as granite.

He frowns and sighs. "I know. It was wrong."

"It was . . ." I twist and lean in eye to eye with him. "Conniving." Fear colors his eyes until I drop my mouth to his neck. "Underhanded." Another kiss. "Desperate." He hums, catching on after my next kiss. "Sweet."

"So you're not mad?" he says in a raspy voice as I drag him back down into our comforter cocoon of love.

"Endearing."

"Some of these things were truly awful ideas." He's trying to point to items on this list now, but I'm not interested.

"Romantic."

"Okay, so I guess we're done with it since you just tossed it across the room like that?"

"Sexy."

Now he's kissing me.

"So you forgive me?" he asks against my skin.

"Yes, but only on the condition that you apply the same amount of dedication to romance to the rest of our marriage."

He gets a devious spark in his eyes when he responds, "Deal."

ROMANCE CHEAT SHEET

Nate, you're out of apples.
- Price

1. ~~Hold hands~~ ✓
2. ~~Food fight~~ ✓ — Surprisingly Sexy.
3. ~~Tuck hair behind ear~~ ✓
4. Dirty talk about sexy hair → hu??
5. ~~Get her favorite flowers~~ ✓ → Green & Pink
6. ~~Touch her arm while talking~~ ✓
7. Fake car trouble
8. ~~Make power go out & light candles~~ ✗
9. Rent out entire restaurant
10. ~~Wink at her~~ ✗ → Derek, you're an idiot – N.
11. ~~Teach her to throw a ~~foot~~ ball~~ ✓
12. ~~Spill something on your shirt~~ ✓
13. ~~Get trapped in elevator~~ ✗
14. ~~Have her favorite candy on hand.~~ ✓ — Starburst
15. Write her a poem → NOPE
16. ~~Rub her feet~~ ✓
17. ~~Kiss her forehead~~ ✓
18. ~~Surprise her at work~~ ✓
19. ~~Dance with her randomly~~ ✓
20. ~~Make out when the moment strikes~~ ✓✓✓

LAWRENCE SUCKS!!! – Jamal

→ Jamal is a tiny baby – Lawrence Hill

YOU WISH YOU HAD MY GAME
– Derell Pendeer

Read on to find out if Bree and Nathan's love defied all odds after their final touchdown, in this exclusive chapter from Sarah Adams!

ONE YEAR LATER . . .

Operation breakup is in full swing. I have a selection of chocolates to my right. At least fifteen different bags of chips are sitting on the coffee table (the individual bags; I'm not a maniac) and my fruity/sour selection to my left. I have my oversize track team T-shirt swallowing my upper half, making me look appropriately depressed, and Betty Boop pajama pants comforting my lower half. I won them as a Dirty Santa Christmas gift. Everyone kept laughing and offering to trade me after the gift exchange and I was like, why?!

Anyway, I have a very sad movie lined up and I'm ready to wallow. The plan is to get all of the pain out of the way in one day, because breakups suck and no one wants that crap lingering on and on.

"Okay, ready to hit Play?" Dylan asks from where my phone is lying beside me on the couch on speaker phone. We might be hours away after he took a styling job on the set of a new romcom movie in Hollywood, but that doesn't mean we can't wallow together. We both went to the grocery store earlier and picked up identical grocery list items and rented the same movie. We'll hit Play at the same time and cry together through the whole thing.

"Yep, I'm ready." I aim the remote at the TV. "On the count of three. One, two, th—"

A thud sounds against my front door, interrupting the countdown.

"Did you order pizza?" Dylan asks.

"No. But dammit, now I want pizza. Hold on, let me go see—"

I'm interrupted again when the door flies open. I gasp and clutch my throat like that's going to protect me from the chain saw murderer breaking in to slice my head off. Oh. It's just Nathan.

Wait! It's Nathan!

"What are you doing here?" I say in a wonder-struck tone as the Jolly Tan Giant strides into my living room, eating up all the space and coming to hover in front of me like a specter here to claim my soul. Even after all this time, his nearness still zings through me with the force of a tsunami.

A line pinches between his sharp dark brows, and his hand juts out and splays across my hip bone, gently pushing me aside. His eyes drop to the coffee table behind me, and I want to stretch out my arms, wave like a hallucinating castaway on an island trying to get a boat's attention. *Here! Look at me!* He's wearing a hoodie and joggers, looking like sex draped in comfort. My mouth waters, even though it has no right to at this moment.

"This isn't what it looks like!" I tell him.

His jet-black eyes meet mine, and the impact of them nearly flattens me to the ground. "It looks like breakup food."

I don't know why, but my first instinct is to deny it. "No, it's not! It's movie night. That's all."

He points a severe finger down at my array of junk food. "You have three kinds of Doritos, Reese's cups, and . . . is that . . . yeah, Sour Mike and Ikes. Wallowing food! Admit it, Bree. You lost hope in me." Gah, he knows me so well. His eyes ram into mine and pin me in place. They dart once to my legs and back up. "Betty Boop. Really?"

Unable to sit under his heavy gaze, I back up and go into the kitchen under the pretense of refilling my already full water glass. "Nathan. You weren't here! What was I supposed to do? I couldn't wait for you forever."

"Forever?!" he asks, anguish radiating through his face. He scoffs and looks over his shoulder while running his hand over his lightly scruffy jawline, bicep flexing like a pulsing light in the dark, drawing me closer to it. "I was supposed to be home in two days. If I hadn't come back early . . . you would have just . . . what, Bree? I want to hear it from your mouth."

The way he says the word *mouth* with his eyes resting heavily on the body part in question has my knees buckling. "I would have gone ahead with the breakup." I dump out my water and return to the fridge and refill the glass, only to give myself something to do. Somewhere to look that isn't Nathan and his all-consuming heat.

He comes to stand right behind me, resting his palm on the fridge above my shoulder and pinning me in. He leans down and his breath slides over my neck, the heat of his chest pressing against my back.

"What a shame . . ." He dips his head and brushes his lips across the exposed sliver of my skin at the base of my neck and the top of my shoulder. His other hand trails fire up the outside of my thigh until it stops at my hip—he grips it. I'm scorching. Lava. The sun has nothing on me. I've missed him too much.

I give in and tilt my head back against the firm wall of his chest as he glides a line up the side of my throat with his mouth. Kissing, nipping, and tasting as he goes.

A desperate desire mounts between us and, unable to withstand it any longer, I set the glass down on the counter and twist around.

Nathan hoists me up and I wrap my legs around his waist, arms locked around his neck. He pushes me back against the refrigerator and takes my mouth in a hungry, crushing kiss.

And then suddenly, Dylan—who I very much forgot was still on the phone—clears his throat. "I know, you two are not over there using my pain and heartbreak as foreplay?!"

I gasp and rip my lips away from Nathan's grinning mouth. I give him a look that says, *behave*! He gives me a look that says, *I'm going to rip these Betty Boop pants right off you.* "Dylan, no! I'm so sorry. We were just . . ."

"Oh, I heard! And let me just say, Nathan, my boyfriend and I broke up three days ago and I tried to wait for your sorry ass to get home from your silly little Promo ball—"

"Pro Bowl . . ." Nathan corrects gently.

"In Hawaii, but I couldn't because my pain was too strong. So how dare you come home and make this about you."

"I'm so sorry, Dylan. I never should have made this about me," says Nathan, doing a fantastic job of sounding suitably abashed while simultaneously divesting me of my shirt.

Nathan and Dylan have become nearly as good friends as Dylan and I have over the last year, and when Nathan heard Dylan and his boyfriend broke up, he wanted to be here to christen the farewell with us. Dylan talked me into going ahead without Nathan, though, because he said his heart was likely to tear down the middle at any moment, and he needed to get the wallowing over with so he could move on. This was all for show, of course, because everyone knows Dylan loves being single and free to mingle. But I humor him because these breakup nights are always a blast.

"You can have Bree back, and I won't interfere with your breakup night anymore."

Dylan's nose is most definitely in the air when he says, "Thank you."

"Just as soon as I'm done with her," Nathan adds with a dark grin while dumping me on the couch. He picks up my phone, ends the call just as Dylan is about to call him a name so ugly Cardi B would blush, and throws it ruthlessly across the room. He couldn't care less what Dylan thinks of him right now.

I prop myself up on my elbows and look stern. "Nathan Donelson! You should be ashamed of yourself . . . there's absolutely no way I'm going to abandon my friend just because you . . ." But my resolve wilts to the ground when Nathan reaches behind his head and tugs his shirt off. Instead, my words sound like, "Guhsldfnso."

His smile widens and he lifts a brow, making him look like the rakish version of Superman. Muscles bulging and trenching in a nearly obscene way. "You don't say?"

He puts a knee beside me on the couch and then hovers over me, sliding his eyes down over my cute new sports bra in his favorite color of yellow. I'm proud of how it matches the scrunchie still tucked away in his memento box. The taut skin over his muscles gleams in the light, and even after a full year of marriage to this man, I still turn into pudding at the sight of him. No, something hotter than pudding. Flambé. A marshmallow caught on fire and rapidly charring.

"I missed you," he says with a note of such longing you would think we'd been separated for more than a week while he was away in Hawaii, playing in the Pro Bowl. I would have gone, too, if I didn't have to stay behind for my dance studio's ballet recital. Nathan was super bummed to have to miss out on it, since it was the first one since moving into the studio and doubling our class sizes, but I filmed the whole thing and plan on making him sit down and watch it no less than three times with me. He'll do the same with Pro Bowl replays, and we'll not leave our apartment for an entire week. Neither of us will be able to recount a single detail of either of those replays, though.

I smile as he touches his lips to both of my dimples. "I missed you too."

"Prove it." He captures my mouth again, and just as our kiss takes a delicious turn, our front door flies open once again.

I scream.

Jamal screams.

Price screams.

Lawrence screams.

Derek screams.

Nathan growls.

"Ew!" Jamal recovers himself first but doesn't have the decency to leave. He walks in farther—with the other guys on his heels and hands all hiding their eyes. "Cover yourselves! Geez, you two are like bunnies. Can't leave you alone for five minutes!"

"Get out, Jamal," Nathan says in a defeated tone while scraping his hands over his face, because he knows these guys aren't going anywhere. I am too busy shimmying back into my shirt to speak.

"And to think that's the welcome we receive after going out of our way to bring dinner over so we could hear how our boy did at the Pro Bowl?"

Lawrence holds up a pan covered in tinfoil. "It's a casserole. I got the recipe from Bree's mom."

"I brought beer," Price says, lifting two six-packs.

Jamal picks up Nathan's shirt and throws it at his face. "Put that on while we're in the kitchen. You're offending my delicate sensibilities."

I run my hand sympathetically up and down Nathan's bare back, unsuccessfully trying not to give in to my laughter. He cuts his eyes to me over his shoulder, and it's clear he's not amused in the least. I, however, don't have the heart to tell them to leave. Each of the guys, except for Derek—who is a self-proclaimed bachelor for life—are married now, and we don't get to see them as often as I would like. I miss these big dorks, and won't turn up my nose at spending time with them.

A moment later, Nathan is clothed and Jamal and the guys reenter the living room where we all squish together on our giant living-room couch—Nathan and I pinned in the middle.

"What are we watching?" Price asks, while raising a beer to his mouth.

Lawrence grabs a box of candy from the coffee table and pops it open.

Derek hands me my phone he picked up from the floor on his way over. "Looks like your friend Dylan is calling."

I smile because I can't help it. My life feels too good sometimes to do anything but that. "Jamal, hit Play when I tell you to."

I answer the phone and all the guys yell hi to Dylan before Nathan apologizes once again. We sync up our movies and settle in for the most epic breakup night anyone has ever experienced where absolutely no one cries and we spend nearly three hours laughing and joking.

Nathan wraps his big arm around my shoulders and pulls me onto his chest, laying a soft kiss on the top of my hair. His thumb rubs back and forth across my shoulder. "Still with me, Bree Cheese?"

I press a kiss to his chest. "Always."

Q&A WITH SARAH ADAMS

What was the inspiration for the characters of Bree and Nathan?

Bree and Nathan were a direct result of needing an escape and a hug through my writing. I set out to write a romance that was so cozy and sweet, it gave me cavities. I had watched *Ted Lasso* when it first aired and fell in love with the way the men in that show interacted, and how anti-toxic masculinity their culture was. I knew that I wanted to incorporate that vibe into Nathan and his friends. As for Bree, I have a history in dance, and it was a blast to write that love for ballet into a character as well as putting the actual dance studio I went to in the book.

What was your favorite scene in this book and why?

My favorite scene to write was definitely the whiteboard scene with Nathan and the guys. I could picture the whole scene unfolding so vividly in my head, and my fingers had trouble keeping up with my brain when I was typing it out. And as an honorary mention, the brownie batter scene was a blast to write! Getting to write both humor and chemistry in one scene was too much fun.

***The Cheat Sheet* features two beloved tropes—friends to lovers and fake dating. What made you want to explore these themes? Why do you think they're so popular?**

Friends to lovers has always been one of my favorite tropes to read because of the built-in trust and loyalty the characters have from page one, and I was dying to write it. And for me, I was craving a romance with this trope where the characters loved each other dearly from the beginning, and always always always built the other up. Friends to lovers can feel so safe and comfy, which makes it a crowd favorite. And fake dating is the perfect accessory trope to friends to lovers, because it allows the characters to explore their desires and feelings without messing anything up along the way. (Or so they hope.)

Why do you prefer writing closed-door love stories?

Prepare yourself; this answer is long. Closed-door romances are so wonderful because they create a safe place for readers of all steam levels to come together and enjoy the same book. Also, if K-dramas and foreign romance shows have taught us anything, it's that love stories can be enjoyable and popular even without sex in the story. I love the challenge of finding different ways to display intimacy between characters, desire unfolding between them, and chemistry sizzling off the page. I have to put everything into those small touches, grabby dialogue, and incredible kisses.

What is your writing process? Does it change depending on the book?

My writing process is similar with each book. I am a plotter, so I like to outline my entire story before I get started. I think it's easier to write if I can see where I'm going with the story. I usually write a first draft and then want to throw the entire thing in a fire and start over. My second draft is exhausting, because I usually end up rewriting a good portion of the story once I can feel my characters and their arcs better. After a second draft, I send it out to a few beta readers for honest feedback. And then, with their opinions in mind, I do a final edit to tighten everything up, make my sentences shine, and add more humor. But in between each of those steps is absolute turmoil and maybe even some job searches to find a new career that requires less vulnerability. :)

What is your favorite thing about writing romance?

For me, I find the romance genre to be mostly hopeful and uplifting. There's something so lovely about getting to write characters with flaws and force them to become completely vulnerable with another person, and then to have them be loved fully despite their flaws . . . it's wonderful and encouraging. Also, I'm a sap and get ridiculously giddy about love in general.

What is the hardest thing about writing?

Writing is the most vulnerable process. I have to dig inside myself in order to put good, complex characters on the page, which means I'm putting a little of myself in every one of my books. It's very difficult to then have to sit back and watch reviews pour in, and the negative ones really cut deep.

What do you have coming next?

I am extremely excited to be introducing a whole new series with a family of lovable characters in the small (made up) town of Rome, Kentucky. The first in that series is called *When in Rome,* and I feel like it's the most romantic, honest, and tender book I've written so far.

ACKNOWLEDGMENTS

It's tough to put into words how I feel about this book and everyone who brought it to life—which is really sad because I'm a writer. However, I'll try.

If you don't know the story of *The Cheat Sheet*'s life, you should know it was first brought into the world as a self-published baby. Honestly, it was a book that I wrote for no one other than me. I wrote it as my therapy. I wrote it to make myself laugh and to get me through a hard time. But when I released it into the world, it became those same things for many other people. The messages poured in; the love poured in, and Bree and Nathan became a hug for readers who desperately needed one. My readers are why this book found a new, wonderful home with Random House and the incredible people at Dell Books. And so I will forever be grateful to you: readers, bookstagrammers, booktokers, and bloggers.

And now, Kim, my agent and fairy godmother. I wish I could hug you. Thank you for coming alongside me and making dreams come true that I didn't even know to wish for! I'm so thankful for your support and hard work in giving this book the best chance of success.

A huge thank-you to my editor, Shauna Summers, for falling in love with Bree and Nathan just as much as I did, and seeing this story's potential. From our first phone call, you've felt like a friend and I knew I could trust this book in your hands.

Ashley, Carina, and Chloe, thank you for your friendship and daily encouragements to keep going and get this story into the world even when I wanted to rip it up and throw it into a bonfire. I love you ladies, and I can't imagine this writing journey without you.

And to Chris, my husband, my heart, by best friend in the entire world. This book is a love letter to you and how safe, cherished, and happy you make me feel daily. I won the jackpot with you.

HEADLINE
ETERNAL